BEARER OF BAD NEWS

The Timekeeper Chronicles

The Chivalrous Welshman
Time to Kill
Tick Tock
Windup
Stopwatch
Free Time
Leap Second
Imminence
Synchronization
Turning Point
The Eleventh Hour

The Fifth Horseman
Famine (Winter 2026)

The Hands of Time
In the Hands of the Enemy
The Hands Pulling the Strings
The Hand Holding the Knife

The Lone Wolf
Wolf Pack
Alpha Wolf
Lone Wolf

The Akari-Bearer
Bearer of Bad News
Right to Bear Arms (Summer 2026)

Singles
Of Saints and Sinners
Chasing the White Bear
Winds of Change (Winter 2025)

Bearer of Bad News
Book One of The Akari-Bearer
The Timekeeper Chronicles

Brooke Shaffer

Black Bear Publishing

Published in Michigan by Black Bear Publishing.

This novel is a work of fiction. Names, characters, places, and incidents are either products of the author's imagination or used fictitiously. All characters are fictional, and any similarity to persons living or dead is purely coincidental.

ISBN:
    Hardcover: 978-1-953113-43-6
    Softcover: 978-1-953113-44-3
    eBook: 978-1-953113-45-0

For Nina and Jessica

JUSTICE
OLDER BROTHER

Miach squatted in the shadows on the street corner, gritting his teeth but trying not to let his irritation show. It wasn't his brother's fault that his stomach was as loud as a dying cow. He was hungry, too. What was his brother's fault was how small and weak and mewling he was. He never seemed to want to change it, either. Twins they were, but MacEoghan never showed any initiative to be a twin and split the labor. He was perfectly content to make Miach do all the work. Twins they were, but the only evidence of it was their looks.

But there were some days when being a twin was absolutely perfect. It afforded them many opportunities to confuse people long enough that they might be able to make a grab for something. Right now, Miach was liking the looks of a purse which some lady left in her car. She and her family were out doing something or other, leaving the purse unguarded.

They didn't need a lot of money, and Miach had learned that the best way to get away with it was to, first, not act like he was stealing. He could casually stroll up to the car and start rummaging around much easier than ambushing the car, drawing attention, and causing a scene. Second, he only took a small portion of what was actually there, and never anything of extreme value. Take all the money, and it would be missed. Take something of great value like jewelry, and it would be missed. A few small bills, some change, things the lady was unlikely to notice immediately and was more likely to brush off.

"Miach, I'm hungry," MacEoghan whimpered behind him.

"I know you're hungry!" Miach hissed. "I'm hungry, too. You know what you're supposed to do?"

"The same thing I always do."

1

"Exactly. Are you ready?"

MacEoghan sounded ready to burst into tears as he muttered assent. After a moment of judging position, crowd, and other factors, Miach made the motion to move out.

Miach had been taking care of his twin brother for almost three years now. Their father had died in the war, mother soon after from sickness. Their older brother had taken care of them for a time until one day he went out and never came home. Ever since, it had been life on the streets. Sometimes they were able to make friends, do a bit of work for a bit of food, and sometimes they had to resort to stealing. After a number of misses and several times almost being apprehended, Miach had wised up and learned a few tricks which had kept them alive and out of the hands of the law.

He strode casually up to the car. That wasn't to say he didn't sometimes entertain the idea of going to a church or a courthouse and explaining their predicament, but two things always stopped him. First, he had no desire to be separated from his brother. There was no guarantee that they would stay together, and for as much of a pain as MacEoghan could be, they were still twins, together from the very beginning to the very end. Second, there was always the thrill of the heist, coming both from walking a knife's edge and hoping not to get caught, but also the small victory at the end that he had provided for them once again. He was only older by a couple of minutes, but he was the older brother, the leader, and he brought home food for them both.

No one even looked his way as he rooted around in the purse, finding an abundance of cosmetics but very little of worth. Maybe that was the reason the lady had so carelessly left her purse; there was nothing worth stealing.

Well, it had been worth a shot, anyway. But there could still be other valuables in the vehicle. Set out the obvious purse as a red herring. Either a thief will get bored thinking there is nothing of value, or it will be in such a time as the thief would be caught and subsequently apprehended with no real loss of or damage to property.

Trying to act as naturally as possible, Miach went around to the other side. He was going for the angle of child sent back to the car to retrieve something but having a hard time finding whatever it was he was sent to retrieve.

At the same time, what if he just took the car? It couldn't be that difficult, assuming he found a way to reach the pedals. It would be a faster getaway, and there had to be someone out there who would buy it with no questions asked, right? Times were tough, people said. Between the Depression and the aftermath of the war, people would do or sell anything to make money. And in order to sell, someone had to be willing to buy.

Miach scrounged up a few pennies, casually stuffing them in the only pocket he had left that didn't have holes. It wouldn't buy much, but it would put enough food in their stomachs that MacEoghan might stop whining.

He looked around the car a little longer, hoping to find something, anything of value; it didn't even have to be money or jewelry or anything of high value. Whoever these people were, either they didn't have anything particularly valuable, or they were smart enough to keep it on them. Judging by the clothes they'd been wearing when they got out, it was probably the latter.

Frustrated at the paltry pull but grateful he got anything at all, Miach slithered out of the car and took several steps back, looking around and trying to judge the movement of the people around him, blend in with the crowd so he could catch up with MacEoghan.

As he backed up, he bumped into someone. Looking up, he could feel the color drain from his cheeks as he found the face of the man who owned the car.

"That's not a very nice thing to do, young man," the man said sternly. "What of mine do you have, I wonder?"

Miach wasn't about to tell him. Instead, he took off at a dead sprint. Behind him, he heard the man begin shouting for help. Miach only vaguely perceived MacEoghan as time seemed to slow down around him. He grabbed his brother and they took off, ducking into an alley.

"You were supposed to keep watch, keep them busy!" Miach growled.

"I did, but you took too long and they were getting suspicious!" MacEoghan wailed.

Regardless of whether he made sense, Miach was still annoyed with his brother, but they also had bigger problems right now.

"Do the thing," MacEoghan said.

"Shut up," Miach hissed.

"Do the thing. Make us go fast!"

"I said shut up."

"There they are!"

They looked up as the man and a couple of police officers appeared in the alleyway. Miach grabbed MacEoghan and they were off again.

Miach tried to do the thing. He wasn't sure what to call it except it usually made him go faster than everything and everyone else around him, even MacEoghan unless he had him by the hand, which he did now. Problem was, the thing wasn't working. No matter how much he willed himself to go faster, they were still just going the same speed they always were, and so was everyone else, including the police.

The only reason they managed to elude capture before the end of the alley was by sheer size and agility. They slipped through a short, narrow opening and were gone. Gaillimh was a large city, but it was also on the coast. If they could find a dock, maybe they could stow away on a boat and escape. Maybe then the thing would work. It would have to.

Miach slowed and ducked into a corner where house met stone wall, dragging MacEoghan down with him and clamping his hand over his mouth. The police ran past. Miach could hear their footsteps, but they slowed as they got farther away. Their targets had disappeared. Did they keep up the chase? Were two little street rats really worth it? Were a few pennies worth so much trouble?

Slowly, Miach released his brother's mouth. Putting a finger to his lips, he nudged MacEoghan along the wall of the house into the small back yard. Then they slipped around to the other side and made their way back along the street the way they had come. Behind them, Micah could hear the police talking to people.

It wasn't the first time they had been pursued. It was the first time they had come so close to being caught. Miach couldn't understand what the thing was or how it worked or, more importantly, why it wasn't working now. They needed to go faster and get away. But that was neither here nor there and the best they could do was find a small shed to duck into, keeping the door open a crack to watch outside goings-on.

"Why are we hiding in here?" MacEoghan whimpered. "Do the thing! Do the go-fast!"

"Shush! I tried, but it's not working," Miach admitted grudgingly.

"How is it not working?"

"I don't know."

"What if we're caught? Where will we run?"

"I don't know. I'm thinking about it."

"Are we going to have to leave the city?"

"I told you, I don't know."

"We're wanted men, Miach."

"Shut up, MacEoghan. It's only a few pennies."

"That's all you got? But they looked so much richer!"

"I said shut up. I know they did. Obviously they had most of their stuff on them. But it's not helping us here."

"What are we going to do?"

Miach ground his teeth. He was going to punch his brother if he kept this up. The shed was small and quickly growing warmer with their sweat and hot breath. They were just going to have to make a break for it and hope the thing worked. It was their only chance now.

"Okay, I have an idea," Miach said.

MacEoghan shifted position, listening eagerly.

"When I say so, grab my hand, and we're going to run and get back into the city. We can't outrun them, so we'll have to hide. We wait until sundown, and then we move on to the next town. Got it?"

MacEoghan grabbed his hand. "Ready."

Miach looked him in the eye, as much to give his brother courage as muster some up for himself. He hoped this worked. He really needed the thing to work right now.

"Ready...steady...go!"

The boys burst out of the shed. Miach hadn't taken three steps before he felt himself being lifted by the back of his shirt. He heard and felt threads tear. He probably could have let go of MacEoghan, slipped out of his shirt, and kept going, but his brother wouldn't be so smart, and he could never leave his brother behind.

"Are these the boys, Minister?" the police officer who held Miach questioned.

"They are," the man, this "Minister," confirmed. "Well done."

Miach reached in his pocket and threw the pennies at the man. "They weren't worth it anyway. They wouldn't have bought anything."

The Minister looked at the pennies and raised a brow. "Did you think I was worried about a few meager pennies? Of course, I, like anyone, do not appreciate being burglarized, but...do you even know who I am?"

"No, sir."

"I am the Minister of Defense. How am I supposed to defend the Irish people if I cannot even defend myself?" He looked at the officers. "You may proceed."

Miach and MacEoghan were set on the ground, but before they could try anything, the officers grabbed them hard by their hands and led them away. It was a long, humiliating walk, but Miach could only think that maybe he should have kept the pennies instead of throwing them at the man, this "Minister of Defense." Maybe the man wouldn't have made a fuss and Miach would have been able to keep his ill-gotten prize.

It was easier and closer to simply walk to the courthouse, which also doubled as the police station, rather than return to the street to find the police car. They were marched inside and taken to see another police officer who sat them down in comfortable chairs, gave them a glass of water, then sat down himself and brought out a bunch of papers.

"Okay, boys, what are your names?" he asked.

"Miach," Miach answered. "This is my brother, MacEoghan."

"Miach and MacEoghan," the officer repeated flatly. "What's your last name?"

"Meagher."

"Miach and MacEoghan Meagher. Where are your parents?"

The boys looked at each other. It was MacEoghan who answered, "We don't have any."

"Oh?" The man shuffled his papers a little. "How long has this been then?"

"We don't know exactly. Three years maybe."

"I see. And you have no grandparents, aunts, uncles, older siblings, any family at all?"

"No, sir."

"No one is watching over you?"

"No, sir," Miach told him. "I take care of my little brother."

"I'm not your little brother!" MacEoghan protested. "I'm your twin."

"You're a baby!"

"Am not!"

"Please, be quiet!" the officer snapped. Both boys shut their mouths and sat upright at attention. The officer took an even breath. "Now then, where are you from? What town or city?"

The boys glanced at each other. Miach replied, "We don't know, sir. It's been a long time. We've been going from place to place."

"Stealing all the way, from the looks of things."

"Please, sir, we don't mean anything by it. We just need some food for the day. Maybe a shirt or a pair of stockings. Honest, sir, we don't take more than we need."

"As noble as that may be," the officer said, standing, "you are still stealing from good, law-abiding citizens. We can't have that. But seeing how you have no parents or family—none that you know of or are admitting to—we can't send you home for your pa to give you a good switch, and it does no one any good to simply lock you up."

"What are you going to do to us?" MacEoghan asked in a small voice.

"I don't know yet. For the moment, I am going to ask my superior where we can keep you. It will be up to a judge to decide your fate."

"We can't get split up!" Miach blurted out. "We just can't! I'm not going to leave my brother!"

"That's not up to me to decide. Now then, stay here for a minute or two while I speak to my superior."

With that, the man was gone, taking his papers with him. Miach looked at MacEoghan. MacEoghan looked at Miach. They looked around the room. It was pretty sparse. Bare floor, metal desk, metal chairs with cushions that had fraying seams. A typewriter sat on the desk, but it looked hardly touched.

"What do you think is going to happen to us?" MacEoghan asked softly.

"I don't know," Miach admitted. "But we can't be split up. I'm not going to leave you."

"And I don't want to leave you. Together forever?"

"Together forever."

They were in the office for another five minutes or so before the police officer returned, sitting in his chair with a big sigh.

"What did your superior say?" Miach wondered. He didn't know what a superior was, but if he could tell a police officer what to do, he had to be very powerful indeed.

"Well, boys, here's what's going to happen—"

"We're not splitting up!" MacEoghan declared. "Together forever!"

"Shut up," Miach hissed.

The officer took another calming breath as he said levelly, "Here's what's going to happen. You're going to go before a judge who will decide what to do with you for the time being. Regardless of anything else, you still committed a crime and you have to face the consequences. In the meantime, we're going to see if we can't locate some family members. It's unlikely you've wandered far from your home town, even in three years. We'll do a county-wide search."

"What if you can't find any family?" Miach asked.

"We'll deal with that when the time comes, but I would be willing to bet that someone out there is looking for you."

"When do we see the judge?"

"Just as soon as he is finished with his current case. In the meantime, we have tea if you'd like some."

Miach took a small cup, even as MacEoghan refused. He'd never been a big tea drinker. Really, they hadn't had any tea in probably over a year. The officer gave him his cup, then left the room one more time.

"Do you think Sean might really be out there looking for us?" MacEoghan asked, referring to their older brother.

"I don't know," Miach answered, contemplating the same thing. If Sean was looking for them, why hadn't he come home that one night, or the many nights after while they waited? Why had no one come to check on them? What had happened?

They sat in silence. MacEoghan's stomach rumbled like thunder. They still hadn't eaten. They hadn't eaten in a couple days, actually. Miach drank his tea and tried to put thoughts of his own hunger out of his mind. They were going before a judge, after all.

It was impossible to say how much time passed until the officer returned. Miach was tempted to think that the thing had worked finally, though in the opposite way he wanted, where he went slow and everything else went fast. But the thing still worked—just a little late. Nevertheless, they were taken out of the office. The police officer handed them over to a court official who introduced himself as Mr. O'Doyle. He herded them down a narrow hallway to a poorly-lit room. There was some spectator seating, though it was empty save for two or three people. The *breithimh*, the judge, sat at his bench at the front of the room. The jury box was empty. At one long table stood the Minister man with another court official. Miach and MacEoghan were escorted to another long table.

"Good afternoon, Minister," the judge greeted. "Making friends with the locals, I see."

The court official with the Minister began to speak. "*A Bhreithimh,* these two scoundrels attempted to steal money and goods from—"

"Yes, I know. I can read, thank you." He looked at Miach and MacEoghan who tried to make themselves small. "Boys, where are your parents?"

"Our father died in the war, and our mother died from sickness."

The judge chuckled humorlessly. "War? Which one?"

"Mama didn't say. Just 'the great war.'"

The judge raised a brow. "How old are you?"

"Ten, I think."

"You do know that it's 1931."

"Yes, sir."

The judge and the boys stared at each other. He was a middle-aged man, perhaps forty, with black hair and angular features. He had an expression that said he was expecting the boys to say something, but Miach wasn't sure what it was. After what seemed like a long time, he shook his head, muttered something under his breath, and addressed the court official standing next to them. "They have no other family? Grandparents, siblings, anything?"

"They claim to be orphans for about three years, *a Bhreithimh*. The police are searching for any remaining family."

"While it is a nice sentiment, *a Bhreithimh*," the Minister's official cut in, "it does not change the fact that they still attempted to take my client's money."

"Yes, I understand that," the judge sighed. "But even if I locked them up, if no family can be found, what use is there? They will still be orphans, without food or money or means. The ordinary citizen is having a hard enough time as it is, what is a child going to do? We are trying to stem the cycle of crime, and it starts with the children."

"What are you suggesting? That we simply give them—"

"Be quiet! And stop interrupting me. I've had more than enough out of you and you only just got here." The judge glared at the man a moment longer before turning his attention back to Mr. O'Doyle. "Mr. O'Doyle."

The man straightened a little. *"A Bhreithimh."*

"Seeing as there is no guarantee that the police will find any family for the boys, I am not going to lock them up indefinitely. But neither am I going to turn them out onto the streets to become a casualty of the economy and steal from someone else who may be of decidedly less influence." He cast a sideways glance at the Minister. "Instead, they will be sent to St. Joseph's Industrial School in Leitir Fraic. There they will be fed, clothed, and housed, and they may learn some useful skills which, with any luck, will turn them into productive adults when they come of age."

"And if family is found for them?"

"Then you'll know where the boys can be found and can direct them there. It's not as if Leitir Fraic is very big. They can't get lost. And it's a long hike between the town and the school."

"So you're going to reward them," the Minister's official stated, sounding unimpressed. "They will serve no punishment for their crimes."

"They're ten years old," the judge told him. "And that's guessing high. Look at them. They're scared out of their minds. Maybe you spent a little too much time in London, Mr. Byrnes. Back here in Éire, we try to help our children and raise them up to be good people, not punish them because life dealt them a bad hand. If you want to punish children because they took your client's lunch money on the playground, go back to London, or try your hand in the bloody partition. Case dismissed."

With that, it was all over. Miach and MacEoghan watched as Mr. O'Doyle, Mr. Byrnes, and the Minister met for a private conference. Mr. Byrnes and the Minister did not look pleased, but Mr. O'Doyle refused to give an inch. At the last moment, the group broke apart before they had to be forced out so as to make room for the next case. Mr. O'Doyle motioned for the boys who followed him meekly out of the room, always keeping one eye on the others.

"Are we going to be locked up?" Miach wondered once they were out of the courtroom.

"No," Mr. O'Doyle said, squatting so he could look them in the eye. "Not at all. Actually, you're going to school. Have you ever been to school?"

"We used to go to school, before our mum died."

"Well, you're going back to school. You'll learn your letters, your maths, history, geography, everything you'll need to make you a literate person. But this is a special school where you'll also learn about farming, woodworking, tailoring, and other trades. If you learn them really well, when you turn sixteen, you can get a job, make money, and be productive. You can provide for yourself and your future families. No more living on the streets. How does that sound?"

The boys glanced at each other. They weren't sure what to think of it. How did it sound? It was Miach who answered, "It sounds good, sir."

"I think you'll like it. Come on, then. We'll grab the court papers from the secretary and then head out to Leitir Fraic. We should get there before dark. Tonight you'll be sleeping in your own beds. How does that sound?"

Well, that sounded pretty good, actually.

CAR RIDE
YOUNGER BROTHER

MacEoghan had never been in a car before. Well, he'd been in one, sometimes to sleep for the night or see what he could steal, but he'd never really ridden in one. It was a fascinating sensation as they rumbled along the roads, passing houses and trees and open fields.

"Where are we going?" MacEoghan asked, ignoring the eye roll from Miach.

A social worker named Padraig accompanied them. He was a young man with dark hair, a pointed nose, gaunt cheeks, and glasses. His dark suit was of a more British style, but he said that was because he'd just returned from studying in London.

"First we're going to Clifden," he answered amiably. "We're going to do a little paperwork at the court offices there, and then we'll be on our way to Leitir Fraic and St. Joseph's."

"What kind of paperwork?"

"We have to establish who you are. If the police can find your family, we have to be able to identify you and get them here to claim you. If they can't find your family, then we still have to have record of you."

"Why?"

"Because we have to. The government has to know who you are, where you're from."

"Why?"

"Shut up, MacEoghan," Miach growled. "You're so stupid."

"Am not!"

"You don't seem very happy, Miach," Padraig observed. "Why is that? Don't you want to sleep in your own bed, a real bed, and be able to eat freely without having to steal?"

Miach squirmed in his seat a little. "But I was good at it."

"Yes, but it is still wrong. On this the government and the Lord agree and say it plain. Thou shalt not steal."

"I don't want to go to Leitir Fraic! I want to go home to my mother! I want to sleep in my bed and eat her food!"

Padraig nodded slowly. Miach tried to remain strong, but his bottom lip quivered and tears flowed from his eyes. MacEoghan wiped tears from his own eyes lest his brother see them.

"I understand," Padraig said slowly. "You want to go home to your old life and the way things were. Believe me when I say that we're trying to help with that. We're going to do our best at locating your family, but we can't have you out on the streets. It's not safe. At the school, you'll get food, clothes, a place to sleep, and you'll continue your education. You probably have some catching up to do since you haven't been to school for a few years, but you're obviously smart if you've lasted this long."

Miach grumpily wiped his eyes and nose and harrumphed back into his seat. MacEoghan sat quietly.

"You said you had an older brother who took care of you," the social worker continued conversationally. "What was his name?"

"Sean."

"And where is he?"

"We don't know. He left one day and never came back. We waited for a little while, but we haven't seen him since."

"I see. Do you have any other brothers or sisters?"

MacEoghan shook his head while Miach stubbornly looked out the window.

"What about your mother? Did she have any brothers or sisters?"

Miach started to say something, then stopped. Padraig shifted in his seat. "What was that?"

"She had lots of brothers who came over a lot. I don't think they liked each other."

"What makes you say that?"

"They would lock themselves in her bedroom, and I would hear yelling and fighting on the bed. Then he would leave. They would both be really sweaty. We would go in her room and she would be crying. She would tell us that she loved us very much, and then she would go out to the market."

Padraig's expression was impossible for MacEoghan to discern. "I see." He cleared his throat. "What do you know about your father?"

"Just that he was a good soldier. He died in the great war."

"How did your older brother take it?"

Miach shrugged. "I don't know."

They rode in silence after that. Padraig looked deep in thought in the front seat, and Miach just stared out the window, fighting tears and being largely unsuccessful. MacEoghan's gaze darted from one to the other, then out his window, then back to the other occupants. The driver of the car was an older man, maybe sixty years old, almost completely bald and what hair he did have left was gray, almost white. He didn't say one word to MacEoghan or Miach, but MacEoghan could see he occasionally exchanged quiet words with Padraig.

"How long until we reach Clifden?" Miach whined after a few minutes.

"Not long now," Padraig replied, sounding a little too cheery about the whole thing.

"I'm hungry."

"If things go smoothly in Clifden, maybe we'll stop at a nice diner and get something to eat before going to Leitir Fraic. How does that sound? Sounds good to me; I'm hungry already. How about you, Adam?"

"Sounds very good, sir," the driver, Adam, replied formally.

"See there? We'll make it an outing."

Starting out on this little adventure, MacEoghan had been more than excited to see new places, meet new people, and experience new...experiences—all without having to worry about getting caught by the police. Now, though, he was getting tired. He was hungry, had been hungry ever since they started out, but fatigue was wearing on him. Only the bouncing of the car and the rutted roads kept him from falling asleep. Looking over, Miach seemed to be thinking the same thing.

Eventually, empty countryside interspersed occasionally by a farmhouse gave way to more clusters of houses interspersed occasionally by countryside. Then the houses gave way to buildings and businesses, streets and people. Fatigue forgotten, MacEoghan sat up and looked around once more. Up front, Adam said something to Padraig who laughed and replied. MacEoghan did not catch the conversation, but he didn't care. They were someplace new.

Clifden was smaller than Gaillimh, but no less busy. They passed tailors and woodworkers and laundromats and pharmacists. But they also passed a lot of closed or empty buildings, too. Briefly, MacEoghan was reminded of one of the last conversations he'd had with Sean. He'd said that something in America had gone wrong and things were going to get a lot harder. MacEoghan asked why that was. Why did a country so far away affect them so much? Sean hadn't answered, just told him to be a good kid. Less than a month later, he was gone.

The empty buildings soon gave way to more blocks of occupied buildings, where businesses were thriving. People walked in and out in a constant flow, and everyone seemed happy. Or happier, compared to those in the car. Miach was still sitting quietly, looking out the window. Padraig rustled around in his briefcase. Adam lamented that there were too many people milling about and he couldn't find a spot to park.

MacEoghan had assumed they were just going to another courthouse and would go before another judge. In actuality, they visited a small office where a secretary struck the keys of a typewriter with lightning speed and absolute precision. She greeted them stiffly and took the papers Padraig handed to her. She regarded the boys for only a moment, then shuffled the papers and continue to strike the typewriter keys.

"It would be a huge service if we could get those papers as soon as possible," Padraig prodded. "I'd like to get the boys to St. Joseph's tonight."

The secretary did not say a word, nor did she pause in her typing as she looked at Padraig with an unreadable expression. She finished up the page she was on, then went to a cabinet to dig around for more paper. MacEoghan saw that she had some pages already pre-typed.

She selected a couple papers and wound them in the typewriter reel, setting them just so, then went for the papers Padraig had given her. She typed out something, moved the sheet, moved the reel, typed out something else, repeat.

Everything had to be done twice, one for each boy, something that took up a lot of time and made the secretary no more pleasant to work with. Padraig waited patiently, saying nothing, looking around a bit, looking out the windows occasionally. MacEoghan felt fatigue creep back up on him. Miach looked forlornly out the window.

"I'm hungry," he mumbled.

"I know, little lad," Padraig said. "These papers shouldn't take long. Then we'll pop out to grab a bite to eat. Miss...ah, what's your name, Miss?"

"Eiligh," the woman replied curtly.

"Miss Eiligh. Where would you recommend as a good place to eat for four hungry young men in this town?"

"Nowhere you haven't already been since the last time you came through here."

Padraig's cheeks turned red. "Right. So then, how about the diner, hm? They've got some lovely sandwiches; I'm sure you'll love them."

MacEoghan was just nodding off when his brother roughly shook him awake, grabbed his hand, and dragged him out of the office. He looked back in the office briefly where Miss Eiligh didn't even give them so much as a goodbye wave before reeling through her next paper and typing away on the keys.

"I'm tired," MacEoghan said, rubbing his eyes. "Can we go to bed and go to school tomorrow?"

"It's barely the middle of the afternoon," Padraig told him, grinning. "Let's get something to eat, and then you can sleep on the way to the school. How about that?"

No, he wanted to sleep now. His tummy didn't even hurt anymore because he was too tired to be hungry. Still, he followed Padraig and Adam and Miach down the street a short distance to a diner. It wasn't overly full, but there was a good crowd and a lot of noise, which only made MacEoghan long for a bed even more.

"Now then, what would you boys like to eat?" Padraig asked, still smiling. "Just name it. Anything you want."

Anything except a bed to sleep in, apparently, though MacEoghan did not say this out loud. Looking at Miach, he seemed just as tired, and more

16

grumpy for it. Sometimes, Miach was able to do the thing, and it seemed like a lot of time passed when it was really only a couple minutes. Sometimes he used the thing to help MacEoghan rest, though he said he couldn't do it for himself. MacEoghan wished Miach would do the go-fast now, let him take a short nap so he could enjoy the nice food they were about to eat. He wished he could do the go-fast for himself. Maybe he could use the go-fast on Miach, and then Miach would be more agreeable and do the go-fast on him. Then they would be happy when they went to school.

As it was, MacEoghan wasn't even sure what he got, or how much he ate of it. He vaguely remembered having food, knew it made his tummy feel better and not so angry, knew it helped him stay awake just a little bit as they walked back to the car, but that was about it.

"Okay, boys, you can go ahead and sleep now," Padraig said, opening the backseat door. "It's not far to Leitir Fraic where they'll put you in a nice, warm bed. All right?"

Miach climbed in first, then MacEoghan. It took a bit of shuffling and stretching and maneuvering, but soon they were sprawled out along the seat. MacEoghan had just closed his eyes when the car gave a lurch and they pulled away from the curb. Adam apologized, and MacEoghan heard Padraig say that it was fine; the boys were sound asleep anyway. At the time it was a lie, but it took only a few seconds for it to become a truth as MacEoghan finally fell into slumber.

The only dream MacEoghan had these days was one of his mother. She held him and his brother, rocking back and forth and telling them that they were good boys. They were such good boys. She would tell them to keep being good, and listen to Sean. He and Miach promised her they would, and they would just keep rocking back and forth.

The only reason he remembered his mother's name was Jenine was because of how often her brothers said it—or yelled it—when they came to visit. He didn't remember any of their names. Didn't remember his father's name, couldn't be sure she'd ever told them.

These thoughts plagued MacEoghan when he woke up. If the police and the courts were looking for family members, how would they even know each other? His mother was dead. His father was dead. His mother's brothers barely said ten words to them in all the years they stopped by. Would any family members even want them? If they did, why hadn't they said so years ago?

"Where are we?" he mumbled, peeking outside the window to view unfamiliar countryside.

"Very near to Leitir Fraic," Padraig answered. "And from there, it's straight on to St. Joseph's."

None of this meant much to the small boy other than they were still in the car and would remain in the car for a while yet. Could Miach do the thing for all of them? The fast thing, so they moved extra fast and could get there quicker. He didn't want to be in the car for so long. His tummy didn't like it.

"You all right there, lad?"

MacEoghan couldn't even comprehend the question before he was vomiting in the man's lap, all the food he had eaten earlier running over his tongue, coupled with the vile taste of stomach fluid. Then he was crying. Someone was yelling. Someone was talking. Then he threw up a second time. He continued to cry. He cried, he sniffed, he gagged on the terrible odor. Then there was wind in the car as windows were hastily opened. They pulled over and everyone got out.

"There, there, it's all right," Padraig said, producing a kerchief to wipe MacEoghan's face. He looked at Miach. "What about you? Is the car ride equally as agreeable for you?"

Miach mumbled something MacEoghan didn't catch.

"Well, we'll stay here for a few minutes until you feel better," Padraig told them amiably. "I'll get cleaned up...somehow...and then we'll make our way this last leg of the journey."

"Tarry too long and they'll be closed down for the night before we get there," the driver commented.

"I can't very well walk in like this. I have to do something. Plus we can't let the smell fester in the car if we can help it. And we can't deliver them two sick boys as if they're a hospital."

"All right, all right. I get where you're coming from—"

"I understand your concern, Adam. We're just resting for a few minutes, not taking time to have a picnic."

18

That was good, MacEoghan thought, because his tummy didn't like the sound of a picnic. Didn't even like thinking about it. He didn't get sick, but food was the last thing on his mind. He sat on the ground, leaning on Miach. Padraig stepped away, and Adam minded the car.

"Do you think this is a good idea?" MacEoghan murmured.

"What?" Miach wondered.

"Going to this school. Is it a good idea?"

"You want to run away?"

"I don't want to get back in the car."

"Neither do I. But if we try to run, they'll just use the car to chase us."

MacEoghan looked around. The countryside was too open; they'd never be able to escape. There wasn't even anywhere they could hide.

"What about the going fast?" the younger twin asked. "Is it still broke? Why is it broke? How did you break it?"

"Who said I broke it?" Miach shot back, though his tone was more grumpy than angry. He sighed. "I don't know. I don't know why it's not working. Maybe it is, but I don't feel good enough to do it."

"But if you can do it, we can run away and the car won't matter."

"And go where?" Miach shifted to face him. "MacEoghan, we don't have a home. We don't know where Sean is, or any of Mum's brothers. If we go to the school, we get a bed and food, we go to school, and Sean can find us."

"Sean could have found us before we ran away," MacEoghan said sharply. "He left us."

"Then we have to go to the school. We have nowhere else."

Now MacEoghan's heart hurt almost as much as his tummy. He looked up at a hand on his shoulder. It was Adam, squatting down in front of them.

"Things will get better for you, lads. I promise. This isn't how your life will always be. And you're luckier than some because you have each other." He nodded as the twins glanced at each other. "Look out for one another. Care for one another. Always stick together."

"Together forever," Miach stated. MacEoghan just nodded.

"That's a good lad. Two good lads. And here's Padraig." Adam stood as Padraig approached, still gingerly wiping at his ruined suit with the dirty kerchief. "Ready, sir?"

"Ready as I'll ever be," Padraig sighed. "I'm afraid these clothes may have to be burned."

They piled into the car.

"Your wife is good at getting out stains, isn't she?" Adam was saying.

"She is, yes, but I don't know about this," the social worker lamented.

"None of your children ever graced your lap with the contents of their stomach before?"

"Of course they did, but it did not set in the fabric for hours before being washed."

MacEoghan looked down at his clothes. They were dirty and stained. He didn't know how long he'd been wearing them. A week? Two? Three or more? Would he get new clothes at the school? Would there be uniforms? He looked at Miach. Would they even be able to tell each other apart?

It wasn't long before MacEoghan's head started to feel heavy again and his tummy hurt. He told Padraig and the car pulled over. They waited a few minutes, but nothing happened, and they continued on. This happened four or five times before Adam said they were about ten minutes from the school.

MacEoghan didn't move, nor did Miach, even as Padraig marveled at the countryside, narrating the scenery. Forests, fields, low stone walls, a herd of deer in the distance. Still, neither boy moved from his position, each trying to lay upon the other. The ride was atrocious and food sounded yucky, yet sleep was entirely elusive as the car struck another rock and bounced roughly.

"Sorry about that," Adam said loudly only the gravelly noise of the road. "It's a bit rocky here. Can't help it if we want to stay on the road."

MacEoghan closed his eyes, wished for sleep, found none.

Then, by the merciful hand of God, the car stopped and the engine went quiet. Padraig's door opened and the man stepped out, telling the boys to get themselves up and around if they wanted to go to bed.

The boys wanted nothing more than to go to bed, but they would have been just as happy to sleep in the car. MacEoghan moved first, stumbling out on watery legs, rubbing his eyes. Miach followed, a little more steady. Padraig came between them and took one of their hands in each of his.

MacEoghan did not see much as the large, church-like building obscured what little sunlight was left. He did not resist as they entered the building and were herded into a small room, a black-clad priest sitting behind a desk. He was a big man, tall, with a full face that spoke of eating well, and a head of thick brown hair.

"Good evening, Father," Padraig greeted humbly, handing over a stack of papers. "I realize it's late. Our trip here was...eventful."

"Yes, I can smell it," the priest commented evenly. He shuffled through the loose pages. "Orphans from the street, picked up for thieving. One older brother, whereabouts unknown. Mother is deceased...I see..."

"There are no uncles, say it that way."

"I understand the implication, thank you. True orphans, then. About ten years old, you say?" The priest glanced at the boys. MacEoghan thought he looked disapproving. He looked back at Padraig. "I'd say eight."

Padraig shrugged. "Father Daniel, we can only go by what they tell us and our own best guesses."

The priest nodded, his expression softening. "Of course. Well, why don't we see about a change of clothes and a bed? Then you and I can talk some more."

"Come on, boys," Padraig ordered gently.

Tired and sore, MacEoghan followed the priest, Miach beside him, Padraig behind.

"I understand that things are a bit confusing now," Father Daniel was saying. "It's late, it's getting dark, you've had a dreadful car ride, and all you want to do is go to bed. Well, trust me, everything will look better in the morning once you're well-rested and well-fed."

Why did adults talk so much? That was all they ever did was talk. Father Daniel and Padraig could have talked even more except the priest seemed to actually notice and care that the boys were so tired. But why did they move so slow? If MacEoghan knew where he was supposed to be going for bed, he would have run there. Or maybe not. He was so tired that even walking felt difficult.

They left the big church building and headed for another building, Father Daniel explaining that this was one of the dormitories for the students. Most likely, where they slept tonight would be their bed for their entire stay, a little place to call their own.

Inside, they met another man who Father Daniel introduced as Brother Michael.

"And this is Micah and MacEoghan." Miach opened his mouth to protest, but Father Daniel continued speaking. "They need a change of clothes and a couple of beds."

"Of course, Father," Brother Michael replied softly.

Before anyone could do anything, Padraig knelt before the boys. MacEoghan could have cried for how tired he was.

"Hey. Look at me. I know things look bad now, but Father Daniel is right. It will all look better in the morning."

"I want to go to bed," MacEoghan whimpered.

Padraig nodded. "Of course." He stood. "Sleep well, boys. I'll try to be back in a few days."

"Bring Sean with you."

The man faltered. "I'll try."

Then he and Father Daniel departed, speaking quietly, leaving Miach and MacEoghan with Brother Michael who ushered them swiftly into the dormitory.

"My name is Miach," Miach said. "Not Micah."

"I think I like Micah better," Brother Michael said, his tone much firmer than before. "It's a Biblical name, one of the minor prophets."

"But my name is Miach."

"This is your home now, boys. A second chance, a fresh start, a new life. And if Father Daniel introduced you as Micah, it's because that is how it appeared on your papers. Your legal name is Micah now."

"What's your legal name?" MacEoghan wondered.

Brother Michael sighed. "Or maybe Father Daniel's been reading too much this evening and went cross-eyed. We can sort it out in the morning, I suppose. Right now, I think we all want to get to bed."

A clean shirt and pair of pants replaced their grubby street clothes. Brother Michael muttered something about giving them both hot baths. But instead of shuffling them to a bath house, he took them to a large, open room, bunkbeds lined up in neat rows, most with sleeping forms under the blankets. The three of them stepped lightly on the floor as they sneaked past.

"You two can share this one," Brother Michael told them, indicating a bunk bed with no occupants. "Now then, get in."

MacEoghan hadn't even needed to be told once as he was already climbing under the covers. Miach scrambled up top.

"Morning comes at six o'clock with morning prayers promptly at six-thirty," Brother Michael said. "Don't be late."

And he left.

ST. JOSEPH'S INDUSTRIAL SCHOOL FOR BOYS
YOUNGER BROTHER

MacEoghan had only been to Mass a few times with his mother, and he couldn't recall that he liked anything about it. Mostly he remembered the whispers and disapproving looks he'd gotten, and the things people said to his mother.

Going to morning prayers the following day—after being startled awake and more following the herd than knowing what was going on—MacEoghan looked around, wondering who was going to whisper and give him and Miach mean looks. As it turned out, no one did. Well, all right, that wasn't entirely true. There were a few glares and shushes as MacEoghan apparently acted improperly during morning prayers, but was it really his fault? He didn't understand what was going on. Sure, he knew about God and Jesus, and he knew that praying was basically talking to Them, but why did he need to talk to Them?

As for reading from the Bible, well, MacEoghan really couldn't read all that well. He knew his letters and numbers, but he wasn't quite sure what to do with them. So he stared at the page, pretending like he understood, turning the page when everyone else did. Beside him in the pew, Miach did the same.

The other thing he remembered about Mass, another thing he didn't like, was that it was so stiff and formal and stuffy. Sing the songs, read the Bible, listen to the priest. The adults got food and drink but the kids never did, which was even more frustrating. Well, his mum never got food and drink, and he distinctly remembered the looks she got when she asked about it. One woman told her, "Women of your affiliations don't get communion."

MacEoghan didn't know what "affiliations" meant, nor "communion," and no one had ever really explained it to him. He got the sense that it was just one of those off-limits things for kids.

Looking around, the boys at the school ranged in age from as young as three to old enough to be an adult. Old enough for "communion" anyway. Maybe they had the right "affiliations."

Morning prayers took forever. A lot of praying, some reading, more praying. MacEoghan wasn't the only one getting squirmy, but he saw that some of the even younger kids were just as quiet and poised as the older kids. This calmness didn't last long once one of the priests rang a huge bell. The quiet stuffiness of Mass suddenly erupted into a mad scramble. MacEoghan startled and grabbed Miach's hand. Miach jumped to his feet, ready for anything but just as confused.

Several mentions of breakfast or breakfast foods cleared up the confusion, and the twins darted into the fray near the back of the crowd. As before, they didn't know where they were going, only that they had to get there with the others.

The place where they ended up was another large room smelling blissfully of food. Long rows of tables and chairs made the room look crowded. MacEoghan could only follow his brother who could only follow everyone else. Along one wall, several priests were standing behind a table. One had a cauldron in front of him, a second had a large covered pan, and a third had an enormous pan of fresh rolls.

The boys lined up at one end of the priests' table. MacEoghan saw the boy up front grab a plate and a bowl. He stopped in front of each priest and was given a portion of food. Soup from the first, something MacEoghan could not discern from the second, and a roll from the third. Then he went and found a place to sit, but he did not dig into his food.

By the time the twins made it to the food table, in line behind Miach, MacEoghan's stomach was howling. He eagerly grabbed a plate and a bowl, both of them made of wood. The first priest ladled some soup into his bowl. Unwilling to wait, he set the plate on the table, tipped up the bowl, and began slurping.

A heavy wooden spoon lashed out and rapped his knuckles. His cry of pain and surprise was muted by his choking even as the bowl slipped. Soup poured all over his front while the bowl dropped to the floor. All activity came to a halt in the dining hall. Shame and embarrassment flooded over

MacEoghan. Chancing a glance at the group, he saw that still none of them had touched their food. And all were staring at him.

"Pick up the bowl," the priest ordered coldly.

Unsure what to do, MacEoghan froze.

"Pick—up—the—bowl."

In front of him, Miach set his bowl and plate down on the table, but before he could do anything, a spoon found his knuckles as well.

"He made the mistake," the priest said. "He fixes it."

"And I help him," Miach retorted.

The priest hit him again, this time on the shoulder. It did not deter Miach who still knelt to pick up the bowl at MacEoghan's feet. The priest continue to hit him with the wooden spoon. Miach set the bowl on the table next to MacEoghan's plate, then picked up his own food.

The soup priest said nothing more as he stopped beating Miach. MacEoghan absently picked up the empty bowl and plate and kept moving.

The second priest was doling out beans and potatoes. He made no mention of the incident, and he did not hit them with a wooden spoon.

The bread priest gave each of them a warm roll, looking like he was trying to smile and be encouraging, but was perhaps afraid of the soup priest more.

MacEoghan and Miach found seats next to each other. MacEoghan sat down sullenly, unsure if he even wanted to eat now. He looked at the boy across from him, maybe thirteen years old, but the boy refused to meet his gaze. MacEoghan did not touch his food, nor Miach.

Once everyone was through the line and seated, they all stood up. One of the priests said yet another prayer. Only when he was finished were they free to sit and eat. Still MacEoghan hesitated.

"It doesn't get better," another nearby boy told him. "You have to learn fast if you want to survive."

MacEoghan did not reply. His hesitation about the food melted away once he took his first bite of the roll. Warm, flaky, and even a little buttery. Soon enough, he could not engage in conversation because his mouth was too full of food.

His mirth ended abruptly when the soup priest walked up behind them.

"Father Daniel will see you after breakfast," he said, just as friendly as when he'd chastised MacEoghan in front of everyone.

Then he left.

MacEoghan had slept well. He liked sleeping in a bed, and it had been a really nice bed. And he liked the food, too. The soup, what he had tasted of it, was good. The beans and potatoes were good. The roll was delicious. It was all very good. And yet, looking at the soup priest as he walked away, MacEoghan couldn't help but wonder just how good it really was.

Once, an exotic peddler had come through, claiming to be someone from the circus. He even had a big, brown bear with him. He could make the bear do just about anything, but he always kept a pistol in one hand. "Just in case." The bear got applause, got treats, and it looked like it had a nice cage to ride around in from town to town. But what if the bear didn't want to do a trick? Or what if it did something wrong? There was always a pistol in the trainer's hand.

Everything will look better in the morning. Well, morning wasn't looking so good, honestly.

On each table was two pitchers of water and one pitcher of milk. MacEoghan was just finishing off a cup of water when a bell rang, very similar to the one from Mass. Apparently breakfast was over.

"Come on," the bread priest said, motioning to him and Miach. "I'll take you to Father Daniel."

And so he did, back to the same office they had come through the night before.

"Ah, welcome," Father Daniel greeted. "Micah and MacEoghan." He looked at the bread priest. "Thank you, Brother Wallace."

The older boy left. Before the father could say anything more, Miach beat him to it. "My name is Miach."

Father Daniel nodded and gestured for the boys to sit in the chairs across from him at the desk, which they did. "Yes, I understand there was a bit of a hiccup with your paperwork, but I'm afraid that my hands are tied in the matter. The papers that were dropped off here will no doubt be filed with the court that sent you here. As of yesterday, your name is now Micah Meagher."

"You can't type up new papers?" Miach asked.

Father Daniel grinned. "I'm afraid it's not that easy. Nothing involving the courts ever is. We may be able to talk to Padraig about it when he returns to check on you. But until something changes, if it changes, your name is now Micah."

MacEoghan looked at his brother. His brother had a new name. But he was still the same Miach. Changing his name didn't change him. Did it? What did it mean to be Micah instead of Miach?

"Anyway," Father Daniel went on, interrupting MacEoghan's thoughts, "I was informed of the incident this morning in the dining hall, as if your shirt did not already give you away. Now, I understand that Brother Simon can be a bit...hasty, with his discipline. And I did not have time to explain last night how things work here, what is expected of you.

"Wake up call comes at six o'clock sharp. You will go to morning prayers, and from there to breakfast. At all meals, everyone receives his food and waits until blessing before eating. After breakfast, everyone goes to class."

"Like school?" MacEoghan asked.

"Sort of. They're trade skills. Farming crops and animal husbandry, woodworking and wooden construction, fishery, logging, masonry and stone construction, some manufacturing, boat building, cooking and baking. There is little here that we cannot teach you. In this way, when you become adults, you will have many fine skills to help you get a job and see you through life. If you are exceptionally skilled, you may even be able to apprentice yourself to a master craftsman earlier than that."

"So where do we go?" Miach—or Micah?—wondered.

"What interests you? Do you have any knowledge or skills already?"

"Miach can do a go-fast!" MacEoghan blurted.

Father Daniel raised a brow. "A go-fast?"

"Shut up," Miach hissed.

MacEoghan did not. "Yeah, he can make it so we go faster than everyone else, and we just run right by!"

To his dismay, Father Daniel just laughed. "Ah, he has fancies! Well, we'll leave the imagination and the storytelling to the literary classes in the afternoon, where you will learn reading, writing, arithmetic, geography, science, history. Then you can tell your stories."

"But it's true!" MacEoghan insisted.

"Shut up," Miach hissed again.

"I'm sure it is," Father Daniel said, still grinning. "Anyway, after morning trades is dinner. Same routine as breakfast, though it will be the cooking students who serve dinner and supper. Then you will go to the classroom to learn all those things I just told you about. Then we have supper, a bit of recreation time, then evening Mass before bed at ten o'clock sharp." He stood. "Now then, first we need to get you cleaned up and into a trade. Most newcomers like to spend time with the animals. Would you like to do that, or something else?"

Miach and MacEoghan glanced at each other. Neither boy had any real experience with animals, but neither had an objection. Father Daniel made a motion, and the two followed him out of his office.

Their first stop was the bath house where they were given lukewarm baths, a haircut, and two changes of crisp, pressed clothing. From there, it was a long distance down a rocky trail to a barn. MacEoghan could smell it long before they saw it as the wind shifted. Looking at the barn, he saw a herd of cows, a herd of goats, a flock of sheep, and a dozen horses milling about in a small paddock. Maybe they should have waited for the bath until after the barn, but before he could say anything, Father Daniel was opening the barn door and calling out a greeting.

There they were introduced to Brother Aubrey and his dozen students, most of them nearly old enough to leave school.

"We're just looking at the animals before sending them to pasture for the day," Brother Aubrey said as Father Daniel left. "Either of you know much about animals? We've got cows, horses, goats—"

"We milked a goat once," MacEoghan piped up.

His last word was cut short as a sudden whistle ended with a crack and a yelp, and pain bloomed on his left calf. Brother Aubrey had hit him with a horse whip. A few of the other boys looked sympathetic, but no one said anything.

"Do not interrupt," Brother Aubrey said coldly. "Speak another word while you're here and you'll get a full hiding. Do you understand?"

"Yes, sir," he mumbled.

The whip cracked again, this time snapping against his right leg. He cried out again, but before Brother Aubrey could do anything, Miach jumped in. He pushed the Brother who stumbled back a step. The rest of the boys backed up several feet, glancing fearfully at one another.

Brother Aubrey regained his balance and turned his gaze, so friendly just a moment ago, on Miach who stood defiantly between him and MacEoghan.

"Don't hurt my brother!" he yelled.

The brother did not say anything as he traded the whip for a rod and began beating Miach. Any bravado Miach may have had quickly buckled under the vicious blows. When MacEoghan dared to try and help, Brother Aubrey brought the rod against him on the backswing, knocking him away.

When it was all over, Miach was whimpering on the dirty barn floor, and MacEoghan and the rest of the boys were watching from the other side of the room. It hadn't even taken that long, maybe fifteen seconds, perhaps twenty. And yet, it felt like forever, like when Miach used go-slow and made it look like he was moving slower than everything else.

Brother Aubrey straightened and looked at the group, rod still in hand. He made a motion. "Well? Carry on with your chores." He kicked Miach. "Get up. No slacking. You have to work, too."

MacEoghan bounced on his toes a couple times, then dared to dart forward and help Miach to his feet. His twin was in obvious pain and there were bruises forming all over his body.

They stayed with a couple older boys as they went about their chores, tending to the cows. MacEoghan did not ask questions. He wasn't even sure if he was allowed to speak yet, and he didn't want to chance it.

"It doesn't get better," one of the boys murmured. "Most of the time, they don't even tell you why they do it. Something about character and discipline and integrity."

" 'Spare the rod and spoil the child' is their favorite verse to quote," another boy said, his tone undeniably acidic.

"This is my fourth school," a third grumbled as he stuck a pitchfork into the dirty straw and tossed it away. He looked to be about fourteen. "Here in Leitir Fraic is the worst of them all, and the others were horrible, too. I'll be glad to leave school."

"How many schools are there?" Miach asked pathetically, casting a quick glance to see if Brother Aubrey was nearby to hit him for speaking.

The older boy sighed as he stabbed the dirty straw again. "Too many. The first one was a dream compared to this place. But the more you mess up, and especially if you're caught running away, they just send you to worse and worse schools. Eventually you come here."

"But we haven't been to any other schools."

The boy just shrugged and tossed away another scoop of straw. "Then you got no luck at all in you."

Brother Aubrey kept a close eye on them throughout the morning, and his demeanor had not improved by midday when he called everyone back into the barn.

"You're all dismissed for lunch, but the last one out of this barn gets a hiding."

He looked at Miach as he said it. Everyone knew exactly what he had in mind, and yet, no one seemed to care as the whole group took off running. Older boys used long legs to get ahead, younger boys used youthful speed and agility. Even MacEoghan would not say he wasn't tempted to leave Miach behind, but he also couldn't bear the thought of going back to the dining hall without his brother.

They walked side-by-side toward the large, open door. As they got closer, Brother Aubrey spoke again.

"Either pick one, or you both get a hiding."

When they were just before the threshold, Miach stopped, turned, and pushed MacEoghan out the door. MacEoghan hadn't even landed before Brother Aubrey descended on him with the rod a second time. This beating did not last as long, but every strike was just as severe. When he was done, Brother Aubrey said, "You're obviously a wily little twat, one of those thieving orphans we sometimes take in. Well, we'll just have to beat some discipline into you, won't we? Teach you how to be polite and proper, a productive member of society. You learn and do as we say, and we won't have any problems." He again kicked Miach. "Get to dinner. Don't be late or Brother Simon will give you a hiding, too. And it won't be with a little wooden spoon this time."

31

Somehow, Miach got to his feet. MacEoghan came alongside him and helped him limp to the dining hall. Surprisingly, they weren't the last ones to arrive. Several students and Brothers glanced over, but no one said a word. Miach sat down in a heap.

"I'll get food for you," MacEoghan told him.

He got in line and waited. The older boys who had made dinner were friendlier than the Brothers who stood behind them, but their expressions were still that of thinly-veiled terror. Every boy got a certain portion, and if the supervising Brothers suspected that one of the serving boys gave out too much, he was rapped with a wooden spoon on the arms or hands and half of the portion was removed from the bowl or plate.

MacEoghan grabbed one bowl and plate for himself, then a second, intending it for Miach. He yelped as a spoon found his knuckles.

"One bowl, one plate!" the soup brother from breakfast, Brother Simon, snapped.

"I need it for Miach." MacEoghan pointed.

"Are his legs broken?"

"Well, no, but—"

"Then he can come and get it himself."

And that was that, and a wooden spoon reinforced the point. MacEoghan glanced again at Miach who was not looking at him, then made his way through the line with only his bowl and plate. When he returned to the table, he set it down in front of Miach.

"Where's your food?" Miach asked.

MacEoghan shrugged wordlessly.

With tears in his eyes, Miach struggled out of his chair and slowly limped up to be the last in line. When he got back, he set the bowl and plate in front of MacEoghan.

Blessings were said, then the boys sat to eat.

"I hate this place," MacEoghan whimpered around a bite of food.

"Everyone does," someone nearby told him. "But they just beat you even worse if you try to run away or tell anyone."

"And you can't get worse than Leitir Fraic," another agreed.

"Is everyone here an orphan?" Miach asked.

"Might as well be. I haven't seen my mum in four years. I write to her sometimes, but I never hear back. I don't even know if my letters get out to her."

"My da sent me here intentionally," a third boy said. "Said it would be my best chance of learning a trade and doing good in the world, be a good member of society and the Church. Haven't seen or heard from him in six years."

"Little orphans like you?" the first boy went on. "They'll love you. Love to beat you, that is. Beat you, touch you. 'Cause you got no one interested in you."

"Yes, we do!" MacEoghan protested. "Padraig said he'd find our older brother."

"How old's your brother?" the second boy wondered.

MacEoghan glanced at Miach who shrugged feebly. A few years, at least. Thirteen when their mum died, so he'd be...older, anyway.

"How long's it been since you seen your brother?"

"Three years? Four?" MacEoghan offered.

The first boy waved a hand. "Never find him. Even if they do find him, they'll still keep you here." He straightened and assumed a deep voice. " 'Boys got to go to school. All children got to go to school.' " He shook his head and returned to his normal posture and voice. "Your brother got money to send you to a nice school? Private tutor? No? Then you're stuck here anyway."

The thought was daunting, and MacEoghan felt his heart racing in his chest.

"Don't speak," the third boy said. "Don't ever speak if you don't have to. Don't question the Brothers, the instructors, or the Sisters when they come by. Don't cry, especially at night. Don't wet the bed. Don't leave stains in the linens when you wash. Don't give anyone too much food at mealtime. Basically, just do whatever task you're told, keep your head down, and look out for yourself."

"But we're together," Miach stated. "Together forever."

"Not here you're not," a fourth boy told him. "Here it's everyone for himself."

"It's not all bad, though," the second boy said, perhaps seeing the look of terror on MacEoghan's face. "You can learn some good skills here."

"Make sure you learn them fast and learn them well," the fourth cut in. "Just as soon as you can leave school, do it. If you got some skills with you, you can get a job and not have to worry about ever coming back to a place like this. And if you can read and write and do basic maths, well, it can only help you, I guess."

"When can we leave?" MacEoghan wondered.

"Got to be fifteen years old before they'll stop hauling you back," the third boy answered. "So you got a few years yet."

"Just do what we told you," the first boy said. "Don't talk, do what you're told, and look out for yourself."

"If everyone looks out for himself, why tell us this?" Miach asked. "If we don't know the rules, you have a better chance of saving your own skin."

The first boy shrugged. "We may not intervene, but that doesn't mean we don't care. Intervening won't stop a Brother from beating you, it just means he'll beat us, too. Then where are we? Two beaten boys and neither one of us better for it."

MacEoghan looked at the bruises on his brother's skin, the mottled colors and swollen muscles. He didn't know what to make of it all.

"And one more thing," the fourth boy said. "There's some here who really do like being here. They like working with the Brothers. And they'll snitch on you just as fast as they can."

"Why?" MacEoghan asked dumbly.

"Gets them privileges," the second boy answered. "They might get a sweet, or they might get to help the brothers beat you. They're the ones the brothers help to get apprenticeships and whatnot so they can brag about how good the school is doing. Watch out for them."

MacEoghan looked around. How would he know them? Were they older? Younger?

"Don't look around," the third boy hissed. MacEoghan looked back at him. "Just keep your eyes on your food, your table, those around you. Never call attention to yourself. You'll get beaten, or worse."

"Worse?" Miach questioned.

The rest of the boys nodded.

"Worse," one said. "You'll find out in the afternoon classes. If the nuns come by and you have a sister for a teacher, it's only pain. But most of the time, it'll be a brother. And it'll be worse."

MacEoghan opened his mouth to speak, but the bell rang and the call went out to clean up and get to afternoon classes. Despite being told that it was everyone for himself, MacEoghan grabbed Miach's dishes and turned them in, then went back to help his brother. If the afternoon was worse, he might just have to defend his brother, like his brother defended him.

THE BROTHERS
OLDER BROTHER

Padraig never came back.

Sean was never found.

And after two years, Micah could almost believe that his name had always been so. Just a typographical error. Just a mispronunciation that had been corrected. It wasn't true, and he knew that in his heart, but there was nothing he could do about it here. It was not a fight worth picking, a lesson he had learned the hard way since arriving.

He tapped a wooden peg into place, then fitted the arm onto the chair, thus completing the project. He didn't know how many times he'd disassembled and reassembled this stupid thing. Roughing in, sanding smooth, varnishing, taking it apart and putting it back together each time so he would know how it all fit together and how it would look and this and that. He knew what a chair looked like. He also knew that if he complained, he would likely get a rod across his shoulders and a lecture on how grateful he should be; when he showed up, he could barely count to ten, never mind figure out larger or smaller numbers. Now he was doing precise measurements and building things.

He thought about that word as he delivered the chair and grabbed another disassembled project. Gratitude. Was he grateful? As he had been asked often enough, didn't he like being able to read and write? Didn't he like using numbers and building things? Didn't he like having a bed to sleep in, three meals a day, and constant communion with God? Did he really want to go back to life on the streets, scavenging for every meal and hoping to evade authorities? Didn't he like being a productive member of society? Was he really just so ungrateful?

He glanced at Brother Jordan, currently hovering over another boy's shoulder. Was Micah grateful to this man who taught him how to work well with wood, how to measure and cut and sand and drill and peg and varnish? Was he grateful to this man who beat him bloody and broke bones when he dared to question something? What did gratitude look like? Was working quietly and just following orders gratitude?

"All right, clean up!" Brother Jordan barked, startling the boy he stood behind.

At least he hadn't threatened them today. It seemed to be a favorite ploy of the Brothers. The last one got a hiding. The last one into class. The last one to clean up. The last one out the door. There always had to be a last one, so there would always be a victim. Some days they were really cruel and declared that the first one in got the hiding.

Don't be first. Don't be last. Just be another face in the crowd. The only time this really didn't apply was when it was one of those the Brothers favored. The snitches. The ones who got the formal apprenticeships just so the Brothers could say that the school was working as intended and to keep sending them money and young boys.

When everyone had cleaned up, Brother Jordan came around to inspect their work areas. Micah tried to remain stoic, if not defiant, as his area was inspected. The boys who trembled typically got a swat with the rod. If they were so afraid that their stations weren't clean, then they obviously needed to do a better job. Then they wouldn't tremble with fear. As if it were so simple.

One boy got a rap on the knuckles, but otherwise it was a pretty tame day, and they were dismissed to dinner. Micah ran to the hall as fast as he could, if only to look for MacEoghan and make sure he was all right. The Brothers had caught on to how Micah would defend his twin and often take his punishment, so they did their best to keep them separated.

MacEoghan had been sent to the kitchens after breakfast. It was actually one of the few places he didn't mind being. Not that he didn't get his fair share of beatings, but he seemed to enjoy cooking. To hear him tell it, he was helping the other boys, everyone else who was stuck under the thumbs of the Brothers. Most of the other trade skills only served the Brothers, or even no purpose at all except busy work.

Micah spotted his twin at the end table, manning the bread with Brother Caleb, looking almost pleased with himself. Their gazes met briefly, but neither said a word. Even when Micah reached the table to receive two slices of freshly baked bread, the two did not speak. Brother Caleb was friendlier than most, but Brother Justin who was manning the vegetables was not, and he kept a close eye on Micah and MacEoghan.

Micah took his food back to the table and waited with the rest. MacEoghan and the other boys who had been in the kitchen that morning joined them last. Blessings were said, and the boys were permitted to eat.

"Delicious, as always," Micah told him, tearing into the bread.

"I tried something different," MacEoghan admitted sheepishly. "I added the flour just half a cup at a time instead of all at once."

"And you got away without bloody knuckles?" a nearby boy wondered.

"Brother Caleb isn't that bad," MacEoghan said, looking a bit guilty for saying so.

"Snitch," someone muttered.

"If he's really all that great, he won't last long," someone else grumbled. "The nice ones never do."

"I'll enjoy it while I can," MacEoghan insisted.

"No one says you shouldn't," Micah said. "Just don't be too sad when it's gone."

"Well, I know I won't be sad when I'm gone from here," the first boy declared. "One year, four months, and twelve days, and I'll be fifteen. Then I can leave this place and never look back."

"Where will you go?" MacEoghan wondered.

The boy shrugged. "I don't know. Honestly, I don't care. I'll live on the streets if I have to. More likely, though, I'll go to work in some factory."

"Where?" Micah asked.

"Dublin. Lots of opportunities in Dublin. All the opportunity in the world. I could start work in the factory, and maybe I can become a salesman."

Everyone in the school had dreams, those hopes and wishes they only spoke aloud at mealtime. But the funny thing was, no one knew how many of those dreams came true because no one ever came back to tell. No one ever visited the school to tell the boys how the training from the Brothers helped them get a good job and stay off the streets. All they heard about was the occasional apprenticeship, and that was it; outgoing boys vanished into thin air.

The bell rang to signal the end of dinner and the start of classroom time. Again, Micah and MacEoghan were separated. Micah went to geography while MacEoghan went to maths.

Any chatter from the boys died instantly when they crossed the threshold into the classroom, making nervous eye contact with Brother Andrew who watched them with a disquieting grin on his face. Again, Micah contemplated gratitude.

On the streets, the only places he knew were where he'd been. Places like England or Scotland or Wales had been just vague concepts, places he hadn't been and would likely never go. Even North Ireland had been merely a name to him. To look at the world map now at the front of the room and consider all the other places that existed...was he grateful? Was he happy to know that he was but one boy upon a huge planet full of boys? Was he happy to think about how other boys in other places lived?

"Edward," Brother Andrew began. "Come here."

No, Micah decided, watching the named boy walk to the front of the room. No, he was not grateful. It was like a magic trick. Look there, not here. Follow the magician's left hand while his right made the magic work. Look at the rest of the world, the big, big world, all the problems everywhere else. Now aren't you ashamed for thinking your problems matter?

The boy said nothing, but his movements were stiff, his face a poorly covered expression of stark terror. Brother Andrew stood to meet him. He turned Edward to face the class and put the boy's arms out to his sides. He pointed to the boy's head.

"Here is the United Kingdom and Ireland, the top of the world, or the only world that matters." He pointed to either arm. "Here is the Atlantic Ocean which leads to the Americas, and here is Asia, in the wings but largely unimportant." He pointed to the boy's feet. "There is Antarctica, clearly cold."

Micah wondered why the Brothers even went through the motions. Everyone knew what came next. Brother Andrew put his hand down the front of Edward's pants. Edward flinched and squeezed his eyes shut. Micah and most of the other boys in the room shifted uncomfortably, chancing a few glances.

"And this is Africa," Brother Andrew breathed. "Large, dark, and savage." He looked out at the rest of the boys. "Would anyone like to learn about Africa?" No one ever volunteered, so the brother picked one at random. Winston was called up and made to put his hand down Edward's pants also.

"What's the matter?" Brother Andrew asked, noting both Winston's and Edward's expressions. "Don't you like Africa? I understand it's a strange and unusual place, but we have a duty to help it."

The only thing Micah saw being helped was Brother Andrew's "Africa."

The Brother straightened, withdrawing his hand. Winston looked like he sorely wanted to, but did not dare until he was dismissed. Brother Andrew regarded the two for a long moment, then sent them both back to their seats with a bit of a resigned sigh. None of the boys said a word.

In the two or so years that Micah had been at St. Joseph's, he'd witnessed such displays at least twice a month from most of the Brothers. Some did not bother with such pretense, instead just calling a boy to the front of the room and doing it. Sometimes it was called a punishment, but most times it was called a reward. Didn't they like being rewarded? Well then, they could be punished in some other way.

Micah had been called up on several occasions. Each time he elected to take the punishment rather than the "reward." When he asked MacEoghan if anything had ever happened to him, he denied it, said he'd managed to escape their notice. Micah figured the brothers were going to try and break him first so that he couldn't or wouldn't defend his brother.

"Now open your geography books to page seventy-five," Brother Andrew ordered, moving on as if nothing had happened.

After geography was history with Brother James. Rarely did anything weird happen there. Was Micah more grateful for this class, then, compared to the other? Maybe. But what use was history when the present wasn't anything spectacular? If the best that all of history—which was riddled with great wars and independence wars and civil wars—could do was this forsaken school out in the middle of nowhere, Micah really didn't see a point.

Reading, writing, maths, all classes he had struggled with in the beginning but was now fairly good at, at least good enough to avoid being punished for being too stupid. He could read and write in Irish and English, and he could fill in a multiplication chart up to twenty-five from memory. He was even pretty good at fractions, too, multiplying and dividing.

"The capacity of St. Joseph's is 190 boys," Brother John said, writing on the board. "Currently, there are 179 boys attending the school. What percentage capacity are we at? Five minutes, go."

Another boy, Oliver, raised his hand first. "Ninety-four-point-two percent."

"Correct. Now, if thirty-two boys are going to graduate this year and forty-four new boys come in, what percentage capacity will we be? Four minutes, go."

This time it was Micah who raised his hand. "Over one hundred percent because there will be 191 boys."

Brother John walked over and rapped him on the knuckles. Not as hard as a true beating, but it still stung. "Be specific. What percentage?"

"One hundred-point-five," Micah answered stiffly.

"When I ask for a percentage, I expect a specific percentage," the Brother warned, and walked away, spouting another complex worded math problem to solve.

It was the worst thing Micah experienced in class that day, and afterwards it was time for supper. Micah caught up with MacEoghan on the way to the dining hall.

"Two years, ten months, twenty-three days," Micah said. "Then we can leave."

"Or you can use go-fast," MacEoghan muttered.

"Even if I did, they'd just catch us again. And you saw what they did to Liam when they brought him back after he ran away. At least if we're fifteen, we can't be forced back."

"Or you can use go-fast. And if they catch us, you can use go-fast again. At least until we're fifteen."

"MacEoghan, we're twelve. Where are we going to go? What are we going to do? You want to go to work in a factory?"

"It can't be worse than here."

"Grown men are maimed in factories. You want to be maimed?"

"I don't want to watch grown men put their hands where they shouldn't." MacEoghan shook his head. "It's wrong, Micah, and you know it. It's even in the Bible."

Micah shrugged. "What do you want me to do?"

"Get us out of here. Get all of us out of here. Stop the Brothers. Do something. Anything."

Desperation caused MacEoghan's voice to crack more than normal. Micah sighed. "I don't know. I don't like it either, but where are we going to go? We're never going to find Sean. We don't know anyone, we don't know where to go."

"Then we can go anywhere. We're not leaving anything behind, that's for sure."

They reached the dining hall. "We need a better plan. We'll talk about it later."

He could see MacEoghan was annoyed with him, but there wasn't much they could do. For one, they couldn't make escape plans right in front of the Brothers in the food line. And for two, where were they going to go? They were twelve. They were only just becoming men. Anyone who saw them was going to know they didn't go to school and ship them right back here to Leitir Fraic.

Unless, of course, he used go-fast to help them escape. Like MacEoghan said, it would only be for a few years, until they were fifteen, or at least looked old enough that they wouldn't be forced to come back. And what was the point of being able to use go-fast except for just such emergencies?

But where to go? What to do? If they were going to run away, they needed a destination, a plan of some form.

Blessings were said and the boys started on their food. Micah looked around, then used go-fast. Everything around him slowed so it seemed to take twice or three times as long to do anything. One boy was sopping up some soup with his bread, and Micah could see every ripple in the soup as he dunked the bread, every drop that fell as he lifted the bread to his mouth. Another boy was drinking from his cup, and Micah watched the backwash as the boy's act of swallowing pushed the water back into the cup so he didn't choke. At another table, a Brother was tearing off a chunk of bread, and Micah watched each crumb slowly make its way to the floor.

He could work with this, couldn't he? To everyone else, it would simply appear as though he and MacEoghan moved extra fast. But no one would be able to catch them. Even dogs couldn't run that fast. The only thing that might prove a challenge was a motor vehicle. So they would have to keep off the roads as much as possible. But they really probably could do it.

He stopped using go-fast. Life resumed as normal. The first boy ate his soup-soaked bread, the second swallowed and put his cup of water back down on the table. The Brother arranged his bread just so and started slathering it with butter. No one appeared to have noticed what he did, except for MacEoghan beside him.

"Can we go now?" he hissed.

"We need a plan," Micah insisted quietly. "We need a destination. We need more than just a wish."

"How do you propose we do that?"

"Take as many outdoor trades as you can. Study the surrounding area. Pay close attention in geography. We can talk at night or in the morning."

If any of the surrounding boys heard their conversation or knew its reference, they knew not to say anything about it. Some were too afraid of being implicated as a co-conspirator and punished, others didn't want to give up someone who was daring enough to try. The few who Micah knew were snitches were not within earshot currently, and it was hard to hear very far at the noisy tables. Supper was the best meal of the day, and sometimes they even got dessert. Tonight was not one of those nights, but it was still the most relaxed time any boy could hope to have in his day.

Supper was also the only meal that did not have a strict ending time as the following couple hours were devoted to recreational time. A boy who wished to stay and savor his food was only taking away from his own play time. This did not mean that slackers were not eventually chased out, but there was a hint of mercy extended at the end of the day.

By the time Micah and MacEoghan left the dining hall, there was already a game of football underway, and another game of cricket was just being set up and teams chosen.

"You think we should start planning now?" MacEoghan wondered.

Micah shook his head. "Not yet. We know the grounds here well enough. It's what's beyond that we need to learn more about."

"Outdoor trades and geography."

"Exactly. We'll start planning in a week, so learn a lot in that time."

"When do you think we'll be able to try?"

"Depends on what we learn. Now let's see if we can't join in on the football. After all, go-fast can only do so much. We're going to have to actually run, too."

They jogged over to the match and manage to weasel their way into the game. After a few predictable incidents where the ball was passed to the wrong twin on the opposite team, they were always put on the same team.

Like most boys their age, they were finally becoming men, though they weren't quite sure what to do with it yet. On the one hand, Micah could certainly outrun the ten year old boys, outrun or overtake them easily. At the same time, he had a hard time keeping up with some of the fourteen year old boys whose legs grew an inch every night, and he found himself the victim of the same slide he used to take out the younger boys.

Telling himself that he needed to practice running in order to get away from the Brothers helped his determination and endurance, even if his concentration suffered equally. He missed several passes because he was focused more on a distant tree, pretending he was being pursued by the Brothers. Finally he pleaded fatigue and left the game. MacEoghan wasn't far behind.

"You really think we can do it?" MacEoghan wondered. "With running and go-fast, you think we can make it?"

Micah nodded. "I think so. If we have somewhere to go. Otherwise we'll just end up right back here, and it might be us who does it!"

"How long do you think it will take to plan?"

Now he shrugged. "Depends on what we learn. You remember what I said?"

"Geography, outdoor trades."

"Right."

MacEoghan nodded, his gaze fixed on the continuing football game. "We have to get out of here, Micah. We have to."

"We will," Micah promised. "Together forever."

The bell rang to signal the end of recreation time. Any relaxation or giddiness the boys may have felt quickly snapped back into the routine of fear as toys and tools were hastily put away in their bid to get to evening Mass on time. Just short of two hundred boys piled into the small chapel, dipping fingers in holy water and grabbing hymnals and Bibles.

If a god could be judged by his followers, Micah had decided that he didn't like God very much. If a father could be judged by his children, then Micah would say that God didn't really know how to parent. He had no control over His children. He couldn't get them to tell the truth, stop fighting, or behave in any good sense of the word. Oh, sure, outsiders might look at the schools and think them well and good, but for the boys who knew... And based on what Micah knew, and what he read in the Bible and how he compared it to the Brothers who were supposed to be wholly devoted holy followers and paragons of righteous living, well, he just didn't like God.

He mouthed the words to the hymns and any verses they were made to read aloud as a group. The only time he did speak aloud was if he was called on specifically to read or sing, which was rare. Beside him in the pew, MacEoghan sang and read obediently, but with no enthusiasm. When Micah expressed his doubts or misgivings, he might conjure up some weak defense about a father not being able to control his adult child's every move and having to trust him, but his commitment to such a defense was lacking. A father might not be able to control his adult son's every move, but if he knew that his son was hurting people, especially children, would he really do nothing to stop him, or just chock it up to being a prodigal?

The worst part was, there was no one Micah could really go to for answers. Most of the boys were of a similar mindset, and any who weren't would likely report him for heresy and he would be beaten, or worse. No one questioned the Brothers. Not the boys, not the nuns, not the support staff. And no one, not even the Taoiseach, questioned the Church.

Mass ended and the boys were sent to wash up and go to bed. Tomorrow was Sunday, which meant an extra long morning Mass followed by some recreational time followed by an extra long evening Mass. Micah suppressed a sigh. He watched as a couple Brothers overseeing the nightly chaos took an interest in one of the younger boys, a new arrival just a few weeks prior. The second day after the boy's arrival he'd wet the bed and been beaten savagely for it. The boy, barely six years old, now put his nightshirt on backwards, somehow still naive enough to grin, and was cuffed over the head for it, for daring to be a little silly. The boy whimpered a little as he put the shirt on the right way. No one around him made a sound, and few dared to look his way.

They had to get out of here, Micah resolved. Anywhere was better than here, even the streets. At least on the streets, they could fight back. On the streets, they didn't have to pretend that everything was fine, that this was exactly as things should be. On the streets, they could make their own rules, set their own schedule, do their own thing. Even working in a factory was starting to feel less demeaning, maybe even a little safer.

He got in bed, taking the top bunk with MacEoghan below. Around them, the rest of the boys did the same. When everyone was tucked in under the blankets, the Brothers wished them a cold good night, turned off lights, blew out lanterns and candles, and left the room.

"It'll be all right, MacEoghan," Micah said. "We'll make a plan."

MANHOOD
YOUNGER BROTHER

Brother Simon said he would become accustomed to it, even get to like it, but after almost three years, MacEoghan could say without a doubt that that was not true by any means.

He didn't like being called up to the front of the class. He didn't like the Brothers putting their hands down his pants, or pulling his pants down so they could "demonstrate" the changes his body was going through as he became a man. He hated that he liked the feeling he got, vehemently hated that the Brothers instigated it, or had another one of the boys, usually a much younger one, instigate it. He hated when he woke up with it, wondering if anything had caused it, if anyone had touched him in the night, and he hated that he might like it.

MacEoghan hated everything about himself becoming a man, and he hated himself for hating it. He'd always wanted to be a man, always looked up to Sean, always looked up to the things he'd once imagined about his father. Even now, he looked up to Micah and how he navigated such things. Micah woke up with it sometimes, too. His excuse usually involved going to relieve himself before the Brothers noticed. They were very rarely in the same class together, and Micah had always taken the beatings over the hands. MacEoghan just couldn't bring himself to quite do that. He'd known pain and hunger and isolation, and he didn't like it. He didn't like the hands or the humiliation either, and he felt ashamed that he would excuse it by saying that at least it felt good.

Micah had morals. Micah had principles. He had the strength and the courage to stand by them. MacEoghan didn't. And he hated himself even more for it. He wanted to leave and run away, and he had sat down with Micah at recreation time and made plans, but for some reason, he just couldn't bring himself to leave. He'd seen what they did to boys who ran away, and it wasn't just a physical beating. Sure, Micah had go-fast. Yes, they'd spent a year making plans and scoring exceptionally well in geography. But what if it just wasn't enough?

Micah wouldn't leave without him, which only further exacerbated MacEoghan's self-loathing. His brother shouldn't have to deal with this. It might have been fine when they were little kids and didn't know any better, but they were nearly men now. Men were supposed to be strong and courageous. They were twins. Why did Micah look and sound and act so much stronger and more courageous? When did MacEoghan get his portion?

Evidently not today as Brother Jude dismissed him and the boy touching him. They hurried back to their seats. The best MacEoghan could do to hide himself at his desk was to bring his knees up and his elbows down so that his trousers tented a bit. They might wrinkle a bit, too, but that was all right. He wanted to hate the feeling, wanted it to go away even as he wanted it to finish as it sometimes did in the morning. From his scrunched position, he watched Brother Jude write on the chalkboard, hating the man for causing MacEoghan to hate what it meant to be a man.

Eventually the feeling went away and he was able to relax some. He could almost focus on the math problem that was written out. Having been humiliated at the start of class, MacEoghan knew he was in no danger of being called on to solve the problem, nor be whacked if he got it wrong. He was the teacher's favorite today. He got special privileges today, like the privilege of not being hit.

He hated himself.

He needed to muster his courage to give Micah the signal for when he was ready to go. He had to get out of here.

Class time ended and the boys made their way to the dining hall. MacEoghan met up with Micah and they got in line for food.

Where would they go? What would they do? They talked about it a lot, but what if things were different than they planned for? Where would they sleep that first night after running away? Where would they get food? If anyone thought them homeless, they would be turned over to the authorities and brought right back here.

No. Micah promised he would use go-fast and they would escape. He tried to use it at least once a week, just to practice and make sure it wouldn't fail again like it did the day they were caught. He didn't know why it had failed that day, but he was determined that it wouldn't happen again.

Maybe MacEoghan should learn how to do it. If he could go-fast, then he wouldn't have to worry so much if they got separated. And maybe his go-fast could combine with Micah's go-fast and they could go twice as fast. Then they could run away twice as fast and would have even less to worry about. Problem was, Micah couldn't explain how he did it. He didn't really know when he'd begun or what made him able to do it. He just willed it and it happened.

MacEoghan had tried willing it a time or two. His will couldn't be any weaker than his brother's at age three or four or whenever it was he'd begun. He'd tried willing it. Specifically, he tried willing the opposite of go-fast. He tried to use go-slow whenever the Brothers called him up. If he slowed down, everything else sped up, and maybe it would be over faster. It never seemed to work. He was always acutely aware of every horrifying moment. Maybe he really didn't have the will. Or maybe, in his fear, he was conjuring go-fast, so that he went faster and everyone else went slower and the terrible experience stretched on even longer.

He needed to get out. He needed to muster his courage, tell Micah that now was the time, and leave. Just leave. Just walk away. Walk out the door for recreation time and just keep going. They could get at least a couple hours' head start.

A warm roll landed on his plate. His mouth watered. His stomach grumbled all the way to the table and he continued to stare at the roll while the rest of the boys got their food and the Brothers said blessing.

"Did you hear the starlings today?" Micah asked him innocently as they sat to eat.

It was one of the many code phrases they had developed, how to talk about their plans in front of the other boys and the Brothers. Listening to birds, seeing deer, seeing an odd formation in the clouds, among other things. Everyone else thought them simply observant and appreciative of nature. The real question was whether today was the day.

He needed to say yes. It was time to go. Time to run. Time to escape. Time to end the Brothers' hold over them, over him.

He took a bite of the warm roll, the outer crust breaking with a satisfying crackle. Well, he had been humiliated today, but he knew, then, that he had at least a couple weeks, maybe even a month, before he was at risk of that again. He took another bite of the roll, the warm butter running down his chin. Besides, it was windy outside, likely to rain tonight. How would it be for them to run away and fall ill? He finished off the roll and shook his head.

Micah sighed and scooped a spoonful of vegetables. He was getting tired of MacEoghan constantly refusing, when he had insisted on all this planning in the first place. A little hesitation was justifiable. A little fear was perfectly understandable. This was just annoying.

He should have said yes. And really, it wasn't as though he couldn't change his answer. He could say something like, "You know, actually I think I did hear them, but the sheep were bleating so loudly it was hard to tell." He'd been out in the barn this morning, so it was perfectly reasonable. He should do that. He needed to tell Micah yes. Yes, he heard the starlings. Yes, he was ready to escape. Today was the day.

But his tongue just would not let him. It wasn't as though he couldn't speak. He could open his mouth, eat food just fine, laugh at another boy's joke or tell one of his own, but he could not look at his own twin and tell him that it was time to leave this terrible place.

What was worse, Micah seemed to see this, too. He knew MacEoghan wanted to say yes, knew that he was in pain. He just wanted to hear him say it. He needed to know that it was his idea, too, that they were in this together. They were two parts, two actors in this plan. This wasn't just Micah dragging MacEoghan around, constantly coming to his little brother's rescue. He needed to know that they were leaving as independent men, not scared little boys.

But MacEoghan was still just a scared little boy. He would rather sit where he was, as terrible as it could be, rather than face the dangers of the unknown. The fear of the unknown. What was, was bad, but what could be, could be worse. But it could also be better. Except he just couldn't convince his mind—or his tongue—of that possibility. He glanced at the Brothers, dining at their own table. If he stared at them long enough, if he thought about what he'd gone through just a few hours ago in class, could he conjure up enough hatred to want to run away?

He could not. In fact, he could only conjure up even more self-loathing. The more he thought about what they did to him, the more his body reacted in the way he hated. Averting his eyes and focusing on his food quelled the reaction but only stoked the flames of hatred for himself.

Why him? If MacEoghan could ask God any question—and actually get an answer—that was it. Why him? Why was this happening? Where were the angels to swoop in and save the day and vanquish evil? Where was the justice for the Brothers and their evils? Where was the mercy for MacEoghan and the other boys who suffered at their hands? And, again, why him? Many boys were touched in such terrible ways, but certainly not all. The Brothers had their favorites. Why him? And why did Micah have to suffer their wrathful hand simply for standing up to them? Was he being punished? Was MacEoghan perhaps in the wrong for resisting? He did like the feeling. He liked it a lot. Was he wrong to hate it at the same time? It was simply his body becoming a man and doing what it did. Was it wrong for the Brothers to show them how it worked? Weren't men supposed to mentor boys?

A rock in his gut said this went beyond mentoring. This was absolutely perverse. But again, where was God? Why did He allow his servants to do this? Why was it on the two of them to have to run away and risk their lives just to escape it? Wasn't there anyone they could tell? Wasn't there any way to stop it?

And here MacEoghan couldn't even tell his brother that it was time to escape. Here he was, just staring at his food, barely engaged in eating or conversation. Now, not only was his tongue fixed in place, but his eyes, too. He couldn't bear to look at his brother. Probably his brother couldn't bear to look at him. Would Micah eventually give up on him and run away on his own? How long would he really wait? How long could he stand to take the beatings? He was strong, but even he had limits. He would use the last of his strength to run, but he couldn't carry MacEoghan at the same time.

The bell rang to signal the end of dinner. MacEoghan followed his brother to drop off their dinnerware, then head outside.

51

"I'm going to bed," MacEoghan said, the first thing he'd managed since turning down Micah's offer to run away.

"It's recreation time, but they'll hide you if they catch you in bed," Micah told him, looking surprised by the statement.

"I don't feel good."

MacEoghan turned away and started toward the dorms before Micah could protest. He did not look back. He couldn't. He didn't want to see the confusion, the hurt, the bewilderment, none of it. He wasn't even sure he wanted Micah to try and stop him, and he couldn't decide whether he was disappointed that he didn't.

He reached the dorms without issue. Micah wasn't wrong. Recreation time was as close to doing whatever they wanted as they would ever get, but the dorms were off-limits, accessible only for sleeping at night and anyone who was tasked with cleaning them in the morning. If anyone caught him here at this hour, he could get a hiding. If he fell asleep and missed Mass, he would be hided until he was unconscious then sent to sit in isolation for at least three days. That was what happened to the last boy who tried such a thing.

And yet, as he lay down, he couldn't bear to be around anyone else right now. He didn't want to see them having fun, playing football or jacks or marbles or whatever else they elected to do. How could they have fun when they were surrounded by this, when they lived under the heavy hand of the Brothers? Was it escapism, or illusion? Did no one else feel like this was wrong? Did no one else feel like something had to give?

He couldn't reconcile it. No matter how hard he tried, he couldn't make it all fit together in his head. There was what the Brothers did, and there was what they preached. Was he the one who was lacking? Was there something he wasn't understanding?

Or he could just give up and accept it. This was life. This was what was supposed to happen. Maybe he was lacking. Maybe he was ascribing too much to things. The Brothers did what they did, from one thing to the next, and they just moved on. From sleeping to eating to teaching, it was just part of the routine. Three times a day, they ate. Once a week, they held Mass basically all day. And once a week or every two weeks, they showed boys what it was to be men. That was all. It was just his own fear getting in the way of things, a little boy who was becoming a big boy who was becoming a man, all involuntarily and entirely unprepared. They were just trying to prepare him.

It still didn't feel right. If that were all true, things would be different. He and other boys wouldn't be singled out. Micah wouldn't be beaten for saying no. And above all, it wouldn't feel wrong. The things of God are good, the Brothers said. Even when they don't feel good, like being punished for stealing, you know they're good, because your spirit knows they're good because they're from God. It's the discipline of a father, unpleasant in the moment, but good in the long-term.

This wasn't good. It couldn't be. Leviticus, Romans, I Corinthians, he had read all of those. It wasn't good. It wasn't even bad. It was worse than bad. It was abominable. Really, really bad. The worst thing ever.

So then, where was God? Even if this was a good thing, couldn't God come and say so? A message? A dream? An angel? If only He could just tell him—no, if He could just tell everyone here, they would have to listen. A burning bush or pillar of fire. If the Brothers were in the right, then the boys would know and they could relax and enjoy it. If the Brothers were wrong, well, they were servants of God and they would have to listen to the rebuke, right? They wanted to walk in the way of righteousness, right? Sometimes people just needed a little correction.

But no answer came. MacEoghan could feel the seconds tick by. He could feel the danger of being caught.

Well, maybe if he wasn't thought to be sleeping, it would be all right. If the Brothers thought he was being productive in some way, maybe they wouldn't beat him if he was caught. Sometimes it wasn't about doing something, like sleeping, so much as just not keeping busy. Sloth was the most reviled of sins here at the school. This was an industrial school where they were supposed to learn a trade and be productive members of society. Anyone could be lazy, but they at the school had to keep busy. And maybe he could take the time, since no one was around, and try to figure some things out on his own. If he did a little self-study and self-reflection, maybe he wouldn't be so self-conscious around the other boys. Like getting called on to answer a question in maths when he didn't understand how to solve the problem. If he understood the problem and how to solve it, he would be more confident when he got called on.

He listened for just a moment, making sure he was alone in the room. His gaze darted to several shadows on the wall, but they were mundane objects only. He leaned over the edge of the bed and looked around underneath, down the row of beds on either side. No one was hiding under any of the beds, and he didn't see anyone under the blankets of the bottom or top bunks when he looked. He was alone, but he still felt like the whole world was watching him somehow. Maybe he shouldn't do this. But then, it would only get worse the next time he was called up.

He lay back down and undid his pants. Even just looking at himself felt wrong. Except even that was foolish because he kind of had to just when he went to the bathroom and when he washed himself. It was his body, as it had always been.

He tried to relax. He was alone, and he was himself. That was all. And yet, images began creeping into his mind. The Brothers, some going through some meaningless speech, pretending he could be used as some object lesson for geography or literature. If this were good and normal, they wouldn't have to cover it up, MacEoghan thought, but his own thoughts felt hollow and distant, belonging to someone else. He closed his eyes as if he could make it stop, but it didn't work in the classroom and it didn't work here.

He felt something touch him, and he did something surprising. He grabbed himself, as if to beat the imaginary hand to it. If anyone was going to do anything, it was going to be him. Not some perverse old man, not some innocent and scared boy younger than he was. It was going to be him. He was going to control the way his body acted and reacted.

And his body certainly reacted. He knew the feeling he liked. He knew what it meant to get hard. But it was going to be him. His hand, his decision, no one else's. He was going to enjoy it because he wanted to.

MacEoghan had always been too afraid to want to know what happened at the end, but he could honestly say it was the pinnacle of his pleasure and self-loathing. He knew he had just done something irresistibly wonderful and yet woefully sinful. He hated himself with fury he could not readily explain.

And yet, it was also kind of like breaking free of some kind of restraint. He had done it. By himself. For himself. Because he wanted to. And that was that. Now he could carry on with his day, finish out recreation time, go the Mass, then go to bed.

Well, maybe not quite yet. He was still a bit fascinated by it, and he would have to clean himself up a little, not unlike he sometimes had to when he woke up. Was this what happened when he sometimes woke up hard or, on rare occasion, wet? Was this something his body did automatically? He didn't know. There was so much he didn't know or understand because he was too busy fending off the Brothers.

Grudgingly, he sat up. Something caught his attention in his peripheral vision, and he looked. Any lingering pleasure or loathing vanished as he made eye contact with Brother David, standing in the doorway.

"Child, do you know what you've just done?" the man asked.

MacEoghan swallowed. "I just did what happens when the Brothers touch me in class. I just went to the end."

Now Brother David approached. MacEoghan, with his pants still undone, tried to stand and be presentable. He was not able to put everything back to rights before Brother David grabbed his arm and started dragging him, using every inch of his own, much longer, stride, out of the dormitory toward the Brothers' residence for punishment.

Recreation time was still going on outside. Across the lawn, MacEoghan spied the football game. A few of the boys on the sidelines took notice of him being hauled away, but none of them said or did anything. Those actively playing football never noticed. And certainly no one intervened. He did not see Micah anywhere.

As soon as the heavy wooden door slammed shut behind him, MacEoghan felt his heart jump into his throat. He'd never been brought here for punishment before; this was reserved for the worst offenses, like running away. What were they going to do to him? Lock him up for a few days? Beat him? He wished Micah were with him. He wished he'd given a better answer to Micah's question; they could have been halfway to town by now, or even farther with the go-fast. Then he wouldn't be here, and he wouldn't hate himself as much as he did.

He was taken to an office and told to sit and wait. His pants were still loose around him, though they'd managed to stay up during the march. After Brother David left the room, MacEoghan managed to get everything back to rights, though he still hadn't been able to clean himself.

All he'd done was what they'd done to him. He'd just finished was all. What had he done wrong? Or maybe this was just because he went to the dorms when he shouldn't have.

He sat. And waited. No one came. Was this what it was like to be locked up for days? Had they forgotten about him? Fear tapered off into confusion, then boredom. Was he just going to sit here until evening Mass? Was he going to be kept from Mass? That seemed like a bigger punishment to the Brothers than to him; he didn't like Mass anyway. On the other hand, sitting here in this office wasn't much fun either.

Maybe they would wait to punish him until after Mass. Maybe the Brothers were going to pray and ask God what kind of punishment they should inflict on him, though he still didn't understand his crime.

He heard the toll of the bell, signaling the end of recreation time. The boys would be leaving the field or wherever they'd hunkered down, and running to the chapel. Should he join them? Mass was mandatory, and punishment for skipping could be severe. At the same time, Brother David had told him to sit here and wait. Disobeying a direct order from a Brother could also be severe.

It was about five minutes into Mass time when the door finally opened and Brother Andrew walked in. MacEoghan braced himself for some kind of rebuke about not being at Mass, but none came. Brother Andrew pulled up a chair and quietly sat down.

"I know what Brother David told me," he began, "but would you care to tell me what happened?"

MacEoghan felt his whole body grow warm with embarrassment. "I just did what..." He mumbled the rest.

"Speak up," Brother Andrew commanded. "Confess it to me."

MacEoghan shifted in his seat. "I just did what you all sometimes do in class."

"But...?"

"I just finished is all."

Brother Andrew sighed and shook his head, his expression unnervingly neutral. "I was a young man, too, once. New to my body, new to growing up. I didn't understand either. But that is what we try to teach you. We want to show you what is good and right about the body God made for you. You are becoming a man, and we are tasked with showing you what that means. You've been a good student, MacEoghan. Surely you've heard the word 'masturbation'?"

"Yes, sir."

Brother Andrew made a vague gesture. "That's what you've done here. Now, understand, sex is a good thing. But it must always be done with someone. Sex comes from the divine. Going it alone is no different than going through life without God. Do you understand?"

MacEoghan nodded his head, but his mouth said, "No."

"No. Of course not. You are, as I said, new. You're what, twelve or thirteen years old?"

"Yes, sir."

"You've been here for about three or four years, right?"

"Yes, sir."

The man remained calm, and MacEoghan didn't know if he should be relieved or afraid. "So you've heard these big words and you've heard about some of these things that are happening, but you are only just starting to experience it for yourself. And sometimes the real thing is different from what we've imagined it to be. Right?"

MacEoghan could only nod, still waiting for the lash of a rod or some other horrible fate to befall him.

Brother Andrew nodded along with him. "Yes, of course. As I said, I was young once, too. Granted, I'm not terribly old, but I'm...experienced. And that's what we really try to impart on you is experience. We want to prepare you, get you ready so that when you start to mature, well, this doesn't happen." He sighed and frowned. "I'm guessing your twin brother has something to do with it."

"What? No!" MacEoghan pleaded, suddenly afraid that Micah would be punished, too.

"He's a strong boy," Brother Andrew went on, his tone finally shifting into something cold, almost sinister. "He's good at physical labor, which is a blessing to be sure. But he is also very stubborn and hard-headed about some things. It's good that he looks out for you, but it seems he is also holding you back."

No, I'm holding him back. MacEoghan almost said it aloud but refrained at the last minute.

"But, now that he isn't here and it's just me and you, maybe we can have a real conversation about manhood. I know that this is a big school, and maybe you've just gotten lost in the shuffle. Maybe you're just a little slower to learn and put things together. Maybe this one-on-one time is just what you need to understand."

MacEoghan didn't know what to say or do, so he just stayed where he was, silent.

"On the other hand," Brother Andrew said, standing, "maybe, since this is what you've come to, you would learn better with a demonstration. After all, didn't I just get done saying that all the explanation in the world is useless if you never experience something for yourself? But if you've never gotten the explanation, then the demonstration can be a little intimidating. Seeing how you've been brought here for the sin of masturbation, I can imagine your discomfort." He began undoing his trousers. "Maybe it would be better if I acted as this demonstration, or part of it. After all, I'm experienced, and I can guide you. No classroom full of spectators to judge you. And you know you'll be safe from punishment. How does that sound?"

MacEoghan could only stare as Brother Andrew's member did the same as his had done earlier, the same as any of the older boys who were called to the front of the class. To get a reward. Brother Andrew was clearly comfortable with it. He was experienced. He knew what was going on, what was expected of a man's body. He knew what was going on and how to prepare boys for when they entered the marriage bed with their wives. That was all this was, right? Did the nuns of the girls' schools do something similar when they became women? And then, once the students were graduated and going to marry, each would know his and her role. That was all this was, right?

The good feeling was good, he just couldn't finish it. Staring at Brother Andrew, he decided that was all he needed to know. He wouldn't sneak off to the dorms anymore. He wouldn't close his eyes in class anymore. He would be good and he would learn.

"I know, it can be scary," Brother Andrew said. "You just haven't grown into your full manhood like I have. But this is still a good opportunity for you to ask questions and do things. And I can show you things. I want to help you. I want to help you not be scared anymore. You can gain valuable experience right here right now that might take years otherwise. You shouldn't be frightened of your own body, or anyone else's for that matter. And a few years is a long time to wait for that kind of experience."

MacEoghan didn't know what to think. He didn't like what was going on. He didn't want to be afraid, but he didn't know what to be afraid of. Brother Andrew said he shouldn't be afraid of his own body. Was he? A little. What would happen if he didn't do it, though? Would he be beaten? Would Micah?

"All right," he said quietly.

Brother Andrew grinned. "Very good. You're a smart lad, not so stubborn as your brother. And you'll be rewarded for it, I promise. Now then, you remember what you did? And you remember what I told you about needing someone else? Well, stand up, remove your trousers, and come here."

PUNISHMENT
OLDER BROTHER

Micah did not see MacEoghan after he left for the dorms. Something bad was going to happen. He just knew it. The bell rang to end recreation time and get the students on their way to Mass. Micah waited outside the chapel as long as he could, waiting for his brother. He didn't see him. MacEoghan might be able to hide during recreation time, but the Brothers were very diligent about recording the boys' attendance at Mass. Something had happened. He'd been caught. He was going to be locked up for days as punishment. Maybe he was already sitting in the cage.

They weren't supposed to know about the cage, certainly not supposed to talk about it. It was hidden under the stairs in the basement of the Brothers' residence. Boys who ran away or who hit the Brothers were locked up in there. They sat there in the dark with no food for two or three or sometimes five days. Micah couldn't stand the thought of MacEoghan being in there.

But he also couldn't leave Mass. He watched one of the Brothers leave shortly after the start, but Micah knew he'd never be able to slip out.

He didn't like not having MacEoghan by his side, especially when he knew that his brother was in trouble. He needed to be there.

Sitting there, only passively listening to the sermon, Micah resolved that they were going to run away tonight. MacEoghan wanted to, but he was too scared. Well, they didn't have a choice anymore. Micah was going to make the decision now. After Mass, he was going to get MacEoghan out of the cage, and they were going to run away.

Mass ended and the boys started back to the dorms. Micah went, hoping for a small miracle that MacEoghan would be in his bed. His heart sank when he saw the empty bed, although the sheets suggested that he had been there at some point.

Micah said nothing about his brother's absence as the Brothers made their last rounds before leaving for the night. The fact that they didn't say anything suggested they knew MacEoghan was gone, locked up as punishment. Then they were gone and the dorms were quiet.

Micah waited for a count of one hundred before sitting up and quietly getting down to the floor. He got about halfway across the room before deciding that they might need a change of clothes. Micah didn't want to be running around in his night clothes, and MacEoghan's clothes would probably be dirty from being in the basement.

"What are you doing?" the boy in the next bunk whispered. "I thought you were heading to the privy."

"You're not thinking of leaving, are you?" his top-bunk counterpart hissed. "They'll catch you and lock you up. MacEoghan is probably already there now for something."

"I'm going to rescue him, and then we're going to run away," Micah said, not looking at them.

The first boy scoffed. "You I could see running away, maybe even escaping capture. Your brother, not so much. Are you sure you're twins?"

"Of course we are."

"He's only going to hold you back," the second boy agreed. "Run away yourself, save your own skin. No need for both of you to get in trouble and get dragged back here."

Micah finished packing and whirled to face them. "He's my brother and we stick together. Together forever!"

The boys were unconvinced as they just shrugged and rolled over. If anyone asked, they didn't know anything.

Micah tiptoed through the dorm and slipped outside without incident. As soon as the door closed, he invoked go-fast. A bug buzzing near his head slowed so that he could see each beat of its tiny wings. One of the barn cats was trotting across the lawn, a mouse in its jaws. He watched the cat's lithe form, every move she made, how her claws poked out of the end of her toes with each slowing step as she headed for home to feed her kittens.

He headed in another direction, toward the Brothers' residence. His count of one hundred obviously wasn't enough, for there were several lights still on. He found a bush to hide in as he waited and considered what he was going to do. He was moving very fast, yes, but he wasn't invisible. The Brothers might still be able to catch him. And he would probably have to get the key to the cage. Now where would that be? Maybe in Father Daniel's office?

He waited about half an hour until all the lights were out. Still using go-fast, he sneaked up to the door and let himself inside.

Straight ahead were the stairs. Moving as quietly as he could, Micah circled around to the back side where the basement door was. Locked. Of course. He stared at the door knob. An idea was swimming around in the back of his mind, but he was too worried about MacEoghan for it to really come to fruition. He would have to find the key.

Father Daniels' office, then. He backed away from the basement door and headed that way. To his relief, it wasn't locked. Everything sat right where he'd left it, quiet and orderly and unassuming in the dark. Micah tiptoed over to the desk. Top drawers, nothing. Middle drawer on the left side had a false bottom, and Micah only found this on accident as he moved a few small books and the false bottom shifted suddenly. He moved everything and popped the secret compartment. A ring of keys.

Micah grabbed the keys and returned to the basement door. It took a few tries, but he found the correct key. The lock ground noisily and Micah paused. Had anyone heard that? He didn't know. Go-fast would buy him some time, but not any that could afford to be wasted.

He opened the door. In the darkness, he could hear something down there. Hopefully it was MacEoghan.

Micah descended the stairs, noting that every single one of them squeaked. Considering the care that went into the maintenance of the grounds, he could only assume this was on purpose, to catch any boys who might try to escape. Between the squeaks and the door, someone was going to come looking.

He had learned that sound was different when he used go-fast. Knowing that it was a bad idea, he let go of it, then peered into the darkness.

"MacEoghan!" he hissed, hurrying down the stairs and turning to face the space beneath.

"Micah?" a blubbering voice questioned half a moment before he burst into sobs anew. "I'm sorry, I'm sorry, I'm sorry."

Micah found the cage, found the door, and began fumbling for keys in the near total darkness. "Did they catch you in the dorms?"

MacEoghan burst into a tidal wave of tears and bumbling words. Micah used go-fast on both of them. As long as they were both in the go-fast, then they could speak normally. But if any of the Brothers yelled at them, it would sound weird, slow and distorted. MacEoghan said that Micah talking inside a go-fast was like the high-pitched chattering of a squirrel.

He found the key and popped the cage open easily, the door squeaking obscenely. They had to move quickly, there was no way no one heard that, and MacEoghan was still babbling.

"MacEoghan, slow down," Micah said, putting his hands on his brother's shoulders. "What happened?"

His brother took several gulping breaths and somehow managed to find coherent words.

"They have been," he wheezed. "They have been. They've been touching me in class."

"What?"

"Ever since the beginning. Since we got here. I never said anything. I didn't know what to do. I w-want to leave, I wanted to tell you that I was ready, but I couldn't. And I was ashamed So I went to the dorms. And I touched myself. And I...I m-m-m-masturbated. But Brother David caught me."

"He locked you up here for that?" Micah asked.

MacEoghan shook his head, snot streaming from his nose. He sniffed hard but it did no good. "He brought me here to see Brother Andrew for punishment. And Brother Andrew said that I had done something wrong, but it was because I was too new and didn't understand my body so he said he could teach me more about it and how it was all done properly so that I wouldn't be scared and I wouldn't sin anymore so I said yes and I didn't want to but I didn't want him to hurt you so he took his trousers off and he was just like me but a full man and he had me do the same thing and then he told me that masturbation was wrong because sex requires two people." He heaved a breath. "But sex is good and he wants me to do it right and know my job as a man so he had me put my mouth on his manhood and he did things and I wanted to get sick but then he stopped and said that was good and then he did the same to me so I would know what it was like and I didn't know if it was supposed to feel good but it did it really really did and I think I finished just like I did when I masturbated and I thought he would get mad and he kind of did but then he said I was just inexperienced and he would show me what it was really for so he had me turn around and then..."

MacEoghan wiped his nose on a dirty sleeve and turned around. Even in the gloom, Micah could see the blood on the back of his brother's pants.

"I cried," MacEoghan whimpered. "But he didn't stop. He hit me for crying, and he just kept going. And then he brought me down here. He said he tried to reward me, to teach me what it was to be a man, but if I couldn't appreciate it and be grateful, if I was just going to cry, then I could sit down here for a few days."

Micah was filled with a rage he could not explain, a wrath that demanded vengeance. Obviously God wasn't going to do anything, but none of the other boys cared enough about each other, and he had little doubt that MacEoghan was not the first.

"Where does Brother Andrew sleep?" he asked.

MacEoghan just shrugged as he turned around, too exhausted to speak or cry anymore.

Micah shoved the bag of clothes into MacEoghan's hands. "Take this. We're going to find Brother Andrew."

MacEoghan fumbled the bag for a second, then righted himself. "What? Why?"

Micah was already heading up the stairs. "He's no man."

Micah didn't know where the go-fast came from. He didn't know when he'd started using it or why MacEoghan couldn't use it. He didn't really understand how it worked, but it was probably the first time he had really felt it as a tangible thing that he controlled. He could control its size, its shape, even its strength, like sculpting clay. Nebulous desire solidified into tangible, iron will. He pulled the go-fast closer around himself and MacEoghan, like a blanket. He made it harder, so that things around them, like the cat that patrolled the building for mice, did not merely slow down, but seemed to stop completely.

"Where are we going?" MacEoghan whimpered behind him as they started up the stairs to the second floor. "We need to be running away."

"No," Micah stated. "No, Brother Andrew can't be allowed to get away with this. Even if we are captured and brought back, he's not going to do this to you again, or anyone else."

There were three stories to the Brothers' residence. The first floor was all offices, and the second and third were the individual chambers. Each door was marked with the name of the occupant, making it easy to find Brother Andrew's room.

"What are you going to do?" MacEoghan hissed as Micah reached for the knob.

Micah slowly turned the knob and pushed the door open. "I'm going to cut off his manhood."

"What?"

Micah looked at his brother, barely perceivable in the dark hall. "He's no man, and he won't do this to anyone ever again."

With that, he crept into the room.

The room was fairly sparse in its decor: a single bed for sleeping, a short nightstand with a Bible on top, a simple wooden chair next to a table with a lamp. An open closet revealed several changes of clothing, all of them basically the same. A crucifix hung on one wall between one painting of Jesus and another painting of the Virgin Mary. On the opposite wall was a painting of a landscape with an eagle soaring overhead, the location and artist unknown. The window was open to the north, revealing more hills and forest and some rocky crags in the distance.

There was nothing especially remarkable about anything in the room, and Micah bet that all of the rooms looked about the same. The only unique thing was the form under the blankets which likely rose and fell in soft rhythm, but in the go-fast were eerily still.

Micah knew what he said he was going to do, he just wasn't sure how he was going to do it. He didn't have a knife, and a quick search of the room and nightstand showed that Brother Andrew didn't either. All he had were blunt objects, rods and paddles to beat unruly children. But what Micah did have were Father Daniel's keys. True, they weren't knives, but there was one key, the old iron key to the cage, that had just a little bit of an edge to it because of its older casting. That would work just fine.

Or so he hoped.

MacEoghan made a high-pitched, strangled sort of sound from the doorway. Micah only glanced at him briefly as he carefully pulled the blankets down to the end of the bed. Brother Andrew wore only his underclothes.

Did he know what he'd done? How many other boys had he abused? Why MacEoghan? Was it to punish him, Micah? Was it because he would rather submit to the rod than have these men put their hands down his pants? What did they do to MacEoghan if he tried to refuse?

Micah did not like others trying to put hands down his pants, and he did not like the idea of putting his hands down anyone else's pants either. But if he wanted to make good on his threat, he was going to have to. Carefully, he took the fabric of Brother Andrew's underpants and started rubbing the sharp edge of the key along the fibers. Some gave way, but the edge was not as sharp as he'd thought, and it took some time before he was able to cut a hole big enough to see the man's parts.

He'd put that in MacEoghan? No wonder his brother was bloody. Stupid, horrid, vile, disgusting piss-poor-excuse-for-a-man! Micah's fury was rekindled, and his anger easily drowned out his disgust at having to touch Brother Andrew. With one hand, he took the man's member, and with the other hand put the sharp edge of the key to the tender flesh.

But the key was not very sharp. It had trouble cutting through simple cotton, and it had just as much trouble cutting through flesh, more trouble even. He drew blood and severed skin, but it certainly wasn't a real knife, and Micah would admit that he was feeling a bit queasy about a quarter of the way through. He felt his go-fast begin to slip. Brother Andrew twitched beneath him for only a blink before he was able to wrangle the go-fast back as tight as it had been.

He repositioned himself and glanced at MacEoghan, rooted to the ground in the doorway, round eyes fixed on the scene.

"Keep going," MacEoghan said, his voice small and tight.

The queasiness passed, and Micah resumed his sawing. He needed to get this done quickly before he became queasy again and lost the go-fast. They still needed it to run away. Flesh tore more than it cut, but at long last, the member was free. Micah got off the bed and stumbled back, stopping himself before he hit the wall.

MacEoghan took a few tentative steps forward. "Is that it?"

Micah held up his quarry. "That's it. It can't hurt anyone ever again."

MacEoghan glanced at Brother Andrew. Outside the go-fast, he had no idea what had just happened. "Should we take his balls, too?"

"This key isn't that sharp," Micah said, shaking his head. While that was certainly true, he also wasn't entirely sure that he would be able to stomach doing much more. He'd choked down his revulsion in the name of avenging his brother, but he still wasn't keen on touching another man's parts. "Besides, we still have to run away."

His brother looked uncertain. "I kind of want to see his reaction. I want him to know."

"He'll know," Micah promised. "But the first thing he's going to do is scream, and we can't be here when the other Brothers come running."

MacEoghan frowned. He spied a rod in the closet and went to grab it. He studied it for a moment, then looked at Micah. "Can you roll him over?"

It took both of them to do so, but Micah was more than happy to let his brother have the honors of shoving the rod into Brother Andrew's nether region. He did it several times, each one harder than the last as MacEoghan vented some of his own fury and pain. Tears streamed down his brother's eyes and more snot from his nose. When he was done, he left the rod where it was and turned to face Micah.

"We can run away now. I think he'll know."

Micah just nodded.

The two of them turned away from Brother Andrew and left the room, Micah locking the door behind them. Then they fled the scene of the crime as fast as they dared, tiptoeing their way up to the front door.

"Why do you still have those?" MacEoghan asked, nodding to the things in Micah's hands.

Micah held up the keys. "So they can't lock anyone in the cage again, and to make it harder on them anyway." He held up Brother Andrew's member. "We'll throw this far away, in a river somewhere. Otherwise they'll just sew it back on and he can keep hurting people."

MacEoghan thought about this for a second, then nodded. "All right. Sounds reasonable."

Micah pocketed the keys and opened the door. "Let's go."

They ended up making a stop in the cafeteria so they could wash their hands and faces and change their bloody clothes. Micah wrapped the member in a towel so he didn't have to carry it in his bare hands anymore. Then they grabbed some bread leftover from supper and some potatoes from the bin.

"Do you suppose we'll need money, too?" MacEoghan wondered.

"The only money I know about would be in Father Daniel's office," Micah mused.

So they returned to the Brothers' residence and helped themselves to Father Daniel's office. They eventually found a locked box, opened with one of the keys on the keyring. Inside were a lot of important-looking documents but only a little cash.

"It's better than nothing," Micah decided, stuffing it in his pockets. "Do we need anything else, or can we run away now?"

"Blankets?" MacEoghan suggested. "Or a tent?"

"We can't carry a blanket or a tent in that bag."

Eventually they concluded that there was nothing more they needed that they could either carry in hand or in the bag. Maybe they would find something later, a bigger bag.

"What if we hitched the horse to the cart?" MacEoghan wondered as they left the residence. "Then we could carry everything we needed."

"We have to stay off the roads, remember? And we have to be quiet. Horses are big and lumbering and noisy." Micah continued before MacEoghan could speak. "Come on. We have to leave now or we never will. We need the best head start we can get."

MacEoghan did not argue, but there was still a great deal of fear in his eyes. Once again, Micah would be leading the charge. Of course, he was also the only one able to use go-fast.

He was pleased to know that the go-fast had worked and not faltered. He got it established as well as he could, then grabbed his brother's hand and started running. After a dozen yards, he let go of MacEoghan and the two continued on, running as fast as they could, heading south.

It was just like a game of football, Micah told himself, except there were no boundaries to this field, and the one with the ball was always one step ahead of them.

It was just like a game of tag; he was "it" and everyone else was ahead of him.

It was just like a game of fast hide-and-go-seek where he only had so much time to find a good hiding spot and there were no limits on where he could go.

Actually, this was exactly like a game of hide-and-go-seek, and there were much bigger consequences if he was found than simply being the next seeker. It was utterly imperative that they not be found.

They followed the road away from the school for about a hundred yards before veering off into the trees and climbing a hill. Briefly Micah wondered if any advantage they gained by not being on the road would be squandered just from the noise they were making, dislodging rocks and snapping twigs.

"Slow down, slow down, slow down," Micah hissed.

He and MacEoghan gradually slowed to a walk.

"What is it?" MacEoghan asked, looking around fearfully.

"We're making too much noise. We have to get farther away."

"Will they notice the noise with the go-fast like it is?"

"Do you really want to find out?"

His brother's silence was answer enough.

They reached the top of the hill and looked out over the valley, over the school, or what they could see of it. Rage again filled Micah. He bent to scoop up a rock and hurl it as hard as he could in the direction of the school. When that failed to sate his anger, he did it again. And again. And again. Even MacEoghan threw a rock or two.

"I hope I never see you again!" Micah said, his words coming out as a gritted, frustrated grunt more than the shout he desired. He picked up another rock. "I hope you rot in Hell!"

He threw a last rock, then just stood there, breathing heavily. A few steps behind him and a few feet to the side, MacEoghan just stared silently, tears streaming down his face, looking both relieved and perplexed.

"You all right?" Micah asked.

MacEoghan nodded quietly a few times. Then, "I am now."

Micah sighed, his rage cooling. He clapped his brother's shoulder. "Come on. We still have a long ways to go. And we need to find a river to toss this thing." He indicated Brother Andrew's member, disturbingly still in hand.

It wasn't hard to find the same river that traveled through the school's animal pastures, and Micah unceremoniously tossed the member in a deep pool of swirling water mostly covered by algae. Even if they thought to look here, they'd never find it, and it would never harm anyone again. Micah was just standing from the water's edge when he was pushed aside by MacEoghan who had found a rather large rock or small boulder. He carried it in two hands and dropped it in the hole.

"Just to make sure," MacEoghan huffed.

"By all means," Micah told him. "Anything else you wanted to do?"

His brother shook his head, still staring at the spot where Brother Andrew's member lay crushed under a rock in a watery grave. "No, that's it."

"Come on, then, let's get out of here."

They turned and continued heading south. Even if they had wanted to look back at the school, it would have been hidden from view. But for as close as they still were to danger, Micah felt an immense sense of relief. Life on the streets was hard, yes, but he'd known since he'd found his brother that it was infinitely better than even the best education the Brothers had to give.

They walked for a while, at least a couple miles, then returned to a steady jog. But between the night's activities, the lack of sleep, and using the go-fast, Micah soon tired. They slowed to a crawl. Micah yawned.

"We're not that far," MacEoghan said. "We have to keep going."

"We're at least ten miles, maybe twenty," Micah told him, unsure if it was true. "And I'm tired." He put up a hand. "I'll stop using go-fast, that should buy us a little time."

"If you stop using go-fast, then Brother Andrew will start hollering for help. And they'll come looking for us."

"It'll take a few minutes for anyone to wake up. It'll take a few minutes for them to get to his room and find out what happened. Then they'll wake up all the boys and do a head count. That will take a few minutes, too. Once they discover we're gone, they'll search the grounds first. They don't believe in the go-fast, so they won't think we've gotten very far. It'll be a while before they realize we are very far away. And we're staying off the roads and walking through the woods, so they can't use cars to follow us." Micah shrugged. "Besides, the only reason they catch the runaways is because someone in a nearby town turns them in for not going to school. They won't actually chase us."

MacEoghan didn't look convinced and he flinched as Micah let go of the go-fast. The only sounds they'd heard for a couple hours now was their feet on the ground, crunching dirt and grass and leaves, as well as the wind. The go-fast did nothing to stop the wind, though thankfully it was only a gentle breeze right now. Now they were regaled by the sounds of owls in the trees, small critters moving in the darkness, and invisible bugs flitting around their ears which they swatted at futilely.

They kept walking.

Micah had suggested that they learn as much as they could about geography before running away. It had seemed like a good and logical idea at the time, except flat maps were suddenly very different from the terrain they now traversed. Micah had also made the mistake of basing everything off of the roads, which ones ran which direction, to and from where. Crossing the countryside, from forest to field and back again, that was something he hadn't really prepared for. He didn't know where Leitir Fraic was, although he certainly wanted to avoid it. He didn't know where Gaillimh was. He didn't want to admit to being lost, for he did not want to see the fear in his brother's eyes, but he would admit it to himself at least: he was lost.

Worse, he was tired. Stopping the go fast had helped, but now he was just tired, and the worsening wind forcing him to squint his eyes almost shut wasn't helping. How many miles had they gone? Was it enough? They neared the edge of the forest again and Micah spied a barn in the pre-dawn light. Could they sleep in the barn? Would the farmer turn them in? They couldn't sleep out in the open, that was for sure.

"Maybe we can sleep in that barn," MacEoghan yawned.

His brother's comment was all that was needed to propel them both in that direction. At least it would be out of the weather. With any luck, the morning chores were done and the farmer wouldn't have to come back to the barn for a while, or at least he wouldn't have to climb up into the hayloft.

They got into the barn without issue; all the animals were out to pasture and the place was quiet. They scurried up a ladder to the hayloft, making for a far corner and burying themselves as much as they dared, all the while being watched by a very perturbed gray cat, six small kittens at her belly.

Micah was ready to just close his eyes and sleep, but then MacEoghan spoke.

"I'm sorry, Micah."

Blinking blearily, Micah looked at his brother. "Sorry for what?"

"I should have said yes. Every day at supper, when you asked if I heard the birds, I should have said yes. When you first asked me if the Brothers were touching me, I should have said yes."

"You were afraid."

"Exactly. I was afraid. I let them do it because I was a coward. I'm still a coward." MacEoghan sniffed. "I'm not like you, Miach. I'm not brave. Maybe we're not really twins. There's no way we could be."

"Don't be stupid, of course we are," Micah said. "But maybe I can help you be brave."

"How is that?"

"Take my name."

MacEoghan blinked, confused. "What?"

"You take my name, and I'll take yours. We're twins, we look alike. If anyone asks, if anyone catches us, I'm MacEoghan. And you can be Micah. So when you're afraid, you can be Micah, and you can be brave."

His brother thought about it for a second. "Wouldn't that make me Miach, not Micah?"

Micah hesitated. "You may be a coward, MacEoghan, but you're not stupid. I know you've done the math. Our father wasn't a soldier in the Great War, and those men who visited weren't our mother's brothers. Our mother was a prostitute. Some man gave her a disease and she died."

"She was still our mother," MacEoghan said quietly. "Why wouldn't you want the name she gave you? Why would you choose the Brothers over her?"

"They're both bad choices. But Miach Meagher was stupid and ran away because he was a little boy. Micah Meagher stood up to the Brothers and took the punishment for others. Who do you want to be?"

"I'd rather be Micah."

"And I'll be MacEoghan. And if the police do catch us, if we do somehow get taken back to the school, MacEoghan is the one who will be punished the worst. And I'll be you, and I'll take it. But you'll be brave, won't you?"

His twin nodded.

MacEoghan and Micah Meagher fell asleep in the hay.

MAKING A WAY
YOUNGER BROTHER

Tables were tipped over and dragged to the middle of the room, forming a kind of loose circle. Drinks were filled and bets made. The barkeep just sighed, his expression saying that this was nothing new for a Saturday night, but he still didn't enjoy the cleanup afterwards. The only reason Micah got as close as he did, and didn't stand back with the barkeep, was because he knew how this was going to turn out. This was the whole reason he'd come, really.

They'd evaded capture by the police and the Brothers for a year now. They were not yet fifteen years old, so they could still potentially be taken back. Life on the road had been hard. They'd tried to keep their heads down and avoid encounters with the law at all costs. They only approached villages in the afternoons an evenings, when children would be expected to be out of school. They didn't steal unless they absolutely had to, instead looking for odd jobs to earn a bit of food or money. And they tried not to stay in one place for too long.

It was a hard life, but Micah would take it over the school any day. He would go to bed starving before he ate at the Brothers' table again.

In an odd sort of way, taking his brother's name did make him feel braver. Brave enough to face the day, brave enough to talk to people, do menial work, and whatever his brother asked him to do.

It did not make him brave enough to enter the fighting ring, however.

It had started about four months ago. A crotchety old farmer had caught them sleeping in his barn. He'd told them that if they worked all day, did whatever he asked of them, then he wouldn't turn them over to the police. They had readily agreed and spent the day in back-breaking labor. The farmer watched them, doing nothing himself all day. At the end of the day, he said he had one more task, then they were free to leave and not come back.

74

Gathering in his barn were a number of men who were spoiling for some unsanctioned prize fighting. He told MacEoghan to enter and fight. If MacEoghan won, the farmer would be a few bucks richer. If MacEoghan lost, well, getting the hell beat out of him ought to teach him a lesson about trespassing.

MacEoghan lost spectacularly. And yet, according to him, it was a thrill. He wanted to get better. He wanted to win.

Since then, they'd been going town to town, sometimes barn to barn, MacEoghan competing in the fights. He had gotten better, a lot better. He won more than he lost now, and he'd bulked up so that he looked bigger and older than just fourteen. It wasn't the most honest of occupations, as such fighting was technically illegal in many places, but it was better than thieving. They fought in taverns, in barns, in basements, even an old mining quarry once. When the arena was in a tavern, such as now, competitors got one free meal a night (the cost more than made up in the amount of alcohol consumed), which the brothers often split, just so they knew they'd both eaten that day. Now that MacEoghan was doing better, Micah was fairly confident in betting on him, and they usually ended the night with more money than they'd started. That money got them food, clothes, hygiene necessities, sometimes rides from town to town, and occasionally a stay at a motel, if the town had one.

They were staying at such a motel now, just a few streets away. The motel manager was across the ring, swinging a stein and shouting for someone to get in there and fight. Just a few hours ago, MacEoghan had been negotiating a room price, pretending to be Sean, fifteen year old Micah's seventeen year old brother, and they were visiting some family friends in town.

Micah peered through the press of bodies and spotted MacEoghan just taking his shirt and shoes off, stretching a little and bouncing on his toes, doing whatever he did to prepare himself for the fight. Micah would not deny that MacEoghan's size did make him look older, but if either of them were able to grow a man's beard, that would certainly sell the image and turn away anyone who thought they might be a little young to be out of school. As it was, seventeen was a bit of a stretch for MacEoghan. Sixteen, at most. But they'd gotten the room, and that was all that mattered.

Micah never cared to learn the more nuanced rules of the fight, who was in charge, who made the matches. In unsanctioned matches like these, the only thing that mattered were the bets. Wagers made on-the-fly and half-drunk had to be keenly tracked. And part of that was watching the women.

The women never fought, but they knew how to fix fights for their brothers or husbands. "Lose to my brother and I'll make sure you win later," was not an uncommon statement, alongside, "Let my husband win, and when he's passed out drunk in celebration, you'll get the real prize."

MacEoghan had reportedly never been approached, but then, he was new to the ring and still quite young. They weren't going to risk a brother's or husband's wrath for a fourteen year old, especially when there was no need because that fourteen year old was still quite likely to lose. Even if they believed him to be sixteen or seventeen, he still lacked a little bit of something that would give him such appeal.

The general din of conversation suddenly shifted, and all attention was turned to the ring as a man boldly walked forward. He was not a fighter, and there were no real referees. He was something of a master of ceremonies, denoting the official start and end of each match. He raised his hands for quiet, but, once drunk, the crowd was never truly quiet.

He welcomed everyone to the match, then announced the first two competitors. Neither one was MacEoghan, so Micah didn't pay much attention except to get out of the way if one or both happened to come near him. The tables that made the ring were arranged in a certain way now, but guaranteed they would be arranged differently by the end of the night.

The first two competitors entered the ring. One was a big, beefy fellow of perhaps thirty-five to forty years, potbellied as a pig. His opponent was a skinny guy somewhere in the neighborhood of twenty to twenty-five with big arms, big shoulders, and a big chest, but who looked like he had as much trouble growing a beard as the twins did.

Somewhere, the bell dinged. The larger man bull rushed the smaller man, meaty fist flying. The younger man swept low but couldn't escape a glancing blow. He stumbled to one side and narrowly avoided the big man's followup. He got in a quick jab to the man's side, but the bull hardly noticed as he whirled around, fists still flying furiously.

The younger man was definitely lighter on his feet, but he just didn't have the room in this ring to use it effectively. He had very few options to get out of range of the big man's swing, and one good slug was all it took to seal the man's fate. He went down quickly and crawled out of the ring before he could be knocked out.

The big man roared his victory and challenged any man to face him. Two more tried, and both fell just as easily. Then the big man declared that he needed to take a piss and get a drink, and left the ring.

The master of ceremonies re-entered the ring which had now shifted a good three feet, gaps appearing between the tables.

"While he's away, how about some mild entertainment from newcomers to the ring?" he posed. He did not wait for an answer as the general response was pretty lackluster anyway. "First up in the ring, we have a savage seventeen year old from Second Street, Renard Lichdhan!"

The named fighter was not one Micah recognized, though that was hardly a surprise if he was a local. He jogged into the ring with some song and dance that was evidently supposed to drum up support from the crowd and instill fear from his opponent. Even Micah was less than impressed. While he did look more seventeen than MacEoghan, he just wasn't all the way there.

The master put his hands up and his tone changed. "And he'll be fighting a newbie, a traveler from the north, come all the way down here because he thinks we southerners are soft."

Claiming to be from the northern partition also made it easier to dodge the authorities, though it did nothing to bolster their image. Sure enough, MacEoghan jogged into the ring, ignoring some of the boo's that accompanied him. Instead he looked around, bouncing on his toes a little, thrilled for the fight.

"What's your name, son?" the master inquired.

While MacEoghan introduced himself and bragged of his paltry exploits in the ring, Micah started placing bets. Interestingly, MacEoghan seemed to be the favored fighter in this round. Glancing toward the ring, he did look a bit bigger in physique compared to Lichdhan, but his still youthful countenance did nothing for him. Surely Lichdhan had more years of experience to call upon?

"I daresay you bear some resemblance to my brother's opponent." Micah's attention was taken by a young woman who approached him. He didn't know much about women; she could have been anywhere from sixteen to twenty-five as far as he was concerned. "Are you his brother, perhaps?"

Micah blinked, initially unsure what to say or do. Then, with a burst of intuition that maybe he should reply to her question, he said, "Aye, he's my brother. My twin brother."

"Twin?" She glanced at MacEoghan. "Well, clearly he's the only one who fights."

"Someone has to take him home."

She laughed. "Of course. Here. One for your brother."

Micah absently clutched the money she handed him. "Didn't you just say that it's your brother who he's facing?"

The woman's expression changed then, to something almost sad. She pushed a bit of hair out of her face and turned toward the light, as if looking at something behind Micah. It was an intentional move as it revealed an almost-healed bruise on her right cheek. "Yes, I suppose I did."

Micah raised a brow. "Shouldn't it be MacEoghan you're talking to?"

"How? They're both in the ring."

She sidled away, her playful demeanor now gone. Micah stared after her, stared at the money in his hand. He didn't know what to do. Sure, he knew how to take and make bets, but usually it was the fighters that the women tried to seduce. Was she trying to seduce him? Honestly, he wasn't sure.

"You heard it here, folks!" the master was saying in the ring. "Sounds like we're going to have a real bloodbath here."

It was difficult to discern just how serious the man was being. Every master of ceremonies was different. In these unsanctioned fights, the master tended to be just some local man, usually a retired fighter, with a big voice and a fun personality who could drum up excitement from the crowd. It was no surprise, then, that he should favor local fighters over travelers, but some just really didn't care for the new fighters one way or the other. They weren't exciting enough. They weren't experienced enough to remind the master or other retired fighters of the thrill and joy of the fight. They weren't interesting enough to excite the crowd.

But that was neither here nor there as the master ducked out of the ring, leaving MacEoghan alone with Lichdhan. The two faced each other, already sweating. Then the bell rang.

Lichdhan initially tried the same tactic as the big man, a simple bull rush to try and end the fight quickly, or at least put MacEoghan ill at ease about the fight. The problem was that Lichdhan was not the same size as the big man, only barely comparable to MacEoghan himself. MacEoghan also had a longer reach, and, with a powerful swing, he was able to clock Lichdhan square in the nose before Lichdhan had the ability to touch him.

Lichdhan's nose exploded into blood, and he stumbled back several steps, stunned though he did not fall down.

There were no real rules when it came to these fights. The only one that was actually enforced was no weapons other than the body. No knives, no broken bottles, no clubs, nothing. Fighters could punch, slap, grab, kick, whatever they needed to do to win. Hair could be pulled, balls could be crushed, nothing was off-limits. There were no penalties for breaking bones, and MacEoghan's decimation of Lichdhan's nose only served to invigorate the audience. More bets were made, most of them in MacEoghan's favor.

Naturally, Lichdhan was unhappy at this turn of events.

"I was right," MacEoghan taunted. "You southerners are pretty soft."

It was unlikely that MacEoghan had ever actually said or thought such a thing; this town just happened to be the next stop on their quest to evade capture and a return to St. Joseph's. But they couldn't give that as their reason for being here, and the crowd usually liked to pretend that there was more to the fights than just two men who wanted to beat the tar out of each other for fun and money.

First injured, now insulted, Lichdhan stepped back into the fight. He was smart enough not to try another bull rush, and the two danced around each other for a good ten seconds.

"One a ye green whelps hit somethin'!" someone shouted.

Sensing the displeasure of the crowd, Lichdhan again made the first move. This time he darted in to the right, taking a swing with his left, trying to get MacEoghan in the side. MacEoghan skittered to the right, knocking Lichdhan's off-hand away but managing to get in a quick jab to the man's floating rib. As Lichdhan instinctively curled over to protect the new wound, MacEoghan bopped him in the side of the head. Lichdhan stumbled to the side, hit one of the tables, and went to a knee. MacEoghan backed off across the small ring, not far from Micah's position.

"Dun show mercy!" someone nearby said. "Finish the lad! Finish him!"

MacEoghan was slow to heed the suggestion, and the hesitation cost him. As he approached Lichdhan to do something to finish, Lichdhan suddenly launched from his kneeling position, catching MacEoghan's middle, and sending them both to the floor. Micah flinched when he saw his brother's head smack the hard wooden floor.

Lichdhan got in one good blow to MacEoghan's ribs as he sat up, trying to pin his hips and give him ample room and leverage to continue delivering punches. But MacEoghan was not as dazed as Micah feared he would be. He took the blow to the ribs, but as Lichdhan sat up and tried to adjust his position, MacEoghan swung hard with his right hand. If he connected, it would be just as devastating as every other blow. Lichdhan saw it coming and dodged, but it still worked in MacEoghan's favor as he put his head perfectly into MacEoghan's left hand. MacEoghan clamped down on Lichdhan's left ear and surrounding hair. The cocky seventeen year old screamed like his mother was pinching his ear, though his cry was cut short as MacEoghan's right fist connected squarely with his jaw. Even Micah heard that crack of bone. Two teeth tumbled out of the man's mouth, and he imagined a couple more might have been swallowed.

MacEoghan let go of his prey, but when Lichdhan fell over to his right, only just catching himself with his right arm, MacEoghan delivered another blow to the man's face, effortlessly pushing him back. This gave MacEoghan more than enough leverage to slide the older boy off him and get to his feet.

By now the crowd was in an absolute uproar. No more bets were made as the winner was clear, and the only cries now were those for MacEoghan to finish off "the paltry charlatan."

Micah couldn't say that he felt any real connection or attachment to a place, a particular town or region, but he couldn't help but feel a little sympathy for Lichdhan, that even his own fellows from his own hometown were rooting for his demise. Even now, as MacEoghan stood and shook himself off—minding some possibly bruised or broken ribs—Lichdhan barely bothered to try and stand, and one hand was always on his jaw. He did not spit, but simply tilted his head and let another tooth tumble to the floor. He got in a very poor, one-handed stance.

"Don't do it," MacEoghan said, relaxing his own posture.

Lichdhan did not listen, but drunkenly leapt forward with a badly projected swing. MacEoghan didn't need to do much of anything as he once again out-reached the man, knocking his arm deftly away with one hand and connecting perfectly with his left eye with the other hand. Again Micah heard the crunch of bone.

Lichdhan went to the floor, limp. Blood was leaking from his left eye, the surrounding tissue already beginning to swell.

The crowd quieted some, everyone straining over the tables. The master of ceremonies scuttled into the ring and knelt beside Lichdhan. He felt his neck, his chest, then nodded and stood. "Aye, the sorry bastard lives." He made a sweeping gesture with his arm. "Now get his sorry hide out of here before that changes because we have a winner!"

Lichdhan was instantly forgotten as the master declared MacEoghan the winner, raising his hand high. The crowd cheered wildly as bets were collected.

MacEoghan was only a newcomer to the fights; he wasn't a seasoned veteran favorite like the big man, and he was dismissed so the big man could come back and start cracking more skulls.

Micah took some of the winnings and went to get food and drink. He then found MacEoghan sitting at a table, still without shoes or shirt, resting from the fight. Micah set down a plate of food and a mug of beer in front of his brother.

"Was the fighting as easy as the betting?" Micah wondered.

MacEoghan stabbed at a chunk of meat. "He'd be a lot tougher if he knew what his body was actually capable of. As it is, he seems to have only an idea in his head that he just can't do."

"Thinks he's the big man—" Micah vaguely gestured to the man still in the ring. "—when he's nothing of the sort?"

"Exactly."

"Aye, but you are the big man, or you could be one day."

"You think so?"

Micah nodded around a mouthful of potatoes. "I do."

MacEoghan thought about this for a minute. Then, "You think I should keep doing this, then? You think I could make a real career out of fighting? Not just these unsanctioned bar brawls, but one of the real, professional fighters? You think I could be a professional boxer?"

Micah shrugged. "I don't see why not. Maybe give it a couple more years before you do try anything professional."

MacEoghan made a vague gesture. "Oh, of course."

He looked ready to say more, but then they were approached by a woman. Micah recognized her as the sister of the man MacEoghan just knocked out.

"Well-fought, sir," she said, looking only at MacEoghan.

"Thank you, ma'am," he replied, looking a shade uncertain.

She smiled. "Forgive me, I should introduce myself. My name is MaryAnn Lichdhan. Renard is my brother."

MacEoghan blinked. "Oh, well... He fought well."

"Please, my brother is a foolish oaf who will amount to little in the ring, and his obsession with it will surely only ruin his honest career prospects." She cleared her throat as if remembering herself. "Nevertheless, I am responsible for him. Seeing how you were the victor, may I inquire a favor of you regarding him?"

"You want me to carry his sorry carcass back to your home?"

She blushed. "Well, yes."

He stood. "I'll be more than happy to help. I expect you just want to rub it in a little more."

"That was one idea, but you are surely famished. Eat, please, and then—"

He waved a hand. "I don't think it will take that long. Besides, Micah needs to eat, too. Look at him, skin and bones."

Considering that both of them, before the school, had been very much scrawny, bony orphans, Micah wasn't sure what to make of the statement. MaryAnn giggled. "Yes, I see. And I see now that you do bear some brotherly resemblance."

"We ought to; he's my twin. Younger twin, but still."

82

MaryAnn wasn't paying any real attention to Micah beyond a mere acknowledgment of his presence. That was fine with him; he was famished and more than happy to finish his meal while MacEoghan did whatever it was that she asked of him.

The master of ceremonies declared another victory for the big man, and the sorry sap who lost was dragged out of the ring. Micah passively watched as the man slowly got to all fours, then found a chair he could use to get to unsteady feet. MacEoghan had looked like that a time or two, in the beginning. He'd also been dragged out entirely unconscious, and Micah had to haul him back to wherever they were staying.

A new challenger entered the arena, convinced that he was the one who would topple the big man. Micah took another bite of potato. It had to happen eventually. The big man was drunk as it was, and he had to be getting tired.

There was the sound of splintering wood and the crowd shrieked in drunken delight as something crashed into one of the table barriers. The table was driven into one of the pub's support posts, splintering two legs. The barkeep shouted something mildly threatening and left his place behind the bar, making a beeline for the master. They argued for a minute.

"All right, gents, let's wrap this up!" the master of ceremonies proclaimed. "Wouldn't want the barkeep to get angry with us."

There were a lot of boo's, more complaints. Some patrons tossed some money in the general direction of the barkeep and stormed out, others didn't even bother with money. A few tried to challenge the barkeep himself to a fight, but the barkeep was no softbelly. He knew how to aim and throw a punch with the best of them. After a couple single-blow knockouts, he was able to return to his post to watch the slow exodus with a certain expression of contempt.

Micah looked around, but he didn't see MacEoghan. Where could the woman and her brother have lived that it was taking this long? Could it have been a way to lure MacEoghan into an ambush? That had happened before, the very first fight he'd actually won. His opponent hadn't taken too kindly to losing and so set up an ambush with some of his friends after the matches were all over. Only because of the go-fast had the two of them made it out.

MacEoghan didn't use the go-fast while in the ring. On the one hand, he said that it was basically cheating. On the other hand, he also said that it was hard to do because he was too focused on the fight which made him too nervous to use the go-fast. He did say that he had done it a time or two, perhaps just reflexively, but it was not a conscious thing.

Micah glanced around again. Seriously, where was MacEoghan?

"Oi, you."

Micah looked up to see the barkeep motioning towards him, wringing up a wet towel menacingly. "We're closin', e'erbody's leavin'. That means you, too."

"I can't find my brother," Micah offered weakly. "He was one of the fighters."

The barkeep was entirely unsympathetic. "Maybe 'e's screwin' that girl 'e was with."

Micah shook his head. "No, he's doesn't do that."

"Maybe 'e's screwin' 'er brother then. I don' care. 'E'll fin' out when 'e gets back that we're closed. Now git."

He didn't have much of a choice, it seemed. Micah left the pub without a fight, stopping on the curb to again look for his brother. The town wasn't that big, almost visible from end to end. Should he go out and actually look? If MacEoghan had been ambushed, it could be the difference between life and death. On the other hand, maybe he just went back to the motel. Unlikely, because he still expected to fight some more, but not impossible.

Well, he couldn't stand there forever. Either he was going to look for his brother or go back to the motel. Maybe he'd take a quick peek at the motel, just to rule that out first. He didn't need to spend two hours searching when a five minute check-up could have solved the whole problem.

There were only six rooms at the motel, and they were staying in room five. Two beds, a small bathroom with hot and cold water, and a small closet for hanging up any nice clothes they might have had. Telegram was available in the main office, should they need it.

The room was devoid of people, and their stuff was arranged exactly as they'd left it. MacEoghan was not here.

Well, great.

Maybe he'd check back at the pub again, just in case MacEoghan had already returned. He'd find it closed and find that he, Micah, was nowhere to be seen.

Again, no luck.

Micah had never really considered the possibility of life without MacEoghan, especially right now while they were still trying to outrun the Brothers. But what if he couldn't find his brother? What if he'd been captured and was even now on his way back to Leitir Fraic? Micah couldn't go to the police or else he would just out himself.

Wait a minute. Hadn't the master of ceremonies announced where the fighter lived? The savage seventeen year old from...from...Second Street? Or was it Seventh Street? Looking at the nearest road signs, it had to be Second. The town didn't look big enough to have a Seventh Street. Maybe he should start there instead.

Second Street was in the opposite direction from the pub, hardly a block away. Micah chastised himself for his stupid idea that MacEoghan would go back to the motel for some reason. Indeed, as he rounded the corner to go down the street in question, he nearly ran into his twin brother.

"Hey, you!" MacEoghan said, looking stupidly delighted. "What are you doing here?"

"You hadn't returned yet, and the pub closed," Micah answered, feeling small and foolish beside his brother. MacEoghan was fine. He was always fine.

They started back in the direction of the motel. "Police break it up?"

Micah shook his head. "No. The crowd started getting rowdy, a couple things got broken, so the barkeep shut it down."

"Ah, spoilsport. Good thing I won my fight, then, eh? Looked like we made good money. According to MaryAnn, Renard is known as one of the worst fighters in town. Anyone looking to make money would do well to bet against him. He's been trying to get her to fix some matches, been beating her because she hasn't been able to."

Micah made a disapproving noise. "That's a sad way to treat a woman, especially your sister."

"Aye, that's what I said."

"What about their parents?"

"Mum dead in childbirth, da a hopeless drunk."

"She gave you their whole life story, then."

MacEoghan shrugged. "She needed a listening ear. And then she thanked me for knocking him out, hopes it will teach him a lesson."

Micah raised a brow. "Why? Sounds like this has been going on for some time. What makes you special?"

"I don't know, but I'm not complaining."

"What are you talking about?"

His brother just grinned. "I'll tell you when we get back to the motel."

It was a short walk, but Micah racked his brain, trying to come up with what in the world could have happened. She asked him to carry her stupid brother's unconscious carcass back to their house. She divulged a tragic story to a passing traveler who didn't already have an opinion of her, and then—

"You didn't," Micah blurted.

MacEoghan grinned but said nothing until the door of their motel room had swung shut. "Didn't what?"

"You fornicated with her?"

"And what if I did?"

"It's wrong!"

"Says who? The Brothers? Obviously they don't care about anything they teach. They say it's wrong, I say, I'm still standing here. I wasn't struck down with lightning. And oh my God, Micah, you have no idea what it's like, how good it feels. To know a woman. Not just something you wake up with, not just something you force on yourself, but to actually be inside a woman, to feel her..."

"But..."

Micah didn't know what to say. For a long moment, he just stared at his twin brother. For the first time, they actually felt like two different people. Finally, quietly, he said, "You hated our mum. Because she was a whore. Because she saw a different man every day and every night. Lied to us, said the men were our uncles, said our father died in the Great War. Those men never looked at us twice, assuming they noticed us at all, and no one in town cared for us either.

"That woman is our mum. No one cares about her, and she goes to the pubs to try and sell herself in order to cover for the failures of her oaf of a brother. She isn't going to look at you twice, and we're not going to be here very long ourselves." Micah pointed. "You are a nameless, faceless uncle."

MacEoghan's jovial mood sobered up very quickly, but Micah took no pleasure or relief in it.

Micah lay in bed that night staring at the ceiling. He'd never known a woman, and any time his thoughts even strayed in such a direction, somehow, he could only imagine her as himself, crying, weeping, begging to stop and being hit for it. Then being locked up in a cage for not enjoying it. In the back of his mind, he supposed it was foolish. Maybe it was different for women, that they found some ecstasy of their own in the act, or maybe they just endured the pain for the sake of children. He didn't know, he didn't want to ask, and he certainly didn't intend to find out any time soon.

Would that woman tell her brother what had happened, what MacEoghan had done? Did she do this with every fighter who bested her brother? Was that the real plan, to enrage her brother so he would fight all the more fiercely the next time? Would he come looking for MacEoghan in the streets? Nothing good could come from it, Micah was sure.

They would have to leave town quickly. They had enough money, maybe they could buy a couple of train tickets. Maybe they should actually go north, to Belfast, make some fortune there, away from the Irish police and the ever-looming threat of the schools. They only had to run for another year or so, and they'd made it this far. How hard could it be?

BIG BROTHER
OLDER BROTHER

Third round of the fight, and final fight of the night. MacEoghan was tired from the fighting but invigorated by the crowd. They loved him. He was fast becoming a favorite wherever he went, and he didn't want to disappoint them. He didn't want to disappoint himself. He'd learned a lot in the year or so since he started fighting. He knew what he was capable of; he just had to grow into it more.

"I think you've got him favoring his left side," Micah sighed.

"Of course I do, after I jabbed him there with my elbow," MacEoghan said, grinning.

"With the full force of gravity and your body weight, pummeling him into the ground."

MacEoghan shrugged. "Obviously I didn't hit hard enough because he's coming back for a third round."

"You hit fine. You don't need to kill him."

Micah wanted to go home, MacEoghan knew. Things weren't like the early days, when it was a fight or two, a cheap or free meal, a drink, and then done for the night. He was getting to be known and liked. And challenged. In the last year, especially the last few months, he had moved from side attraction, something to fill the time in between main fights, to a primary fighter himself. That meant more rounds, more fights, later nights.

"I'm not going to kill him," MacEoghan sighed. "I'm just trying to make it a profitable night for us."

His brother said nothing, just gave him a look. Likely there would be words later, when they returned to the motel. "Another motel," Micah would say. "We're fifteen, near sixteen now, and you look older at least." Bigger, maybe, but neither one of them could grow a real beard yet. But most importantly, "We're not in danger of going back to school. Let's find a room to rent and a job to do."

"This is a job," MacEoghan would reply. "It makes money."

"And finding a doctor to bind your broken bones takes money."

"We get food, we get to travel."

"We have to show ourselves as more than just street ruffians and vagabonds."

MacEoghan shook his head, telling himself that he needed to stay focused. One last fight, he could make it. He had to. If he could keep this up for a couple more years, maybe he could become a professional boxer. When they went to larger towns and cities, it wasn't impossible for talent scouts to be in the crowds. MacEoghan had seen at least two men get recruited. His time could come. Now that he was getting bigger in size and name, he would get noticed. For the right reasons.

The filler fight ended, little more than a couple of thirteen or fourteen year old boys wrestling in the dirt. Of course, MacEoghan had been one of them not long ago. Sometimes he still was the filler, when they went to cities where the real competitions were. But if he could win this, and keep it up, he'd be recognized. He'd be picked up by a talent scout.

The ringmaster entered the ring, declaring the winner and shooing the fillers out so the real fighters could get back to work. MacEoghan did not look at Micah, but he could feel his stare. One more fight for tonight, but if they did go to a city, and if he did get noticed, how much more would be expected of him? How many more fights? How long would Micah follow him around?

That didn't matter right now, he told himself, walking into the ring. All that mattered was the here and now, this fight, this man in front of him.

He was indeed favoring his left side, and basic human nature demanded that he protect the injury, a large bruise flowering just above his left hip. Considering that he was unable to pretend that it didn't hurt or didn't need such heavy protection, it was probably a pretty serious injury.

Stay to his left, put him on the defense, MacEoghan told himself. *Force him to keep his weight on that hip and exploit the injury.*

If it was bad enough, MacEoghan might not even need to use go-fast.

In his own defense, he didn't use it often. If he had, he would never suffer injury and he would already be the best of the best in the professional world. The only time he used go-fast was to protect his face and maybe occasionally cover up an otherwise potentially fatal mistake, such as if he got his feet mixed up and almost went over, avoiding a groin shot, things of that nature. But he could take a hit, and he had.

On the one hand, Micah said that using the go-fast was cheating. On the other hand, as he said often enough, doctors cost money which they did not have a lot of. Maybe he just didn't like the go-fast being used because if MacEoghan used it too much, he would be in the professional world with the more numerous fights and later nights.

On the third hand, he should stop worrying about it because the fight was about to begin. That was the problem with these fights. They always took too darn long, and the longest part was that time in between the realization of a swing and when it made contact. And it had nothing to do with the go-fast.

Already MacEoghan could feel things start to slow down. He studied his opponent's movements, his feet, especially his favor. He tried to judge the likelihood of a feint, trying to bait him into a trap, decided it was highly unlikely given the bruising. But a bruised hip did not make the man's fists less powerful, and MacEoghan could still feel a little smart in his left side right under his armpit where the man had gotten in a lucky strike. Likewise, the man sized him up as well, trying to judge his best shots while protecting his injury.

"And so, for the third and final time tonight...!" the ringmaster boomed, working the crowd as much as he could, an easy thing by this point, "Begin!"

The bell echoed for a long moment as time seemed to slow even more. MacEoghan shuffled his feet, put his hands up defensively while keeping an eye on his opponent's first movements. His opponent turned slightly to the left, keeping his injury protected near the outer edge of the ring, making it harder to exploit the injury directly but also putting himself at a disadvantage.

MacEoghan shifted to the left. The man couldn't put his back to him, but the best he could do without exposing his injury was turn to the side. MacEoghan had a thought that the man really should have just tapped out, except his honor wouldn't let him. These weren't professional exhibitions for advancement and large purses, these were unsanctioned tavern brawls where the real prize was honor and pride and maybe some cheap beer. None of which would pay the bills.

All of this crossed MacEoghan's mind in about the time it took to take half a step forward, trying to frighten the man into giving away or giving up on his ploy. The man flinched, weakly shuffled back half a step.

MacEoghan did this a few times, seeing if the man might do all the work for him. Turn this way, wrench that way, exacerbate the injury so that he went down on his own with no contact needed. When that didn't happen, he made his move.

If he only went after the man's left side, the man would only turn away, offering his shoulder as a more obvious yet sturdier target. But if he went the other way, danced to the man's right, he could force him into a precarious position. The man would either have to expose himself in order to keep a halfway-decent stance, or else risk MacEoghan getting behind him.

He chose to get in stance, but even that decision was delayed and hesitant. MacEoghan got in two good swings before the man got his arms up and managed to block, taking advantage of MacEoghan's cockiness and getting in a rib shot of his own.

Were MacEoghan younger and less experienced, he might have retreated after being struck, even just half a step. Now, though, he just gritted his teeth and refused to give up his advantage. The man's momentum was spent on impact, and MacEoghan managed to sneak in a chest shot, glancing though it was as the man managed to snap his arm up and brush him off.

The man tried to retreat, but it was clumsy. MacEoghan could have backed off, taken a breath, maybe even given him a chance to back down. That might have been more polite, more sporting. Maybe it was something a professional boxer would do. But he wasn't a professional yet. He was still trying to prove himself. One way to do that was to win quickly.

He stayed on the man. For every half-step the man took in his retreat, MacEoghan moved in a step, never letting him maneuver as well as he wanted. He got in a couple less effective blows, tried to get around the man's front. He was too close for either of them to punch well, but where strength could not reach, precision more than made up for it. Although the man's left side was injured, a blow to the right side was painful enough to almost break the man's defense. MacEoghan knew a moment of mild admiration that he didn't go down immediately, but it didn't stop him from delivering the second blow that caused the man to nearly crumble.

Once the man's defense was broken, a simple one-two punch put him on the ground, heavily dazed and moaning in pain. Some in the crowd cheered, others cursed. Most bets were handed over, a small fight broke out over those that weren't. One man was thrown out of the pub.

The ringmaster came and officially declared MacEoghan the winner, then hurriedly shuffled him out to make room for the next fight.

MacEoghan staggered over to the table where Micah was waiting and sat down in a heap.

"See?" he puffed. "That didn't take long at all."

"For a second, I thought he was going to tear himself apart for you," Micah admitted.

"I was trying, hoping. Bastard stuck it out, for a few seconds anyway." MacEoghan finished off his pint. "All right. Let me sit for a few minutes, then we'll be off."

Those few minutes weren't for the rest so much as to bask in the glory an admiration of some of the spectators who came up to slap him on the back and congratulate him on the victory. When one man offered to buy him a drink—"just what a successful young buck needs to celebrate"—well, he couldn't turn that down, could he?

"You really think there will be talent scouts who will pick you up?" Micah wondered, sounding mildly curious.

"Why wouldn't there be?" MacEoghan countered. "We've seen them. We've watched others get picked up."

"Aye, but those are long odds, aren't they? Some get picked up, others are passed by."

MacEoghan shrugged. "Can't win if you don't play."

Micah opened his mouth, but it was another voice that met MacEoghan's ears. "Excuse me."

He looked up though he did not stand right away. The voice belonged to a man who looked a little too ritzy for the establishment he was patronizing. Hope flared in MacEoghan's chest even as some part of his brain, the small part that hadn't fully succumbed to the alcohol, said that this was too small of a ring for talent scouts to consider.

"Yes sir?" MacEoghan inquired, hoping he didn't sound too eager.

"You are MacEoghan Meagher?" the man asked.

"Aye, that's me. Can I help you with something?" That same non-drunk part of his brain told him he should probably stand and speak to this talent scout face-to-face as respectable men. The best the drunk part of his brain would allow was to straighten up from his lazy slouch.

The man gave him an odd look. "Is MacEoghan your given name? Are you related to the Mag Eochagáin or Mac Eochaidh clans?"

MacEoghan shrugged. "It's the name my mum saw fit to grace me with, so that's what I go by." He could feel Micah's gaze on him.

The man frowned, made a "Hm" sort of noise, then appeared to remember himself. "My name is Lorcan Kearney—"

MacEoghan threw out his hand. "Pleased to meet you."

Lorcan Kearney did not look enthused about having to shake MacEoghan's hand, but he did so anyway, briefly. "Yes. Anyway, if you are able, I would like to take a walk and discuss a matter with you."

The odds were low, especially in a place like this, but never zero. MacEoghan's thoughts were racing as he stood. "Of course, Mr. Kearney." He made a vague gesture. "Lead the way."

As Kearney moved off, MacEoghan turned to look at his brother. Micah looked unequivocally stunned. MacEoghan did not say anything, but he made sure his expression and mild gesture conveyed a certain sense of "I told you so." Micah blinked, his stupefied expression breaking. But instead of grinning and encouraging this meeting, he seemed to be mildly cautious and trying to tell him to be careful and watch himself. MacEoghan sighed as he turned away and followed Kearney through the mass of spectators loudly cheering for the current fight. Only once were they outside in the cool night air did MacEoghan realize just how loud and hot it was inside.

Kearney did not speak right away, but moved off several yards first.

"Now that we can hear each other..." he began.

"Are you a talent scout?" MacEoghan blurted. "Are you here from one of the professional boxing leagues?"

The man shifted his stance. "No, not as such. Although the organization I work for and the interests I represent have been watching you and your brother for some time."

MacEoghan's hope slowly morphed into fear. "Why do you say that? I'm the only one who fights. He just drags my sorry ass back home and calls a doctor. And we're too old for school."

"Perhaps we should speak of the job, the real reason I brought you out here."

"Job?" The elder twin's foggy mind was struggling to keep up. Something was off about this, but he couldn't figure out just what.

"Yes, a job. Just a small one." The shifty man shifted his stance once more. "A client of mine betrayed me and my business, and I have had some trouble finding him. I have reason to believe that he is somewhere in this town, but if he sees me, he'll run. He's a Runner, that's what he does. But if you could find him, that would be most helpful."

MacEoghan folded his arms. "And what is it you expect me to do once I've found him?"

"You're a boxer, are you not? It is true that I myself am not a talent scout, as you disappointingly discovered, but I may have some connections in that realm. I could help you. I could recommend you to one of them."

"You want me to beat him up?"

"Rough him up a bit, yes. And when you're done, he should have a key on his person. It opens a—well, it doesn't matter what it opens. But it is my property."

Something about this still seemed off, but then, it always did when it came to these shady dealings done outside the law. "And what's this man's name?"

"Nolan Kane."

"If he thinks you might be after him, you think he might be using a different name?"

"It is absolutely a possibility, as possible as him seeing me in this pub or talking to you. Are you interested or not?"

MacEoghan shrugged. "I'll give it a go."

"I would appreciate it if you set about it sooner rather than later. It may be that he has already spotted me or gotten wind of my pursuit and is already packing his bags." Kearney turned, then looked back. "He's not a big man, perhaps around your brother's size. Black hair, clean-shaven last I saw. But he is a bit of a scrapper." He gave MacEoghan a look. "And if he does anything...interesting...let me know."

"What do you mean 'interesting'?"

"You'll know it if you see it. Meet me at the motel a few blocks from here tomorrow night with the key." He started walking away, shouting over his shoulder, "Happy hunting!"

MacEoghan watched him go, turning their conversation over in his mind. How strange. Kearney wasn't the only man who had ever asked a fighter to rough up some kind of competition, and he wasn't the only rich man to do so, but something about this still seemed...off. Maybe it was the beer just trying to make things make sense. After all, he was promising a great reward, the one thing MacEoghan had been looking for. Was it some kind of divine providence, or just an eerie coincidence?

He shrugged to himself as he went back inside, suddenly barraged by heat and noise and the stench of sweat and beer. He returned to the table where Miach, upon noticing him, looked up expectantly.

"And?" his twin wondered. "Is he a talent scout?"

MacEoghan shook his head. "No, but he apparently knows some."

Miach raised a brow. "But...?"

MacEoghan shrugged. "He said he'd introduce me to them, but first I have to find some guy who's here in town, beat him up, and take a key off him."

Miach sighed heavily and shook his head. "I hope you didn't say you'd do it."

He shrugged again. "I said I'd think about it."

"If he really does know talent scouts, then if you do this, you know what he's going to do? He's going to tell them that you're a no-good, rough-housing hooligan, and you'll never get into professional boxing."

MacEoghan gave his brother a look. "You'd like that, wouldn't you?"

Miach blinked and did not answer for half a moment. Then, "If you're going to not be a professional boxer, I'd rather it wasn't because you did something stupid like this. What's this key open anyway? How do you know you're not doing a thief's dirty work for him?"

"He didn't say what the key was. He said the guy was a business partner who betrayed him and stole this key on his way out."

"So why isn't he telling the cops where the guy is?"

MacEoghan shrugged dramatically. "I don't know." He stood again. "Maybe I'll ask the guy when I find him."

Miach gave him a severe look but did not stand. "MacEoghan, don't do this. You want to keep fighting, fine, but do it honestly."

MacEoghan was no longer listening. He ambled away from the table and up to the bar. The keep glanced at him. "Another?"

He shook his head. "Any men in here by the name of Nolan Kane? Smaller than me, black hair, clean-shaven, maybe on the run from the law?"

The barkeep laughed. "Any of the men in here could fit at least two of those descriptions, if not more. As for a man who fits all of them, I couldn't tell you."

Even in his drunken state, MacEoghan knew that was a lie. Barkeeps were more attentive than that, especially on fight nights. They knew everyone who came and went from their pub, fighting or not, drinking or not. And if a patron wasn't local, barkeeps went out of their way to know who was who, just in case things got rough.

Barkeeps were also seasoned fighters themselves with lips of steel. He wasn't going to tell and MacEoghan wouldn't be able to pry it out of him if he wanted to. Instead, he watched the man turn his attention to another patron demanding beer.

He turned at a tap on the arm and found himself looking at an older man, maybe in his late sixties, bloodshot eyes, two-foot beard, and a half-drunk beer. Speaking through a bushy mustache and a total of four teeth, he jerked his thumb in a wayward direction and mumbled, "Dunno if 'is your guy, but a guy like that wen' out the back door a minute ago."

Well, his only options were to return to Miach's disapproving stare or follow the vague lead. MacEoghan chose the latter, thanking the old timer and heading for the back door. Maybe he'd get lucky and be able to wrap this up in ten minutes or less. If he met with Kearney tonight and gave the man this alleged key, he could be meeting with talent scouts that much sooner.

Outside in the alley, he initially found nothing remarkable. A little trash, some mice, a couple alley cats, and blessed silence. Cobblestone paving made it impossible to determine footprints, at least to his eyes. Or maybe that was his head which was starting to throb. Maybe he should wait and pick this up in the morning. Maybe he should return to Micah and go back to the motel for a good night's sleep.

Movement caught his eye, and he spied a man at the end of the alley. The man did not appear to be suspicious, or he wasn't worried about appearing so, as he leaned against the building, smoking a pipe.

"'Ey! You there!" MacEoghan called, ambling toward the man.

The man glanced at him. "You wanna fight, go back inside."

Getting closer, MacEoghan was able to make out black hair and common clothes. "You know a man named Nolan Kane?"

The man puffed again. "Maybe I do. Who's asking?"

About four paces away, MacEoghan stopped. "I am."

The man chuckled. "You're, what, sixteen? Eighteen at most? Don't even have proper whiskers on your cheeks." He made a flippant motion with his pipe. "Go back inside and watch the men fight."

MacEoghan blinked and shifted his stance indignantly. "I'm a fighter."

Now the man laughed. "Going around beating up a few drunk vagabonds and ruffians? Hoping a talent scout might come by and scoop you out of the trash in the alley in the morning? Ha! Is that what you think?"

MacEoghan took a step forward, trying to appear big and menacing. "I've won all my fights tonight."

The man set his pipe aside. "Not yet you haven't."

MacEoghan got in stance, briefly wondering just how well this was going to go. He was an experienced fighter, true, but his record was hardly unblemished. Plus there was always a limit. He'd never gone into a fight with the intent to kill his opponent, nor had he ever been truly afraid that his opponent was trying to kill him. Suddenly, that was looking like a very real concern.

Even before the first punch was thrown, MacEoghan decided that he was going to use go-fast to give himself every advantage. Lorcan Kearney and his key didn't matter if MacEoghan was dead. As soon as he saw the man, presumably Nolan Kane, move his arm, whether or not he was actually moving to attack, MacEoghan invoked go-fast. MacEoghan watched the punch move through the air in slow motion, easily avoided the blow and moved in to strike. One, two, three times he hit Kane, then stepped back. After a moment to catch his breath, he released the go-fast.

Kane's punch diverted into something wild as he suddenly reeled from three blows he hadn't seen coming, and he staggered to one side. His hand went to his face and the blood that was now streaming from his nose. Then he looked at MacEoghan. "So. That's how it's going to be, then, eh?"

Then Kane did something MacEoghan did not expect. With a sudden burst of red light, Kane also invoked a go-fast. MacEoghan was too slow to do anything more than realize this before he, too, was reeling from several blows that Kane delivered to him.

"I bet you thought you were pretty special," Kane said, suddenly appearing several paces behind MacEoghan. "Question is, who exposed you?"

"What?" MacEoghan asked dumbly.

"Who exposed you?" a new yet familiar voice inquired. In another flash of bright red light, Kearney appeared in the alley beside Kane. "You were only a child, so it must have been someone close. Mother? Father? An older sibling?"

The beer had to have been spiked with something, MacEoghan thought. He was going absolutely mad. The only thing he could manage was, "Who are you people? Obviously he's not an estranged business partner."

Kearney grinned. "Obviously not. As I introduced myself before, I am Lorcan Kearney. I am the Captain of this District. Mr. Kane here is my Lieutenant. We are the Timekeepers your mentor might have warned you about."

They were the only three in the alley. Was anyone back in the tavern going just as mad? "Timekeepers? What are you talking about? And what do you want with me?"

"Only a fiend would murder a Brother," Kane sneered. "And only someone with the ability to Band could pull it off the way you did."

MacEoghan felt the blood drain from his face.

"We are willing to entertain the idea that it was not you specifically," Kearney said calmly. "After all, you're hardly a man now, so you would have been but a child back then. So tell us, who was it?"

MacEoghan opened his mouth but no words came out.

"Who taught you how to Band?" Kearney pressed. "Was it your father?"

"M...m-my mum was a whore," MacEoghan sputtered in a small voice. "I don't know my father. And our older brother left when we were small."

"You were taken to St. Joseph's shortly thereafter. Was it another one of the Brothers?" The "Timekeepers" frowned, perhaps troubled by the prospect.

"I don't know what you're talking about," MacEoghan insisted. "I've been able to use the go-fast as long as I can remember."

"Go-fast?" Kane echoed. "You weren't even taught proper names?"

"It's all I know, I promise. It's something I've always been able to do."

"Then it was you who murdered Brother Andrew," Kearney stated. He went on before MacEoghan could speak. "There is record of your being punished. The same night, Brother Andrew was murdered and the twin orphans Micah and MacEoghan Meagher escaped St. Joseph's, not to be seen or heard from again. Until recently, when someone made the connection between those twins and these twins moving from place to place in the amateur fight leagues."

MacEoghan swallowed, seeing his odds of a successful fight and flight very rapidly dwindle. They hadn't said anything about Micah yet, but he wasn't sure that was a good thing. While he'd been out here with Kane, had Kearney been in the tavern doing something to Micah? Was his brother all right? Was there any way he could still warn him?

"What are you going to do?" he asked, trying to buy some time.

"We're going to take you before the Grandfathers for trial, for misuse of Time," Kearney explained. "Then, when they're through with you, assuming they haven't left you a drooling idiot, we'll send you to the local authorities in Leitir Fraic so you can be tried for the murder of Brother Andrew."

MacEoghan swallowed again. "All right. I guess you got me. But before you—"

He invoked go-fast at that moment, as strong and as hard as he had done since the night he apparently killed Brother Andrew. He ran past the two men back to the tavern, ripping open the door and barreling inside.

He hadn't meant to kill Brother Andrew, or he didn't think he had. He'd just wanted to make it so he couldn't hurt any of the boys ever again. Well, he certainly wouldn't be, but still, MacEoghan hadn't meant it like that.

Once inside the tavern, he spied Micah almost immediately, just standing up from the table. MacEoghan hastily walked toward him, extending the go-fast—the Band? as Kane had called it—around his brother, almost running into him.

"What the—?" Micah wondered, momentarily disoriented.

MacEoghan grabbed his brother's arm and started for the door, pushing past patrons who were moving so slowly they could as well have been standing still. "We have to leave right now."

"What? Why?" Micah stumbled but MacEoghan dragged him along anyway. "MacEoghan, what's going on?"

They burst out of the tavern where MacEoghan made a hard right and headed for the motel. There he fumbled with the key and nearly forced his way in out of sheer fear and frustration. Once inside, he started frantically grabbing their few worldly possessions.

"Damn you, MacEoghan, what's going on?!" Micah demanded from the door.

MacEoghan snatched up a shirt. "You remember Brother Andrew?"

Micah folded his arms. "Of course I do, and I'd rather not."

"The man who approached me and the man he wanted me to find, it was all a setup. They're here about Brother Andrew, and they figured out it was me."

"Who cut off his cock?"

"Micah, he died from that. They want to try me for murder."

Micah cursed.

"What's worse," MacEoghan went on, "is they can use go-fast, too."

Micah blinked. "What?"

"They called it Banding, said they were like Timekeepers or something. I don't know, they said something about Grandfathers and a trial. They might be some part of the IRA."

Now Micah raised a brow. "Are these men actually Irish?"

"One had an Irish accent, the other an English one, so I can't say for sure." MacEoghan slammed his suitcase shut. "But I'm not going to stick around and ask questions. Are you?"

Finally Micah felt compelled to help pack, saying, "No, I guess not. But where do you think we're going to go?"

"Step one, away from here."

It didn't take but a few minutes for them to gather everything they owned and run out the door, leaving the room key behind with a hastily scrawled thank you note.

"All right, where to?" Micah asked. "Train station?"

"Of course not," MacEoghan told him. "All they'd have to do is ask if we'd been there and they'd meet us wherever we're going. We'll take a cab, get as far away from here as possible. Then take another cab even farther." He went on, "We'll take the first cab together, get to a big city. After that, we'll split up, take separate cabs to somewhere else."

Micah did not slow necessarily, but MacEoghan could still feel his hesitation. "Are you sure? Is splitting up really a good idea?"

"We'll still be going to the same place, but then the cabbies won't be able to say that they took twins wherever it is we're going. Just a man with a suitcase."

Micah hummed a sigh. "You do have a point. But how long do we run? Where do we go? Most of Ireland knows us, or knows you."

"They know me as a fighter, a boxer." MacEoghan was suddenly hit with the realization that he wasn't likely to become a professional boxer. He pushed it aside for the moment. "And there are a few places we haven't been. But first, the city."

There were only a couple cabs in town, but they stayed busy with the number of men too drunk to even walk home from the tavern after the fights. Only as they approached the tavern and saw everyone standing still did MacEoghan consider that he was still using go-fast. He couldn't decide whether it was the alcohol or the go-fast that was giving him a headache right now, but he didn't want to let go of the go-fast. The Band.

"What do we do?" Micah asked. "Can you use the go-fast on one of the cabs and drivers?"

MacEoghan shifted his stance. "I don't know, maybe. But I think that would be too obvious. If we take someone's car—one of these sorry blokes— then it will be at least morning before it's noticed missing."

"You want to steal a car?"

"What do you want me to do, *a Mhicah*? I'm already on the hook for murder, stealing a car is nothing."

Micah sighed and looked around. Finally, "Fine. I suppose I'll have to drive. You're too drunk and too tired."

"I am not too drunk," MacEoghan protested. "But I am tired. And I want to hold the go-fast as long as possible."

They made for a neighborhood a block away from the tavern and picked a car from a dark house. MacEoghan slid in the passenger seat. He was tired standing up, but sitting down almost put him out.

"Aw no," Micah said, punching him in the arm. "No, you stay awake, you keep that go-fast going. We have to get out of here."

MacEoghan rubbed his eyes, startling back to wakefulness as the car roared to life and leapt forward with the clunky mannerisms of a driver who had been behind the wheel of a car all of twice before.

"We're going to make it," MacEoghan mumbled, "as long as you don't kill us first."

"Oh, quiet, you," Micah scoffed, grinning humorlessly. "I know what I'm doing. You just make sure you don't fall asleep for a while."

The best MacEoghan could do was try, and the two of them disappeared into the darkness of the Irish countryside.

BED AND BREAKFAST
OLDER BROTHER

Five cabs and eleven days later, the brothers found themselves beyond the end of the cab routes, walking along a dirt road pitted with holes and washouts as it wound down to a small fishing village on the south shore of Ireland. It probably had a pub, maybe even had some unofficial fights, but it was too out of the way for anyone other than the locals to try and make themselves known. Neither brother had known this village existed except that the fishermen apparently exported some of their catch to surrounding towns. MacEoghan had spied the name of the village in one of these town markets and, on a whim, made it their next destination.

They'd traded their suitcases for backpacks, but they still looked a sorry pair scuffing up puffs of dust that were rapidly swept away by the sea breeze.

"You really think we can hide here for a while?" Micah wondered sullenly as they paused and surveyed the town from above.

"If we can't hide here..." MacEoghan trailed off. If they couldn't hide here, then what? Where could they go? What could they do? Did they dare try to go back north, maybe sneak across the border to Belfast? Could they sneak over to England? If Kearney and Kane were to be believed, then it was likely that any law enforcement would be looking for them. Looking for him, anyway, but poor Micah was going to get caught up in this against his will just for being his twin.

Finally MacEoghan sighed and started off down the twisting road to the village. "Come on. We need a place to stay the night anyway."

On the road but nowhere to go, he thought ruefully. As the sun beat down on them, he found himself almost missing the school. He hated himself for it, but it didn't stop the thoughts from penetrating his mind. It had been predictable, comfortable. A bed to sleep in, meals every day, work to keep them busy and prepare them for the world so they could enter the workforce and not be wandering vagabonds and drunks.

If that was all the school had been, if it had lived up to such a shining reputation, then, well, they'd probably still be there. At the very least, they wouldn't have run away. They could have gotten respectable jobs. Instead, Micah had been horrifically abused and they'd spent the last few years roaming from town to town in pursuit of some foolish boxing dream. Of course, that dream had apparently saved them from earlier apprehension.

So, what now? Lay low in this little fishing village and become fishermen? Was that all this escapade would allow them to amount to in life? If it had been normal police officers on their tail, MacEoghan would probably be a lot less worried. Maybe his boxing dream could not be pursued, but there were other things he could do. But with Kearney and Kane being able to use go-fast...

MacEoghan had never understood go-fast. Didn't understand exactly what it was, how it worked, or why only he could apparently do it. It was simply something that was part of him, a talent he alone possessed. He wasn't sure what to make of other people being able to do it, nor the implication that there were a lot of someones, those someones had rules about it, and he had broken them.

Or maybe he had gone mad. Maybe his drink that night had been tainted with something. Maybe this was all in his head. Wouldn't that be a frightful and maddening thing? He might have entertained the notion that it was some kind of setup from a competitor to get him out of the league, except no one knew about St. Joseph's, and, more importantly, no one knew about Brother Andrew.

The only thing left, then, was that it was real. Kearney and Kane had the ability to use go-fast and they were some kind of law enforcement, pursuing him for the murder of Brother Andrew.

If only the dark cloud over his mind could have covered the sun, just for a moment. The breeze intensified as they reached the village and neared the shore, but it did little for the stark heat coming from the sun and reflecting off the water. MacEoghan shaded his eyes as he paused and looked around for some sign of a motel, tavern, or any social establishment.

As it was, the village wasn't much to look at. A couple dozen boats bobbed in the water, a couple dozen more fishermen gathered in one spot with some nets and tools having some discussion. Wind-battered homes sat quietly on various levels carved out of the sand and cliffs. A few children played in the street. MacEoghan spied signs for a few stores: a general store, a clothing store, a recreational fishing store, and a couple others he could not readily identify.

"So, we're here," Micah observed dryly. "Now what?"

That was the question, wasn't it? It wasn't as though they had family to surprise with a visit. They didn't even know anyone here.

"Do you suppose they even have a motel?" MacEoghan wondered, heading in the direction of the stores.

"We've yet to visit a town without one," Micah offered. "But then, this appears to be an end or a destination, not a stop on the way to anywhere else."

MacEoghan grunted in agreement as they passed by each store. Many had signs warning potential customers of a possible shortage of some goods owing to disturbances from England and the European mainland.

"What do you suppose they're on about?" Micah wondered, gesturing to one such sign that was a little flashier than the others.

MacEoghan shook his head. "I'm not entirely sure. I think it has to do with the Germans again, or that's what I gathered from some of the other fighters. Said they were training up real good in case they had to fight them, but I'm not sure what it's all about."

Micah considered this for a moment. Then he shrugged and went on his way with a casual, "Huh."

They entered the general store, bypassing a similar sign with a similar message. Indeed, some shelves were a bit sparse. Others had had more of the same inventory spread out so they did not appear to be empty, though the lack of variety was perhaps more noticeable.

"Help you boys?"

They turned to see an old shopkeep leaning on the counter, reading but not reading a newspaper.

"Do you...?" MacEoghan began, then paused. They were both quite hungry, but, glancing at himself and his brother, they also still wore the road. "Is there a motel in town?"

The shopkeep frowned, though he kept his eyes on the paper. "Motel, sure, if you don't mind a few fleas. If you want something a little nicer, go down to the shore and look for Sarah. She's got a bit of a bed and breakfast going right now, get you bathed and fed real well."

He gave them directions. MacEoghan thanked the old man, and he and Micah left the shop.

"A bath does sound nice right about now," Micah commented, giving them a once-over.

"A bath and a meal," MacEoghan agreed.

Following the old shopkeep's directions took them to a large home near the shoreline. The porch sagged a bit and the paint was peeling, but there was plenty of evidence of residence as a woman, appearing in her forties, swept the porch and yelled at a couple of small children playing on the beach nearby to get washed up.

MacEoghan could feel Micah's expression, a silent question. He led the way toward the porch, pausing just long enough for the children to run past them into the house.

"Help you boys?" the woman inquired. "I don't recognize you. You from up the road?"

"We were told Sarah has a bed and breakfast around here? Might have a room?" MacEoghan ventured.

The woman straightened, her broom stopping midstride. "Aye. I'm Sarah." She studied them, leaning mildly on the broom. "You been on the road long? You're filthy. Your clothes, too. And you look like teenage boys so you must be starving."

"Yes, ma'am," Micah blurted.

That got Sarah to laugh. "I thought as much. Well, come on up. Get your hands and faces washed, let me see your bags; I'm assuming you got clothes in 'em. You got money or you want to trade favors? My husband could use some strong young men to help."

"Either is fine with us, ma'am," MacEoghan told her, walking up the porch steps.

106

"All right then." She nodded once then popped her head inside the house. "Shay! Show these boys to the wash! Ciara! Set two extra plates!"

MacEoghan surrendered his bag to Sarah, then followed a thirteen year old boy to the back of the house to a washroom. The smell of food in the house made his stomach grumble hopefully. As much as he wanted to make himself presentable for dinner, he wanted dinner more. He passed Micah on the way out to the dining table. The arrangement looked small even for the gathered family, never mind having to add two more settings.

"Come on, sit down," Sarah ordered, she and her daughters busily carrying food to the table. "You're guests here. Padraig will put your backs to work well enough afterwards."

MacEoghan chose a seat. When Micah appeared a moment later, he sat beside him.

The woman's husband, Padraig, walked in the house just as Sarah was placing the last dish of food. He was a big man, bigger than MacEoghan, but easily thirty years older, skin hard and leathery from years of labor. He looked at the twins through bushy eyebrows and spoke through a bushier mustache and beard.

"You staying long?"

"We don't know, sir," MacEoghan answered lamely. "We don't have much money, but we can help however you need us."

The man grunted and took his place at the head of the table. The children, ranging in age from about fifteen down to four, took their places, Sarah seating herself last. Blessings were said, and chaos ensued.

The older children seemed to understand a policy of feeding the guests first. The younger children did not take kindly to this policy, at least until Padraig intervened, with a deep, slow, steady, slightly muffled voice promising them a good switchin' if they didn't listen to their mother at the dinner table. The threat worked to stem the blatant whining, but it did not improve the sullen attitudes. The Brothers would have had a field day with them, MacEoghan thought, accepting portions of food with a word of gratitude but little more.

"So, where are you boys from?" Sarah began once all the children had been served.

"Ah, north," MacEoghan answered evasively. "County Gaillimh."

"Gaillimh, really? What brings you this way, then?"

"Just..." MacEoghan glanced at Micah. "Traveling."

"Is it the war?" Padraig asked pointedly.

"Honestly, Padraig," Sarah hissed, "we agreed not to speak of this at the supper table."

"What war?" Micah wondered.

Sarah just sighed.

"The war, brewing on the mainland," Padraig said. "Again. Germany's angry about losing the Great War, so now they're going to retaliate."

"It has nothing to do with us," Sarah commented, glancing over her children.

"Aye, but that doesn't mean we don't end up getting involved in some way anyway. Damned English, dragging us into their bloody wars. Starting wars all over the damned place."

"Padraig, language."

"But if Germany is getting upset, why is that England's fault?" MacEoghan wondered.

"Don't encourage him," Shauna hissed at him, looking and sounding exactly like her mother despite being only six years old.

Padraig grunted. "You boys got an education? You follow the news?"

MacEoghan nodded. "Yes, sir. And no, sir."

"How old are you? Fourteen?"

"Fifteen, almost sixteen."

"You learn much about the Great War?"

He knew that they'd once believed their father to have been a noble soldier in the Great War, knew now that it was a horrendous lie. Actually, he knew plenty about it thanks to the Brothers, though he was unwilling to give them any credit for it.

"Honestly, Padraig," Sarah cut in, sounding annoyed, "you can talk politics with them while they work for you. But not at the table!"

Padraig huffed a sigh but agreed.

"So anyway," she went on, grinning hugely, "tell us of your travels. Surely you haven't walked all the way from Gaillimh!"

"No, ma'am," MacEoghan told her. "We've walked, taken trains, cabs. We've been all over."

"Ah, lovely. You're on a bit of a holiday from family, then? Do they know of your travels?"

Micah just cleared his throat.

"How have you been funding your trip?" Padraig asked. "You work?"

"Prize fighting mostly," MacEoghan answered before thinking.

Sarah scoffed and waved a hand. "Honestly. Nasty business. So barbaric."

"You any good?" Padraig wondered, looking intrigued.

MacEoghan shrugged. "I'm great. Just, sometimes, the other guy is better."

"Then I have to drag your sorry, bloody hide back home to fix you up," Micah laughed, jabbing him in the ribs. "At least you won more than you lost."

"I almost had a talent scout approach me." MacEoghan looked at Padraig. "I was going to be a professional boxer."

"He thought he was," Micah cut in. MacEoghan did not miss the sudden sharpness of his tone.

Now Padraig chuckled. "Well, you might find a few fights down at the pub, but there'll be no talent scouts here."

MacEoghan thrust a thumb at Micah. "He's trying to talk me out of it. Part of the reason we started down here instead of continuing on a proper circuit or league."

"At least one of you has some sense," Sarah commented. "Where did you say you went to school? Or, if you can afford to travel and get in bar brawls, maybe you had private tutors?"

They really should have come up with some kind of a story. As it was, MacEoghan answered, "Private tutors," at the same time Micah said, "St. Joseph's." To rescue the situation, MacEoghan clarified, "It was St. Joseph's, but the education was so good it was like having private tutors."

He invoked go-fast just enough to give Micah a look. The best his twin could do was a guilty look and small promise to keep his mouth shut.

Sarah broke into an enormous grin. "Oh, wonderful!" She glanced at Padraig. "We heard about the industrial schools, of course, at Mass on

Sundays. So much good they're doing, and you were blessed to go there. Did they teach you many skills?"

MacEoghan noted how Micah seemed to shrink in his chair. He shifted uncomfortably and answered, "Yes, they taught us a lot."

Now she frowned. "You don't sound very enthusiastic."

"You must have just recently graduated," Padraig observed, looking thoughtful. "Fifteen years old."

MacEoghan seized on the comment. "Yes, very recently. That's part of the reason we're out traveling, because the only thing we've seen for many years is that school. We want to see the rest of the world, too, or at least the country."

Sarah nodded. "Well, if you're from Gaillimh—and I'm not quite sure where St. Joseph's is—then you're probably heading back soon. I mean, you've come as far south as you can go, unless you want to visit some small, rocky, useless islands."

"We have no desire to visit the islands," Micah said, his tone suggesting he didn't know what to say and wanted only to turn the conversation.

"Well, we're glad you've decided to stop here. You seem like hard-working yet well-mannered young men."

Conversation then steered away from the twins specifically and more toward their travels, the places they had been and things they had seen. Sarah and her daughters were more interested in the travels and scenery while Padraig and his sons wanted to know more about MacEoghan's prize fighting. MacEoghan was happy to brag about himself while Micah placated the women with the pettier tales.

The conversation meant Padraig was late to get back out to his afternoon chores and he hurried out of the house, his older sons following, Micah and MacEoghan trailing a step behind.

Padraig Dearbhfhine was no one special. Like most of the men in town, he was a fisherman, owned a small business his father and grandfather had built. Every morning he went out in his boat, cast his lines, cast his nets, and prayed to catch something that would then be shipped to various markets. Every afternoon was then spent inspecting the boat, inspecting the lines and nets, doing proper maintenance and making any needed repairs.

MacEoghan didn't know anything about fishing. He couldn't say he was smart enough to identify too many fish. He might have said that even the five year old knew more about what was going on than he did.

"Didn't that school teach you nothin'?" Padraig asked.

"It was an industrial school, sir," MacEoghan offered helplessly. "And we were far from any water."

A sudden memory of tossing Brother Andrew's severed penis into the river flashed through his mind.

Padraig made a disapproving sound as he turned a net over, fingers working deftly to repair a tear. "Industrial school. Teaching you things for the cities, work in the factories, make tools and weapons for the war."

"They taught us farming, too," Micah mentioned.

The man barked a laugh. "A noble skill, aye, but not the most useful skill here. The women tend their gardens, but the only real industry here is fishing."

Padraig was not a perfect teacher, nor the most patient, but he was never cruel. MacEoghan saw Micah wanted to learn and be helpful, but he was also very uncomfortable. MacEoghan couldn't say he didn't understand. At one point, he messed up something on a net. When Padraig came to examine it and correct him, MacEoghan visibly flinched, expecting a hand or a rod to come down on him. But the man just took the net, turned it over once, then leaned in close to explain how to do it again and do it better.

MacEoghan silently cursed himself for his weakness. It was years ago, and in the time since, he'd become a strong fighter. He would never be afraid again. He would never allow himself to be pushed around again, at least not without a good fight. True, Padraig was a big man, strong and weathered from his trade, but to flinch away and cower like he had was unacceptable.

The sun went down, reflecting off the water with a burgundy glow. The man and his boys and Micah and MacEoghan all stood on the rocky beach, simply watching and enjoying, until Sarah called them in for supper. The table arrangement was the same, and the twins sat down easily, grateful for the meal which proved to be fish soup.

"So, did they earn their stay tonight?" Sarah inquired of her husband, sitting down.

"Aye, I'd say so," Padraig answered. "They don't know nothin' 'bout fishin', but they're quick study." He ladled out some soup into his bowl. "How long you expect you'll be here?"

The twins glanced at each other. It was MacEoghan who answered, "We're really not sure. If you want us out, we'll go, but as long as we're here, as long as you'll have us, we'll keep working."

He could see that the couple found the answer strange. He found himself wishing for a motel; at least they didn't ask questions. As long as you had money for the room, they were happy to leave you alone. Except their money was all but gone, and motels didn't like to barter. And a home-cooked meal was a welcome thing.

Supper conversation revolved around planning for the next day. Micah and MacEoghan were informed that their help would be enlisted for the morning cast, although, with the skills they displayed that day, or lack thereof, their participation would likely be minimal. But, once back on land, they could help load the catch to be taken to the nearby towns. The twins had no choice but to agree, at least, if they wanted to stay more than one night.

They were shown to the room they would be sharing. Two small beds, each with a crucifix on the wall over the head, were the most exciting part of an otherwise bare room, a single window providing a view of the street to the north. Their clothes and bags had been washed and neatly folded, two stacks on each bed. Sarah wished them good night and closed the door.

"No uncles," Micah said after a moment, expression grimly melancholy.

"Aye," MacEoghan murmured.

"Is this what a family is like?"

MacEoghan shrugged as he sat down on one of the beds. "I don't know. We've only been here half a day, but they seem nice."

Micah nodded silently and bent to put his clothes back in his bag. Then he sat down on the bed, facing MacEoghan. "How long are we planning on staying?"

MacEoghan opened his mouth and shrugged again, only able to manage an unintelligible stutter at first. Then, "I don't know. I don't know what to do, Micah. We're at the end here. There's nowhere else to go, not in Ireland. I suppose we could try to go to England, see how far that gets us."

Micah's expression twisted into anguish. "If there's a war going on, MacEoghan, I don't want to get conscripted."

"Who says you won't get conscripted here?"

"We're out in the middle of nowhere."

"If we go to a city, we can find work in a factory. Can't conscript the people making the things needed for the war."

Micah thought about this a moment, but MacEoghan could see he still wasn't convinced. "You think they'd let us stay here a while?"

MacEoghan blinked. "I mean, a few days, sure, but we're still only guests."

"But they're really nice."

"It's a bed and breakfast and they have kids. Of course they're nice." MacEoghan sighed and rubbed his face. "We're fifteen, near sixteen, Micah. No one's adopting us. No one is coming to our rescue. We're too old. We're too skilled—"

"Obviously not if we can't help a fisherman more than his six year old son," Micah sputtered, but MacEoghan could see his eyes were wet.

"No one is coming, Micah," MacEoghan said as gently as he could. "We're all we have. And I know I messed that up for us. I messed it up real bad."

"You saved me."

"Aye, well, no good deed goes unpunished." He cut himself off, sighed, lay down, and closed his eyes. "I'm sure we'll figure something out in the next day or two."

He could hear the bed rustle and creak as Micah also lay down, saying, "I know you will."

MacEoghan had just gotten comfortable when the door opened and a light hit his eyelids.

"Up and at 'em, boys, the fish are running!" Padraig said loudly.

Already? Had he even fallen asleep? Through bleary eyes, he could see Micah roll over, pulling a pillow over his face.

MacEoghan sat up. Judging by the messed up blankets, he must have slept. He just couldn't remember it. Well, time to pay for the beds they just slept in.

Padraig and his sons had a well-rehearsed routine, and MacEoghan and Micah were not part of it. There was some bumping and shoving and a bit of a slow down. This did not please Padraig and he was quick to snap at everyone to hurry up and get out to the boat. Sarah barely had time to kiss her husband goodbye and wish them well before the crew was out the door.

Only the boys who were ten and older actually went out on the boat, but the younger ones still ran after them in the dark, telling them to fish good and be home for dinner. Padraig, his mind focused on only one thing, paid them no mind.

MacEoghan got in the boat, then turned to help his brother. Having packed the boat the previous evening, they were underway within minutes.

The sun was nowhere to be seen and MacEoghan had a hard time believing that there was any color change on the horizon. The lights on the boat were already poor, and the way they swung about as they crashed over waves did little to illuminate anything. What they did illuminate only exacerbated MacEoghan's growing nausea. Micah didn't look much better as he knelt near the railing.

Once they got out past the rocks and shoals, the sharpness of the waves ebbed and they were left with a more gentle bob. Only pinpricks of light gave any indication of other boats in the area. Padraig was already giving orders to his boys who didn't look like they really needed to be told their jobs. MacEoghan and Micah tried not to get underfoot even as they also tried to help.

"You two really don't know nothin' 'bout fishing, do you?" Padraig wondered, finally stepping down from the helm to assist.

"No, sir," MacEoghan said. "I promise, we weren't holding out on you."

The man frowned and made his disapproving noise. "Well, do what you're told for now. We'll see if you can be of any more help when we ship out our catch."

The man headed off to talk to one of his older boys, but MacEoghan couldn't move for a long second. He couldn't pinpoint exactly what it was except maybe a little annoyance coupled with a bit of astonishment. He didn't like not knowing something. He didn't like feeling dismissed because of it. He wouldn't mind learning so he could be helpful. On the other hand, if he and Micah were only supposed to stick around for a few days, well, what would be the point? Use them where they are most helpful and send them on their way.

He held no ill will for Padraig on account of the comments, but it still bothered him as they bobbed out in the water. Padraig and his sons did their work, and the twins were mostly relegated to fetching items.

Discernible color appeared on the horizon. Soon, MacEoghan could make out the others on the boat. Then the other boats and the people on them. Then the lamps became unnecessary. By the time the sun sat upon the water, they had a respectable catch of fish and were lazily turning back toward shore. They did not rush, but continued to cast lines and nets, seeing what else they could bring in on the return.

When they reached the shore, the docks were in a frenzy. More men went to work in the various warehouses, hastily processing the fish and packing them in large crates. Several delivery trucks rumbled to life, black smoke puffing. MacEoghan might not have understood the nuances of fishing, but he could haul and load with minimal supervision. Now more impressed by his houseguests, Padraig sent the twins with the trucks to help offload at the various surrounding towns. Some of the fish went straight to market, and some went onto bigger trucks destined for canneries and other processing plants.

By the time they returned, it was about dinner time. MacEoghan spied the boys on the docks, and they informed the twins that their father was doing book work in the office.

"Think we should help?" Micah wondered.

MacEoghan shook his head and started back toward the house. "No. Business is for them. We're just hired hands."

"So, how did it go?" Sarah inquired as they walked in the door.

"We caught fish," Micah offered uncertainly.

"Well I saw that much. Did you learn something?"

"We learned that we don't know anything about fishing," MacEoghan said.

She waved a hand. "That's all right. You'll get the hang of it, even in a day or two. You want to call them in for dinner for me?"

115

So they did. It took a few minutes for Padraig to wrap up his business, but then he and his sons returned to the house for dinner.

"How did it go?" Sarah asked of her husband, just as interested in his answer as the twins'.

"Old Kenny being a miser again," Padraig grumbled. "We have an agreement by the pound. He doesn't—"

"Not at the table," Sarah told him firmly. "And how did the boys do?"

Padraig's attitude shifted into something resembling pride as he recounted things his sons had done out on the boat. MacEoghan did not understand the significance of everything the man said, but he found himself a bit jealous.

"And did our houseguests earn their keep?" his wife inquired.

Thankfully, Padraig nodded. "Aye, they did. I don't expect them to learn much in just a few days out on the boat, but they do good dock work. Load, unload, they're good at it. Saves my back anyway."

"Wonderful. And I'm sure they'll learn plenty; they seem to have their wits about them. They must if they went to St. Joseph's."

Padraig waved a hand dismissively. "Academic types don't go to places like St. Joseph's. It's an industrial school; boys go there to learn how to work. I'm sure the teachers and priests there are more than adequate for teaching them how to work."

MacEoghan kept his mouth shut, instead focusing on the meal before him. He could feel similar unease from Micah beside him. If either Padraig or Sarah noticed their discomfort, nothing was said about it.

After dinner was another afternoon and evening of inspecting the boat and the equipment, performing maintenance, and making any necessary repairs. Then some minor chores around the house. Then it was time for supper, a nightly Scripture reading, a little free time, and finally bed.

"You really think we'll learn anything about fishing?" Micah wondered, most of his question enveloped by a yawn.

"I don't know," MacEoghan mumbled, pulling a pillow over his eyes. "Maybe."

At least that night he knew he got to sleep before he was woken up again.

So it was for the next three days. Wake up early, light breakfast more often taken on the boat than at the table, go out fishing, process the fish, take the fish to the markets, dinner, maintenance on the boat and equipment, supper, Scriptures, some free time, then bed. MacEoghan liked to think he learned a little about fishing in that time. Padraig told his wife that was the case, anyway, although he still didn't feel as knowledgeable as the other boys.

It had been Monday when they first approached the Dearbhfhine family, and it was Friday night when MacEoghan decided that it was probably about time for them to consider their next move. He knew Padraig was expecting them to work in the morning, so maybe he could broach the subject at dinner the next day.

Saturday, the trucks were late to the docks which meant they were late to leave the docks which meant they were too late for dinner. None of this put Padraig in a good mood by the time supper came around. Sarah did her best to break up the awkward tension at the table.

"So, Micah, MacEoghan, why don't you tell us about your family?" she began. "You don't hardly talk about yourselves." When the twins hesitated, she asked, "What's your mum's name?"

"Jeannie," MacEoghan answered simply. He was fairly certain that was true, except he was having a hard time recalling her face, never mind her name.

"Lovely name. And—"

"And your father?" Padraig cut in. "What's his name? And I want you to answer at the same time."

"Padraig!" Sarah hissed.

MacEoghan used go-fast to exchange a glance with Micah.

"What should we say?" Micah wondered, looking distressed.

"I don't know," MacEoghan said, searching for an answer. "Ah...Kevin."

"Kevin?"

"You got a better name?"

Micah shook his head, eyes huge. MacEoghan heaved a breath and released the go-fast. Before he had a chance to open his mouth, Sarah spoke.

"The reason we ask..." She shifted in her seat. "We've heard some of your conversations through the wall at night. Once, we heard one of you crying." Her expression was gentle. "You don't have a family, do you?"

MacEoghan let go of his breath. He looked at Micah who stared at the table. Finally, "No, ma'am. We never knew our pa and our mum died when we were young. We were sent to St. Joseph's as orphans."

Sarah nodded. "We suspected as much."

"Got into prize fighting to support yourselves," Padraig stated, still grumpy. "Why not use the skills the school taught you?"

Micah just shrugged; MacEoghan did not answer.

"Where do you plan to go?" Sarah wondered. "What will you do?"

"We don't know," MacEoghan answered honestly. "To tell the truth, I might have gotten into a bit of trouble at my last fighting match, came down here to escape and lie low for a little while."

"I see. What kind of trouble?"

"The unsanctioned fighting kind of trouble."

"Hm. And you have no family whatsoever?"

"We had a brother once," Micah said. "Older brother. He left shortly before our mum died. Never knew what happened to him."

"No aunts or uncles? No grandparents?"

"Our mum was a whore," MacEoghan said venomously. "Almost every night there was a different 'uncle' in the house."

One of the little girls gasped while a couple of the boys giggled. Sarah and Padraig exchanged a glance.

"If we had any family, we never met them," Micah said, his tone less acidic. "We don't even know where we were born, barely remember where our mum died, and we have no idea where our family is actually from."

"You've never searched for the Meagher family?" Padraig questioned.

"We were shipped off to school."

"Surely they must have searched."

"If they did, they didn't find anyone."

Sarah's frown deepened. "That's so sad." She shifted again. "Well then, I suppose it makes this next inquiry a bit easier on you, or I hope it does." She cleared her throat and glanced at her husband who shoved a bite of food in his mouth. "Would you like to stay with us?"

MacEoghan blinked. He looked at Micah who appeared equally stunned.

"I know it must seem strange, but—"

118

"Yes," Micah stated sharply, eagerly.

Sarah made a sound that was somewhere in the realm of a sigh, a giggle, and the bark of weeping. She grinned. "Yes. Good. I mean..." She wiped away a small tear. "You see, our first child—" She gestured to herself and Padraig who was still silent but absolutely scarlet. "—well, they were twins. And they were stillborn." She wiped away another tear. "And they'd be your age now." She managed a small laugh. "I was praying to God at Mass recently, asking Him about them, asking Him what they're like in Heaven, wondering what they'd be like if they were here with us. And then you two showed up."

"I think your sons would be better fishermen than us," MacEoghan said, heart racing.

"That's nothing a little time and teachin' won't fix," Padraig told him dismissively. "Assuming you're able and willing to learn."

"Aye, sir, we are," Micah agreed excitedly.

"Does that mean we have to listen to them?" one of the boys asked, his tone whining.

"You should anyway because they're older," Sarah informed him. "It's respectful."

"But they don't know nothin' 'bout fishin' and such!"

"They'll learn," Padraig said. "Won't you?"

"Yes sir," Micah agreed again.

Sarah looked at MacEoghan. "You don't look as certain. You don't want to stay?"

MacEoghan shrugged. "It's always just been us two, even at the school. Always me and him. I always looked out for him, came to his rescue."

"Yes, but who looked out for you? It's all right, lad. You can relax."

"I don't know if I can."

"You been fightin' too much," Padraig told him. "Been fightin' so much, you don't know what to do without the fight. I'll bet that's how you ended up in whatever trouble you're in. You learn an honest trade, do honest work, the fight won't matter so much."

"We'd love to have you," Sarah continued. "At least sleep on it. Maybe pray about it at Mass tomorrow. Then we'll see what happens."

MacEoghan had no real reason not to, he supposed. Micah was clearly all for it. And why not? Just a few nights ago MacEoghan had told him in no uncertain terms that they were on their own. Now, it seemed, they weren't, or they had the option.

But what about Kearney and Kane? Were they still on the hunt? Would they hurt Padraig and Sarah and the other children?

MacEoghan lay awake that night, turning it over in his mind. Maybe he should leave Micah here and go off on his own. Micah wasn't the one in trouble. Or would he be punished anyway? Who would save him then? And besides, this was a nice family. It was nice to have a good bed to sleep in and home-cooked meals. Maybe they wouldn't stay forever, but they could rest here for a little while.

DEARBHFHINE
YOUNGER BROTHER

Micah would admit, he kind of enjoyed annoying MacEoghan in the morning, shaking him awake and telling him to hurry up, the fish were running. MacEoghan would groan, roll over, mumble something into the mattress, then crawl out of bed while Micah was already halfway to the toilet. From there it was out to the kitchen where Sarah had a light breakfast packed for them to take on the boat. He took the bag, kissed her on the cheek, then bounded out the door toward the water. MacEoghan, meanwhile, stumbled around, half-awake and in no mood for joyful frolicking.

Micah ignored him.

Padraig was always the first one in the boat, but Micah was almost always second, tossing his breakfast in the crate they used to carry their breakfast bags, and going about his morning chores. Prepare the nets, prepare the lines, light the lanterns. One by one, the younger boys and MacEoghan climbed into the boat. Shay, thirteen years old, Cillian, eleven, and, very rarely, Brendan, who was eight. Once the crew was accounted for, they shoved off into the darkness.

He still didn't understand everything about fishing, but he knew a lot more than he had when they first showed up two months ago. He knew how to tie eleven different knots and for what occasion. He could cast lines and nets, though he wasn't the most accurate. He wasn't allowed to drive the boat quite yet, but Padraig promised that it was coming soon.

He'd also learned a great deal about the ocean, the currents, the weather, even how the fish might respond to the changing elements. And, of course, different fish could respond differently.

It was a lot to learn, and sometimes he got it wrong. He'd broken lines, lost his hold on a net. Padraig had thought it odd at first how he'd flinched when he did something wrong. Now the man simply ignored it, decided it was just a personal quirk. Micah couldn't help it, but he was trying to be better about it. Padraig didn't beat him for making a mistake or asking questions. He might raise his voice in frustration, and Micah had watched him switch Brendan once for backtalk, but it was nowhere near the cruelty of the Brothers. And never, not once, did Padraig ever touch Micah, MacEoghan, or any of the boys in their pants.

It was odd, but it felt right. It felt genuinely good, as if this was the way things were supposed to be. This was what life should have been like. No more nightly uncles, no disappearing siblings, no judicial or papal guardians. A mother, a father, and many siblings. Even better that he and MacEoghan were the oldest of the bunch. He stood at the prow and looked back at the others. Everyone was awake to some degree, but only he and Padraig looked really excited. MacEoghan ambled up beside him.

"You are far too happy this morning," his twin grumbled.

"You say that every morning," Micah told him.

"And it's true every morning."

"Now you know how I felt waiting for you every night at your boxing matches."

MacEoghan made a disgusted sort of sound. "Aye, but that was at night when we could just go to bed and sleep how we wanted. This is...early. You can't just go to bed, you got to get up and stay up."

"This is life. We were the odd ones, MacEoghan. This is how things ought to be, how it should have been."

"We weren't odd." When Micah started to speak, MacEoghan beat him to it. "We weren't the only orphans at that school. We're not the only orphans in Ireland or in the world. Being orphaned is a common thing; we're not special."

"Common, sure, but still not normal," Micah said. "And we're not orphans anymore."

MacEoghan just folded his arms, huffed a sigh that turned into a yawn, and looked out into the darkness. Micah watched him for a long moment. In the dim light of the lanterns, he thought his brother looked like a man, a real man, big and strong and thinking about many serious things. Micah was thinking about the fish they were going to catch and possibly one of the pretty girls in one of the towns on his delivery route that day.

The boat slowed and finally came to a stop. The other boats did the same and the sound of engines faded into the darkness until all that was left was the slapping of waves against the hull and the noise of the boys as they raced to cast nets and lines.

"And now we wait," MacEoghan mused.

"What would you rather we doing, fighting sharks?" Micah teased.

"I could fight a shark!" Cillian declared.

"You couldn't even wrestle me the other night, and I was going easy on you," MacEoghan told the boy. "What are you going to do to a shark?"

"A shark would eat you for a snack," Shay agreed.

"Not if I fed you to it first!" the eleven-year-old said smartly.

"You'd have to catch me first and I'd outswim you easily."

"No one's getting eaten by any sharks," Padraig interrupted, his tone all business. "Now pay attention to the nets."

Each of the boys was assigned a net or a line, and Micah turned his attention back to his charge. Once they'd caught a fair amount in this location, they'd bring everything back in, move to another spot, and cast out again, repeating until they had to return to shore to meet the delivery trucks.

Shay was the first the call out a catch. It wasn't a Biblical haul, but respectable. Unfortunately, it was also the best one they got that morning, and their offering to the trucks was less than anyone hoped for. Micah and MacEoghan helped load while Padraig waited to collect the money for that day. Once the fish were loaded and the money paid out, the twins climbed in their respective trucks and rumbled off on their routes.

Micah wasn't actually driving, just helping the driver, a man in his sixties, once a fisherman himself. Rory was his name, and he always had a story to tell. They weren't always true stories, but there was usually a good laugh to be had somewhere in the telling.

"So, you going to talk to this girl today or what?" Rory asked as they pulled away from the warehouse and started up the road.

"I don't know," Micah said, squirming in his seat a little.

"She's a pretty girl, you're a handsome lad. You could say hello."

"Maybe, but looks aren't everything."

Rory made a scoffing sound and waved a hand dismissively, not taking his eyes off the truck in front of them. "That's an excuse and you know it. At your age, looks are the only thing. But you are right. Looks aren't everything. She's got to be smart, too. And loyal, that's a big one. And loving, too, for your children—"

"I'm not going to say hello and then ask her to marry me," Micah cut in.

"Maybe not, but these are things you need to think about when you're looking at girls. Breasts are a fine thing, don't get me wrong, but you got to think beyond the end of your cock." He shifted in his seat. "I once knew a man, an Englishman, name of David. Nice guy, real nice guy, well, for an Englishman, and anyway..."

So began the story of David, a man who most likely didn't exist but whose story Rory was somehow intimately familiar with, at least enough to impart a life lesson to Micah.

They arrived at the first town. It wasn't much to look at, and they offloaded at a couple restaurants and pubs. With the war looming in Europe, as well as the lingering effects of the economic depression in the United States, one might have expected tourism to be slow or nonexistent. In fact, the opposite was true. Some, especially the English, were taking extended holidays in places like Ireland, trying to escape the tension and maybe not be home if the bombing started.

Walking into a pub that also boasted a few motel rooms, Micah saw that the place was unusually busy so early in the morning, and most of the chatter he heard had a British accent. True, it was a Saturday in August, but it was still more than he was prepared for.

"Things must be getting bad, eh?" Rory inquired of the pub manager.

"Aye," the manager said sharply, sounding harried and in no mood to talk. "There's talk of invasion."

"Germany invading the UK?" Micah asked.

"Nah. Poland."

"So what are these English doing here?" Rory asked.

"Afraid they'll be next, I guess."

"Shouldn't they be getting ready to fight, then?" Micah questioned.

"I suppose, once they're done drinking." The manager paused, a crate of fish still in his arms, and looked at Micah. "Thing about war is, the waiting kills you more than the actual fighting. You start thinking and imagining and worrying. By the time the fighting breaks out, you've already fought a whole battle and ten more besides. These sops might look and act like mewling kittens now, but once something does happen, it'll break that trance and they'll run home to fight." He shrugged. "Well, most of them. There's a few that's real cowards, I suppose."

Micah and Rory finished their delivery, then hopped back in the truck to move on to the next town.

"You fought in the Great War, didn't you?" Micah asked. "Is it true, what he said about the waiting?"

Rory was unnervingly serious in his answer. "Well, he's not wrong. When you're waiting, all you think about is the hunger, the sickness, your feet rotting off, your girl back home, your mother wringing her hands. And yes, you start wondering about the guys on the other side of no man's land. What are they thinking? What are they planning? What do I do if something suddenly happens and the guns start firing? Waiting is bad, yes, but the fighting will still kill you, too."

"Do you think Germany really would invade Poland? Or the United Kingdom?"

Rory shrugged, his demeanor suggesting he wasn't overly concerned. "I mean, they're not exactly thrilled about what happened to them after the war, and I commend their national and ethnic pride. Italy, too. I was here for the War of Independence and the Civil War; I know the feeling. To hell with this partition business. At the same time, if Germany wants to gather up all the German-speaking regions, I don't know what Poland has to do with it. Last I knew, Poland was Slavic, like the Soviets."

Micah was silent. Sure, he and MacEoghan had gleaned some of the mainland happenings while out on the fighting circuit, but only now were they really exposed to a continuous stream of information, and it only sounded like bad news.

"What do you think Ireland will do if Germany does invade Poland or England?"

"Oh, I expect we'll join them and go fight," Rory sighed. "Probably some appeal to the might and sovereignty of the United Kingdom of England, Ireland, Scotland, and Wales."

"But we're already independent and Parliament has said they want to remain neutral."

The old man barked a laugh. "Ha! Politics change quickly, lad. Neutrality today is allegiance tomorrow and hostility the day after that."

"Do you think they, Germany, they'd attack us first? Would they invade Ireland?"

Rory waved a hand. "Doubt it. We don't speak German, not historically German, and we're not antagonizing them. They don't give a rat's ass about us long as we don't do nothing."

Micah frowned and fell silent once more. He didn't know what to make of it. Sure, at the school they'd learned geography and history, but they never really talked about real, in-depth politics. He knew all the countries in Europe and he knew their leaders, basically knew about how they got there and some of the history leading up to the present day, but only now was he being exposed to the real how's and why's, the intrigue and ideologies. He didn't understand it, and he didn't like what he didn't understand. In this case, he didn't like what he did understand either.

"But, I will tell you this, lad," Rory went on. "Talking to you and your other self on these routes, you need to keep an eye on your brother. He's a fighter. Not just a boxer, a fighter. Strong, strong-willed, but impulsive, rash, even stupid sometimes."

"He does what he thinks is necessary," Micah said, taken aback.

"Aye, but that doesn't automatically make it the right thing, or the smart thing. It might have served you just fine before when it's a couple of kids trying to survive, but this is war."

"But if Ireland is neutral—"

"Officially, sure. You think that stops the likes of the IRA? And there's always the British Army; if they go to war, they'll be happy for every hand they can get."

Micah hesitated. Then, "He wouldn't listen to me. We might be twins, but he's always been the older brother."

"Aye, because you let him. You need to stand up for yourself, too, be your own man."

"And what if he doesn't listen to me?"

Rory shrugged. "Then he doesn't listen, and you need to decide what you're going to do. Are you really going to follow him out into the line of fire, or are you going to stick to your own principles?"

"What if I want to fight, too?"

"Do you?"

He didn't know. Brother Andrew notwithstanding, he'd never really hurt anyone before, at least not intentionally. He didn't like being hurt, so he tried not to inflict pain on others. Obviously MacEoghan was not so reserved. What if he did go off to fight? Micah didn't know that he would be able to follow. But why should he? Was he his brother's keeper? Well, yes. He had been as long as MacEoghan had been fighting, dragging his bloody hide back to the motel room or to a doctor. Maybe he could work in a hospital, or maybe as a medic. He could stay by MacEoghan and tend his wounds in the field, assuming he had any. And his brother still knew how to use go-fast. He might have refrained from using it while in a fair fighting ring, but surely he would not continue to hold to such morals while in an active war.

"Here we are," Rory announced, cutting into Micah's thoughts as he pulled up to their next stop. "Next delivery. Time to turn your thoughts back to fish."

That was easier said than done as the two modes of thought only blended together. One of the downsides of living on an island was being so dependent on others. There were talks of serious rationing on the wind, both food and fuel. Would their fish be confiscated to feed the soldiers? What if the fuel was rationed and they couldn't go out fishing? What if they couldn't use the trucks to deliver the fish?

If they had any meaningful conversation with the store owner, Micah did not remember it. The next thing he knew, he was climbing back in the truck and they were rumbling off to their next stop.

"I don't mean to worry you, lad," Rory said apologetically. "You have the look of a frightened hare about you. Why don't we speak of other things, like what you're going to say to Shannon at our next stop?"

The thought of the pretty girl at the next market was enough to break Micah's dark brooding, but it did nothing for his anxiety. What did he think he was going to say to her? What could he say to her?

"Can I suggest you start with, 'Hello'?" Rory teased, as if reading his mind. "Maybe even introduce yourself. 'Hello, my name is Micah.' "

"She already knows my name," Micah said weakly.

"Well, there you go, step one accomplished!"

"But then what do I say?"

The older man shrugged. "Oh, I don't know. You might comment on the nice weather; it is quite lovely today. You could compliment her on her pretty dress, her nice hair, her beautiful eyes."

Micah felt his chest tighten. "How do I do that?"

Rory laughed, but it was more disbelief than humor. "Lad, you just come out and say it! 'Your dress is pretty.' 'Your hair looks nice today.' Say anything, lad. If you and I didn't talk, she'd think you were a mute!"

As it is, I'd rather be a mute than a coward. But a coward was all he knew how to be. He wished MacEoghan were with him. At the same time, if MacEoghan were there, he'd already be talking to her. On the days he rode with Rory, well, he probably already was. Why should she look at him, Micah, when MacEoghan was probably talking circles around him?

The Kilkenney Market was a butcher shop, the Kilkenney family selling their own beef and lamb and goat, but the fish was all Dearbhfhine. Cillian Kilkenney was usually busy cutting up a carcass, leaving his son Aiden and daughter Shannon to manage the store. Aiden helped to unload the fish while Shannon drew up all the receipts.

Today, Rory made sure that he and Aiden were entirely unavailable to handle the paperwork, leaving Micah standing there awkwardly, his hand on one side of the papers, her hand on the other. He was unable to let go, for he needed the receipts, but she wasn't exactly giving them up. Their eyes met. He stared at her, blue eyes set against pale skin framed by perfectly red hair. Perfectly round breasts. Beautiful body accented by a slender shirt and skirt. He tightened his grip on the receipts.

"Thank you," he managed, voice small, chest tight.

"He does speak." She flashed him a smile. "You're welcome. Micah."

As soon as she released the papers, he turned and made straight for the truck. He climbed in the seat and just sat, keeping his eyes fixed straight ahead on nothing. A minute later, Rory helped himself to the driver's seat, started up the vehicle, and off they went.

"One last stop," the old man commented. Micah could see his knowing expression in his peripheral vision. "You talk to her?" Micah nodded stiffly and Rory laughed. "I knew it. I can tell. You are straight up and down, and I don't mean your spine."

Micah swallowed, another wave of heat flushing his skin. Rory reached over and gave his shoulder something like a half-pat, half-squeeze.

"Ah, don't feel bad. Every man was young once. Every man has looked on a pretty girl before and had improper thoughts."

Micah didn't know that he'd had any thoughts, improper or otherwise. He just knew that she was pretty and she'd spoken to him and he'd said something back. At least his words had been appropriate. He had thanked her for the receipts, right? That was what he'd said? Now he couldn't remember. What if he'd said something stupid? No, he was pretty sure he'd at least thanked her. But had he said anything else?

Now Rory was frowning. "What's wrong, lad?" When Micah didn't answer, he went on, "All right, now you're just beating yourself up over it and I don't know why." He shifted in his seat. "I don't understand you, Micah. You're so uptight about everything, but when it comes to anything, you just sit back and let your brother deal with it."

"I don't know," Micah stated, and that was the most he could get out.

"Are you sure you and MacEoghan are brothers? If you didn't look alike, I'd really be questioning you both."

Micah just shook his head, unsure what to say or do.

"You got a mouse in your ear, lad," Rory said, tone concerned. "What's it telling you?"

"I just..." He trailed off.

"Every good lad knows the women he looks at are well too good for him, and he might be a bit shy. And everyone compares himself to everyone else, even his own family, and especially his brothers. But you seem to be taking it a little too seriously. Your brother beat you or what?"

"No, but the Brothers did." The words were out before Micah could think to call them back.

"Brothers?"

"At the school, St. Joseph's."

Rory's expression was puzzled. "Lad, a rap on the knuckles or swat on the behind is hardly a beating; it's just good discipline."

"It wasn't just a rap or a swat," Micah cut in. "They beat us with rods, locked us in cages!"

"Bah!" Now the man's expression was cold dismissal. "Nonsense! I've known several boys who had delightful experiences at the industrial schools. They never said one word about anyone—themselves or any other boy—being beaten in such a manner." He made a sound like a humorless laugh. "You keep talking like that, people think you're a damned Protestant."

"But it's true!" Micah insisted.

"Even if it were true, I highly doubt they'd just go around beating kids with sticks. You have to do something bad to be punished, and to be punished in such a fashion, what was it you were doing?"

Micah could not answer, wasn't sure he wanted to. Rory already didn't believe him, so telling more of the story wasn't going to make it any more believable. Micah didn't believe it himself sometimes. Beaten for arbitrary reasons or no reason at all. Beaten because the alternative was potential sodomy. Rory would never believe that.

After a moment of silence, Rory continued speaking, his tone carefully neutral. "Talking to you, talking to your brother, and talking to Padraig, I understand you two have had a hard go of it. I'm sorry for that. But you've had a good education with respectable men and now you've even been blessed with what sounds like your first real family. Thank the Lord for what He's given you, in spite of everything, and make the best of it. One of the fastest ways you can destroy all of it is by bad-mouthing the ones who have helped you."

"But—"

"Now that's enough, you understand me? I don't want to hear any more of that in this truck."

Micah took a slow breath and let it out just as slowly. "Yes sir."

"Good. Whatever did or didn't happen, that's all in the past. You've got a good thing going here with Padraig and Sarah. Good chance to start over. But gossip is a real easy way to undo all of that. Understand me?"

"Yes sir."

The old man's expression softened some. "I can see you're a good lad, Micah. A little lost, a little confused, but I'm sure you'll find your way. You seem to embrace the family more readily than your brother."

Micah sighed again. "I suppose."

Conversation sputtered to a halt after that. Micah respected the old man. He just wished someone would just consider the possibility that maybe he was telling the truth. He couldn't be the only one who had ever been savagely beaten and sodomized by the Brothers. He knew of at least three others at St. Joseph's alone. What had happened to them? Did they tell no one? Did they ever hint at the mistreatment?

The following day, at Mass, Micah studied the priest, studied the altar boys and girls. Was the priest too friendly with any of them? Did any of the children look scared? Everything Father Flynn did looked right and proper, and he paid no special attention to the children. The children, likewise, did their duties, minding the priest as appropriate. As far as Micah could tell, none of them bore the vacant, haunted look that the boys at St. Joseph's did at Mass. A few looked bored, a few were too young to appreciate any of the ritual beyond doing what they were told, and a couple actually appeared to enjoy their duties.

He'd done this every week, looking for any clues that something was amiss. He hadn't really said anything, but some of the questions he'd asked of the children—roundabout-like inquiries, nothing direct yet—had garnered some strange looks from both the children and their parents. He'd laid off, lest someone think of him as a queer or a dandy, but the confusion remained. The altar boys and girls really didn't have anything bad to say about the priest. He was about fifty years old or so and appeared to genuinely care for the children—and the adults, too—as the children and grandchildren he did not have.

Mass ended and was always followed by at least an hour of chitchat and gossip outside the church doors. The younger children went to play with their friends while parents and grandparents congregated in their circles to talk. Micah watched it all unfold, just another beat in the weekly routine. By the time he turned around, MacEoghan was gone and Father Flynn was approaching.

"Hello, son, how are you?" the priest greeted amiably.

"I'm good, sir," Micah replied mechanically, not meeting his gaze.

"Rory McKenna suggested I speak with you, said you expressed some...concerns while on the road yesterday."

Micah swallowed nervously. "Idle talk, sir, nothing more."

Flynn raised a brow. "Oh? He seemed to think it was more than that. Your demeanor concurs, even if your words do not. So, which part of you is lying?"

Micah visibly flinched, expecting a rod to the back of his legs.

"He mentioned that you had some...unpleasant experiences at St. Joseph's School," the priest pressed. "Would you care to tell me about them?"

Now Micah looked at the priest, a kernel of either courage of stupidity in his heart. "To what end, sir? Nothing will change."

"Aye, that's true. Nothing will change as long as you keep silent about it. Can't fix a problem no one brings to light, and it's much harder to rebuild a dam than repair a small crack."

"Did Rory tell you what I said?"

"Not specifically, no. He just said that you had some unpleasant experiences that you believed were beyond the authority of the church."

Micah grinned foolishly. "Is that what he said? Is that how he sees it? Is that how you see it?"

"I don't know what 'it' is, so I don't know." Father Flynn's tone was tinged with both concern and annoyance. "Now please, tell me what it is that has you so worked up. Does it have to do with the way you stare at the altar boys and girls?"

Micah looked around, suddenly self-conscious. On the one hand, he wanted everyone to know. No, the schools were not so lavish as they were promoted. No, the Brothers were not so friendly to the children. Yes, the boys who ran away had very good reasons. On the other hand, he did not want to admit his own shame, the shame of what Brother Andrew did to him, the crime of what MacEoghan had done in return. Surely Father Flynn would call the police on them for it. He couldn't betray his brother like that, regardless of what Brother Andrew did.

"No," he said sharply. "Forget it."

"We can go somewhere more private if you prefer," Flynn goaded. "The trees over there, back inside the church."

Micah just shook his head and started backing away, looking for his twin. "No. Never mind. Forget I said anything. Forget whatever Rory told you. It's nothing."

He walked away, heedless of Father Flynn's protests. It was said that anything spoken in confessional couldn't be used in court. That was well and good when it came to petty theft or thinking bad thoughts about someone, but did it really cover murder? Would it really have been different if Brother Andrew hadn't died? Would Father Flynn understand, or would he seek to punish them personally?

He found MacEoghan talking to a group of boys around their age. Three were also sons of fishermen on other boats that went out in the morning, one was the son of the general store owner, and the last was the son of another of the delivery truck drivers.

"Don't let her fool you," the delivery driver's son said seriously. "She'll sweet talk any man who makes a delivery."

"Yeah, I'd like to make a personal delivery myself," one of the fishermen's boys laughed knowingly.

"You got no chance," another told him, punching him in the shoulder.

"What about that girl in Fishtown, eh?" the store owner's son brought up.

"The one with the lazy eye?"

"Aye, her."

"You know she's looking at two men at the same time," the third fishing son chortled.

The rest of them got a laugh out of that, but Micah just inwardly rolled his eyes. He wouldn't say he hadn't laughed at a few dumb jokes, nor that he hadn't told a few himself, but he just wasn't in the mood right now.

"Got the twins here, would she even know that they're two people, or would they come into focus as one man?" the first fishing son questioned.

That, too, elicited some dumb chuckles and several speculations that all talked over each other. Micah still did not laugh. MacEoghan slapped him on the back.

"Come on, Micah, lighten up."

"I can't right now," Micah stated, his tone rote.

"So why are you making that our problem?" the store owner's son wondered.

"Padraig and Sarah want to get going?" MacEoghan asked, unconcerned.

"Aye," Micah lied.

No surprise, his twin waved a hand. "Well, they can go ahead. It's Sunday; they don't need us. We'll be home after a spell. Or you can go with them if you want."

Everything in town was within walking distance, so it wasn't as though anyone would get lost on their way home. And everyone knew everyone, so the chances of running into trouble were basically nonexistent. If anyone did get into trouble, well, the news would travel fast enough that parents would find out long before their child showed up at the door with some wild lie.

Micah frowned and turned away. Might as well go home, take a Sunday afternoon nap, play some games with the younger kids when he woke up. MacEoghan could do whatever it was he was figuring to do. If it was bad, they'd hear about it.

He walked home. The doors were unlocked, as always. With the house empty, it was easy to lie back on his bed and drift off.

He wasn't even sure he slept before he heard the door slam open, then slam shut, then slam open again, then slam shut again. Then there was Sarah's voice, shouting at the kids not to slam the door, open or closed. He heard footsteps, then his door opened. He looked over at Sarah.

"You not feeling well, love?" she asked.

"Fine," he told her, looking up at the ceiling and closing his eyes.

"Father Flynn said you had something on your mind."

"I'm fine," Micah repeated.

"Well, if you're fine, then you know that we stick together as a family." Her tone was not unkind. "That means good times, bad times, and walking to and from church."

"Yes, ma'am."

"I don't know where your other self is, but I'll find out soon enough, I'm sure."

Micah just smiled, eyes still closed.

"How can you look so alike but be so different?"

"Aye, we look alike. Neither of us wants to get blamed for the actions of the other, so we have to make ourselves different somehow."

Sarah sighed dramatically, and he could imagine her expression. A second later, the door closed, and her light footsteps walked away.

Either MacEoghan wasn't gone long or else Micah slept the day away because it didn't seem like too much later when he heard his twin's voice. Micah sighed and opened his eyes. The sun had definitely changed position, but it wasn't quite sunset yet. He lay still, straining to make out the conversation. It wasn't an argument exactly, just Sarah chastising MacEoghan for wandering off after church. Again. When her lecture was over, MacEoghan came down to the room.

"Something wrong with you?" MacEoghan asked, two steps into the room. "You ill?"

"I'm fine," Micah told him blandly.

"Well that's a bald-faced lie." MacEoghan sat on his bed and took his socks off. "What's wrong?"

Micah just sighed and asked levelly, "Where have you been?"

"Out. What's wrong?"

"I'm fine."

MacEoghan stood suddenly. "Damn it, Micah, we're not doing this again! We are not kids anymore and you are not going to keep stuff like this from me. If something's wrong, I want to know about it."

"I tried to tell Rory about the school," Micah said, cutting into whatever MacEoghan was going to say next.

His brother was silent for a moment. Then he sat, slowly. "What brought this on?"

"I don't even remember now. I think it was something about your fighting —your prize fighting, I mean. And I tried to tell him about how the Brothers beat us."

135

"He didn't believe you."

Micah shook his head, staring at the ceiling. "No. Called me a damned Protestant and said he didn't want to hear anything more about it. And apparently he told Father Flynn to talk to me."

"Did you say anything to him?"

Now Micah looked at MacEoghan. "How could I? He's one of them. If I said too much and he looked into it, he could figure out what we did and come after us."

MacEoghan made a sound of reluctant agreement. "You're not wrong." He shifted position. "But if that's the case, then you can't say anything to anyone. Ever. Catholic, Protestant, priest, layman, no one. Not about Brother Andrew, any of the other Brothers, the school, nothing. We went there, we graduated, that's all. And if we can help it, since we're here, we didn't even go to the school. We're MacEoghan and Micah Dearbhfhine, always have been."

Micah shifted uncomfortably, turning his gaze to the ceiling again. "I guess I would rather live that lie than pretend nothing happened at the school." He paused, then stole a glance at MacEoghan. "And I suppose we should do better about acting the part. Listen to our mum and pa, maybe actually call them Mum and Pa."

His brother squirmed. "But it's still strange, isn't it?"

Micah shrugged. "Maybe. But it's the truth now as far as we're concerned. We're Dearbhfhines, always have been."

MacEoghan continued to squirm. "I guess I haven't been the best son."

"We don't know how to be sons," Micah said frankly. "I barely remember our mum's face, don't remember her voice at all. Except the crying."

"Except the crying," MacEoghan echoed. "And then she was gone."

Micah studied his hands. "You think things would be different, if she hadn't died?"

MacEoghan shook his head mildly. "I don't think so. There were more than a few boys at school who were sons of whores like us who became wards of the state. I think they would have caught up to us eventually."

Micah didn't like that answer, but he couldn't refute it either. And would life have really been better? Or different? Maybe MacEoghan would have become a prize fighter anyway, to make money. Maybe Micah would have been taken advantage of in some other humiliating way. Nothing about their life had ever risen above the gutter. Except, maybe, now, with the Dearbhfhine family.

"So then," MacEoghan began. "What do we think? We've been on the run a good portion of our lives, and imprisoned for the years we weren't running. Do we think we can really stay here voluntarily and be good?" The way he said it evoked an image of tasting new food and being unsure whether it was palatable.

"We've been here for a couple months now," Micah said.

"Aye, but the novelty is wearing a bit, don't you think? Something new and exciting is becoming mundane."

"I'm fine with mundane. I think the real question is, do you think you can handle it? You're bolder than I am, no one can deny that. You think you can trade the excitement of fighting and being on the run for the mundane life of a fisherman?"

Micah knew his twin too well. He knew the exact expression MacEoghan got without even needing to look. He practically knew the thoughts inside his brother's head. MacEoghan just wasn't made for sitting still and idling away his time. He needed the fight, the adversity, the opposition, the excitement.

"I won't blame you if you leave," Micah told him, now looking at him. "We may look alike, but you're not me. And I'm not you. And we're near grown men now; we won't be so close together forever."

"Maybe not," MacEoghan conceded, "but I don't think it would be right if I just threw away the very thing we've been looking for, for years. Maybe the mundane won't be so bad, if I can get myself to relax a little. Padraig is a good man and a better teacher than the Brothers ever were. And it's real nice to have good food on the table every day."

"Aye," Micah agreed. "It's nice to have a mum and pa, and not an endless stream of so-called uncles."

MacEoghan nodded emphatically. "Aye." He sighed, still nodding. "I suppose I can try this mundane home life of a fisherman for a while longer, make myself a presentable man. If things don't turn out here, well, sounds like there may be a war effort that's going to need some help."

Micah frowned. "Please don't, MacEoghan. I can't lose you."

"I still have the go-fast I can use if I need to."

"Please don't," Micah repeated.

MacEoghan made a sound that was somewhere between a sigh and a humorless laugh. "Well, it's only a thought. Besides, if I leave, how can I stand the thought of you running off with Shannon?"

Micah blushed.

TIME
OLDER BROTHER

News of the impending war persisted, although any official missives directed people not to use the word "war." It was a "concern," a "conflict," an "emergency," even. But not a war. Not yet anyway.

"It's a bloody war," one of the market managers growled, taking the last crate of fish. "The shooting's already started, just waiting on the invasion."

"You think it will really happen?" MacEoghan wondered, slamming the truck door shut.

"Armies don't muster for nothing, lad. They're up to something, mark my words."

Before MacEoghan could say anything more, the manager wandered off, still growling to himself.

"You know how he can be," the truck driver, John, said, patting MacEoghan on the shoulder. "Take a minute to yourself. Someone I got to talk to in town here."

He walked away, stride long and purposeful. Well, it was the last stop of the day, so it wasn't as though there were still fish that needed to be delivered. MacEoghan leaned on the front of the truck and looked around. The days were cooling off once more, and multiple layers of clouds had been raining on them off and on throughout the day. Storefronts wanted to keep their doors propped open in hopes of catching a warm breeze, yet some refrained because they didn't want to get rained on indoors.

"Well, it's not the best day, but it's not the worst day," a new voice said. MacEoghan looked to see a man approach, stop beside him, and lean against the truck also, folding his arms. "It was nice to see the sun and clear blue skies yesterday."

"A rare treat," MacEoghan agreed.

The man made a slight turn to look at him. "You have a twin, don't you? Or at least a brother?"

"Aye, Micah. I'm MacEoghan. We trade off which truck routes we run."

"Ah, I see. And where do you live?"

"Oh, we live in little Slieveport, between Bantry and Clonakilty."

The man's expression turned surprised. "Oh, so these are your fish."

MacEoghan nodded. "Aye, some."

"Oh, excellent, carrying on your family tradition, then?"

"Aye."

The man nodded and stepped away from the truck, facing MacEoghan. "Good on you, lad. You're doing good work here."

"Go raibh míle maith agaibh," MacEoghan said, shaking the man's hand. (Thank you very much indeed.)

The man had no sooner turned to walk away than John returned, motioning for MacEoghan to get back in the truck.

"You find who you needed?" MacEoghan wondered. "You weren't gone long."

John waved a hand. "Oh, it was just a quick question."

This quick question was soon followed by a rather lengthy story that took up the entire ride home. It might have gone on even longer if they weren't the last ones back and John needed to get home to his wife who was likely annoyed by his tardiness.

Not that Sarah would be any happier about MacEoghan being late, but she knew that he was at the mercy of the drivers. He knew what her expression would be, what minor lecture he would receive. It was just her being a concerned mother. It had taken some time for him to get used to the idea that her fretting was indeed harmless and concerned and not a real challenge or accusation.

What he was not prepared for, however, was to walk in the door, expecting a late dinner, and see the same man whom he'd been speaking with in town while John had been away.

"Ah, hello again," the man greeted. He stood in the front room, speaking amiably to Sarah and Micah. Padraig and the rest of the boys were already back out on the boat.

"Do you also have a twin?" MacEoghan blurted. "How did you get here?"

"I drove, same as you," the man replied, still grinning, his posture nonthreatening. "No, I don't have a twin."

"He was impressed with your work in the market," Sarah said, beaming at the apparent praise. "He wanted to have a word with you two."

The man made a friendly, waving gesture. "Come on outside. Let's have a talk."

Micah, oblivious to any shenanigans, followed the man readily. MacEoghan trailed behind a step or two. He used go-fast on himself and his twin, bringing the man to a near standstill.

"What's wrong?" Micah wondered.

"There's no way," MacEoghan stated. "I talked to him in town. He walked away, we got in the truck and came straight back. How long has he been here?"

Micah shrugged. "Five minutes? Ten?"

"Why come here? How did he know where we live? Why not follow us to the warehouse?"

His brother's expression looked a bit disturbed, but he clearly wasn't of a mind to question things. MacEoghan briefly wondered if he was being foolish. This was about fish. This was a fishing village. He looked past Micah and studied the strange man a moment longer, then released the go-fast.

They left the house and made their way down to the rocky shore not far away. The boats bobbed quietly at the docks a short distance down. The only activity in the area now was some children looking for goodies in the tidal pools.

"You seem to know us well enough," MacEoghan said, "but I haven't heard your name."

"Yes, forgive me. My name is Sean McKeogh."

"And after we spoke for all of thirty seconds, you just hopped in your car and drove all the way down here to talk about fish?"

Now the man frowned. "Well, regrettably, no. Actually, I'm here to talk about a couple of men I'm told you had a run-in with. Lorcan Kearney and Nolan Kane."

141

MacEoghan used go-fast just so he could buy time to maintain his composure before answering, "Never heard of them."

Sean McKeogh let out a breath and pinched the bridge of his nose, closing his eyes. Without opening his eyes, he invoked go-fast, but he did it with a flash of red light, just as Kearney and Kane had done. MacEoghan and Micah recoiled, and MacEoghan quickly looked around for either a weapon or means of escape. The best weapon he had was either a rock or his fists, and the area was too open for an effective escape.

"Please, MacEoghan, I promise you, I'm here to talk," Sean sighed, lowering his hand and opening his eyes. "I'm trying to sort out a huge mess, and I think the majority of the blame lies with Mr. Kearney and Mr. Kane."

"Who are you?" MacEoghan demanded.

"My name is Sean McKeogh. I'm one of the Lieutenant Timekeepers of District—"

"One of them said the same thing. The other said he was a captain. You with the IRA?"

"Is this why we had to leave town?" Micah asked.

"The Timekeepers have no affiliation with the IRA. Kearney and Kane are Timekeepers, yes, but they are not officers. However, they like to masquerade as officers when they hunt down Runners. Intimidation is all it is."

"Am I a Runner?" MacEoghan demanded. "Are we Runners? I don't even know what that means."

"Yes, I've gathered this. You and your brother are both very strange. Is it true that you have been able to Band since you were children?"

"Only him," Micah said. "I don't have the talent."

Sean frowned. "I see. And you don't know anything about how it first came about?"

MacEoghan gave a stiff, "No."

"Hm. I looked into your family some—your birth family—and I found precious little."

"What do you want? Why are you here?"

"Kearney and Kane were investigating the murder of a priest at St. Joseph's Industrial School for Boys. Their investigation led them to you. The first challenge is simply that you were children, and very rarely do children learn how to Band. It is unheard of that you should be both self-actualized and self-taught. The second challenge is that Runners are only Runners if they steal Time, which, if you are involved, didn't happen. And Time theft is typically found among Harvesters—"

"What in the bloody world are you talking about?" Micah asked, echoing MacEoghan's thoughts.

The man sighed again and murmured. "A child has been given control of a vehicle. He knows not where he got it, who gave it to him, where he is going, the finer points of how to operate it, nor the rules of the road and driving. Yet, because he has figured out simply how to make it stop and go, he believes himself invincible."

"We never had a problem until Kearney and Kane showed up," MacEoghan said defensively.

"Well, I regret to inform you that the direction and outcome of this conversation could influence the number and severity of some impending problems." Sean shifted his stance, trying to appear nonthreatening. "All right, maybe I'll start with the basics."

"Please do."

"There are people in the world who can manipulate Time, make it go slower or faster at will—but never backwards, regrettably. These people are called Timekeepers. The world is divided up into Regions and Districts and the Timekeepers oversee these Regions and Districts. Their job is to ensure that Time is used...legally."

"Didn't know Time could be used illegally," MacEoghan remarked.

Sean made an odd, vague gesture. "Well, there are other people who are called Harvesters. When someone is dying, it is their job to Harvest their remaining Time. For the elderly, this may be only a few seconds. For someone who has been fatally wounded, it could be years, decades, all the time they would have had if not for said fatal wound."

"That sounds horrible," Micah commented.

The man's expression suggested that he did not disagree. "This Time can then be given to others, and it extends their life. So if someone were to consume the years of the fatally injured man, they would absorb all of his years, however many there were left. Eventually, the aging process slows to the point that it seems to stop."

MacEoghan raised a brow. "You're bonkers."

"And you can control Time. Who's really bonkers here?" Sean challenged. "Sometimes Harvesters—and even some lesser Timekeepers—go bad. There is a process in place for how Time is acquired, refined, sold, and consumed. If this process is broken, if that Time is stolen, that person is called a Runner. They are pursued, arrested, and punished."

"Did we do something wrong?" Micah wondered.

Sean hesitated and finally shook his head. "Everything I've been able to find says no. You're Banding, not Harvesting. And even so, you were too young to know what you were doing; you had no guidance."

"So we don't have to worry about Kearney or Kane?" MacEoghan asked, wondering if he should dare to feel hopeful.

"Let me worry about Kearney and Kane. As I said, they've a history of pretending to be officers in order to intimidate others." Sean shifted his stance again. "But that doesn't mean I should just let you go."

"Why not? You just said we're not doing anything wrong."

"Yes, that is true, but I'm afraid that, now that you have been enlightened, you are now faced with a choice. This kind of power cannot simply be left unchecked and unsupervised. At this point, you have two options. I can train you in how to wield this power more effectively, more efficiently, more powerfully. I can teach you to hone your skills. Or I can Suppress you, and this will prevent you from ever Banding again, or until the Suppression were to be lifted by me or someone of equal talent."

MacEoghan glanced at Micah. Micah's expression was puzzled and bewildered. MacEoghan looked back at Sean. The three of them stood in the middle of this so-called Fast Band on a beach in the south of Ireland, everything around them slowed to a stop: the waves, the birds, the little tidal creatures and the children who chased them. Everyone else, outside the Band, was concerned with fishing, children, and the impending war—ahem, emergency. And here they were, talking about manipulating Time.

MacEoghan wasn't sure what to make of it. He'd always considered the go-fast his little secret, his little weird ability that only he could use, his way of keeping Micah safe and ensuring the two of them had what they needed to survive. Kearney and Kane had shown him that he wasn't the only one, and it had unnerved him. Maybe because others could do it, maybe because the pair had seemed to use it for more nefarious reasons. And now, here was Sean, telling him that not only were there others, but there was a whole system built around it, and he was on the weak end of it, almost on the illegal side of things although he still didn't fully understand that bit.

And Micah, too? The idea that this was something that anyone could just learn...well, MacEoghan would be lying if he said he wasn't jealous. This was his thing. Even if others could do it, too, having it as a kind of birthright or something, he could accept that. But to just give it out to anyone who was interested...

"Can I learn this, too?" Micah asked of Sean, as if knowing MacEoghan's thoughts. "Or is it only for those like MacEoghan, who were born with it?"

"I don't know the cause of your brother's talents," Sean said, his tone suggesting he had said this several times already but somehow they had missed it, "but yes, you can learn as well, if you so desire."

Micah grinned hugely and looked at MacEoghan. He'd worn a similar expression those first few weeks when Padraig and Sarah opened their home to them. He was overjoyed. He was getting something he'd always wanted. A family and loving home. A job he was good at. And now, the talent that he had so far only been able to observe from afar.

MacEoghan found that he could not muster up the same enthusiasm. He couldn't put his finger on it, but he really wasn't happy for his twin. Actually, the whole thing was a little upsetting. He'd put the time and effort into this. He'd spent years trying to get it right so they'd never get caught again. He'd led them from place to place, tried to protect them both, tried to provide for them both. And now it seemed as though Micah was just being handed everything. They were old enough now that they didn't absolutely need a family, a mother whose skirts they could hide behind, a father whose career would be the life and death of him in mundane drudgery. And, really, they didn't need this whole Time business either. If they were free and clear with no wrongdoing, then they were free and clear. They could walk away, no harm done. He could probably find a way to get rid of the Suppressing or whatever Sean called it; he would just have to wait a little while, until he was sure they weren't being watched. And he suspected that Sean and the others would be watching them for a while, just to make sure nothing happened.

"You should understand," Sean went on, "that this is not merely a bit of schooling or education in a minor hobby. If you were to learn, you would be expected to work. Now, it's not very difficult work, but you would be involved in the pursuit and apprehension of Runners."

"Law enforcement," MacEoghan stated.

"Basically, yes. And it wouldn't be right away. Timekeeping requires months and years of training."

"Years?" Micah echoed, turning pale. "Would we have to go somewhere? Like school?"

Sean shook his head. "No, not at all. You could continue living and working here as normal. Obviously I know where you live, and I know part of your truck routes. I can easily come to you."

MacEoghan wouldn't say that he hadn't been a tad uneasy about the prospect of going to a school, but he also couldn't say that he wasn't a tad disappointed that he wouldn't be going anywhere. He shifted his stance. "So, do Pad—our pa and mum know about this? Did you talk to them?"

"The average person has no inkling of the work we do or the power we have, nor should they. Some of the things I am going to teach you will go beyond your mortal understanding, at least initially. The older someone is when they are exposed, the harder it is to accept. You are an exception, I think, since you've grown up with it, but even so, you are of a prime age to start such training."

"What's the oldest someone can be?" Micah asked, his tone and immediate expression saying he might not have intended to ask the question aloud.

Sean shrugged. "There's no limit. The person just has to be willing to accept what they see and work with it. The oldest that I personally have heard of is a man in his late forties or early fifties. That really is an exception, because there is a bit of a statistical drop-off after age thirty." The man shifted his stance, his posture and sudden change in tone saying that he wanted to wrap this up. "I'll let you think it over. I know this is a lot to take in. I'm just glad we were able to have a productive conversation; I know Kearney and Kane can be rather...abrasive to some people."

"That's putting it mildly," MacEoghan grumbled.

"I'll take care of them, don't worry."

"Can I try it?" Micah wondered. "The go-fast, or the Banding, I mean?"

Now the Timekeeper looked uncertain, his pleasant expression turning into a disapproving frown. "If you haven't been exposed to the degree that you can do this on your own, I don't want to push you over that edge only to just take it away in a few days." He made a sound that resembled a relent or internal compromise. "At the same time, not doing so does diminish your ability to make an informed decision."

"I've only ever watched MacEoghan," Micah pressed. "I've only ever been able to follow him around like a child. What do I need to do?"

At his twin's statement, MacEoghan knew a moment of offense, though he couldn't pinpoint exactly which nerve was struck. That Micah was degrading himself? That he wanted to learn? Immediately on the heels of the offense was a sense of relief. He wouldn't have to drag Micah around anymore. He wouldn't have to worry about his twin. If Micah could learn to look after himself, MacEoghan could worry about himself. He could go back out and start boxing again. He just might do that, now that he knew he didn't have to worry about Kearney and Kane anymore; that was a hugely welcome relief. Given that Sean wasn't bringing up Brother Andrew's murder—and he was not about to bring it up himself—then maybe they were clear of those charges as well.

And if he didn't have to worry about Micah or Kearney or Kane, maybe he would let Sean stifle this go-fast ability, let him go on with his life. He never asked for this. At the same time, it was a pretty handy little tool. It had saved them from the Brothers and aided him here and there in the ring—not all the time, only in real emergencies. But if he couldn't keep the ability—Time, Banding, whatever Sean was calling it—without becoming one of these Timekeepers, this mysterious sort of law enforcement, did he really want it? Was it really all that great? MacEoghan had never really been interested in law enforcement, and even throwing in this odd element of Time wasn't really sparking a sudden interest.

147

Well, it sounded like he might have at least a few days to think about it. A few days of trying to keep Micah from hurting himself or anyone else. And then there was that lingering question: if Sean was having to show Micah how to Band, who had shown him, MacEoghan? How had this all come about for him?

"MacEoghan?"

MacEoghan blinked back to the present moment and looked at Sean. They still stood in the red-tinted Fast Band. In his periphery, he saw Micah had what looked like a secondary red-tinted film-like appearance around him.

"I'd like to see you Fast Band once; I'm curious how you do it," Sean said.

MacEoghan blinked again, shrugged casually, then invoked the go-fast, the Fast Band. Staring at the red tint of Sean's Band, and then at Micah's red film, MacEoghan realized that his Band did not have such a tint. Was he doing it wrong? Was there really that much more to learn? Thinking about it, he managed to bring about a red tint to it, though he didn't know how. The color darkened some as his Band matched his twin's. As he took a few steps toward his brother, the Bands seemed to merge and he took them both in hand as it were.

The first thing he noticed was that Sean's method of Banding felt very heavy, if he could appropriately describe it as such. He was accustomed to a lighter, more airy feel within his mind and body, maybe within his soul, that feeling that he was moving and interacting with the world as it was meant to be, that feeling of becoming so intimately familiar with his opponent in the arena that their match was more of a perfectly choreographed dance. This Band, however, was less like the dance and more like the punch that followed, and the headache that started poking around his brain only reinforced this feeling.

"Is this what it's like?" Micah wondered, looking around uncertainly.

"I suppose so," MacEoghan answered lamely. "Come on, let's get out of here."

He dropped the Band before his brother could protest, returning them to Sean's Band.

"Very good," the man said, nodding. "Micah, you are going to be a quick study, I can tell. MacEoghan, you are obviously already quite skilled. It may be that we can accelerate your training even more."

"Assuming we choose to pursue this," MacEoghan stated.

"Of course. I don't mean to put any undue pressure on you. Please, take a few days to think it over, talk it over, experiment a little. I will catch up with you on one of your delivery routes to get your answer and make any necessary arrangements."

"We run separate routes," Micah informed him, "and we change routes every day."

Sean nodded. "I know. You let me worry about that."

He dropped the Band. Immediately, low-tide waves crashed onto the far shore, birds in the air continued their glide on cooling currents, tidal creatures scuttled about and children chased them, laughing hysterically.

"I wish you both a good day and happy Banding," Sean said formally.

"Aye," was the best MacEoghan could manage even as Micah replied, "Thank you very much, sir!"

They watched him go, gave him a good fifty yard start, then returned themselves to the house.

"I saw Mr. McKeogh leave," Sarah said, meeting them on the porch. "What did he want? Good news about the fish and the business, I hope?"

"Aye," MacEoghan answered before Micah could speak. "We had a good talk and he said he wanted to speak to us again in a few days. In town when we're on our routes."

"Oh. So, is he a market owner? A distributor? Is he asking for more fish? I know you men do the best you can, but there was some talk of petrol rationing."

"Calm down, Mum," Micah told her tenderly. "There's no need to worry about any of that."

He always was better at that sort of thing, MacEoghan thought. Sarah smiled, took a breath, and nodded. "Of course. 'Who by worrying can add a single day to his life?' I trust you, I trust your father, and I trust the Father."

"That's all we can ask."

Micah's grin was genuine, MacEoghan knew, but not for the reason that she thought. Still, she gave them both a kiss on the cheek, then handed them a packed dinner for them to take to the docks while they continued their afternoon chores.

As if either of them could focus long enough to do their chores well. Micah was too distracted by his sudden, newfound power to make himself go faster than everyone around him, and he spent more time playing tricks on their pa and brothers than actually working.

MacEoghan, meanwhile, was still wrestling with the idea of his power suddenly coming with strings attached. He didn't know what this Timekeeping business was, other than general law enforcement, and it didn't sound like a lot of fun. Sean was a welcome relief from Kearney and Kane, but none of them had left an exemplary taste in his mouth about the whole business. He just wanted to do what he wanted to do; was it really too much to ask? And what was so unreasonably astounding about it that people over thirty just couldn't handle it?

More questions began popping up in his mind, things he wished he'd asked Sean. Few of the questions had anything to do about the Banding, most related to the man himself. What was his real name? Where was he from? If Time or Harvesting or whatever slowed a man's aging, then how old was he? What was his story? Keep the man talking and maybe MacEoghan could catch him in a lie.

But then, with all of this new information, how would he even know what the truth was? On what basis could he call Sean a liar? If the man claimed to be much older than he was, simple appearance would determine that to be a lie. But if this Timekeeping business somehow slowed one's aging, how would he, MacEoghan, be able to call him a liar?

As if his own abilities weren't strange enough, now he found himself wondering if he weren't a madman. Just what sorcery was this? Should he perhaps seek out Father Flynn instead? Or someone else knowledgeable of such things?

He observed several flashes of red as Micah continued to experiment with his own new power. It was like watching an infant play with its food. The child cared little for the taste and nothing for the nourishment, for its joy was found in the texture and the ability to manipulate squishy objects. MacEoghan wouldn't say it wasn't a little amusing to watch, but mostly it just annoyed him. For years he had used his abilities to look out for the two of them, had honed his skills so as to ensure their very survival as they ran from law enforcement, the Brothers, and an occasional drunken brawler. Now Micah treated it like a game, a toy.

He told himself to let it go. There was no sense in getting upset about it. No one else would understand why he was upset; it wasn't as though he could just show them. Or could he? What if he did perform a demonstration in front of a large group of people? What if he did it in the middle of Mass? What could Sean really do about it? At the same time, what would be the point? What did he want out of all of this? He couldn't do what he wanted without someone looking over his shoulder. Maybe it would be better to walk away. He was already a good boxer on his own; he could improve without his minor party tricks.

His sour disposition lasted through the evening, but Micah's suddenly cheerful demeanor kept any attention off of him. Only once they were laying down to sleep did Micah bring it up.

"What's the matter?" Micah wondered, his tone suggesting he sensed MacEoghan's bad mood but was truly ignorant of the possible cause.

MacEoghan sighed. "What happened to just me and you against the world? When did this all open up and now suddenly there are others who can do what I do?"

Micah was silent for a long moment, invisible in the darkness. Then, "I think that's because for a long time there was only me and you. We were the only ones who mattered. No one at the school was overly friendly. Once we got out into the real world, suddenly, real people existed. And apparently some have your same abilities."

"Yes, but when? Why? How?"

"I don't know." MacEoghan could hear his brother's frown.

MacEoghan sighed again. "Used to be that it was just something I could do, something that got us out of a lot of trouble. Now—"

"I can do it, too," Micah cut in. "Why does that make you mad?"

"I didn't say that."

"But it's true. You asked Sean if it was something he was born with, if Kearney and Kane were born with it, if you had likely been born with it. You were interested in what he had to say as long as that was the case because it meant that you were still special. But if it could be taught to anyone, then suddenly you weren't special anymore. And now that I can do it, you're no longer the mighty big brother."

MacEoghan did not reply, but his brother wasn't wrong. He didn't like being pinned so accurately even as he clung indignantly to that assessment. He wanted to be special.

"Well, guess what?" Micah went on. "I can do it, too, now. You know what else? I think I might just join Sean and his Timekeepers."

"Why?" MacEoghan wondered. "You've never been confrontational, and this sounds like some kind of law enforcement which tends to require a measure of confrontation."

"I can learn. I want to learn. I don't want to have to rely on you all the time; it's embarrassing. Eventually, you and I will marry and have families and go our separate ways. Who's going to save me then? And how better to save my family than with the same abilities you used to save me?"

Again MacEoghan did not reply, but these comments cut him in a new way. Micah wasn't trying to spite him. He was trying to imitate him.

A million thoughts ran through his mind, many of them more like fleeting images and impressions and emotional reactions that anything coherent. He didn't want to share. He was humbled by his twin's admission. He was glad Micah wanted to fend for himself for once. He wanted to still be the big brother, even if the age difference was only a couple minutes.

"I still don't know about his claims," MacEoghan said finally, changing the subject. "It sounds too weird."

"Have you seen what we can do?" Micah countered. "Did you ever wonder if maybe that's why they sent us to St. Joseph's, the worst of all the schools?"

"No one saw me use it."

"They must have at some point."

"Me not being able to use it is what got us caught in the first place. That much I remember for certain."

He could hear Micah shift position. "I still think someone saw it and that's why they sent us to St. Joseph's."

MacEoghan looked in his general direction. "Then why did the Brothers never ask about it? They would have loved to have made an example out of me for it. It never came up."

"I don't know. But that's what I think."

MacEoghan just sighed and shook his head.

They lay there in the dark for several minutes. Finally Micah asked, "So are you going to do it?"

"Do what?"

"Take the training, become a Timekeeper, keep your abilities?"

MacEoghan sighed once more. "I don't know..."

"Come on..."

"I'm a fighter, Micah. I'm a boxer. I'm not a policeman, going out on patrols and writing citations."

Micah chuckled dryly. "I don't know, the police got involved in several brawls in the pubs where you fought."

"Aye, a few times only. Probably the highlight of their week. Or month. I need something more. This fishing business bores me."

"Maybe you can ask Sean about it. If there's a whole system, I can't imagine that everyone is a stuffy old policeman on patrol."

MacEoghan shrugged though his brother couldn't see. "Maybe."

"Come on, MacEoghan..."

"This sounds more like your thing," MacEoghan whined.

"But you still like your abilities," Micah stated.

"Of course I do."

"So use them for good. If nothing else, at least learn how to improve them."

Well, there was that, he supposed. He rolled onto one side. "What do you think the rest of the family would say if we showed them?"

"You know Mum is too religious for that. She'd probably call for Father Flynn to exorcise the witchcraft out of you."

"Who's to say it isn't witchcraft? Maybe our birth mum was a witch as well as a whore. Maybe she was a whore because she was a witch. Maybe she did something to me or I watched her do something and it changed me."

"You think Sean is a witcher, then? Or Kearney or Kane?"

MacEoghan scoffed. "With the way those two treated me and with what Sean said about them, it wouldn't be impossible, I think. As for Sean, though...I don't know. I always thought witches were supposed to be ugly and outcast. I don't think Sean is ugly and no one seemed to have any problem with him."

"No one can explain this," Micah said, his tone suggesting MacEoghan had made some kind of point although he himself apparently missed it. "You've never really been able to explain it. I can't explain it. Anyone else is going to call it witchcraft or sorcery. But maybe Sean can explain it with this Timekeeper training."

"You think there might be more to it than just Timekeeping? Maybe there are other options?"

He could imagine his brother shrugging. "I don't know. Maybe. Only one way to find out."

MacEoghan sighed. "I guess you're right."

"Come on," Micah goaded. "Let's do it together. For once."

"All right. All right, fine, I'll...think about it and give it a shot. It would be nice to know what exactly this is and what else I can do with it. What we can do with it."

He still couldn't deny that saying such a thing felt like swallowing a massive pill of pride. It had always been him. His power, his abilities, his duty to save the day. At the same time, there was also a little spark of pride, too. Micah was finally going to understand. He was going to learn and be able to use all of this himself. He would be able to save himself. He might need to save MacEoghan one day. For once, they might actually be twins instead of merely identical-looking brothers.

"Do you think—?" Micah began.

"I'm going to sleep," MacEoghan cut in, rolling over. "Whatever we do or don't do with these abilities, it's still going to be a few days before we're supposed to see Sean again. Until then, we still have to get up early to go catch fish."

Micah mumbled some sort of agreement and started rustling around in his own bed, trying to get comfortable. MacEoghan just lay there, staring into the darkness, thoughts racing.

Once more, a chance encounter had turned their lives upside down. Again, it had to do with his abilities. The go-fast. The Time Bands. Just what were these abilities? What did it all mean? How did it work together with this Harvesting and Running and whatever else Sean had talked about? Was this really something he wanted to get mixed up in? It sounded amazing, but what exactly did it entail? Was there any way to know without becoming one of these Timekeepers?

MacEoghan rolled back over. A moment later, Micah did the same.

"You asleep?" Micah asked.

"Nope."

"Do you think it's possible to use the go-fa—I mean, the Fast Band, on someone else so they could get a full night's rest in just a few hours? Or minutes? Or even seconds?"

MacEoghan shrugged. "I mean, I used to do that to you when we were on the streets."

"You want to try it? You can do me and then I can actually return the favor for once."

MacEoghan yawned. "No, not tonight. Maybe some other time once you know what you're doing."

"Oh." Micah sounded disappointed. "All right."

MacEoghan chuckled weakly, suddenly exhausted. He yawned again. "If Sean is right, and this does somehow slow aging, you're going to have more than enough time to sleep."

Without waiting for his brother's reply, he again rolled over, shifted several times, closed his eyes, and drifted off.

REGISTRATION
YOUNGER BROTHER

Micah watched everything around him with bewildered interest. They were moving so slowly, and yet, he himself moved normally. But to those outside the Band, they were moving normally and he was moving very quickly. Or he would, if he moved too much or too far. He didn't want to spook anyone. He was spooking himself well enough; he didn't need to cause public panic.

But then, what if he did? It felt like an evil thought, but what if? He'd played a few minor tricks on his brothers when they were out fishing, but that had been harmless stuff. It wouldn't have been recognizable as anything overtly strange or impossible to explain away. What if he did do something like that, though? What if he decided to just run through town? He would only be jogging normally, but with the Band, everyone would think he was racing the wind...and winning. It was harmless enough; it wasn't as though he were thinking about stealing anything or touching a girl and getting away with it. It was just a little fun for his own amusement.

He couldn't quite bring himself to do it, and he dropped the Band. He might be mischievous sometimes, but he wasn't quite that brave. He was working up to it, though. If this Timekeeping was some form of law enforcement, then he would have to work on his courage and confrontation. Granted, confronting a criminal might not be the same as playing a prank on the public, but he could respect building blocks.

He looked around, wondering if Sean were watching him right now. The market wasn't overly packed, but it was busy. A fair portion of those out and about were from more populated areas. Ireland might not be involved in the "Emergency" but they were still trapped in the same isles as those who were. Goods and services were fast becoming more difficult to come by as rationing orders started coming down concerning fuel and staple foods. Micah heard plenty of discussion around the docks in the afternoon. Fishermen and similar producers were supposed to take priority so as to keep people fed, but what good would it do if no one could come to buy the fish, or if they couldn't deliver?

Briefly he wondered how long it would take to learn how to Band as well as Sean, to be able to bring everything around him to a complete standstill. If he could do that, maybe he could just take some nets out and scoop the fish right out of the water. They wouldn't have to sit and wait and wonder and pray, bobbing along in the boat in this place or that one, just go straight to the fish and nab them. What would Padraig think of that?

Sorcery, Micah thought. Evil witchcraft, the kind condemned in the Bible. But was it really evil if they used it to help people? Could they use this simply as a tool? What if something happened to Padraig and he couldn't go out anymore? Whether it was a physical ailment or misfortune befalling the boat or equipment, it would be devastating. To be able to continue the work —with far less labor and fewer things that could go wrong—could be life-saving.

It wasn't the first time he'd had such thoughts in the last few days. What if he Banded the truck so they could make deliveries faster? He could be home in time for dinner, the same time every day instead of early one day or late the next. What if he Banded everyone so they could get a full night's rest in only a few minutes? No more slogging out of bed with only a few winks in their eyes, but bright-eyed and full of energy, ready for the day. What if he Banded MacEoghan's Bands? They'd tried that once, but with no real results. Given that they really didn't know what they were doing or expecting, it didn't feel like any great loss.

What if, what if, what if. And all the things Micah imagined himself doing. Helping people, talking to girls, doing things with MacEoghan, doing things on his own. He had very few specific ideas or dreams, but any that he did have typically fell into one of those broad categories. For once, things seemed to be going his way. He had a chance to be himself, defend himself, and be there for others. Maybe he could help MacEoghan help others instead of being the one constantly in need of rescue.

A sudden tint of red and the feeling of being struck in the chest alerted him to mischief. He barely turned when he saw Sean.

"I know that look," the man said, smirking a little.

"What look?" Micah wondered.

"That dreamy look of someone who's been given a great gift and is thinking about all the ways he's going to use it." Sean laughed. "You're not the first, nor the last."

Micah felt his skin flush. "Is it really possible to help people, even if they can't know what this is? Or is it all just this Timekeeping business and law enforcement?"

"It is absolutely possible to help people," Sean told him, nodding emphatically. "Helping people is one hundred percent encouraged. Even if they can't know about it, you can think of yourself as a quick and quiet guardian angel. As for your law enforcement analogy, well, that's more easily explained on the way to registration. Assuming you are interested?"

Micah nodded. "Aye, I am interested. But MacEoghan..."

Sean raised a brow. "He's not?"

"He thinks it's going to be boring. Writing citations, checking papers, standing around, lots of rules."

"Ah." Sean nodded again. "I understand. Well, I can't say there aren't rules, but the rest of his concerns are moot. There is a remarkable amount of freedom with what we can do. We are not so terribly busy that we can't live our own lives. Believe it or not, Kearney used to be a lawyer. He worked as a lawyer right alongside his Timekeeping duties with almost no issues. And Kane was a cigar dealer, imported them from around the world."

"So I'd still be fishing."

"If that's what you want to do. And your brother could still pursue his boxing goals."

"He'd like that very much, I think. And I'm sure he would do it without needing to use Bands. That'd be cheating after all."

Sean's expression turned unreadable. "Well, the Laws of Time are unflinchingly stringent when it comes to how Time is to be gathered and consumed, but the loopholes and freedoms they allow are breathtakingly enormous."

"How do you mean?"

The man waved a hand. "As I said, easier to explain at registration. I just wanted to make sure you were interested before I went through the hassle of arranging your registration."

"Oh." Micah blinked. "Do you need anything from me? Papers of some form?"

"Not necessary. I'm going to go speak to MacEoghan, get his answer. Then, later today or tonight, I will come get either you or both of you and take you to be registered."

"Late at night? Is it at the police station?"

Now Sean grinned. "No, no. It's in the Wheel of Time. I promise everything will be explained later. I just needed an answer, and I got one." He did an imaginary tip of the hat. "Until this evening."

And as quick as he had come, he was gone. The red tint vanished along with the man, although Micah thought he could see something like a residual trail heading east. Then he blinked and the trail was gone. A trick of the eye, maybe.

"All right, you ready to go?" the truck driver asked, opening his door.

Micah stumbled in place but used a Band to recover quickly, blindly reaching for his own door. He yanked it open and clambered into his seat. "I'm ready."

He wasn't much for conversation on the drive, so it was a good thing that this particular driver was talkative enough for a whole room full of people. If he ever noticed that Micah didn't appear to be paying attention, he gave no mention of it. Well, Micah didn't think he did.

He himself was too consumed with his own issues. He couldn't quite graduate them to "problems" per se, as he seemed to have the ability to walk away from them if he so chose. But this Timekeeping business was certainly bigger than a mere passing concern. The last few days of using Bands and getting used to them and playing pranks and thinking of all the things he could suddenly do, it was all coming into focus with this new thought of registration. He was actually going to do this. He was going to step into a new role as a Timekeeper. He didn't know what that meant. It was frightening and yet he was also eager to find out.

They returned to town without incident, dropped off the truck. Looking around, Micah spotted the truck MacEoghan had ridden in, but there was no sign of his brother. But he didn't worry about it, just wished his driver a good day and left, heading for home.

MacEoghan was just heading out the door with their pa and the rest of the boys when Micah arrived. He tried to judge his twin's disposition, gauge whether he'd officially accepted Sean's offer. If he'd known how to Band himself and others, maybe he could have done so and just asked. As it stood, however, the best he could do was try to read his brother's body language. Pretty good chance, he thought. MacEoghan still had a bit of a bewildered expression, as if trying to figure out exactly what he'd just agreed to. Micah probably wore a similar expression, though with far less subtlety, as he walked in the house.

"Too late to sit with the family," his mum tsked mildly, "but not so late the food's gone cold." She made a gesture. "Might as well set you down a minute. Here's a plate for you."

He wasn't going to turn down the opportunity, and he certainly wasn't going to disobey his mum. Micah sat, accepted the plate, and started eating.

"So," Sarah stated, leaning against the table.

Micah glanced at her. "What?"

"Marie Clemens."

"What about her?" Micah felt his skin flush, but he couldn't say just why.

"She's been making eyes at you at Mass for weeks now and you've not said a word. Barely look her way." When Micah did not respond except to take another bite of food, she continued, "She's not a bad-looking girl, *a Mhicah*. She makes all her pretty clothes herself, cooks half the food for the church dinners, looks after her little nieces and nephews with care, and she's smart. True, she didn't go to as prestigious a school as you, but she's not dull."

"I know that," Micah said, shrugging.

"So what's the problem? Why don't you talk to her?"

Micah shrugged again. "I don't know. I just..."

"Just what? Come on, Micah, you're a good man working a good trade. You should have a good wife and family, too. And with this 'Emergency'—"

The disdain in her voice was evident. "—going on, there's no telling what could happen. You should know the joy of a family—"

"Before I die?" Micah raised a brow, but there was no real malice in his tone.

His mum gave him a look, the one she got when someone interrupted her. "At least talk to her."

Micah shoveled the last of his food in his mouth, barely chewed, and forced himself to swallow as he stood. "Maybe later. Right now, I'm late to help the others."

The best Sarah could do was sigh and take the plate. Micah headed out the door before she could rope him into some other trifling conversation. The fact that Padraig made no mention of his being late to help with afternoon chores suggested that he'd known that his wife had planned to corner him on the subject. Had they had the same conversation with MacEoghan, too? Which girl were they trying to match him with?

It was a couple hours later when everything around him came to a halt with a red tint. He looked up at MacEoghan who was the only other moving person in the vicinity. His expression said that he was not the source of the Band.

"Is this a bad time?" Sean asked, making his way toward them on the docks, neatly weaving his way around people and obstacles.

"We're just doing chores," MacEoghan said, indicating the nets in their hands. "Does registration take long?"

"Not at all." Sean stopped about ten feet away. "In fact, to everyone here, it will be like you never left."

"Where are we going?" Micah wondered.

"Like I told you earlier, the Wheel of Time. Just watch."

Micah and MacEoghan exchanged a glance. Then there was a bright light. Micah dropped everything to put his hands up, though the light faded quickly enough. When he dared to look, it was as though a door had opened up in thin air. There was no real frame to it except a mild white glow, and there was, impossibly, no apparent depth to the passageway either. Cautiously, Micah stepped to one side and MacEoghan the other. Viewed from the side, it was no thicker than a piece of paper, and even that felt generous.

Micah looked at the door again from the front. Yes, there did appear to be some kind of room on the other side. The best he could tell was that it had a metal floor and metal walls and there were other doors, too, as if in a hallway.

"Follow me," Sean squeaked. His skin was beet red, veins bulging, sweat pouring down his face. With stiff, exhausted motions, the man seemed to force himself forward, through the door. Micah watched as he walked into this metal hallway and completely disappear from the docks. A paper-thin door to an enormous room.

MacEoghan went first after him. Micah figured he could be forgiven for hanging back for just a second, just to see what happened. As each man went through, his foot crossing the threshold, it was as though they began to slow. Were they stepping out of the Band? Where were they going? What was going on at all? Doors in thin air?

Micah swallowed. He wanted, needed to be brave. He wanted the courage of his brother. Well, this would be a good first step. Taking a breath, he followed.

Walking through the door was like walking into the grip of something that regarded him as little more than an insect or small mammal. Just one squeeze and he would pop. His chest tightened, his lungs screamed for air, his heart raced. By the time these realizations made it to his brain, he had no time or ability to react and try and save himself. Panic set in, but he felt paralyzed. Was that his own fear, or some other, more terrible sorcery? Were the others experiencing the same thing? Where was his brother? And then, mercifully, he blacked out.

He was not out long enough for the fear to wane, but it was long enough to have sapped his whole body of strength. Feeling as though he'd laid down to sleep five minutes before having to get up for another day of fishing, Micah blinked open his eyes.

The room was indeed made of metal, but it was much, much larger than a mere hallway. The ceiling was easily hundreds of feet above his head, and it, too, was made of metal. This metal ceiling, as well as the walls, what he could see of them, had geometric veins running through them of a variety of colors, red and blue being the most prominent.

With his eyes adjusting and no apparent danger, Micah tried to sit up. Nausea overwhelmed him immediately and he involuntarily heaved up his entire lunch. His only saving grace was that he'd had just enough time to get on all fours so most of it went on the ground and not on him. Only a few feet away, MacEoghan was in a similar position. Sean was standing, but he was just as pale as the two of them.

"If this..." MacEoghan wheezed, "...is going to be...a regular occurrence...I want...nothing to do...with Timekeeping."

"It's not," Sean said, his voice soft and level. "Believe me, if this were a regular occurrence, I'd likely be a Runner myself."

It was still a few minutes before Micah felt well enough to move, and the best he could do was just try to sit upright and take in his surroundings.

The peculiarity of the room quickly took second place—and maybe even third or fourth place—to what was arguably the bigger oddity. Micah would not deny that he had learned many sophisticated words while at the school, but beholding the creature before him now, all of them escaped him. It was big, easily fourteen feet tall, its rubbery-looking skin a dull orange color. Its feet were like those of an elephant, and it moved just as slowly, yet it walked upright. It had four arms, and its hands, if they could be called such, had only three digits arranged in a more symmetrical formation than a thumb and fingers. At the shoulder, it was only perhaps six to eight feet. The remainder of its height was expended in a laughably long neck that appeared to end in a single eyeball. A dozen rubbery appendages stuck out around the neck near the eyeball. Micah saw no discernible nose, mouth, or ears.

Meanwhile, just a few feet away, walking down the hall giving no thought to any of these marvelous things, was a creature that had the stature and near-appearance of a man, but its skin was so pale as to be translucent and there seemed to be lights in its forehead. Coming from the other direction was a beast that resembled a dog but with six legs and skin like a frog.

"What is this place?" Micah asked, his nausea being fast replaced by wonder.

"This is the Wheel of Time, the portal room to be specific," Sean answered, sounding better himself. "This is where creatures and species from all over the universe converge."

"What?" MacEoghan wondered.

Sean nodded, slowly and deliberately. "This is why it is difficult for almost everyone over thirty years to accept. They've become too set in their ways, convinced of the ways of the world. I won't say it isn't still overwhelming for the young, but you are more apt to accept it."

Micah felt around on the floor as best he could, avoiding his vomit. He got to his feet and took a few tentative steps. "Is this real?"

"Absolutely." Sean moved to give MacEoghan a hand up. "As real as anything on Earth."

"Are they all Timekeepers?" MacEoghan asked, looking around.

Sean shook his head and motioned for them to follow him. They were indeed in a corridor, but it more resembled a field hospital, Micah thought. Each door, or portal, he supposed, hung hastily upon a rod to provide only minimal privacy in the middle of a massive room. In between portals, which were spaced maybe six feet apart, he could see hundreds and even thousands of them in the room.

"No, they are not," Sean said, answering MacEoghan's question. "As I explained before, there are Harvesters who Harvest Time. They sell it to the Merchants who then make it universally available. The Timekeepers simply enforce the Laws of Time, at the bidding of the Grandfathers and the Hands of Time."

"And the Runners steal the Time," Micah stated.

"Yes. All in all...it's why we call it the Time industry. It's a business. Nothing more, nothing less. There is no real noble cause to fight for here. This is a mode of employment. A job. Some worlds are what we call Openly Engaged, where everyone knows about Time and the Time industry. Their Timekeepers are held in high regard and often make very lucrative careers. Earth is what we call Unengaged, meaning the general public has no knowledge of Time and it needs to stay that way. Our jobs, our role, have very little impact on anything."

"Why bother, then?" MacEoghan wondered.

"Because it's required. Once a Runner or a Harvester pops up on a world, who is part of that world, that system, that society, there must be Timekeepers to keep them in check. Again, sometimes this turns into a big deal. Sometimes it doesn't. On Earth, it isn't a big deal. But if it ever became a big deal, then we would be needed."

It felt like a few miles before they reached the end of the room, where everyone seemed to file through a single, very large door. Before that, however, Sean led them over to a small machine. It was rather unassuming, looking no more significant than an inset in the wall. But when Sean pressed his finger into a particular button, a needle popped out and pricked him, drawing blood. A moment later, a small device popped out. He picked it up and started fussing. One part of it looked like a priest's collar which he put around his neck, and the other part went in his ear.

He motioned for the twins to do the same. MacEoghan went first, flinching at the needle prick. Micah copied his brother, also flinching. Sean helped them to properly place the odd devices.

"This will allow you to understand others, and for others to understand you," he explained, adjusting Micah's collar. "As you might have guessed, not too many people speak English or Irish here."

Micah might have considered such a thing in the very back of his mind, but at the forefront was currently a revelation that the sounds that some of these other creatures were make were actually words and the semblance of a language. He saw another one of the six-legged dog creatures, except this one was walking upright. As another creature bumped into it, he—or she? Or it?—snapped at the thing to watch where it was going.

"That six-legged dog?" Sean guessed, gesturing. Micah nodded. "That's a Lixon. They're called anthromorphs, meaning they can stand upright or on all paws with no issue; both postures are natural to them. Generally very agreeable, but also very business-minded. They make good secretaries."

Micah had no room to question, argue, or complain. He had no room to do anything. Any thoughts or dreams he might have had the last few days when he was first getting used to the idea of Time and Timekeeping were now gone, washed away in this tide of revelations.

"Come on," Sean said, moving off. "Let's get you registered and then back home. You'll want to sleep this one off, I think."

Micah might have made a break for it immediately, but looking back at the rows upon rows upon rows of portals, he knew he would never be able to find his way back. Which row was theirs? How far down? What happened if he walked through the wrong one? Was that possible?

He and MacEoghan kept hard on Sean's heels as he headed for the big door, wondering what new and exciting and terrifying thing could possibly be waiting for them on the other side. Micah wanted to know everything. He wanted to believe none of it existed. He was terrified that this was all real. He was more afraid that he had gone mad and was hallucinating dreadfully. What was all of this, really? Fine, so a few future-thinking media entertainers invented a couple grand stories about space and life in the greater universe, but...it was real? All of it? Were those entertainers part of this "Time industry" and so pulled their stories from real sources? He asked this of Sean.

"Some probably do," their guide answered. "I would be more surprised if none of them did. I expect such stories will become more popular over the coming years as humanity advances and starts to toe the line of becoming Engaged."

Engaged, meaning, everyone would know. Everyone would know about this. About Time, the Wheel, these aliens, all of it. Could they handle it? Micah didn't know if he could.

They pushed through the crowd and emerged into a room that seemed impossibly large. There was nothing of real significance that Micah could tell; to him it simply looked like an enormous cube. The intriguing part was that people—could he rightly call aliens people?—walked naturally upon every surface. The floor, where they were now, the walls, even the ceiling high above. A few flying creatures floated by here and there, but otherwise, everyone moved upon the surfaces.

"This is the Cube," Sean introduced, moving them away from the door they'd just come from before stopping to speak. Micah noted that the door—all of them, in fact, the dozens and more—were like the portal from home: paper thin, assuming the third dimension even existed. Sean gestured around. "This is the hub of all activity in the Wheel. You've got your marketplaces, which make up the majority of doors. Then you've got places like the Food Court, the Archives, the Arena, the Judgment Wing, and the Seat of the Hands."

"Arena?" MacEoghan piped up.

Sean chuckled nervously. "Well, it's not the kind of arena you're thinking of. It's where we'll spend some time training. It's a controlled environment for you to learn new skills. There is some combat training involved, but that comes much later."

MacEoghan's disappointment was evident.

"The Judgment Wing sounds like court," Micah reasoned. "The Food Court sounds like some kind of market or restaurant. The Seat of the Hands, well, if the Hands are the rulers, then it's some sort of governmental or Parliamentary building. The Archives sounds like a library or record-keeping place, so I assume that's where we're going?"

"Very deductive of you," Sean praised. "Unfortunately, while it does make some sense, we are actually going to the Seat, to bring you before the Hands before registration."

"An interview?" MacEoghan questioned.

"Sort of. It won't take long. They just want to see all the incoming recruits." Sean made a motion and they started walking.

Micah looked around. "But with how many...different people are here...how do they do it? Doesn't it take a long time? Won't someone start to miss them, miss us?"

"As I said before, we can spend as much time as we need here, but as long as our portal stays open, no time will pass at home. It'll be like we never even left."

Micah puzzled over this, trying to make it make sense. None of it made sense, yet here it was before his eyes. He couldn't make sense of people walking on walls, but then, suddenly, he was doing the same thing. They just approached the wall where stairs made up the entire crease, walked up the stairs, and then the cube seemed to shift, or maybe it was just his perception. The wall was suddenly the floor, and everything was relative again.

"How...?" Micah began dumbly.

"There's a lot about this place that even I don't understand," Sean laughed. "As long as you don't try to force it to make sense, you'll be fine. The secretaries keep everything running."

"Secretaries?" MacEoghan echoed. "Shouldn't there be engineers or...construction workers or something?"

"They are. Secretaries is simply a catch-all term for those who keep things running behind the scenes as it were." Sean paused and turned to face them. "But make no mistake. The secretaries here, whatever their role, have more influence and more authority than almost every Time Agent here. They'll smile, they'll nod, but they hold no loyalties beyond the Wheel and themselves. And they have eyes and ears everywhere in here. So be very cautious."

He continued walking. Micah followed, trying to process this new information with all of the other new information churning in his brain. Was there no end to this information onslaught?

"And here we are," Sean announced suddenly. He did not stop or even slow as he simply approached one of the many thin-air doors and walked through. Micah and MacEoghan hesitated and slowed. MacEoghan went through first and Micah timidly followed. There were no issues. No physical maladies befell them; it was no different than walking through a regular doorway.

The sight before them now was no longer geometric, but historical, as they beheld the Roman Coliseum. Or it looked like such. The picture Micah remembered showed the Coliseum being made of stone, as one would expect. This Coliseum, however, was made of the same metal panels as the portal room, though there was a certain translucent quality to them so they were neither wall nor window.

"What's this place?" MacEoghan wondered.

"The Seat of the Hands," Sean answered, pausing just long enough for them to catch up. "Colloquially known as the Coliseum. Conspiracy theories abound among Earth Timekeepers as to who influenced whom. Unfortunately, there is only one Time Agent from that era and he doesn't know, and the Hands will never admit to being the second ones to discover or create anything."

"There's a Roman Time Agent?" Micah questioned.

Sean nodded, still walking. "Aye, from the time of Christ, even claims to have witnessed the Resurrection, for what it's worth to you."

"Did he?"

The man made a so-so gesture but appeared generally unconcerned.

"Well, I'm not one to call a man a liar when it comes to his religious beliefs. And I've no way to prove it one way or the other. Best anyone could do is take him at his word."

They reached the Coliseum and entered the first of, apparently, several concentric tracks that ran around the structure. In spite of the oddities like the metal construction and alien life forms, just being present and having such activity going on around them made the Earth history come alive for Micah. Was the whole thing true to form, or just the exterior?

There were a number of doors that they passed by on their trek around the building. When Sean finally chose one, they found themselves in what amounted to little more than a government office. There were service desks, attendants, and a line.

"You mentioned a Judgment Wing," MacEoghan said. "Is this it? Is the Judgment Wing part of the Seat?"

Sean shook his head. "No. Think of this, like your brother said, as a governmental or Parliamentary building. The Judgment Wing would be your police station, courthouse, and jail."

Micah just nodded quietly and looked around. All the shapes and sizes, all the colors, all the extra or missing organs and appendages, and they were all the same standing in line, waiting to be seen.

It didn't take long for them to get up to a counter. Sean gave the attendant —one of the secretaries, apparently—something called universal coordinates and explained that he was going to introduce a couple new probationary Timekeepers and get them registered. The secretary reacted in no discernible way, and they were made to wait in another room.

"Will we have to wait long?" MacEoghan asked, looking around and sounding a bit annoyed.

"Well, time is fairly relative here. I suppose it depends on how you define a long time," Sean answered evasively.

"Can't you just use Time and make it go faster?"

"Not here, not in the Seat. There's a dampening field so no Time can be used."

"Why?" Micah asked dumbly.

"Security measure. That's the rule and I see no reason to change it."

"But if something were to happen, we'd be at the mercy of everything bigger and stronger than us," MacEoghan protested.

"And we are bigger and stronger than some others." Sean shrugged. "Besides, we'd only have to make it out of the Coliseum. And there is more security here than you can appreciate. Even if someone wanted to try something, it would never get very far."

Micah could see his brother was not pleased with the answer, but he had no choice but to accept it.

Despite the grandeur of the structure overall, decorations were so sparse as to be entirely nonexistent. The only interesting thing to look at were some carvings above the doors. Sean explained that they were simple symbols. There was no universal language in the Wheel, but symbols could guide them anywhere they needed to go and identify key figures. The sequence above the doors now included symbols for "Hand" and "Seat" as one might expect.

"When we get in there, just let me do the talking," Sean told them. "This is only an introduction and we don't want to give them cause to doubt your abilities or your loyalties."

"Loyalties?" MacEoghan echoed.

"Don't give them a reason to think you're going to take everything I'm teaching you and use it to become a Runner."

MacEoghan frowned but said nothing more. Some part of Micah found Sean's statement a bit odd, but his brain was becoming burned out on all of this new information and new experiences. His ability to care about any of this was dwindling quickly. He hoped this wouldn't take very long.

Then the door opened and a new secretary, this one having the appearance of a giraffe mixed with a peacock, informed them that the Hands were ready to see them.

Micah and MacEoghan stayed close behind Sean, nearly treading on his heels, as they walked down a dimly-lit hallway—hallway being a bit of a misnomer as it was easily thirty feet wide and just as tall—to a gated door. The secretary cranked an old-fashioned wheel over and over, lifting the medieval gate ever so slowly. Were there lions waiting for them at the end of the short tunnel in the great room beyond?

"The Hands are ready," the secretary stated once the gate was fully open.

The secretary did not lead or follow them, but Sean walked confidently down the hallway, twins following dutifully. They emerged into a spectacularly white room. Once Micah's eyes adjusted, he saw that it appeared to be solid marble, as if the entire room had been cut from a single, perfect block. They had entered on the floor of the room and approached another symbol. There Sean turned around and they looked up to see a group of figures looking down on them from the stands.

More aliens, Micah thought. By this time, he shouldn't have been surprised. He wasn't surprised, really, because it came across as more of a resigned mental sigh. Oh, more aliens. Of course. Why not? He hoped this wouldn't take long.

It really didn't, actually. Sean introduced them, explained that he would be taking on both of them as probationary Apprentices and possibly both as full Apprentices. Then the Hands were less concerned with the twins and more interested in how Sean expected to handle such a task. Micah might have been more interested, except he was starting to get tired, a little hungry, and he kind of wanted to go home where things made sense. Where it was just him, the boat, the nets, his pa and brothers beside him, his ma and sisters cooking up a nice meal for them when they got done. Then they would have the nightly Scripture reading and a little free time before heading off to bed so they could get up early for more fish.

But, apparently, simply introducing them wasn't enough. Once the Hands gave their blessing to Sean, then he had to take them back to see another secretary elsewhere in the Seat to actually register them.

"You can register under any name you like," Sean told them. "Meagher, Dearbhfhine, something else entirely. You could switch first names if you wanted to." Micah and MacEoghan both snapped their gaze to him. Did he know? How could he? Upon realizing their expression, Sean put his hands up in mild surrender. "I'm joking. Well, I mean, you could do that, but if you don't want to..." He appeared genuinely confused, Micah thought.

They registered as Micah and MacEoghan Dearbhfhine. MacEoghan wanted absolutely nothing to do with the Meagher name, and Micah liked being a Dearbhfhine and having a family, even if they could never know about this.

"Congratulations," Sean told them once the record was entered. "You are now officially probationary Timekeepers."

"What does that mean exactly?" MacEoghan asked. "Do we start training or what?"

They started out of the room, out of the Coliseum at large.

"Not immediately," Sean explained. "I know that today has been very stressful, maybe even a little traumatic. You need time to think about it, maybe go back to something familiar for a while. At least this evening. And I imagine you're getting tired. It's normal, I promise. Instead, I'm just going to take you home for the evening. We'll actually start training in a day or two."

"How is that going to work?" Micah inquired.

"Training works best, I think, when done in the evening. It's hard work, and it will be easier to just send you home to bed rather than put you through everything and then expect you to still go about your day. I may not be a fisherman, but I know that you do a lot of hard work out there. You'll want every bit of your strength throughout the day and I won't rob you of that.

"So what I'll do is I will come to you. Don't worry about the details; you just leave that to me. But when I do show up, I expect that we will be training, no excuses."

"How long is our probation?"

"It will be about a year, maybe less." Sean looked at MacEoghan. "Maybe much less for you because of how developed your skills already are."

MacEoghan looked pleased at the idea, Micah thought.

They left the Coliseum, passing through the thin-air doorway back into the Cube. They appeared to be on the floor, but then, Micah knew for a fact that they had walked onto a wall. Or was this, perhaps, the ceiling instead? Did such words even have any meaning here?

They approached the crease between...walls? They walked up the steps and then, suddenly, the world seemed to shift. But there was no head rush, no physical disorientation. One minute they were walking normally on one wall, and now they were walking normally on another wall. Micah remembered the awe, still felt a bit of that same awe, but he was just so tired of the barrage of weirdness. Sean was right; he wanted to get back to something normal so he could think about this, make sense of it all.

Somehow Sean got them back to the door that took them to the portal room. They returned their speaking devices, then made their way down a row of portals.

"How do you know which one is ours?" Micah wondered. "What if it's three rows over? What if we miss it?"

Sean shrugged. "It's just something you get used to, I suppose, needing to remember where you parked."

"And how often do we have to come here?" MacEoghan questioned. "Do we really have to go through all that every time?"

"No. You probably won't be back until your Apprentice review. Your probationary period is not especially rigorous. There is no real need to utilize the Arena. Meeting near your home will do just fine."

It was a relief Micah didn't realize he needed until he was suddenly faced with the daunting task of walking back through the portal to get home. His stomach churned at the thought.

"There's no other way?" he whined.

"Afraid not," Sean said apologetically. "Only way out is through, and I have to be the last one." He made a motion. "After you."

Micah glanced at his brother who looked just as uneasy. Then, taking a breath, MacEoghan walked through and Micah followed.

It was no more pleasant exiting the Wheel of Time than it had been entering it. If Micah had any food left in his system, he would have given it up. As it was, he was left dry-heaving pathetically on the docks.

True to Sean's word, everything was exactly how they'd left it. The people remained frozen, the sun still peeped through tiny gaps in the clouds, and the tide hadn't moved one inch one way or the other.

"I expect it will be a few days before we actually begin," Sean said behind them. Micah looked. The portal was gone but Sean looked no better than either of them. He went on, "Take the time to digest everything you've seen and heard and learned. Keep practicing with what I've already shown you, what you already know. Then we'll see what we can do to improve it."

WILD HEART
OLDER BROTHER

MacEoghan was never so grateful for his abilities than during the winter, especially now that he was out fishing with his pa and brothers almost every day. Being able to Band meant he could react faster to sudden changes in wind and waves, whether it was making a correction with the boat or catching a brother or an item before it washed overboard. And if utilizing his Time abilities in such a way didn't qualify him for an early Apprenticeship, he didn't know what would.

Sean had talked about some residual abilities that would start developing more quickly now that he was under formal training and guidance. One such ability was a Reflexive Band. As the name implied, he would Band reflexively so he could better analyze a situation. His brain knew that something was wrong, but his mind might be a few seconds behind. Seeing how rescuing things from potentially being lost at sea was his most common use of Banding—or the most high-stress use of Banding—that was when the Reflexive Bands started to really develop.

Another residual ability was called Predict, where he could visualize or even truly see the path of an object in motion. Combined with the Reflexive Bands, there was very little that he could miss while out on the boat. Assuming he was paying attention. These residual abilities weren't that strong yet, and he could easily let them slip right by if he was too focused on something else.

As they returned to shore, cold and wet but no worse for wear as they offloaded a respectable haul, MacEoghan just kept telling himself that an early Apprenticeship meant an earlier Journeyman. Like the traditional trades, as a Journeyman Timekeeper, he would be expected to travel and learn from other Masters. Considering he was basically an adult now, there were any number of ways he could get away from here to pursue such a thing. He could pursue boxing again. He could cross the border to England and enlist in the army. He could travel to mainland Europe for some odd reason.

He got in the truck, grateful that his driver today preferred to keep things quiet. The man would make small talk if necessary, but otherwise he was a quiet man.

MacEoghan wouldn't mind returning to boxing. It wasn't as though he had lost any strength or dexterity while working as a fisherman, and Reflexive Bands and Predict could really come in handy in the ring. The problem was that the war—ahem, Emergency—was straining goods and resources in the country, and boxing wasn't considered a necessity. As a fisherman, he could buy certain things that regular people couldn't, like fuel. If he tried to get into boxing, well, there was a good chance that he would be biking everywhere.

They arrived at their first stop. Shops were still open and people still walked here and there, trying to stay lively and optimistic. MacEoghan wondered if things were so normal in the larger cities. He started unloading fish, listening to various conversations going on in the immediate vicinity.

"I'm sorry, I can't deliver," one shop owner was saying, looking a bit helpless to satisfy a customer. "My truck is broken down and the parts aren't coming in."

"Well they're not needed for the war effort," the customer was saying, his attitude dismissive.

The shop owner turned a bit defensive. "Maybe not for us, but the Germans don't know that. You know they captured two merchant vessels just last week off the coast, boarded them, searched them for contraband, anything that people might be trying to smuggle into England. Made off with a lot of goods for their own use, the pirates."

Somehow this did not seem to register as important in the customer's mind. "Are our own factories abandoned?"

"No, but prices for raw materials have gone sky high. Iron is a premium, steel a luxury." The shop owner put up a hand and cut off whatever the customer was about to nitpick next. "I'm sorry, sir. Unless you can produce the part to fix my truck, or even provide a horse and cart, I can't deliver."

MacEoghan Banded and paused in his work for just a minute, glancing at the engine of the truck he was currently riding in. England was scooping up vehicle parts as fast as they could be produced, leaving only a trickle for the rest of them. The truck was running fine just now, but what if that changed? One of the other trucks needed some work, but they were limping it along the best they could. What if they couldn't get the parts? Fishing might be important, but what if they weren't important enough? What if the boat engine broke down? What was more important, one little fishing boat on the southern coast, or a submarine?

He dropped the Band and continued working, fulfilling the order and getting back in the truck.

What could one soldier with the ability to Band do? If he could bring everything around him to a standstill, he could probably wipe out an army. If he could do that, he could single-handedly end the war and things could get back to normal.

But what if the other side had someone who could Band? What if both sides had Timekeepers? Sean hadn't broached the subject of Time in combat, or Time as combat. If MacEoghan got out there and was faced with an enemy combatant who was a more skilled Timekeeper than him, well, it probably wouldn't be pretty, regardless of his boxing prowess.

On the other hand, what were the odds of that? It wasn't as though Timekeepers—or any Time Agent—were hiding behind every rock and tree. MacEoghan had thought he was the only one for a long time. Considering that his Region encompassed all of Europe and Scandinavia and his District was the entirety of the UK and Scandinavia, he might have gone his whole life believing he was the only one except for his actions at the school prompting a more determined investigation.

They arrived at their next stop and began unloading.

"The nice thing about keeping things local," the shop owner declared, taking a crate of fish, "I don't have to worry about whether a ship is going to refuse to come in our waters, and I don't have to hope that ours can make it out to them, get the goods, and bring them back without being attacked or boarded."

MacEoghan again considered what could happen if the truck broke down. Would the man come to get the fish himself? Not likely seeing how he got no rationing privileges. Maybe he would make the trip once or twice, just to try and keep things running, hope that deliveries would resume in good time. But as they waited on the part and got excuse after excuse, he wouldn't come to get the fish and they couldn't deliver the fish to him.

MacEoghan tried not to dwell on it. Things weren't so bad. They were still operating, the sun still rose—somewhere behind the clouds—and everyone was still in good health. Ireland remained officially neutral and so enjoyed a tense peace among the people, this often marred by news of their ships being boarded by German pirates and the rationing on certain goods. Otherwise, things were well and generally peaceful. But how long would that last? What if the Germans decided to really cross the channel, try to take England by force? Would they really let Ireland be? For how long?

Again he wondered if he wouldn't be better off crossing the border and enlisting. Even if he didn't Band in order to wipe out the opposing side, just being able to help his fellow soldier ought to count for something.

Another stop, more fish, repeat until everything was offloaded and they could return home. No side trips, no idling. They were fortunate to have gas ration privileges, and they didn't want to squander those privileges.

With everything trimmed down as much as it could be, MacEoghan and Micah were never late for dinner anymore, and the two of them walked in the door just in time to wash up properly and sit down at the table.

Sarah didn't like political talk at the dinner, but with the rationing and everything else, sometimes it could be hard to avoid.

"Seamus said he thought he saw something up near the north shoal," Padraig began. "We'll have to avoid it for a few days."

"What did he see?" Brendan asked. "Sharks?"

"We're not worried about sharks," Cillian told him, his tone suggesting it was something way cooler. "We can catch the sharks. He probably saw one of those German U-boats, right, Pa?"

"U-boats need deeper waters than that shoal," Sarah said, her words curt, tone dismissive, expression telling her husband to steer the conversation in another direction.

"Are they going to bomb us, Papa?" Shauna asked fearfully, eyes huge and terrified. "Miss Agnes at the shop said kids in England are being sent away." Tears started running down her cheeks. "You won't send us away, will you, Papa?"

"No, dear, of course not," Sarah said, sighing with some resignation. "We're safe here. Ireland isn't involved in this emergency, and we're just a little fishing town. There is nothing here the Germans could want."

"Well what do they want with anything else except they want it?" Shay questioned. "What do they care about England except they want it?"

Sarah's expression said his words were not helping things.

"We'll adapt," Padraig cut in decisively. "We're fishermen, it's what we do. Be it weather, tide, misfortune, or war—"

"Padraig!" Sarah hissed. "It's an emergency."

He gave her a look and continued, "—we adapt. The fish haven't stopped swimming and we're not going to stop catching them. We will continue to do our work the best we can. If that means avoiding the north shoal for a few days, so be it. Understood?" He nodded, which elicited more nods. "Good."

"But what if there really are Germans out there?" MacEoghan asked, deliberately looking at his food as he spoke. "I mean, we're as far south as you can get, and they're only right across the channel."

"They would have to get past both the English and the French."

"Which they've already done." Now he looked up. "They've attacked ships already in the west."

"Cargo ships. Not small fishing vessels." Padraig shot a glance at Shauna.

"But what if?" MacEoghan pressed. "The English and the French know to protect the bigger ships and bigger ports, but what if the Germans tried to come here, sneak in a smaller passage?"

"Ireland isn't involved," Sarah said tightly.

"And you think it would be some grand inconvenience for them if we were?"

"You will not speak to your mother like that," Padraig told him. "And this conversation is over."

MacEoghan stood suddenly and left the table, ignoring both of them telling him to sit down. If he felt bad about anything as he stormed out of the house, it was that he heard Shauna start to cry. He didn't mean to upset her, but he was tired of pretending that they were immune to the effects of the war that was going on right next door and across the channel. It would be one thing if it were farther away or if England weren't involved, but that wasn't the case. And they couldn't just ignore the possibility of danger. Seamus had likely only seen some large fish or odd shadow on the water, but was his own theory really so far-fetched?

He avoided the docks and instead walked down the shoreline a fair distance. He stared out at the ocean and the rocks jutting up from the shallows and the depths. What would it look like for German ships to appear on the horizon? How would it be for a bunch of submarines to suddenly emerge from the waves? The town would be helpless and they wouldn't be able to get anyone out in time to warn nearby towns.

Was everyone else being naive? Was he being overbearing and paranoid? He didn't understand. It was like living next to a pub that was in the middle of a massive row and somehow believing that your house wasn't going to be harmed in any way.

He heard Padraig coming but chose not to react.

"I know I don't look it now, but when I was a younger man, I never looked my age." Padraig stopped to stand beside MacEoghan, looking out to sea. "I always looked much younger. When I was twenty, I looked fifteen. When I was fifteen, I looked ten. Wasn't until I got married and started having my own children that my physical appearance caught up to my age."

He paused for a long minute. "During the Great War, there were a lot of young men who lied about their age in order to join the army. My older brother didn't need to lie, but I did. Unfortunately, because of how young I looked, I probably wouldn't have been accepted even if I were of age. So my brother had to go by himself. You know what happened?"

MacEoghan bit his tongue so he wouldn't be tempted to answer, though Padraig continued anyway. "He died. Wasn't a bullet or bomb or glorious charge; he died of sickness sitting there in those infernal trenches."

Despite biting his tongue, some words managed to slip through, and then they came tumbling out. "I don't remember a lot about my birth mum, but I do remember that she always told us that our father was a soldier in the Great

War, that he died nobly, heroically, fending off the Germans. But that wasn't true. It couldn't be."

Padraig nodded slowly. "Aye, it's a hard thing to learn that our parents lie. Some more than others. I don't expect you to understand until you have children."

"Lying to children about fairies and goblins is one thing. Telling them that their father is a dead hero as a cover for her whoring is—"

"In the past," Padraig finished, not unkindly. "It's in the past. A different life, a different family. And it's quite obvious that you have not adapted half so well as your brother to being in this family."

MacEoghan huffed a sigh. "Aye, the good son."

Padraig waved a hand dismissively. "You're both good sons. You're just different from each other. You have to be, I think, especially being twins."

"Is this what you had in mind when you used us to replace your own children?"

Now the man hardened a little. "Frustration is no excuse to speak ill of the dead, especially a man's children."

MacEoghan sighed again, relenting just a little as he stared at his feet and muttered, "Sorry."

"I have a notion of what you're thinking about doing," Padraig went on. "I can't make the decision for you, but just consider who and what you'd be leaving behind. You have a brother who likely won't go with you, or whom you would worry about terribly if he did. And if you have any love and respect for Sarah as your mother, don't grieve her with the worry of the loss of yet another child."

"But if Ireland were involved, it would be different?" MacEoghan challenged. "If we got involved this year, next year, the year after? Then it would be all right?"

Padraig was remarkably calm in his answer. "Right now, you're thinking about going because you've conjured up ghosts and scenarios and what ifs in your mind. And I can't say they're all unreasonable. What if Seamus really did see a U-boat? But ghosts only, still. If Ireland were to get involved, I think your frame of mind and your priorities would be a lot more serious and more carefully considered."

With that, he turned and started walking away. After a few yards, he paused and looked back. "Right now, the Germans are still many miles away. But the fishing nets are right on our stoop and they need tending to."

MacEoghan watched him for a few seconds, then sighed and slowly followed.

He had the drive, but he also had the abilities. He could help people, soldiers and civilians. He could save men from being shot, he could decimate enemy lines.

No one said anything to him as he reached the house and grabbed a net. He could feel the eyes on him, but he ignored them.

Whenever any of the boys protested the Brothers' horrific treatment—be it physical or sexual in nature—the Brothers always had some excuse for it. If pressed or confronted directly, they always tried to sidestep the issue by asking if the boys were ungrateful for the things they were receiving at no cost to them. Food, shelter, clothing, education, work prospects, the hope of a life out of the gutter.

Now MacEoghan found himself pondering those same questions, except he was the one on trial. Padraig and Sarah had done nothing wrong. Food, shelter, clothing, work, the hope of a life out of the gutter. Family, security, purpose, usefulness. Was he ungrateful? If he wanted to be honest, he wasn't sure he was grateful or ungrateful. He had been doing just fine on his own. He could be working for Padraig just fine as an employee without needing to be his son.

Was it pity, then? Had Padraig and Sarah taken pity on Micah but took MacEoghan in as a formality? Everyone expected twins to do a lot together, and they had. Why not adoption? Not that any papers had been signed or anything; the two of them had just been kind of absorbed into the family and accepted with nary a word from government official, church leader, or common townsfolk. It was just something that happened, apparently.

MacEoghan Banded so he could look around at the others without making it obvious. Who and what was he leaving behind? Shay, who had been the oldest until he and Micah showed up. The fourteen year old complained about it, but he also watched everything MacEoghan and Micah did, at least as far as talking to girls and stepping into their own adult lives.

181

Cillian, twelve, who was just coming into manhood and looking to his father and older brothers for what to do and how to navigate his sudden size, strength, and interest in girls.

Brendan, nine years old now, too young to be a man quite yet but too old to be a child. Every day was an adventure.

Darren, just old enough to start helping with the boats and nets and other chores. He was thrilled to finally be able to leave his mother and sisters and join the men of the house.

Inside the house, there was Ciara, fierce and independent and still not yet a woman. Sarah sometimes muttered that her own mother's curse had come true and her eldest daughter truly was just like her at that age.

In contrast, there was little Shauna, small and delicate in both mind and body. She had a way she liked things and she didn't like that way to be disturbed. MacEoghan still felt bad about making her cry earlier. He would have to apologize.

Finally there was Kayleigh, just starting to let go of Sarah's skirts and branch out into the world. She was a quick learner, already knew her letters and numbers, simple reading and math, and was constantly asking questions.

He dropped the Band.

There was nothing that MacEoghan held against any of them, but he couldn't say that he cared about any of them the same way he cared about Micah. And even then, Micah was an adult, too. They would be going their own ways, living their own lives. MacEoghan found himself almost offended by the thought of Micah going to war just because he was.

Except he hadn't made that decision yet, not officially. And why not? He should just do it and be done with it. He was tired of hearing news and rumors and not being able to do anything about it. Eventually the war would reach them. The Germans only knew how to take and take, and they were never satisfied. If they took France, it was only a short hop across the channel to England. If they took England, there was no reason to think they wouldn't come for Ireland, too. But by then it would be too late to do anything.

His thoughts were too focused on his brooding to notice the Reflexive Band that popped up half a blink before he stuck himself with the needle he was using to finesse the lines on the fishing net. He jerked his hand back instinctively and nursed a bit of blood that welled up. No one said anything about it. They'd all done it more times than they cared to count.

He again Banded and looked around at the others. Why should he feel the need to fight if not for them? He'd been all around Ireland, beating the shit out of men in pubs, trying to avoid the authorities or anyone who might report them and get them sent back to the school. Why should he fight for any of that? What was he defending exactly? He didn't care for England. He'd fight for Ireland, but was his homeland really the thing he held in the highest regard? Was he really more willing to fight for land than these people here?

Again he dropped the Band and focused on his work. What was he fighting for? What did he hope to really accomplish? Did it matter? The Germans didn't get to take something just because they wanted it. They didn't get to run around unchecked. If they took the mainland, why wouldn't they come for the islands?

The same arguments ran around in circles in his mind all afternoon. When the smell of supper started wafting out of the house, MacEoghan knew a moment of guilt. He wasn't Padraig's employee to be contractually paid, nor Sarah's houseguest who owed her rent and compensation for food. He was their son. He worked in his father's business and his mother took care to keep him fed and clothed. Shay might gripe sometimes about no longer being the oldest child, but Kayleigh didn't really know the difference.

But then, didn't he owe it to them to keep them safe? Didn't he owe it to Padraig to ensure that the shoals and the channel were free of threats, be they sharks or Germans or German sharks? Padraig was getting too old and Shay was still obviously very young, so the responsibility, logically, fell to him, MacEoghan. Well, him and Micah, but he knew Micah was not so inclined. Therefore, MacEoghan had to be the fighting man of the family. Even better that he had his Time gifts.

It wasn't long before Sarah called everyone in for supper. Darren and Brendan jumped up, and Micah barked at them to pick up their tools and put things back the right way before going in. MacEoghan did his part dutifully, if silently, and somberly went to wash up and take his place at the table.

Before he could sit down, Sarah stopped him. Her expression was serious, but not angry.

"Are you ready to be part of this family again?" she asked sternly.

"Yes, ma'am," MacEoghan mumbled to the floor.

"Look me in the eye, child."

He didn't want to, but if he wanted to eat, he had to.

"I know I've told you this before, but this table is a sacred place," she told him. "It's a place for family. As long as you're part of this family, you'll have a place here. But that also means you don't get to just walk away. Understand?"

"Yes, ma'am."

"Good." She looked him up and down briefly, checking to make sure he'd washed up to her standards. Then she nodded. "Sit down. Supper's just coming out."

He did so, feeling very conspicuous.

Supper was quieter than dinner, but there were no outbursts, arguments, disagreements, or political discussions of any kind. Padraig mentioned a few extra projects he wanted to get done on the boat in the next couple weeks, and he praised Brendan for being a good little worker. The child basked in his father's praise. Not to be outdone, Kayleigh bragged that she had helped to make dinner and Sarah echoed this with a bit of her own praise.

No fear, no worry, no beatings, MacEoghan thought. The trials of daily life, but otherwise carefree. Unconditional.

He said little at the table except to apologize to Shauna for upsetting her, and after supper was over, he headed outside to stand on the porch. Sean came around about once a week or so for training and it was again within his timeframe to appear.

Instead of going down to the beach like he might normally, MacEoghan instead walked through town and headed up the road to the top of the cliffs. The wind was much fiercer here, but it was a good walk anyway. It was probably half an hour before Micah found him.

"If you're planning on running off, you should still pack a bag," his twin said, looking out over the town and the ocean beyond.

"I'm not running off," MacEoghan told him.

"Sure looks and feels like it." Micah still did not face him. "Why is it so hard for you to have a family?"

"I don't know what to do with them. For the longest time, we were the only family worth having, me and you." MacEoghan made a vague gesture. "What am I supposed to do with this?"

"With what? Proper guidance, a family business, a home-cooked meal every day, beds to call our own?"

"Love. Respect. Even the Brothers provided food, shelter, and clothing. I did that just fine for both of us while on the road. But what do I do with this?"

Now Micah glanced at him. "Reciprocate it. Give it back."

MacEoghan studied him. His twin looked so...full of life. He again made a vague motion. "How? How do you adapt to this so quickly while I'm...up here?"

Micah shrugged and returned his gaze to the ocean. "I've already had plenty of experience with it, being dependent on someone else and being grateful for it."

MacEoghan sighed. "I'm not a fisherman, Micah. I can't just sit back and listen to all of these rumors and reports from the war. It might be far away now, but it could get closer. And if it goes on a long time, even if it doesn't come here, the rationing and the economy are only going to tighten. Things are going to get harder. What happens if we can't export the fish? We might be able to fish for ourselves, but—"

"And what do you expect to do?" Micah wondered.

"I don't know. My part. One man doesn't mean much, but many men make a formidable army. And with Time, I think I can help our side a lot, even if it's just pulling men out of the line of bullets."

Micah nodded slowly. "Aye, maybe. But what if the Germans have Timekeepers, too? Sean said there are no real rules about using Time, other than just don't steal it. We're only probationary. You think you could go up against an officer? A Master? Even just a Journeyman?"

"I can't do nothing," MacEoghan repeated.

Micah opened his mouth to speak, but before any words came out, they were pulled into a Fast Band. They turned to see Sean approaching.

"Decided to change things up on me, did you?" he asked lightly. "I was just about to give up for tonight, figured maybe you were doing other things, and then I thought, 'I need to go up and take a look around, just in case.' Lo and behold, here you are."

"Sean, are you sure there are no rules for Time on the battlefield?" Micah asked.

For a moment, Sean did not answer, apparently caught off-guard by the question. Then, "The Time industry is too big to make such blanket rules. It's left up to each species or each planet. Because Earth is Unengaged, there is no good way to establish such rules and enforce them."

"Why not make a rule that says, 'Don't use Time on the battlefield'?" MacEoghan wondered.

Sean raised a brow. "What do you think a battle is, exactly? Two armies lining up on the field to fight for king and country?" He shook his head. "It's not. Battle, especially these days, is burning villages, bombing cities, destroying bridges and infrastructure. When a city is a battlefield, should a man not be permitted to use Time to defend his family? Should a soldier not be permitted to use Time to save his brother in arms?"

MacEoghan shot his brother a look. Sean apparently caught it because he shifted his stance and said, "I have a feeling that at least one of you is up to something."

"And you're just being polite about which one of us it is," Micah stated.

"Are you going to tell me not to go, too?" MacEoghan asked.

Sean shifted his stance again. "It's a good and right thing to defend one's homeland. And under normal circumstances, I might even encourage it. But I think you are severely misinterpreting what battle is and overestimating how useful your Time abilities are going to be."

"But you've said that battlefields are huge honey pots for Harvesters and, more importantly, Runners. So we need to either protect the Harvesters or catch the Runners."

Sean frowned. "Why don't we go through tonight's training as usual? In the next few days, I'll see if I can't find someone who can help me open a blind portal. Then we'll take a little field trip to a battlefield so you can see just what war and battle is."

"A blind portal?" Micah questioned.

"Aye. The majority of portals go to the Wheel, and they're the easiest to open because the Wheel has the technology to carry them. But it is possible to open a portal directly from here to there, without needing to go through the Wheel. It is much more difficult, however, and I am not confident enough to do it on my own. At the very least, I'm not willing to risk your lives."

"So if a portal collapses when you're in the middle of it, you die?"

Sean shrugged. "There are theories about there being another in-between dimension, but seeing how no one has ever returned from this mythical dimension, it feels more honest to say, yes, you die."

Micah glanced at MacEoghan. Then they looked back at Sean.

"All right," MacEoghan said with a resigned sigh. "What is tonight's training?"

Sean studied them a moment longer, MacEoghan for two moments. Then, "We're going to start on External Banding. So far, we've been focusing only on standard Banding, that is, just yourself. It's a logical place to start, but if you want to—"

"I can already Band other people," MacEoghan interrupted.

"Without initially touching them?" Sean raised a brow.

Well, he hadn't done that, no. He'd always had to have a hand on Micah, but it couldn't be that hard, could it? It was just forming a Band and applying it to the two of them.

Not to be humiliated, MacEoghan put a Band up around himself. Micah and Sean hadn't been moving much, so the relative strength was a little difficult to tell, but the visual tint of the Band suggested it was about one hour inside to one minute outside—not the strongest, but good enough for the demonstration. He looked at his brother, resisting the habit of reaching out and touching him. And what was the point of that anyway? As boys, fine, they'd needed to stick close together. As adults, unnecessary, right? He knew what he was doing.

The physicality of a Band was difficult to describe except perhaps as a tight-fitting suit around the body, like the kind gymnasts at the circus might wear. It was intended and form-fitted for him and him alone. Even when he touched Micah, that suit stayed around the two of them with only the slightest expansion. He just needed to recreate the suit without any physical contact.

He would not admit this aloud, but he attributed his success only to sheer memory of what it was like to touch Micah and extend the Band. Turning his attention to Sean, he faltered.

"You can do it," Micah encouraged.

MacEoghan was uncertain. He knew Micah, knew how it felt to have Micah in the Band with him. He didn't know Sean especially well, hadn't touched him beyond a handshake once or twice. He was a stranger, really.

He couldn't let it slow him down. What if there was a real emergency on the fishing boat and his only option was to Band Padraig or one of his brothers? He needed to be able to do this. If he could do it the hard way, with a stranger, he could do it the easy way, with a family member. And if he did go off to fight in the war, he would have to be able to do it with a bunch of strangers with not a lot of time to think about it.

Still, he couldn't quite manage it. Just like the water distorted one's vision of fish or stones, he couldn't quite get a handle on Sean. Reluctantly, MacEoghan dropped the Band entirely.

"It was a valiant effort," Sean praised, gesturing emphatically. "You did successfully bring Micah into your Band without needing to touch him, and you were definitely trying to bring me into the Band as well. Don't think I didn't notice."

"It's like trying to catch fish with your hands," MacEoghan said, trying not to whine or show his dejection. "I know the water makes things appear to be where they're not, but I don't know how to compensate."

"That's all right; that's why we're here to learn and practice. And if you can get a handle on this, then we can spend a little more time going over some of the more mundane, logistical information. Then you'll be ready for your Apprentice review."

"Both of us?" Micah questioned. "So soon?"

Sean nodded. "The probationary period, while providing an introduction to the basic abilities, is a test of character, integrity, mental fortitude, and the ability to grasp the fundamentals of Timekeeping. It's a way of evaluating the likelihood of you yourselves turning Runner."

"You don't think we could?" MacEoghan wondered. He shrugged. "Just as a hypothetical."

"Anyone could. I've seen Masters turn Runner, but that usually has to do with prolonged politics and personal frustrations. For a probationary, well, how do you two respond to having the ability to manipulate Time? Considering that you—" He gestured to MacEoghan. "—have had these abilities for many years, even if you didn't understand what they were, it really speaks to your character. You're here for your brother. Maybe you get a little selfish in the boxing ring, but I can't say that I'm a saint with my abilities either. But your heart and your morals are in the right place for the job at hand."

MacEoghan didn't know how to take that, honestly. It was a compliment, and it sounded like a hefty one. Like Padraig's speech earlier, MacEoghan was just at a loss. Did he say thank you? Was he supposed to reply with some like compliment about Sean's mentorship? Was he supposed to deflect and say something nice about Micah? He looked at Micah, but his twin was already looking at him expectantly. He was supposed to say something, but he just didn't know...what.

"Thank you," he managed finally.

Sean nodded once and moved on. MacEoghan slowly let out a sigh of relief.

Because of the Banding, it was difficult to say just how long the training actually lasted. What was certain was that neither brother felt like they had made much progress. They could Band themselves and they even managed to be able to Band each other with minor pauses and delays and a few misfires which could be worked out with practice. But Banding Sean was a little more difficult and neither of them were able to do it by the end of the session. Whether it was because he was a stranger to them or he was intentionally resisting them somehow, they could not say. MacEoghan had come close, but then the fish slipped away, the water distorting his perception.

"We'll try again in a few days," Sean promised them, the only one who seemed optimistic. "Keep working at it with each other, and don't be afraid to try it out on other things, preferably inanimate objects or animals."

"Can animals learn to use Time?" Micah wondered.

"Unfortunately, no. They can be exposed to that degree, but it usually drives them insane so they have to be put down. But, you never know, maybe it will help with your fishing endeavors."

The three of them parted ways. By the time MacEoghan and Micah got home, it was near time for bed.

"Where do you two wander off to?" Sarah wondered, her tone curious rather than accusing. "Some nights you just seem to disappear."

"That's a secret of being twins," MacEoghan said before Micah could open his mouth.

"Is it now?" Her tone and expression said she knew he was brushing her off, but it was no great concern yet. "Well, I suppose the rest of us peasants will just have to wonder."

"I suppose you will."

MacEoghan and Micah headed down to their room. As MacEoghan sat down on his bed, Shay appeared in the doorway, looking mischievous.

"So where do you go, really?" he asked, grinning.

"Like I told Mum, it's a twin secret," MacEoghan replied, shrugging.

"Oh, come on," the teenager begged. "You can tell me!"

"You're not a twin," Micah informed him.

"Please!"

MacEoghan made a shooing motion. "No. Now get your own self to bed."

Shay wandered off, but MacEoghan had a suspicion that he was still hiding within earshot. Before he could do anything, Micah had Banded himself. After a few seconds of struggling, he brought MacEoghan in as well.

"A twin secret?" Micah wondered, raising a brow.

MacEoghan matched him. "What were you going to tell them?"

"I don't know. A walk around town?"

"You know Mum would think we were out seeing girls, and she'd want to know which ones."

"You know she thinks that already, she just wants us to admit to it."

MacEoghan waved a hand dismissively. "Enough out of you, go to bed."

Micah laughed and dropped the Band. They got ready for bed and slunk under their respective blankets.

BREDAVAD
OLDER BROTHER

It didn't take two days for MacEoghan to be able to Band both himself and Micah with ease. Micah got the hang of it, too, eventually. Being able to Band each other without needing to touch made it much easier to hold private conversations or relay important information. This was especially useful when they were out fishing. On rough days, they needed to be able to communicate amid wind and waves and little brothers. On calm days, it was taboo to talk too much or too loud. Banding let them circumvent both situations.

About six days after that training, MacEoghan and Micah were just getting up and around for another early morning of fishing when they were suddenly swept up in a suffocatingly strong Fast Band. A moment later, Sean walked in their room.

"You'll pardon the lack of social graces," he began, "but there is something rather important I need to show you."

MacEoghan glanced at his brother, but they followed him out of the house. Once outside, they were introduced to another man, a Norwegian Timekeeper.

"There's been an incident in Denmark," Sean explained. "I don't know that it could be classified as a battle now, but the early morning surprise might give you a taste of what war is." He gestured to the Norseman. "Hedvig here will assist with the blind portal. It is imperative that you go through just as soon as we tell you."

There wasn't a lot of room to argue, and neither twin said anything.

MacEoghan remembered the strain Sean had displayed when he opened a portal to the Wheel, the near-physical pain he appeared to have experienced. Seeing that again, but worse, in two men, MacEoghan began to wonder.

The portal sputtered open like a shorted wire, and the best that either Sean or Hedvig could do was motion for them to hurry through. MacEoghan ducked through dutifully, followed by Micah. The two Masters hardly waited for them to get all the way through before they, too, pushed their way in. MacEoghan, struck in the back by a falling Micah, stumbled forward, catching himself on a low wall. Micah landed in the grass beside him, and Sean and Hedvig went face-first into a brick walkway.

As MacEoghan straightened and got his head on straight, he saw everything was tinted red. Somehow, not only had the two Masters opened the portal to this location, but erected a Fast Band on the other side also. No one at home would miss them, and no one here would notice them.

Looking around, MacEoghan discovered that they had landed in some kind of garden in someone's backyard. What it grew was anyone's guess as it was apparently still too early to plant. Prep work had begun, however. Old winter mulch was in the process of being turned under; tools were being dusted off, cleaned, and sharpened; and trellises, climbing wires, and guides were in the process of being erected. The wall that surrounded the yard was partly stone and brick, and partly wrought iron. The house itself looked to have been quite old—not that MacEoghan was any judge of historical architecture—yet maintained so that it may as well have been almost new.

But this little plot of paradise was wholly disrupted by the soldiers hiding behind the stone portion of the wall. They looked tired and disheveled in the gray dawn light, and he was just able to make out the embel of a Danish flag MacEoghan followed their line of sight down the road leading out of town, squinting in the haze. Armored cars and panzer tanks rumbled up the road, flanked by motorbikes, bicycles, and soldiers on foot. Craters in the area suggested that some fighting had already occurred, the Danish forces falling back, perhaps looking for better cover in the gardens of this otherwise quiet village.

"What's going on?" Micah wondered dumbly, looking like he was struggling against a headache. MacEoghan could relate.

"The Germans began their invasion early this morning," Hedvig answered when Sean could or would not. "Norwegian intelligence thinks they are trying to capture Denmark in order to launch an invasion on Norway."

"And you're part of Norwegian intelligence?" MacEoghan inquired, looking at the man. The two were of a height, but Hedvig had a kind of natural bulk to him that MacEoghan could only work to achieve.

"That's not your business."

"Why does Germany care about Norway?"

"Iron, and other commodities."

MacEoghan looked back at the Danes. They were wide-eyed and terrified, fueled only by fear and adrenaline seeing how their sleep had been forfeited. With exception of a handful who might have been in charge, every single one couldn't have been over twenty-five.

"Where are we?" MacEoghan asked.

"Bredavad," Hedvig answered. He gave its geographical location relative to other places MacEoghan had never heard of. The Norseman gestured around. "A little nothing town, with only little nothing boys fresh from bootcamp to defend it."

MacEoghan looked at Sean. "We could help them." When Sean hesitated and looked to reply, he pressed on. "Right here, right now, in this Band. Go over there, disable all the armored cars, disable the tanks. Kill the soldiers, too, if we wanted. We could do it." He gestured to the nearest Dane, a boy who couldn't have been older than fourteen. "He doesn't have to fear for his life; he can grow up and marry and have children one day."

Sean frowned and made a motion. "Follow me."

MacEoghan sighed and stuttered through a few more vague reasons and statements, but ultimately followed, Micah behind him, Hedvig bringing up the rear. There was a certain rigidity in his stride, a seriousness about his countenance, that suggested he had to be Norwegian intelligence.

Walking through the town gone silent in the middle of an invasion was more than eerie. MacEoghan felt the skin on his arms prickle with unease. He couldn't quite pinpoint it except he had the sneaking suspicion they were being watched. Not simply by eyes blind to how fast they were moving, but as if someone were here in the Band with them.

They approached the German advance, veering off the road as if they might still be struck by the vehicles. Sean paused in the middle of a group of bicycle soldiers. He gestured to them.

When MacEoghan looked, he saw that many were also young. Sixteen, seventeen, eighteen, eyes wide and sleep-deprived, not unlike the Danes.

"Are you going to save him, too?" Sean wondered. "You think he cares about Denmark, about being here? Or do you think he was woken up at some godawful hour, told to grab his gun, grab his bike, and head out? You think he doesn't have a girl waiting for him at home?"

"With blond hair and blue eyes no doubt." MacEoghan touched his beard, somewhat scruffy, which he knew to be an atrocious conglomeration of red, brown, and blond.

Now Hedvig spoke with a mild shrug. "Der Führer views the Danes as pure Aryans, has been wanting to ally or annex them for years. Honestly, he'll probably treat them well, comparatively speaking. Might make an ally of them yet."

MacEoghan could feel his brother's gaze. "Fine. So let Germany and Denmark fight it out between themselves. Or fight together. But I fight for Ireland."

"But Ireland isn't fighting," Sean reminded him. "And Britain isn't going to fight for Ireland; they would sooner invade Ireland themselves again if they thought it beneficial to their cause."

"Everyone has a reason, but you have to pick a side!" MacEoghan declared, frustrated. He made a wild gesture and walked away several steps to another bicycle soldier. This one was older, his eyes glinting with experience and resolve, but he was peeking at a picture of a woman that was attached to his rifle. Brown hair, brown eyes, two children by her side.

"You're right, MacEoghan," Sean said behind him. "Right here, right now, in this Band, we could help them. Denmark, Germany, Allies, Axis. We could kill them all if we wanted. We could disable the vehicles and send every single German right back to Berlin. And then what?"

MacEoghan growled to himself and turned to face Sean. "Did you stay out of the Civil War, too? What about the Anglo-Irish War? Did you at least fight for Éire independence?"

"At least that was for Éire," Sean replied hotly. "That was directly for our people. This..." He looked around. "We're in Denmark standing in the middle of a bunch of Germans."

MacEoghan pointed. "Then why is Hedvig here? More than just a good Timekeeper who can open a blind portal, he's here because a German advance puts his people in jeopardy." Sean flinched. "Britain would love to invade us, I know. But the Germans want to invade Britain, and then who are we?"

"If Britain had stayed out of things, it wouldn't even be an issue."

"Well, they didn't, and it is." A new thought occurred to him. "Unless you want the Germans to invade."

"It would certainly teach the British a lesson," Sean growled.

MacEoghan huffed in disbelief and turned around several times. Tanks, cars, bicycles, soldiers everywhere, all converging on some tiny town in the south of Denmark. Somewhere in the back of his mind, he still felt like they were being observed. He looked back at Sean. "So which side would you choose to help? Danish or German?"

"I have no argument with the Danes," the man replied levelly.

"That wasn't my question. Would you choose the Danish or the Germans?"

"Éire is neutral," Sean insisted.

"You would side with the Germans."

"I side with Éire! I side with our people!"

"But if Ireland were to join the Allies—"

Sean cut in with a stomp of his foot. "Damn you, MacEoghan, I'm trying to keep you out of the war if at all possible!"

MacEoghan raised a brow. "But if I were siding with the Germans, if only because they're fighting the British, you wouldn't be trying so hard. If I were fighting for your cause, it would be all right." He shifted his stance. "I'm going to place a bet that you were an Anti-Treaty IRA. Tell me, did you kill any Pro-Treaty men? How is that helping Éire if you're killing your own people?"

Now Sean suddenly calmed, his face going white. "You were too young to appreciate the wars. Be glad for your schooling then."

MacEoghan paced several steps, acutely aware of Micah and Hedvig watching them. "So what are we supposed to do? Kill the Danes? Kill the Germans? Go back home and pretend like none of this ever happened?"

Sean took a breath, his color returning. "I'm only your Timekeeper Master. As I've said, there are no real rules governing the use of Time outside of official business. This was intended to be an object lesson, a way to dissuade you from jumping into war just because you can pull off a few party tricks."

MacEoghan glanced around nonchalantly. "I don't see anyone here using Time. And again, if I agreed with your politics, you would have no problem with it."

Sean took an even breath, then grabbed a rifle from the loose grip of a nearby soldier. "You keep trying to make this about me. But it's you making the decision." He held the gun out to MacEoghan. "Let's see how much of a problem you have with it. Here's a German, and you know where the Danes are. Pick your side. Pull the trigger. Then do it again and again and again and again and again. When you've exhausted the ammo in that gun, well, there are plenty more around. Kill one side or both sides, do it with rage or in cold blood, I don't care."

MacEoghan stared at the gun for a second before snatching it out of Sean's hand. He'd never held a gun before. It was heavier than he expected. And cold, too, in the early morning hour.

An image flashed through his mind. Brother Andrew, lying in his bed, his male member missing, a rod shoved into his nether region, but the blood not yet flowing. Eventually he would succumb to the wounds, though MacEoghan hadn't known that until later. He had killed a man. He still fully believed that Brother Andrew deserved it. Had he known the man would die anyway, he might have done a little more, just to make sure the pedophile suffered as much as possible.

The image in his mind began to morph, including all the little details he wished would happen and had learned later. Brother Andrew came screaming awake, his groin and anus spurting blood. He writhed and thrashed as other Brothers ran into the room, wondering what was happening. One party of men was sent to find the perpetrator while another party hurried to reach the doctor who lived in town many miles away. Brother Andrew died, drenched in blood, clutching for something that was no longer there, something he had used as a terrible weapon to hurt so many boys.

196

MacEoghan blinked, trying to clear the image from his head. He shifted his stance to focus on the German soldier in front of him. Twenty-five, maybe a little older. The woman in the picture was probably the same age or close enough. The children in the picture were not yet six years old, the same age he had been when he and Micah had been orphaned. Was this man a good father? Was he teaching his children about being good Aryans?

Only if he returned. Maybe he would survive the day, maybe not, but in this moment, MacEoghan could make that decision. He could decide whether this boy, this man, this soldier, this Nazi, lived or died. He could decide this man's fate, at least for the moment. If MacEoghan decided to let him live, well, there was no saying that the Danes wouldn't do him in anyway.

In Denmark. In the middle of a bunch of Germans. So far from home it took a blind portal to get here with any speed.

He looked at Hedvig. Not his country either, but if Germany took Denmark, it was only a short hop over to Norway. Germany wanted to make an ally of Denmark, these supposedly pure Aryans, and they were still invading. Germany was actively at war with Britain, hadn't said much about where the Brits and her neighbors stood in the racial pyramid. Britain would not fare so well if they were invaded. They already weren't faring well with the bombings.

Dublin, Baile Átha Cliath, had been bombed. Only a few planes who had wandered off course in bad weather on their way to London or Belfast, the Germans said. Even paid for some of the reconstruction as a sort of apology.

Belfast, Béal Feirste, and North Ireland were as Irish as Ireland. Germany only targeted them because they were under control of Britain. But then, those Irish wanted to be British. Was it a bit of poetic justice, then, letting them know the consequences of their actions?

Did that mean Sean was right? Was it better to sit back and let things happen, let Britain suffer the consequences of her arrogance?

Denmark had had a treaty with Germany. The Germans broke it. How long until they decided to ignore Ireland's declaration of neutrality? How long until Ireland could no longer passively observe this "emergency" because they were suddenly engaged in an actual war? And who would be able to stand alone against the whole of the Third Reich?

MacEoghan continued to study the man before him, weighing the gun in his hand. Was he going to kill just this one, or all of them? Could he really go it alone? Hedvig might help, if only in the interest of protecting his country and people, but Sean and Micah wouldn't. He looked around. Despite never being in such a situation before, he knew this was only a small force. A small force coming to take a small town. If this was an invasion, it was not what MacEoghan had in mind to overthrow a whole country. There had to be more units in other areas, maybe parachuting into bigger cities. Considering the landscape of the country, the bulk of the invasion was probably taking place at sea.

Did he plan on killing everyone here, then going from town to town looking for the rest of the invasion and doing the same? Was he going to scour the European countryside looking for Germans to kill? Was he really going to be a one-man army? Even if he did find a few Timekeepers to help him, were they really going to take down the Axis by themselves? In the name of what? Their respective countries? God? Something else? Would it make them heroes, or just murderers? No one would understand what they did, why they felt it necessary.

He raised the gun to the man's head, trying to muster up some kind of anger or motivation. He wanted to help. He wanted to defend Éire from those who would do her harm, be they British or German. But here he was. Actively looking for trouble. In Denmark, hundreds or thousands of miles away. In the middle of a bunch of German boys who got woken up at a tragic hour, told to grab their guns, grab their bikes, and move out.

Several things happened at once, and not in the correct order, or so his mind said. First, the gun dropped to the ground of its own volition. No, he had released it intentionally. Flinched. He flinched. Burning pain began working its way up his arm. Once it got past his elbow, his entire right side was engulfed in pain and he doubled over. A flash of light blinded him before he could figure out what was going on.

It took at least ten seconds for the spots to clear well enough for him to study his arm, although the sudden, growing nausea was making his assessment brief at best. Micah was immediately by his side.

"You've been shot," his twin said, eyes huge.

That was kind of what it looked like, MacEoghan thought. There was a rather unnatural hole in his arm and quite a bit of blood coming from it, although the pain seemed to be subsiding for the moment and he managed to get himself together. The best MacEoghan could manage was, "Oh."

Micah ripped a piece of the soldier's uniform and pressed it against the wound. "We should have Mum look at this, but she'll probably call a doctor."

MacEoghan blinked, his mouth forming words that his brain could not immediately comprehend. "And how the blazes are we going to explain it? We just got up. We're supposed to be going fishing in the bay, not getting shot in Denmark."

Micah tore another strip. "What do you want to do? Ask the Danes for help? Ask the Germans?"

MacEoghan wasn't fond of the sight of his own blood, yet he couldn't look away. It was fascinating, almost mesmerizing. This was coming from his own body. Normally it was supposed to be inside, under his skin, but here it was.

Then the pain really hit and he went to a knee. Greater than before when it had been simply a reflex, his body telling him something had happened, now this was his body letting him know in no uncertain terms that something was very wrong. His hand and fingers stiffened, unwilling to even twitch for fear of increasing the agony. He let out a delayed cry of pain and hot tears snaked down his cheeks unbidden.

He wouldn't say he'd never been struck in the boxing ring, had never broken a bone in his life. God knew he'd taken plenty of physical punishment from the Brothers. This went far beyond that. He could not describe it for he had never experienced anything like it before, and he wasn't of a well enough mind to be thumbing through a mental thesaurus for anything more than "painful."

He knew when someone approached, knew from the shoes that it was Sean, but he did not look up even as Sean knelt beside them.

"Does the Wheel have a hospital of some kind?" Micah demanded.

Sean made a sound to the negative. "Too many alien species, no one wants to be responsible for all of them, and no one wants to be experimented on by something that isn't their own kind."

"So what do we do? We're supposed to be fishing at home, not getting shot in Denmark," Micah said, echoing MacEoghan's sentiments.

"Don't worry, there's a doctor who can help. Hedvig and I are going to fetch him now."

"What happened?" MacEoghan gasped. Speaking it aloud somehow brought some clarity back to his mind and he looked around. "Who shot me?"

"A German," Sean told him curtly. "A German Time Agent. Hedvig took care of him, don't worry. You just sit tight and we'll bring the doctor to you." He shifted his kneeling posture. "Micah, I'm going to hand the Band off to you."

"Me?" Micah questioned.

"Your brother isn't capable right now." Sean stood. "It won't be but a moment, I promise."

If Micah said anything more, Sean did not pay him any mind. MacEoghan felt the Band wobble and waver as his brother took over control from Sean and Hedvig. How much time was lost in that wobble and waver? Sounds were distant and fuzzy to MacEoghan, but when he managed to chance a look around, it did not appear that anything had changed. Maybe it was just him.

"Still think you want to run off to fight?" Micah demanded of him, his tone partly worried and partly accusing. "You couldn't kill a man and a man nearly killed you. And this is about as controlled as you're going to get. If this Band weren't here—"

"Shut up," MacEoghan hissed.

"I don't know how Time is going to fix this either," his twin went on, heedless. "A bloody nose always stops bleeding. A broken arm can be Banded to heal once set. I don't think Time can perform surgery."

"We don't know what Time can do at the higher levels," MacEoghan growled through gritted teeth.

Truthfully, deep down, MacEoghan was very afraid that was the exact case, that there was something Time couldn't do. It had served him well in his life and it seemed like such an amazing thing, almost limitless in its application. Well, he may have just found one of those limits.

Three figures appeared around them: Sean, Hedvig, and a third man he did not know.

"MacEoghan, this is Doctor Haunstein," Sean introduced.

"A German?" MacEoghan asked. "Or a Jew?"

"An old blood Swiss," the new man, Haunstein, answered, his accent well proving his statement. "The one who has control over how your arm heals—or doesn't."

He did not wait for MacEoghan to react, apologize, or invite him to examine his arm. Rather, he helped himself to the injured appendage, ignoring MacEoghan's yelp of pain while Hedvig intercepted the reactionary flying fist.

"Not horrible," the doctor determined, "but still not a good thing." With one hand, he held MacEoghan's arm. With the other hand, he rummaged around in his doctor's bag. "A shot of heroin should take the edge off the pain enough for me to work without needing armed security at the ready."

The heroin did something all right, MacEoghan thought, feeling every part of his body relax. It started out well enough, the pain subsiding enough that he could think and look around and take in his surroundings. Then it kept going, his alertness fading away again, but in a more pleasant manner. He wasn't completely out of his mind, but he was far less concerned about what Haunstein was doing to him.

A voice in the back of his mind said he probably should care more. Just because Haunstein was Swiss didn't mean he wasn't a Jew. There was a reason Ireland was refusing Jewish refugees, and it wasn't just to avoid Germany's ire.

Apparently, however, his drugged voice was just as strong as his drunk voice, because his sober voice was again dismissed. He could generally feel Haunstein working, although Micah blocked any kind of view. Was the man digging out a bullet? Repairing bone? Stitching muscle and skin? Did MacEoghan really want to watch any of that? Considering how he'd felt when he'd witnessed his own blood bubbling up from the wound, maybe not.

Then the mild lethargic fuzz began to recede from his brain. He became alert just as if waking from a nap. At some point, he reached an invisible threshold because it was like he'd been shot anew, fresh fire searing through his arm. He barked in pain and cradled his arm, but as soon as it had come, it had gone. His arm didn't hurt, and there wasn't even any residual blood on his skin. There was no hole, no bone, no tissue, no blood, no stitches, and only the faintest hint of a tiny scar. He flexed his hand, twisted his wrist, twisted his elbow. Pain had waned into pins and needles, and then it was gone.

"Good as new," Haunstein declared, looking no happier for it as he put his instruments back in his bag.

"What did you do?" MacEoghan asked, studying the pinpoint scar.

"Everything I would have done in a normal patient. I simply condensed the healing time between steps so that all steps could be completed in only a few minutes rather than weeks."

"Oh." He still did not look at the doctor.

"You're welcome," Haunstein said pointedly, grabbing his bag and standing. "May I recommend staying away from battlefields if you don't actually intend to fight?"

He did not wait for an answer, and Sean and Hedvig did not need to be prompted to open a portal to send the man back home.

MacEoghan still stared at his arm, at the place where he was fairly certain he'd been shot. Had that even happened? He remembered the pain, remembered the blood, but there was nothing. Nothing but a tiny scar that looked like it could have come from anywhere, but it was probably long ago when he was still a little boy getting into mischief. Certainly it wasn't from running around on a battlefield and being shot by a German. It had all happened so fast, couldn't have been more than ten minutes from start to finish.

He got to his feet, Micah by his side. Sean meandered his way over. MacEoghan decided the man's slight stagger was more from opening so many portals in a row rather than any attempt at being casual or smug.

"So, yes, there are Time Agents in war, on the battlefield," Sean said, breathing heavily. "They exist on both sides." He nodded slowly and looked around at the war scene still frozen around them. "Utilizing Time in war requires a much higher level of situational awareness than you are prepared for. I still can't say that I am fully prepared for such a thing as this, and yes, I did fight in the Civil War. And the Anglo-Irish War. Here, it was Hedvig who identified and apprehended the man even before the bullet was fully through your arm."

MacEoghan had spent years being beaten in order to feel guilt over crimes he had not committed. He was unaccustomed to feeling guilt for something he did do. Maybe he had gotten a little cocky about his abilities. Maybe he had underestimated just how powerful Sean and Hedvig were, how much more he still had to learn. It wasn't just about himself and one other man in a boxing ring anymore. This was an entire battlefield with hills, valleys, streets, houses, enemies out in the open and enemies hidden in places he would not have before imagined.

This was war. Hedvig was here to help Sean, but also to help his own country. He wasn't just out lackadaisically looking around and trying to prove something; he had a plan and a strategy in mind. Sean already had that experience. He might have questionable motives and loyalties, but if MacEoghan must make a decision, he was trying to ensure he didn't make a hasty one he would regret later.

These thoughts flitted through MacEoghan's mind as more vague impressions and mental and emotional revelations rather than word-for-word sentences. He studied his arm again to try and cover the worst of his humiliation.

"All right," he said quietly, lowering his arm. "Let's go home."

"Take a minute to look around a bit more," Sean told him, sitting down on a rock teetering on the edge of a crater. "I need to rest a moment before opening another blind portal."

"Does it ever get easier?" Micah wondered.

"'Easier' is a relative term," Hedvig answered. "Your brother is stronger than you, can probably do things you cannot. But even he has limits."

And if they wanted to stop reminding him of those limits, that would be great, MacEoghan thought, turning his back and pretending to survey the scene. He had a lot to learn. He understood that very well now. But that only made him more determined to better himself. Maybe this war would be over by the time he was ready to tackle something so chaotic, but if humanity did anything well, it was wage war. There would always be another.

The German force here wasn't very large, he noted, nor was the Danish defense anything noteworthy. But then, Bredavad wasn't exactly a bustling metropolis. It probably had, what, two or three thousand residents? For the Germans, it was just a pit stop on the way to somewhere larger and more consequential, likely Copenhagen. Studying the scene, there couldn't have been more than half a dozen dead between both sides, probably incidental only, maybe even friendly fire. The Germans didn't care about the Danes and the Danes didn't care about the Germans. They just didn't want to exist in the same place at the same time.

Would the Germans invade Ireland to get to Britain? Would it even really be an invasion or just a convenient landing spot? Would the British invade Ireland to keep it out of German hands? Would they let it go again after the war was over?

The Brothers had made it sound so simple in the classroom, a classroom blissfully insulated from the realities of the Anglo-Irish War and the Civil War. In the classrooms that they controlled, the Brothers always framed it as the United Kingdom on top of the world. Their needs were greater, their motives purer, the ends always justifying the means. Infighting was just something that happened, with no lasting consequences.

MacEoghan didn't know what to think. The Germans clearly thought the same thing. Their needs were greater, their motives purer, the ends justifying the means. They needed resources. Norway had those resources. Denmark was in the way. This was just a little infighting between two Aryan groups.

Britain and Germany were enemies, and Ireland was an asset and liability for both. MacEoghan glanced at his arm, the scar that almost didn't exist. The needs of the Irish were best served in neutrality.

He felt no deep, soul-searching conviction in this line of thought, but it made more sense now.

"This is only a tiny glimpse into war," Sean said, walking up behind him. "One small skirmish in a country people barely remember exists, a handful of men on each side, and you are staring at what amounts to a single picture. If we had the time, I'd drop this Band so you could just how fast and slow it moves."

"That's an oxymoron," MacEoghan remarked.

"And perfectly true. And I hope you never have to experience it the hard way." Sean shifted his stance. "We control Time through our will and a lot of discipline, but every man has some innate, watered-down, latent ability. If you were to talk to an average soldier, he would tell you about such-and-such a time when time seemed to slow down or come to a stop. Or when it went by so fast he had hardly blinked."

"He created a Band."

"Brief, undisciplined, unable to be replicated by his own sheer will, but yes. Sometimes it saves lives. Now imagine every soldier had the abilities you do. Imagine they had the abilities I do, or Hedvig." When MacEoghan did not answer, Sean continued, "Extended lives mean a lot more years to rejoice or regret. One comes more easily than the other."

MacEoghan still did not respond.

"Well, let's get you home." Sean patted him on the shoulder. "It will be a few more days before our next training; I expect you'll have a lot to think about in the next few days."

Now MacEoghan broke his silence, saying, "Think only, seeing how I can't tell anyone about this."

Sean gave him a look. "You have one."

With that, he made a few vague motions and everyone got in position, ready for a portal. As one sputtered to life, MacEoghan found himself wondering, not for the first time, about what would happen if the portal closed before they were all the way through. Death, most likely. Another dimension, Sean had postulated, not seriously. Something else? Who knew? Who was willing to risk himself to find out?

The portal became stable enough that Hedvig motioned for them to go. MacEoghan and Micah jumped through first. As MacEoghan stood and turned, he had just enough time to see Hedvig and Sean step back and deliberately close the portal, not coming through themselves, but remaining in Denmark.

And there they were, back in their bedroom, allegedly just woken up to go out for another ordinary day of fishing. The Band had disappeared with the two Masters, and for a long moment, the only sound was the hustle and bustle of the rest of the family getting ready for the day. MacEoghan looked at Micah. Micah looked at MacEoghan. It was as if they had never even left. Never gone to Bredavad, Denmark. Never investigated a battlefield. Never been given a gun and given a choice to kill. Never been shot. Never been healed.

"Did we really just do that?" Micah whispered.

MacEoghan studied his arm. That tiny scar was still there. "I think so." He straightened and shifted his stance, trying to acclimate himself to his new yet familiar surroundings. "And we're just supposed to go fishing?"

Micah blinked and shook his head in disbelief as he slowly straightened and cracked some joints. "I think so."

How?

Ireland's needs are best served by its neutrality, MacEoghan told himself, unsure if he believed it. *We're serving our people by fishing, keeping them fed while the rest of Europe is in shambles, rationing everything from fuel to grain. We declare, we get involved, we take on all of their problems. Their problems become our problems. Hunger is not one of our problems, nor should it be.*

"We fish," MacEoghan stated, answering a question he knew had not been asked aloud.

Such motivation only lasted for a couple of days. MacEoghan kept his head down and worked hard, helping to haul in more fish than any other boat. Padraig praised him well enough, called him a good luck charm, then sent him out on the truck, telling him to keep up the luck and get them some good prices. And maybe make it so the trucks didn't use so much fuel. MacEoghan just said he would do his best.

It was on the start of the route that day, two mornings after traveling to Bredavad, that MacEoghan learned that Denmark had surrendered to the Germans. Germany had indeed launched a number of invasion points by air, land, and sea, including Copenhagen itself, and taken the country within just a few hours.

Sean had been right, MacEoghan reflected. There was nothing he could have done. Even if he had killed every German in Bredavad, it wouldn't have mattered in the grand scheme of things. He would have had to have held a Band, traveled the entire country—including going out to sea—and defeated every single invading force. Killed every single soldier, or at least three-quarters of them probably. Could he do that? He thought of the gun Sean had given him, told him to kill the man who was looking at a picture of his wife and children. Could he kill a defenseless man in cold blood?

But this was war. This was the nature of war.

But Ireland wasn't involved. The needs of Ireland were best served with neutrality. If Ireland was neutral, and if it was right, he should align himself accordingly.

But what if it wasn't right? Would he know before it was too late?

Thousands of Irish soldiers had gone to fight with the Allies anyway. The newspapers and common folk called them cowards at best, traitors at worst, demanded they be court martialed and even executed upon their return. But were the soldiers really wrong? One man might not do much, but a hundred, a thousand, ten thousand could. But what if their involvement jeopardized Ireland overall?

"You look deep in thought, lad," the driver observed as they pulled into the next town and made their way to the market.

"Why Denmark?" MacEoghan wondered.

The driver shrugged. "Hitler's had an eye on them for a while, I think. Calls them 'true Aryans,' or so I hear. But they weren't interested in anything more than non-aggression. Well, I guess he didn't like that, and the man has a knack for getting what he wants."

"What if he decides he wants Ireland?"

The driver made a noise that was somewhere between a scoff and a laugh. "Britain wants Ireland more than Germany does. I'd be watching the east more than the south if you catch my meaning."

MacEoghan did catch his meaning, and he elected to say nothing more about it. He didn't know what reaction he expected to get, or what he was trying to do beyond pick a brain for ideas or opinions. He wasn't trying to start trouble, rally men to his side for a cause. He didn't know what that cause would be. The Irish government had declared neutrality as the best course of action. The IRA was more than willing to defend the homeland and take the fight to the Brits if necessary, but they had neither the interest nor the manpower nor the resources to side with the Allies or the Axis.

So what did he want? Ireland was safely neutral, probably one of if not the most well-off country in Europe right now. He could endure the same mild hardships and inconveniences as everyone else with no problem. If he wanted to fight for Britain, well, they weren't going to say no. If he wanted to fight against Britain, the IRA would be more than happy to have him.

He didn't know. He just didn't know. One war, three avenues. Which one did he pick that he wouldn't regret? Was there any way to know? Regardless of their great skill, Sean had said on several occasions, Time only moved forward. There was no going back and changing things.

They continued their route. Most places, if Denmark was mentioned at all, brushed it off as best they could. It was Europe's problem. It was their emergency. Not war, Emergency. By the middle of the afternoon, people had determined—whether through news or their own logic—that Denmark would be fine. It was Norway that Germany was after. They just needed Danish ports. The people would be fine. MacEoghan wondered how true that was, wondered if there might be a way to find out, wondered why he was so concerned.

He couldn't be concerned. Ireland was neutral. The Emergency was on the mainland. If something happened to Ireland, he was more than able and willing to do whatever it took to defend her. But only Ireland.

The route finished, they returned the truck and went their separate ways. MacEoghan returned home where Sarah was just setting out plates at the table while the children all got themselves cleaned up.

"Far be it from me to look a gift horse in the mouth," Padraig began upon seeing MacEoghan, "but I think my good luck charm needs to be a little less lucky."

"Why is that?" MacEoghan washed his hands and sat at the table.

"Jacob and Marcus aren't paying their bills. They don't get the same rations we do and they can't deliver their goods like they used to. They're falling behind."

"So we redistribute to the other markets and vendors."

Padraig shook his head. "Supply and demand. People can only stand so much fish, and when there's a surplus, they want a discount. They get too many discounts, we make no money." He talked over MacEoghan as he started to protest. "We're not going to starve them or price them out of house and home. Absolutely not. But for as privileged as we are to get fuel rations, those rations are expensive. Plus we have to ensure everyone gets paid. More fish, more sorting, more processing, more driving, all of it costs money." Padraig shook his head. "Like I said, we're not going to starve the people or demand they hand over their gold and silver. We just have to cut back a little in order to better balance the supply and demand."

MacEoghan frowned but did not reply. He knew Padraig was right; he glanced at the accounting books a time or two. Still, it felt...unfair. Ireland was neutral. So far, both sides had no problem with that. Still they had to adjust their lives because of the war. Could they hope for a speedy end to the war? And which side would be better to win?

FATHER AND SON
YOUNGER BROTHER

All the power to manipulate Time in order to catch more fish or help the business in other ways, and it didn't do a thing for the economy, Micah thought as they returned to the dock. They could have caught so much more, but circumstances just didn't allow them to seize the opportunity. Some of their clients had fallen behind on payments—not just to the fishermen, but to other industries also. The rationing was beginning to spread from fuel to other goods, almost all of them due to the price of fuel or having to import past naval blockades, wartime tariffs, and other threats.

So, yes, the fish was local, caught just off the coast. The fishermen were good, loyal, hardworking Irishmen. Very little about the job itself was dependent on foreign entities. Except for the fuel.

They tied off and started unloading the catch of the day. It could have been so much more, Micah thought. They should have been able to send out all of the trucks and stocked their clients' shelves or booths so full, they wouldn't know what to do with it. And the people would come and buy the fish, a smile on their faces as they fed their families well that day without any concern for whatever was going on over in the mainland.

The fish offloaded, swiftly processed, just as hastily sorted, and packed in ice, MacEoghan jumped in a truck. Micah watched him go. They used to trade off on trucks; now they traded off on days while most of the delivery trucks sat quietly in the warehouse. Just a few loads of fish. Hardly felt worth the effort to get out of bed in the morning.

Micah turned to leave with his younger brothers when Padraig called to him. He turned back around to see his father standing in the door of the office. The man waved him over and Micah made his way, stomach twisting in knots over what more bad news he was about to hear.

It wasn't until he was in the office—taking a seat as Padraig bade while he himself sat behind his desk—that Micah considered that any news about the business ought to be shared either at home or during afternoon chores, when everyone could hear it and give input.

"This is new," Micah observed. "Is something wrong?"

Padraig sighed and shook his head awkwardly. "That's an odd question to be asking in times like these. Of course something's wrong; the whole world's gone straight to Hell while we stand here hoping nobody notices us." He sighed again, but his expression changed into something slightly more optimistic. "But I don't want to talk about the political state of affairs. I want to talk about the business, specifically the future of the business."

"Sir?" Micah's stomach churned uneasily around a sudden rock. "Are we closing up shop?"

His father shook his head confidently. "No, nothing like that. I know we're all feeling the strain, but our straits are not so dire." He shifted position. "Maybe I'll just say it outright and avoid any confusion." He cleared his throat and shifted again. "I want you to take over the company."

Micah blinked, unsure he'd heard Padraig correctly.

"Well, come on," Padraig goaded. "Tell me what you think."

"Me?" Micah squeaked. "Why?"

"For one, you're the oldest—"

"Technically, MacEoghan is older. He's always loved reminding me of it."

His father's expression turned very frank. "MacEoghan has had his life planned out his own way for quite a while, before your mother took you in. This here for him is only a temporary stay. I think you know this as well as I do. He's got other ambitions. And even if he weren't so unsettled here, he's more aggressive in his approach to things. Anything at all, he prefers brute force over your patience. Fishing is a matter of patience. Business, however hectic it can get, is a matter of patience, thinking things through, analyzing them, and being forceful if necessary. And your schooling has gifted you with a proficiency in letter and number that I could only dream of."

Micah could only stare at the man. Was he hearing this right? It wasn't as though anything his father said was untrue. MacEoghan did kind of have his life planned out, even if that plan was as vague as "not fishing" and "maybe boxing." Micah couldn't say that he had any real plans for himself. Wake up in the morning, go fishing, do his chores, help out the family as best he could. He couldn't say that he was craving any major ambitions.

"If there's any area where you might need a little guidance," Padraig went on, "it's standing up for yourself and being just a little more assertive. You're good at it when it comes to saving life and limb, but you're a bit limp when it comes to any other kind of confrontation. I figure that giving you a little more responsibility and some guidance over time, we can get you where you need to be."

"What if I can't?" Micah wondered. "Or what if I don't want to?"

His father frowned as if disappointed. Then, "Well, then I suppose I would have a talk with Shay about it, perhaps sooner rather than later. I've no need to turn over the company right now or even in the next couple years, but I would very much like to have everything ready for when the day comes. Maybe I'll step down and just do the fishing without the extra business stuff, maybe I'll fall overboard in a storm, or maybe I won't give it up until the Lord pries me off this earth, who knows? You know how I got this business, don't you?"

Micah knew very well, but Padraig saw fit to recount the tale again anyway. "My da and his da were fishermen, just them and me and my three brothers in our time. We had one boat, a few lines, and a few nets. We provided for this town and no one else, got us through a lot of war and strife. It was my next younger brother who was the ambitious one, especially in the wake of the Great War, wanted to turn it into a proper business. Problem was, no one really knew how and my granddad didn't like the idea. My da could barely read or write, did all his figures in his head and he still wasn't very good at it. My brother was a little better, but not as good as he thought he was. After my granddad passed, they got the business grown up a little, bought a truck or two, started delivering. Then a storm came in and swept them both out to sea. Never saw them again. The business fell to me. I didn't hardly know what I was doing, but somehow I got things under control and grew it into what it is today."

"And what do you expect me to do with it?" Micah asked.

Padraig shrugged. "Whatever you want. The first order of business for either of us is keeping it afloat during this Emergency we've got going. After that, we can talk about growing it back to what it was when you first arrived and then growing beyond that. Or maybe you want to be like my granddad and keep things local."

"There are too many fish in the sea for that," Micah said. "It would be too easy for other fishing companies to come in and roll right over us with cheaper prices for larger catches."

His father nodded, expression thoughtful and proud. "As I said, you're quick with your numbers. And you're absolutely right. It's hard to be a little fish in a big ocean."

"But being the biggest fish isn't the best idea either. If something happens to the big fish, all of the fish suffer for it."

Padraig continued to nod. "You are absolutely correct. Again." He made a vague gesture. "See? You're good. You'd be good in business."

Micah wanted to believe him, couldn't help but bask in the praise just a little. It just felt...misplaced.

His father seemed to pick up on this as he stood and said, "Well, I don't need an answer today. Think it over a little, see if running a fishing business is really what you want to do. It's not what MacEoghan wants, and I respect that. That's why I'm not asking him. At the same time, I don't want to turn it over to someone who doesn't want it. If you don't want it, I'll ask Shay. If he doesn't want it, I'll ask Brendan. And on and on until maybe this business dies with me."

"It won't," Micah said, standing. "It's just easy to think that way when the whole world is going to Hell and we're here sitting in our fishing boat."

"You're not wrong." Padraig made a motion. "All right, out you go. You don't get to learn all of my business secrets until you want to learn them."

Micah couldn't help but grin as he turned and left. He didn't know what he was supposed to do with all of this. Take over the fishing business? He couldn't say it was a dream come true or something he had been aiming for, but even he knew it was a high honor. This wasn't something he could accept or reject on a mere whim. He would have a life career, a steady, worthwhile job where he could work hard, help his community, and raise a family.

His steps slowed as his thoughts veered off in another direction. Sean had said that most Timekeepers were afflicted with slowed aging. The more he and MacEoghan used Time, the slower they would age until it seemed to stop completely. Even just pursuing standard studies up to Master level would affect them in such a way. It didn't mean that they couldn't marry and have children, but they would far outlive their families. They would watch grandchildren and possibly even great-grandchildren die of old age before it even became a threat to them.

Could he really do that, then? Could he run a business for two hundred years? Unlikely. People would get suspicious eventually. Could he marry and have a family, then fake his own death, get washed out to sea perhaps? Maybe, physically, but emotionally? How could he abandon a family so heartlessly? Could he sell the business in the future? Well, there was always someone who would buy, most of them wealthy corporate men, many of them British. He didn't like the sound of that.

Maybe he could just tell Padraig he wasn't interested; give the business to Shay. Shay was a smart lad, good with his letters and numbers and knew his duties well on the boat. He was also more assertive than Micah without being as aggressive as MacEoghan. He would be a good businessman one day.

Unfortunately, that didn't solve Micah's sudden dilemma. What did he do with himself? Theoretically, he could do anything he wanted. Most men only got to live one life. He inherited or chose his profession or trade as a teenager or very young adult, and he typically stuck with that trade his whole life, barring some form of military service.

Micah, on the other hand, would have to change it up. Maybe he could pretend to look young for a while as he reached twenty and then thirty years old, but if his aging slowed so that it seemed to stop, could he really pass himself off as forty? Fifty would be a huge stretch. And over sixty would be impossible.

Padraig wasn't the most learned man; he had really only known this one life, and he just did the best he could. Sometimes he made mistakes. But he would never be accused of being rash or foolhardy. If anything, one might rightly accuse him of being too slow and careful, at least, when it didn't come to catching fish. Deciding whom to ask to take over his family business? He didn't just wake up that morning and decide to ask Micah, say it that way. Likely he had been thinking about it for a while, weeks or months. Maybe he had been considering it for many years and only just found the man he was looking for in Micah.

Micah couldn't let him down, didn't want to disappoint the man who had shown and given him so much.

Maybe the better option, then, was to give up Time. Let Sean Suppress him so he could more confidently take over the business. Time wasn't doing much for him anyway. Sure, it was fun to play pranks, and it had come in handy at times out on the boat, but it just wasn't the game changer he might have expected. Escaping from the Brothers, absolutely necessary. Living an honest life and working an honest trade, less necessary.

But what about the war? Micah thought back to Denmark. Had the Danes expected to ride it out like Ireland? What if the Germans came? What if the British came? Being able to Band to protect the family would be invaluable. Sure, MacEoghan might be around, but he also might not. He was more apt to go and fight, on the line, in the street, didn't matter. Micah would be tasked with their parents and siblings back home.

It seemed a long shot, though, however much they had to cut back on their fishing. The Germans were so close yet so far away, the British were waiting right next door, and here they were still just a little fishing town of no real importance.

And what about after the war was over? People would still need to eat, and someone had to catch the fish for them. Whatever the world looked like after this Emergency, Micah was willing to bet that Time would still be only a very small part of it. Other than Sean, Hedvig, Kearney and Kane, and that one Timekeeper on the battlefield, they'd had no real contact with any part of the Time industry. They hadn't encountered any Harvesters, Merchants, or Runners of any kind. Sean assured them that they were out there, but the war was making things challenging.

What wasn't challenging, at least not in the same way, was fishing and business. Normal things for a normal life. MacEoghan might want to become a boxer or chase Runners or do whatever else that got his adrenaline up, but Micah was perfectly content with mundane business.

The next thing to do, then, would be to tell MacEoghan. That would obviously be tonight when they went to bed. How was his twin going to take it? Micah had a sneaking suspicion it wasn't going to go as well as he might hope. MacEoghan either wasn't going to care at all, or else he was going to somehow take it as excruciatingly personal. Either reaction would hurt. Micah just wasn't sure how to make him understand.

Maybe he should think about it a little while. Padraig didn't rush his decisions, and he respected others who did the same. He might be offended if Micah were too quick with an answer. Maybe this was a kind of test.

Micah found himself grateful for the dull monotony of chores throughout the day that let him think and brood.

The word "Suppression" suggested that it could be undone later if he changed his mind. At the same time, he couldn't tell his father yes, he'd take over the business this year, and then give it back next year. That just wasn't how things worked. But what about in five years? Ten? No, that was dishonest. He made a decision, he stuck with it. That was called loyalty, integrity. Keeping his word to his father to manage the business—maybe even grow it bigger and better than ever—was honorable. It showed that he could be trusted and relied upon.

But what if he couldn't do it? What if he couldn't get the business to rebound after the Emergency? What if he couldn't get it to grow? Was letting it succumb to circumstance really any nobler than simply shutting it down intentionally? But then, was it really such a difficult business to begin with? If an illiterate could get it started and a not-so-learned man could grow it to what it was, surely someone with some learning and some experience could handle it well enough to keep it running. He didn't need it to be a massive enterprise, just a respectable size that could employ men to feed their families and provide a necessary commodity to the community. It couldn't be all that difficult, right?

Padraig made no mention of their conversation at all that day, whether at the supper table or in private. If he'd told Sarah—and there was no reason to think he hadn't—she also kept silent.

"So, what'd Pa tell you?" MacEoghan asked once they were safely in their room getting ready for bed.

"What?" Micah asked, wondering if he himself had accidentally said something.

MacEoghan gave him a look. "I saw you follow him into his office this morning after I got on the truck, and you've been distracted all day. What did he say?"

"Oh." Micah blinked. Was is that obvious? Lord, let him never have to rely on his own skill to have to lie his way out of something. "Um..."

"Well...?"

So much for thinking about it for a few days. "He said he wanted to turn the business over to me. Not right away, but train me up, like a partner, for a little while. Then, if something happened to him or when he was ready, he'd sign it over to me fully."

MacEoghan stared at him for several seconds, expression puzzled. Then, "Oh."

"I don't know if I should," Micah blurted. Several incoherent excuses and vague worries about Time came tumbling from his mouth.

MacEoghan's expression remained puzzled, but it was a different kind of puzzled. Finally, "Really?"

"Really what?"

His twin shrugged and looked around. "This is it? This is where and how you just want to be with your life? Don't you have any ambition? Any drive? Even a little bit of curiosity?" He did not wait for an answer. "We have the ability to live ten lives, a hundred lives, and you want to waste one on fish?" He continued, speaking over Micah. "If we have a hundred years to spend, spend one life as a fisherman, fine, but spend another life traveling the world. Spend another life doing whatever it is you want to do. And every life after that. Time is a gift, Micah. Don't waste it on fish."

"What about family?" Micah asked quietly. "Are you going to marry a new woman every ten or fifteen years? Are you going to have children with each wife? Are you going to abandon every family you ever had?"

"I've never abandoned you," MacEoghan shot back hotly. "If you want to stop and while away here, that's your business. If anything, I'd say that's you abandoning me."

They stared at each other, sharp words still hanging in the air.

"Go to bed," MacEoghan said finally.

"But—"

MacEoghan got under his blanket. "Just go to bed."

Micah followed suit, though he couldn't say he fell asleep right away. Even when he did sleep, it was not very well nor for very long. He would just start to dream, then suddenly jolt awake. He would roll around for a bit, then drift off again, only to repeat the process.

"You awake?" Micah inquired quietly. He had no idea what time it was, nor how long until it was time to get up.

For a long second there was no answer. Then there was a huff of a sigh and, from the darkness, "Aye, unfortunately."

"You want to Band each other so we get more sleep?"

"What do you care? You want to be a normal person. Mum and Pa don't get to Band each other when they can't sleep."

Micah sighed.

"I don't understand you, *a Mhicah*," MacEoghan said. "Is there nothing you want to do with your life? What were you going to do if we hadn't been taken in? What if we were still out and about, hm? What if I were a boxer? What if I did decide to join the war effort? Then what?"

"I don't know," Micah admitted. "But tell me this: what were you going to do with your life? Before you knew that our aging would slow and we could live these ten or one hundred lives, what were your plans?"

"I mean, before the war, boxing seemed a very likely avenue."

"Before the war? Or before Kearney and Kane?"

"Pretending that hadn't happened, boxing was still very likely."

"And if not? What if you weren't recruited? What if you were too injured?"

MacEoghan made an annoyed sound. "Questions are fine, but we can't plan for everything. I don't know, all right? Is that what you want to hear? I don't know exactly what I would have done, what I want to do. I just know that I can't stay here."

"Why?" Micah pressed. "What are you running towards? Or from? You want to travel the world, fine, that's a goal. You want to be a boxer, fine, that's a goal. But just running off into the horizon...I don't understand it."

"And I don't understand just idling away here. Aye, it's a nice view, a quiet life, with decent people, but there has to be more out there. There must be if the world is losing its mind over it. I want to see it, too."

Micah nodded even though his brother couldn't see. Heck, even with a mirror he himself wouldn't be able to see. "I can't deny that it might be nice to see the world once, or what's left of it, if the news and rumors are to be believed. But I also want my own home to return to and my own bed to sleep in. Not on the streets or in a motel, not in a dormitory with fifty other boys and the Brothers. I want something that's mine." He gently tapped the bedframe. "This is mine. This pillow is mine. These clothes are mine. Aye, maybe I have to share the room with you, but we're brothers. And this is our family home."

"Why do you think you can't have both?" MacEoghan wondered.

"Why do you think I can? You live and work here; you know we don't exactly have a lot of free time in the day."

He could feel his brother's frown. After a moment, "Can I ask one thing?"

"What's that?"

"Don't quit now. We've only just started, or you have, and there is still a war going on over in the mainland. Stay with it at least until the end of the war. Maybe we'll never need it here, and that's fine. But if the Germans or the British do come, I don't want you to be defenseless. It will take both of us to keep the family and the town safe, or as safe as it can be. Once the war is over, then if you want to quit..." He trailed off a moment. Then, "Can I ask that much?"

Micah nodded invisibly again. "Aye, that I can agree to."

He could hear the relief in his brother's voice. "Good. I've spent too many years defending us by myself. It's time for you to pull your weight around here, I think."

"Let's not forget which of us was asked to take over the business. You could be talking to your future boss."

"Psh. 'Could be,' 'future,' sounds like a lot of talk to me."

Micah stifled a laugh. "All right, then, what do you say? You think we could Band each other to try and get some more sleep?"

MacEoghan rolled over noisily in his bed. "Oh, I suppose we could try."

It came easier to MacEoghan than to Micah, but he managed, or he thought he did. Whatever the case, when all Bands were dropped, it wasn't ten minutes before Brendan burst into the room saying it was time to get up and they'd better hurry or they would miss out on the eggs. MacEoghan just gave him a customary, "Sure, sure," to the boy's back as he darted out of the room.

Another day of culling the catch and only sending out a few trucks. This was Micah's day to ride, so he hopped in a truck. As they pulled out of the warehouse, he noticed in the mirror Padraig motioning for MacEoghan to follow him into the office. Padraig couldn't think that Micah hadn't told his brother. Was he telling him anyway, to be fair? Or maybe to gauge MacEoghan's reaction?

Micah thought over their conversation the previous evening. At no point had MacEoghan expressed jealousy over the offer being presented to Micah. If anything, he was probably relieved. He was still free to do his own thing. Micah just wished he understood what that actually was, what it meant.

There were no new developments regarding the mainland Emergency, and everyone was happy to just leave it at that and instead focus on their daily lives. Micah thought they were a little more intent on ignoring the war than going about their lives. No news might be good news, but any news tended to be heavy-hitting these days, and not in the Allies' favor.

Just through the war, Micah thought. That was all MacEoghan was asking. He really couldn't argue with his brother's logic; he himself had the same thoughts. At the same time, how long was the war going to last? Two more years? Five? Ten? Just reaching Master rank would be enough to make his age questionable. Would he really be able to take over the business then? When did he decide to just walk away? What if he couldn't?

No, he told himself, mentally shaking his head and offloading a crate of fish. He couldn't afford to entertain every wild thought. If things started to look a little tense regarding Ireland—and only Ireland—then he would start worrying. As it was, people were still buying fish, still going about their daily lives. He hopped back in the truck and they made their way to their next, and regrettably final, stop for the day before returning home for dinner and chores.

With such small hauls and shorter delivery routes, the afternoon chores were starting to feel less like necessary upkeep and more like cumbersome burdens. Giving the same care to the nets and the boat now that they had just a year ago when production was twice as great really felt like a slap in the face. Conversation had always been limited, but light-hearted. Now it was a drudging silence, at least, until Brendan finally spoke up.

"Papa, can I go play with Jacob and Aaron?" The boy put down his net, expression barely hopeful that Padraig would say yes.

The rest of them stopped working, waiting to hear their father's verdict. He looked around at each of them. The man looked exhausted, Micah thought, his expression saying that there were things he would much rather be doing as well. Finally he sighed and nodded. "Off you go. All of you. But not you, Micah. You stay here."

Brendan scampered off right away, immediately excited and not bothering to take his leave. Shay also jogged off, and Micah had a suspicion that he was going to go find his friends and they were going to go look at girls. MacEoghan needed no encouragement to leave, but he was thoughtful enough to at least put away the tools first.

Micah watched them go, then turned to Padraig who hadn't moved, just sat in his seat, also watching the rest of them leave.

"Did I do something wrong?" Micah wondered.

His father shook his head. "No." He made a motion. "Sit." Micah sat. "Pick up your tools. The work still has to get done. This is part of running the business."

"But..." Micah made another stitch, then paused. "The whole point..."

Padraig sighed. "I know. Why do we do the same work with less to show for it? How do we justify it?"

"Exactly."

Padraig made a motion for Micah to continue stitching. Micah sighed but plodded along. Padraig spoke. "If you made the decisions, what would you do?"

Micah thought about it for a few minutes. Then, "There's no need to keep half a dozen trucks if we're only using two or three. No need to keep so many boats and nets if we're only using a fraction of them."

"You'd sell them? What about the men who do maintenance on them? The men who drive them?"

"They only rotate their days and trucks. Each man used to work five or six days on his own truck, now they're down to one day, sometimes not even that."

"Keep three or four men employed full-time over a dozen or more occasionally."

"Aye."

"Then how would those other men hope to provide for their families? Isn't making a little money better than making no money?"

Micah thought back to being a child on the streets. Every penny helped, and every scrap of food was a godsend.

"Furthermore," Padraig went on, "how do you choose which men to keep? Do you tell the old man that because he is old and moves slower that he is less valuable? Do you tell the single man that because he has no family he has no worth?" The old fisherman never looked up from his work. "The Lord provides for all of us, Micah. Far be it from me to tell any man that he is somehow less valuable."

"Will it matter if we don't make enough money to pay them and everyone loses their job?" Micah countered. "We can only cut back and strangle ourselves so much."

"It will matter." Padraig nodded slowly, still staring at his work, fingers moving deftly over the knots. "That's when your reputation carries you. If people know you were honest and hard-working, that you valued them even when it would have been more profitable to be selfish, that they know you tried your best to give everyone a fair chance, it will come back to you. But you start cutting back, firing people, assigning such worth to them or not because they are young or old or married or single or for no reason at all, they remember that, too."

"You cut back in the hard times, save the business, there will still be opportunity to grow and re-expand in the future," Micah said. "We lose everything by slowly draining the finances with only the hope of things possibly getting better, then even when things get better, there's no money to buy the boats back, no business for anyone to come back to."

Padraig frowned. "Well, I can't say you're wrong there either. We've watched a few of those in the last year or so, haven't we?" He shifted in his seat. "I spoke to MacEoghan earlier today."

"I already told him about your offer," Micah said.

"I figured you would. Actually, our conversation ran more along the lines of this one right here just now."

Micah paused in his work and looked up. "Are you firing MacEoghan from the family business?"

Padraig shook his head, but his expression lacked conviction. "No. Family is the last one you fire. But I may have been inquiring about his life plans in the near future. With my offer to you and his...restless nature, I can't imagine he would want to stick around here longer than necessary."

"Last I knew, he still wanted to be a boxer."

"He did make some comment about that. He also stated that he did not intend to leave until the Emergency on the mainland wrapped up. If nothing else, he was going to stay close in order to defend the family if need be."

"You think he'll need to?"

Now Padraig looked up, but he didn't answer for a long moment. Then, "There's no violence quite like revenge, especially when everything else has been taken away."

Micah said no more on the subject, although Sean echoed similar sentiments at Time training a few nights later.

"You think the British will invade?" MacEoghan inquired of the Master Timekeeper.

"It's more likely than the Germans," Sean said casually. "Germans still have to cross a channel, and everyone's worried about them. British are right next door and to the north. They already walk among us. Would be a lot easier, I think."

MacEoghan looked at Micah. "You see? You can't quit now."

"Quit?" Sean also looked at Micah.

Micah gave his brother a look but nodded. "Aye. Our father offered me the family business. MacEoghan thinks I could run the business and stay with Time. I don't think so. But he made me agree to keep training at least through the war, just in case someone decides to invade."

Sean nodded, expression thoughtful. "Not a bad idea. But you know you could keep Time and the business. You think I sit at home all day twiddling my thumbs? No, I work, too."

"Aye, but the thing about a family business is that's it's in the family, typically for a good long time. How can I have a family? How could I abandon them after ten or twenty years because I stopped aging?"

Sean shifted his stance. "All very valid questions. I cannot rightly fault you for them."

"I think he's being stupid," MacEoghan commented bluntly, shifting his stance. "He can live ten lives and be a different man in each one. He can do anything he wants."

"It is nice being able to experiment with different things," Sean agreed, his tone cautious. "It is nice not to have to choose so severely or consequentially, wondering if we might reach our deathbed with a million regrets of things we didn't or could never do. At the same time, more important than what you do is who you are, the man you want to be. Some men figure that out with only one life to live, and some Timekeepers are still searching for it after twenty lifetimes." Sean looked back and forth between them. "Oddly enough, I think you are both correct in your assessments."

Micah felt relieved, but MacEoghan looked offended. "But—"

"I can't force him to stick with it," Sean cut in, not unkindly. "Neither can you. He's a grown man, MacEoghan, you can't tell him what to do or not do. You are living your life and he is living his. As you each see fit."

MacEoghan's expression said he had a thousand things running through his head, all of them desiring to come out but all getting stuck in his mouth.

"And yet—" Sean continued, apparently sensing the awkward tension, "—you did agree to stick with it until this mainland Emergency pans out. That is an agreement I will hold you to." Micah nodded. "That said, I am satisfied enough with both of you that I think I can schedule your Apprenticeship review in the very near future."

"You think so?" MacEoghan sounded excited by the prospect. Micah, while grateful for the vote of confidence, simply accepted the notion, knowing it was just something to do and not necessarily a step toward some greater goal he had.

Sean nodded enthusiastically. "Absolutely. With Micah expressing his desire to be Suppressed, well, I'd like to get him as much training as possible beforehand." His expression was more severe. "You can always have the Suppression lifted if you change your mind, and I'd hate for you to be left too vulnerable."

Micah just nodded coolly.

"What does the review involve?" MacEoghan inquired eagerly.

"It comes in three parts. First, a knowledge test, questions and answers, can you explain what you are doing? Second is a skill test, mostly rote demonstrations, all of it very by-the-book. It's like doing numbered math problems in class. Then there is a brief combat portion—"

"Combat?" The twins said it at the same time, but their dispositions were quite different.

Sean put up a hand as if to quiet a rowdy crowd. "Believe me, compared to higher exams, this is nothing. It's just a little thing to get you to think on your feet. The rote demonstrations, like I said, are the numbered math problems, and this is like the worded math problems. You have to be able to apply what you've been learning."

Micah didn't like the sound of that. At the same time, would it be any different if he had to use it here to defend the family in case of invasion? At least in a formal review it would hopefully be a more controlled environment with set expectations, rules that were a little kinder than simply "Hope to live."

"The third and final portion is a psychological exam," Sean went on. "It's a way of testing your motivations, seeing how likely you are to turn Runner. It's a lot easier to weed it out now and Suppress any bad apples than to let that tree grow and suddenly they're Wardens walking around with no one able to stop or Suppress them."

"Isn't a Dominion over a Warden?" Micah questioned.

Sean shrugged. "Aye, the only one over a Warden, and even then, by that point, it's more about pretty titles than great differences in skill. You only need to be a Gatekeeper to run for a Hand position, if that tells you anything."

"And Gatekeeper oversees the planet, right?" MacEoghan wondered.

"That's right. I know we've done a lot of skill training and very little knowledge training. So the next few weeks are going to be spent on more book type learning. You'll need to know all the ranks of the Timekeepers, all the titles of the Hands—"

"All fifty-one?" Micah asked. His tone was whiny, but he didn't care.

"All fifty-one," Sean confirmed. "And if you really want to impress them, you'll have to address each one individually by their full title." He nodded, looking a bit unenthusiastic. "You'll have to be able to define a Band, Fast Band, Slow Band, how to read strengths, and a thousand other possible questions that they could come up with on the spot. The good news is that each Hand only asks one question, so the maximum number of questions you'll answer is fifty-one."

That, at least, was a minor relief. Actually, it was a huge relief. Micah remembered math tests that had been one hundred questions long. Fifty-one would be a breeze.

"So is the psychological exam written or demonstration?" MacEoghan asked.

"It is unique to the individual and cannot be spoken of," Sean informed him, his expression suggesting there was no room for questions. "Your experiences will be different, and you do not share."

Micah glanced at his twin who was already looking at him. Sure, they each had things that they kept from the other, but to be under orders to not share felt...unfair.

"Or I can Suppress you both right here right now and we can all go on with our lives," Sean said, shrugged casually.

"No," MacEoghan stated forcefully. "I can pass one little test. Or three of them, I guess."

Sean nodded and looked at Micah. "You?"

Micah took a breath but nodded slowly. "I gave my word that I would stick it out through this Emergency, and I will honor my word."

"Good to hear. Now then, find a comfortable spot in the grass and listen carefully."

A SECOND ENCOUNTER
YOUNGER BROTHER

Three weeks sounded like a long time, until it wasn't. Suddenly, it was time for the Apprentice review. In the middle of dinner one day, Sean had appeared and announced that it was time. Micah and MacEoghan glanced at each other, shocked. It wasn't as though he hadn't given them ample warning or study time. But still, that was today? Already?

Micah had inquired about waiting until after dinner, but Sean shook his head no. He said something about the time and calendar discrepancies between Earth and the Wheel of Time, how they had to be worked and calculated. Short answer, no, they had to go now. It wasn't as though they were going to miss out on anything; the portal to the Wheel would remain open, ergo, no time would actually pass on Earth.

Micah still tried to wrap his head around such a concept as they followed their Master through the Wheel. He looked around at the portals in the portal room, a million doors leading to a million worlds. Not one of them would experience the passage of time. And yet, here were a million people milling about in the Wheel on various modes of business. They were all experiencing the passage of time from one second to the next. Weren't they?

He puzzled over this as they found their way to the Seat of the Hands. The dull drudgery of office work was an odd comfort, Micah thought. Thousands or maybe millions of species across the universe and not one of them had developed a more efficient way of doing things. It was mildly funny, but also a bit disheartening considering how many of those species were capable of space travel.

They were called up to the next available secretary.

"Two probationaries here for their Apprentice review," Sean told him—or her? or it?—and relayed whatever information the secretary asked for.

The secretary studied Micah and MacEoghan as if it had never seen twins before. Maybe it hadn't.

"Both?" it questioned.

"Did I stutter?" Sean countered, remarkably cool. "Yes, both."

The secretary did not argue, nor did it appear to react to Sean's sarcasm. Of course, Micah wasn't sure he would be able to read the body language of an alien that was four foot tall, unbelievably round in shape, had claws more than fingers, and was covered in orange fur with a mane running the circumference of its round body. What was this thing called? Where was it from? What was its name? Its purpose in life? He didn't need to know any of this, but he kind of wanted to.

Whatever the conversation between Sean and the secretary, it ended abruptly enough to pull Micah from his musings about the odd, round, orange creature. The three of them were led by another secretary deeper into the Coliseum and left to wait in the boxy, white room.

"How do the Hands get so much done in a day?" MacEoghan asked. "If it were just Earth, maybe I could see it, but with thousands of species and thousands of reviews..."

"That's where Time comes in handy," Sean told him. "When you have the ability to manipulate Time and can appear to create more of it out of thin air, well, it can make for a very long workday."

Just another reason to leave, Micah thought to himself. If he used Time to sit out on the boat until he caught every fish in the sea, well, it might take a while. Or if he had Banded to finish all of the nets in one day instead of letting himself stop for the night after supper, he probably wouldn't be in a very good mood. He also probably wouldn't have had a minor epiphany that night about how to fix one particular net that had been giving him trouble all day.

At the same time, using Bands to give himself those minor breaks every now and again was kind of nice.

"Have you said anything or should I say anything about what I intend to do?" Micah wondered evasively.

Sean shook his head severely. "Not a word."

He left no room for questions or argument, and Micah was fine with that.

He couldn't say he didn't understand. How would he feel if someone in the company asked for more training and a raise when this person had just proclaimed that he intended to leave in a few months? It very likely wasn't going to happen.

"Am I going first, then?" MacEoghan asked.

"Actually, I want Micah to go first," Sean told him. "I believe the Hands will want to review you both and then deliberate and render a verdict for both of you at the same time. I'm kind of hoping that they'll act on the premise of recency and maybe your identical appearance will blur over any mistakes one of you makes."

"They won't be able to remember who messed up and on what," Micah stated.

"Something like that."

"You think I can't do it?" MacEoghan wondered.

"Not at all." Sean looked annoyed by the suggestion. "Actually, I'm betting that your demonstration and combat test will be a little more...flagrant, and will cover for any of Micah's mistakes. I also expect that the answers on his knowledge test will be a little more thorough than yours and cover up for any of your mistakes. It's simple teamwork."

Micah could see what was going on, but maybe he felt more relaxed because he found the stakes to be far lower. He wasn't overly concerned whether he passed or failed because he wasn't going to be continuing his studies for that much longer, or so he hoped.

"What happens if we fail?" MacEoghan pressed.

Sean shrugged. "More to me than to you. I get reprimanded for wasting the Hands' time and being a poor instructor. You just have to study and practice more. They say that you have to wait a full year before trying again, but I know of at least a couple people who managed to try again in six months."

Before anyone could say more, the door opened and a secretary who bore great resemblance to an enormous anthropomorphic bat entered the room. It still a good eight or nine feet tall and used massive, leathery wings as a sort of cloak around its body. It did not appear to wear any kind of clothing or other bodily markings designating it as a secretary. Micah saw that its mouth was slightly ajar, and he wondered if this massive beast was truly blind like a bat and using echolocation to form a picture of the room.

"Micah Dearbhfhine," Sean said, projecting his voice so as to slightly babble over top of the Bat's request for one of them. Sean looked at the younger twin. "You're up. Good luck."

Despite the cool confidence of telling himself that it didn't matter because he wasn't going to be doing this much longer, Micah still found his knees a little shaky, palms a little sweaty as he followed the creature out of the room.

"Can I ask your name, sir?" Micah inquired politely, trying to mask his growing fear.

"I am called the Bat," it answered, not breaking stride or looking at him. "The other is called the Day."

Other? Other what? Did he dare ask? Would it betray his limited knowledge and mess up the exam? Was it even something he had studied? Sean hadn't mentioned anything about knowing much about the secretaries. Was it impolite to ask? Would he need to know for a future test?

They stopped in front of the same medieval gate as before, its presence striking in an otherwise highly technological landscape. The Bat took hold of the mechanism and cranked it hand over hand. The gate opened with neither scrape nor scratch, gliding open like a ghostly apparition.

"Your review begins now," the Bat said. "It does not end until the Hands have rendered judgment. You are not to discuss any part of the review with anyone who is not present, including your mentor. Do you understand?"

"I understand," Micah answered.

"The Hands await," the Bat said once the gate was all the way open.

That was it. No final words of encouragement, no tips on how to make it easier on himself, not even a rote, scripted, soulless, "Good luck."

Walking down the tunnel to the center of the Coliseum, Micah could feel his heart start to beat just a little faster and he could feel heat on the back of his neck accompanied by a single bead of sweat. Why was he so nervous? He was just going through the motions. This wouldn't matter in a year or two years when he was Suppressed and settled into his life as a fisherman.

He wouldn't say he didn't want to do well. He didn't want to reflect poorly on Sean who really was a good teacher, and he also didn't want to feel like an absolute failure that he couldn't even make it past probationary level. But this was it. This was all.

The tunnel opened up into the massive arena where Micah still expected to see lions and gladiators and was more unnerved by the silence. He reached the symbol on the floor and turned to face the Hands.

"Micah Dearbhfhine, probationary Timekeeper, you approach the Hands today for your review, your intentions to advance to the rank of Apprentice Timekeeper," the Zero Hour stated. "Is this correct?"

"Aye," Micah replied, feeling another bead of sweat snake slowly down his side under his arm.

What followed was a good ten minutes of introductions, rules, and general housekeeping, with multiple prompts of, "Do you understand?" By the fourth one, Micah began to wonder what would happen if he said he didn't understand.

By the time the Zero Hour indicated that the test was to commence, Micah had basically ceased being nervous. Instead he was just bored.

"Name all of the Hands of Time," was the first question, and "Name all of the ranks of the Timekeepers," was the second. These were followed by having to name the ranks of the other Time Agents, Harvesters and Merchants.

For the Hands of Time, there were fifty-one of them. The first fifteen could be arrayed in a matrix by their scientific and engaged representation. Scientifically Superior, Advanced, Advancing, Modest, and Primitive. Then they were either Engaged, Engaged Privilege, or Unengaged. These were as easy to remember as those representing the various Time Agent divisions. Hand of the Timekeepers, the Harvesters, the Merchants, the Scouts, the Secretaries, even one called the Hand of New Blood which dealt with probationaries or prospective Time Agents. Then there was also the Hand of the Hands, more commonly known as the Zero Hour. There were other, more obscure Hands that were more difficult to remember, but Micah got through all fifty-one.

For the various Time Agent ranks, more rote memorization. Timekeeper ranks were entirely linear. Probationary, Apprentice, Journeyman, Master, Lieutenant, Captain, Manager, Gatekeeper, Warden, Dominion. Harvester ranks were also fairly linear, except only the top two were considered officers. After Master, their ranks went into Assistant, Physician, Surgeon, Doctorate, Intervention, and Triage. Merchants, once they became Masters, instead began training for a specific market. This started as a Negotiator, then branched into either Merchant, Auctioneer, or Investor.

Rote information, lists, not unlike a lot of the things the Brothers had made them memorize. Names, dates, places, just simple facts, and Micah had learned a dozen ways to commit such dull information to memory.

Then there were more in-depth questions, like describing the nature of the calendar in the Wheel—the system the secretaries used to schedule things like these reviews—compared to the greater universe, specifically his home planet. The way Sean told it, no one actually quite knew what the Wheel was, never mind where it was located. There were some theories, the most prominent being the center of the universe, and the farther away one was from the center, the harder it was to open portals. It didn't explain everything, such as why time at home paused while one was in the Wheel, though only if the portal stayed open. But for an Apprentice review, Micah hoped it was good enough.

Similarly, he could name the parts of a Band easily enough. There was the wake, which was, as the name suggested, the temporal energy disturbance left behind a Band when one either moved or when it was dispersed. Someone walking through a wake was subject to mild disorientation, minor forgetfulness, and possible bouts of déjà vu. Then there was the interior of the Band, which contained everything inside that was affected by the Band. There was also the exterior of the Band which defined its limits and determined its strength. When someone tried to break into or out of a Band, they had to overcome that exterior shell. It was manipulable by other forces, too, so a Band could be passed off to someone else, among other things. The last part of the Band was the tether, which was exactly how it sounded, and it anchored the Band to one or more holders. It was also like a power conduit of the Band, but it could only be held by conscious will. If someone holding a Band became unconscious for some reason, the Band dissipated.

Because Bands only dealt with temporal energy, they had little to no effect on air or gases; a Band wouldn't save someone from toxic fumes. They were also very finicky when dealing with high-energy reactions such as fire. Containing a candle was typically a non-issue, but anything larger than a small campfire could potentially cause big problems and bigger explosions.

Then they got into more open-ended questions, ones that Micah was far less comfortable with. The question was, "What is the role of a probationary Time Agent of any discipline and is it an effective role?" Well, it was a role used to judge skill and interest as well as personal integrity and character. Micah didn't see a problem with that. But was it really necessary for the probationary period to last for so long? And he and MacEoghan had been in an accelerated program because of how much they already knew.

Describing the role of a Hand was simple enough, but then being asked if fifty-one Hands was too many and if the Time industry would benefit from having more or fewer Hands...that felt like a huge trap. Was there a right or wrong answer? Was this just about being able to defend his position? But why? And why ask it of a probationary Timekeeper from an Unengaged world? He didn't know enough about the Time industry to formulate a fair argument. Had they somehow gone from the knowledge test straight into the psychological evaluation and he didn't realize it?

Micah had tried to keep track of the questions, but as dry information turned into thoughtful opinion, he'd lost count. And interest. He was done with this test, and in a few years, he would be done with Timekeeping. In the moment, he was kind of ready to move on to the skill test.

Finally, the Zero Hour stood.

"Micah Dearbhfhine, your final question."

At last.

"What is Time?"

Micah blinked. What is Time? Were they looking for a dictionary definition or something more esoteric?

He'd been told that if at any point he did not know the answer to a question, he could simply answer "Unknown" and move on. He really didn't want to do that. He didn't like crediting the Brothers, but he would have to agree that trying and failing was better than not trying at all. He just wished he knew which way they were going with the question because he only had one answer he could confidently give.

"Time," he stated, "noun, the system of sequential relations that any event has to any other, such as past, present, or future, an indefinite continuous duration regarded as that in which events succeed one another."

After a brief pause, the Zero Hour, in its shroud, made a motion. "Thus concludes the first test of the Apprentice Timekeeper review for Micah Dearbhfhine. Thank you for your time and thoughtful consideration of all your answers. You have performed admirably and are a credit to yourself and your mentor. We will now move immediately into the second test, the test of skill. Micah Dearbhfhine, are you ready?"

Considering they had announced the test before asking if he was ready, he really didn't think he had a choice in the matter. Still, he nodded once, glad for the mental reprieve. "I am ready."

"The second part of the review is a test of skill, and this test will be done in two parts," The Zero Hour went on. "The first test is a standing test. You will be asked to create Bands with specific parameters which will not exceed the reasonable limits expected of a probationary Timekeeper. If we the Hands are satisfied with the results of the standing test, then we will move on to the second test, that is, the reflexive test where you must create Bands reflexively in a variety of scenarios."

The combat portion, Micah thought.

"The test will end when we the Hands are satisfied with your performance," the Zero Hour added. "Do you have any questions before we begin the test?"

It would end when they were satisfied? There was no set limit, either the questions they asked or maybe a time limit? This was wholly open-ended? Micah did not like the sound of that.

"Do you have any questions?" the Zero Hour repeated.

"No," Micah answered blankly.

"Commence now the first test of the second portion of the review."

The Zero Hour sat and another Hand stood.

"Fast Band, hour:minute," it commanded.

Fast Band, so Micah would be moving faster than everything around him. Specifically, one hour spent inside the Band was one minute spent outside the Band. The nice thing about the Time industry was that, somehow, the base lengths used for seconds, minutes, hours, and so on, coincided with those used on Earth, or close enough. One Base Second on Earth was the same as one Base Second used in the Time industry. Either that or, like the pausing of Time while a portal remained open, there was some odd technology in use which made it so it always aligned with one's home time measurement.

Micah had created the desired Band and held it for no more than a few minutes before it was ripped away. One of the Hands had effectively grabbed the outer shell, sunk his own figurative claws in it, and ripped it away, snapping the tether like worn thread. Micah stumbled standing up but recovered in time to hear the next command.

"Slow Band, five minutes:six hours."

Slow Band, so he would be moving slower than everything else. Five minutes in the Band was like six hours outside. This time, once he achieved the desired strength, he held the Band for what felt like only a couple seconds before it was taken away. Again he stumbled. Though he did manage to stop himself from falling, he was not completely upright before the next command came down.

"Fast Band, six hours:ten minutes."

Micah did so, and on it went, back and forth between Fast and Slow Bands, the ratios becoming wider and ever more specific, even down to seconds. Training in Time, especially Timekeeping, sharpened one's perception of the passage of time. He became more attuned to what really constituted an hour, a minute, even a second. He became more aware of everything that happened in that time frame, and he naturally honed his reflexes. Micah had noticed this on the fishing boat a while ago, and though he did use this heightened perception to assist in fishing, only now did he appreciate the real mechanics of it.

Each time, his Band was ripped away from him. Eventually he learned to stop fighting it and just go with it. Stop trying to fight the waves and keep his land legs and learn to use his sea legs instead. It made it much easier, though he was no less relieved when the Zero Hour finally stood.

"Begin with a Fast Band, day:second. Slide into a Slow Band of second:day."

Slide? Take a Fast Band and make it into a Slow Band without losing the

Band? Sean had touched on it a little, had made them try it a couple times, but Micah didn't have a full grasp on it.

Didn't matter, he told himself, forming the Fast Band. This test didn't mean anything, not really. He was just going through the motions for a couple years at most.

Manipulating the Fast Band wasn't difficult, bringing it down to just hovering around Base Time. Now he had to turn it into a Slow Band without actually losing the Band. Fortunately, he had an idea of how to do this, something he had tried in the few times Sean had made them practice this. It was very similar to making a drastic course change with the boat. If he could do it fast enough, he could use the momentum to carry the Band and pop it from a Fast Band to a Slow Band, like bouncing off a wave to force a sharper turn. Granted, he was talking about physical motion versus temporal motion, and even trying the aforementioned maneuver in a boat was extremely risky, but maybe he could make it work.

It was clumsy, but he managed. He still almost lost the Band, fumbling it as it popped over into a Slow Band. Once he got a better hold of it, he easily strengthened it into second:day as requested.

He'd no sooner locked in the Band than it was taken from him. He let it go, grateful to be done.

"And so concludes the first part of the second portion of the review," the Zero Hour said formally. "You have performed admirably and may take the second test. Are you ready?"

He was tired, physically, from making so many Bands, and mentally, from both the stress and boredom of the test.

"I'm ready," he told them.

"The second part of the test is a test of reflexes. As you do not yet possess the skills to perform Outside Bands, this test will be brief." Actually, Sean had showed them External Bands, but he wasn't going to correct the Hand. "For this test, you must use Fast and Slow Bands in order to defend yourself. Do you have any questions before we begin?"

"Defend myself from what?"

"A variety of projectiles and assailants."

Not the most helpful answer, Micah thought, though he did not say so out loud. That could be anything from pebbles to bullets, small children to enemy soldiers.

Or, as it turned out, the Bat itself. Micah wasn't sure just which reflex was tipped off—sound, hearing the Bat rush up behind him; air, feeling the Bat's hot breath or maybe the beat of its wings; or something else entirely—but it saved him from being effectively hit by a train. He contorted his body while grabbing the Reflex Band and trying to strengthen it on the fly. He bent backwards and found himself looking at the underside of the Bat's leathery pinion, easily ten feet long, four feet wide, with a foot-long claw at the joint and the tip. A three-foot tail tipped with a barnacle-looking thing streamed out behind it.

The Bat wasted no Time throwing up a Band of its own, whipping around faster than Micah was prepared for and reaching for him with a four-taloned hand. Seeing the muscle in the Bat's unusually long arms up close, suddenly he had an idea of just how heavy the gates that led into the Coliseum really were.

Micah wasn't sure what to do next. Try an even stronger Band? Trade out a Fast Band for a Slow one? Was he actually supposed to lay hands on the Bat? Would it actually hurt him? His last question was answered quickly enough and it was a definite yes. The Bat would hurt him, and if he didn't defend himself quickly, it could very well kill him.

Again, Micah decided to just go with it. As the Bat's claws met his body, Micah rolled with the motion, reaching for a Fast Band to try and put a few feet between them. As he did so, with the Bat's hand still in motion, it seemed to physically grab his Band. Then, even more frightening, it not only moved the Band, but him within it. How was that even possible? And why couldn't he let it go? It was as though the Bat had glued the tether into him. What was going on?

Then the Bat grabbed him, physically, Band, body and all, and threw him. Once he was well in the air, Micah was able to release the Band, though it did nothing to change gravity or momentum. He hit the ground, rolled, and slammed against the wall. He'd only just gotten up on all fours when his reflexes kicked in again. He grabbed the Band, and at the same time, he dropped back to his stomach, pulling the Band in as tight as he could manage. Above him, the Bat was coming at him, fangs and claws outstretched.

Micah slowly crawled out from under the Bat, got to his feet, and sprinted a good ten yards away before turning and daring to release the Band. In theory, the Bat was going to slam into the ground with no prey to show for its efforts. Instead, it again whipped around faster than the laws of physics said it should have been able to, planted its three-taloned feet on the wall, and used it as a launch pad, covering that ten yards in less than three seconds and that was without a Band.

Micah just stood there. He didn't know what to do. The Bat closed in like an arrow, then suddenly flared its huge wings, coming to a near complete stop. The wind pushed Micah back a few steps. Then the Bat landed, folded its wings like a cloak, looked up at the Hands, and nodded once.

"Thank you, Bat, you are dismissed," the Zero Hour said.

The Bat nodded again, then turned and left the Coliseum, as if it hadn't just tried to kill him. Micah watched it leave, then looked back at the Hands, hoping for an explanation.

"The purpose of the test was to assess your ability to act on instinct," the Zero Hour explained, "to Band as reflexively as throwing up an arm to protect yourself, and to be able to think on your feet and incorporate Time and Banding in combat."

"Oh," was all Micah could manage.

"Thus concludes the second part of the Apprentice Timekeeper review for Micah Dearbhfhine," the Zero Hour decided. All the Hands stood. "The third part of the review, the psychological exam, will commence shortly. You will be returned to your waiting room where food and drink will be provided."

Well, he certainly wasn't going to argue with that. He thanked the Hands, then turned and headed out of the Coliseum. The gates were open and the Bat waited patiently. It gave no indication of what had just happened, just directed him back to the waiting room.

In theory, it should have been the same waiting room that he had left, the one where Sean and MacEoghan were still waiting. Maybe MacEoghan would be brought out for his first two tests so Micah had a chance to rest for a bit. That seemed logical, right?

Instead, when he opened the door—the door that the Bat had indicated and now confirmed—he froze. Inside was not Sean nor MacEoghan. It was someone Micah knew he should not be seeing because this man was dead.

"Ah, welcome, Micah," Brother Andrew said cheerfully. He stood behind a chair at a table in the middle of the room. Though the room remained white and bland, the furniture had come straight from St. Joseph's. Brother Andrew indicated the chair across from him at the table. "Come, right here."

He didn't want to. He didn't even want to be in the same room as this man, though the Bat forced that issue, pushing him inside and closing the door behind him. This had to be part of the psychological exam. Brother Andrew was dead, long dead for years. Time only moved forward, and no one had admitted to being able to travel into the past, so either the Hands possessed some obscene technology to bring a dead man from the past here, or else he had been drugged. But when? How? What was going on?

"Come here," Brother Andrew said, more forcefully now. "Stand behind your chair. It's mealtime and the food needs to be blessed. I prefer my food to be warm."

"How are you here?" Micah asked, voice wavering. "You're dead."

"Am I?"

"Kearney and Kane said so. That's why they were hunting us."

"Kearney and Kane also said they were officers, but that wasn't true."

"You're a Timekeeper, then? Or a Time Agent?"

"You think an ordinary man could just accidentally make his way here? The Wheel would be difficult enough, but this far into the Coliseum..." The man gave him a look. "Honestly, Micah, you were the studious twin. I thought we taught you better than that." He gestured toward the table. The spread looked like chops with vegetables and rolls. "Now then, would you like to sit and eat like civilized men?"

Micah was hungry after his recent ordeal, and he didn't think hallucinations could involve such wonderful smells.

"Where is MacEoghan?" he asked suddenly.

"I'll be visiting him, too, don't worry. I thought some one-on-one time was in order. MacEoghan was always hot-headed; I was hoping for a more rational conversation with you."

Fury flared within Micah and he strode toward the table. "The last conversation we had—!"

"Ah-ah," Brother Andrew interrupted, getting an expression and making a gesture Micah knew all too well. He wanted to defy it, but habit dictated he stop moving and shut his mouth. "There we go. Now then, first we bless the food, and then we speak."

Standing right there at the table, so close to food, Micah was torn. He didn't want to eat at the Devil's table. At the same time, he was hungry, and he would be waiting for some time while MacEoghan took his review. Finally he sighed, nodded, and made a motion for Brother Andrew to bless the food. The man wasted no time lifting his hands and launching into a bombastic prayer. Micah's ears grated at the sound of it, like nails on chalkboard. He dug his nails into the back of the chair where he stood, just waiting for it to be over.

Then it was, and they took their seats. Guess it couldn't be a hallucination if they could sit down at a table, Micah figured. Brother Andrew immediately cut open one of his rolls and started slathering butter inside. Micah was slower to pick up his utensils.

"Honestly, Micah, you know the power of the Church," Brother Andrew said, pushing the butter toward him. "If Kearney and Kane could find you, what makes you think the Church couldn't do the same? If you killed a clergyman, the Church would not simply let it slide. Given what you did to me, simple justice in a courtroom would not be enough of a punishment."

"And what about what you did to me?" Micah rebutted, slicing open his roll and pushing a bit of butter around until it was melted.

"I helped you become a man. Some people can be told, others have to be shown. You were one who had to be shown what a man's body is capable of."

Micah slammed a palm on the table. "That's no excuse!" He went on before Brother Andrew could speak. "If a priest refuses to teach on a subject, it's because he is guilty of that crime. None of you ever talked about Sodom and Gomorrah. None of you ever talked about certain chapters of Romans or I Corinthians. Because they would damn you."

Brother Andrew frowned as he forked off a tender bite of chop. "We teach what we believe and know to be true, child." He took a bite and made a vague gesture with his fork. "You think any of this is Biblical? Did God create the Wheel of Time? Is every sentient race created in His image?"

Micah blinked. "You don't believe in God?"

Brother Andrew shrugged. "*A* god, maybe. Maybe even multiple gods, a kind of cosmic pantheon. The rest? Does it matter? It is a system of power and order and justice." He made another gesture. "It got you off the streets, didn't it? Gave you an education, some discipline, helped set you up for success."

Micah frowned. "But what about *me*?"

The priest took another bite of chop. Lamb, Micah thought. "What about you? I told you what happened, why I did what I did. I did my best to help. What you do with it is up to you. But take another look around this place, Micah. You don't matter. You are one of billions of humans, and humans are one of thousands or millions of species. The universe is full of planets and races and is constantly expanding. God can't be everywhere at once, and caring about one little orphan on Earth is a little ridiculous, don't you think?"

Micah didn't know what to think. He still couldn't believe this was real except he was sitting in a chair at a solid table eating food which he could smell and taste.

Brother Andrew never broke stride. "I'm here to help, Micah. Truly I am. Now then, finish your meal, and then I will take you back to the Inner Sanctum for your psychological review."

"I think this is part of the psychological review," Micah stated, peeling off a bite of meat. "If you really are here and not dead, I think they brought you specifically to test me. And when we walk back into the Inner Sanctum, it will be for the end of the review so you can tell them whether I passed or failed."

"And which do you think I'm going to say?"

Micah glanced at the man. "I don't know. You could fail me, just to make a point of it. Or you could pass me because you know I'll be thinking about this for a long time."

The man shrugged again. "True on both accounts. Guess we'll just have to finish our meals and find out."

Suddenly, Micah wanted to pass the test, just so he could shove it in Brother Andrew's face. At the same time, if he failed, well, he was bowing out anyway, so what did it matter?

They finished their food in silence. Then, as promised, Brother Andrew led Micah back out of the room toward the Inner Sanctum. The Bat again raised the gates and saw them through wordlessly. Once inside, the Hands were waiting patiently. Brother Andrew opened his mouth to speak, but Micah beat him to it.

"I know this is a hallucination," he stated. "I don't know when or where or how, but I know it is."

Brother Andrew raised a brow. "Oh? And how is that?"

Micah grinned as he looked at the dead man. "Because I'm not Micah."

Brother Andrew blinked, then vanished like fog. Micah let out a slow breath, then looked up at the Hands. "Clever trick."

There was a long moment of silence. Then the Zero Hour spoke, saying only, "Indeed."

A bit of nausea began swimming around in the back of Micah's brain, but he fought it back long enough to ask, "So, do I pass?"

The Zero Hour said something to the effect of, "We will review your performance," but if he said anything more, Micah did not hear it before he passed out.

His sleep, if he got any, was dreamless. When he managed to crawl back to consciousness, he initially thought he had been bound, perhaps in a straightjacket. Why? Had he said or done something violent? What was going on? Then, after a minute or two, once he got his limbs sorted out, he realized it was not a straightjacket, only sheer exhaustion. He was lying on the floor, and that was about the extent of his observation. Even opening his eyes was a chore, though when he did open them, the sudden light forced them closed again for another minute.

"Well, well, welcome back." It was Sean, his location impossible to determine. "How'd it go?"

Micah just groaned for about ten seconds, then opened his eyes and forced them to look around. Then, "The combat was tough, but hardly the most physical thing I've ever done. So why do I feel so horrible?"

Sean spoke as he walked over and knelt to Micah's left. "It's the drugs they give you for the psychological exam. And don't ask me what they are because I don't know."

Micah closed his eyes again. He intended to sigh, but the best he could do was a small huff. "How long does this last? I've had bad hangovers but this is like nothing I've experienced before."

"Oh, you'll be up and around in an hour or so, I imagine. When MacEoghan recovers from his review, we'll go and get the results of both your reviews. Then we'll go home and you're probably going to want to sleep for a few days." He went on before Micah could summon the will to speak. "Don't worry, I'll Band you. I know you've got dinner to eat and fish to catch."

Micah did not reply, just tried to get his bearings. Somehow, exhaustion was mightily uncomfortable, and yet he found that it took too much effort to relax. It wasn't for another fifteen minutes that he felt all the tension in his muscles release and he was able to relax. Another five minutes and he could sit up and drag himself over the lean back against the wall near Sean.

"So, how'd that conversation go?" Sean asked.

Shrugging was about the limit of Micah's physical ability at the moment. "The Hands didn't have much to say."

"I mean with Brother Andrew."

Micah's mind lurched into panic mode, then settled into confusion. "How do you know about that?"

"You were here. I saw it. A Master always knows his Apprentice's hallucinations. MacEoghan was taken out allegedly for his own test preparation, mostly just so the surprise wasn't spoiled for him."

"But, what you said about not talking about the exam..."

"A minor test, to see how you would handle such a thought."

"A lie," Micah stated.

"One we have to tell, at least until you actually go through it."

"Sounds ridiculous."

"Most things about the Time industry are." Sean's laugh was empty, bitter, and he quickly grew serious. "But, truly, how was it? I know what was said, but..."

243

Micah hesitated for a long moment. Then, "We had been planning to run away for a while. I was too scared, and Miach wouldn't leave without me."

He could feel Sean's gaze. "I'd heard rumors about the schools, some of the things they did. They did them to you."

"Aye. Micah came and found me, rescued me. We ran. And we switched names. I always admired him, wanted to be like him in every way, not just appearances. He thought that giving me his name would make me brave." He shook his head. "Even if it was all fake, I should have taken that hallucinated knife and cut his hallucinated throat."

Sean made a noise like he agreed. "Well, I can't say I wouldn't have thought something similar."

"Why him?" Micah wondered. "How did the Hands know about him? That was long before Time."

"I don't know how the drugs work specifically, but they infiltrate your mind, sifting through your most vivid emotions and memories and constructing a fantasy that you can interact with. There is also some kind of technology in the Coliseum it interacts with so I can at least see and hear what's going on. All of it scripted, of course, designed to test your psychological fortitude and your loyalty to Time."

"How did a conversation with Brother Andrew accomplish that?"

The pause said the man had an idea, but his words were, "Only the Hands know, and they're the ones who will make that determination."

Micah frowned. "Do you think I was really talking to Brother Andrew, how he might have been if all that were true, or do you think I was actually talking to myself?"

"I don't understand," Sean said quizzically. "And I never knew the man, so I can't gauge his authenticity."

"Do you think I was really just arguing with myself over the existence of God?" Micah managed to turn his head stiffly to look at his Master. "Do you still believe in God?"

Sean's expression was sympathetic. "Time turns many people into atheists, those who live long enough to think about it anyway. As for me, I don't think I could ever go quite that far. The Wheel is weird and complex, but it didn't build itself. Time didn't invent itself either. Now whether it's the

244

Catholic God, I can't say for sure. If it is, well, I think a few more books might need to be added to the Bible."

Micah turned his head stiffly back into a forward position. "He said he was just using the institution for its power."

"Did he say that, or did the hallucination? I know it felt very real, you could see, hear, taste, smell, touch, but it was still all in your head."

"But—"

"All in your head. You can't take a ghost at its word."

This time Micah did manage to sigh, and he even nodded. "All right. You're right. It was all some drug-induced hallucination scripted and skewed a certain way so the Hands could see just how loyal I really am."

Sean nodded emphatically. "Exactly. And another thing: with this kind of review, you either figure out it's a hallucination, or you very likely die in the process."

"What?"

"Loyalty in the Time industry is absolute. You thought getting away from the school was difficult? Try crossing the Hands and see what happens."

A SECOND ENCOUNTER
OLDER BROTHER

Micah had not returned by the time the Bat came to retrieve MacEoghan. He thought it a tad odd until the Bat mentioned something about being taken for test preparation. Well, considering how many reviews the Hands probably saw in a day, it made some sense, he supposed. If they could cut some time off the process here and there, it probably added up.

He was taken to another room and left there. He waited. Was there something he was supposed to be doing? Was someone going to come and give him a last-minute quiz, maybe some helpful hints, ask if he had any last-minute questions? Was he supposed to take time to pray? What was the protocol here? Sean hadn't said anything about this pre-test preparation time, but then, it sounded like there might be a few things Sean wasn't allowed to tell them.

It wasn't more than ten minutes before the Bat came back and ordered him to follow; his test was set to begin.

"Was there something I was supposed to be doing here?" MacEoghan wondered, looking around at the room.

"Preparing for your exam, however that means to you," the Bat replied. It turned and stalked off, not bothering to check if MacEoghan was following.

Was there some reason he couldn't have done that in the normal waiting room with Sean? Or did they think Sean might have been a distraction, or a crutch? Get him alone and see how he does.

Whatever the case, the test was beginning. MacEoghan jogged up behind the Bat, following it to the tunnel where the great beast turned the mechanism hand over hand. The gate on either end of the tunnel slid open.

"Your review begins now," the Bat said. "It does not end until the Hands have rendered judgment. You are not to discuss any part of the review with anyone who is not present, including your mentor. Do you understand?"

"I suppose so," MacEoghan answered. What else was he going to say?

"The Hands await," the Bat said once the gate was all the way open.

MacEoghan ducked unnecessarily as he entered the tunnel, then straightened and jogged the length, finally slowing to a walk as he neared the inner gate.

Sure, being interrupted in the middle of dinner had been annoying and inconvenient, but he was ready for this. He was more than ready. He'd been a probationary for years, basically his entire life. He knew his stuff and he was ready to move on and learn more, improve his skills, expand his knowledge. He'd been ready for this a long time ago. Damned formalities anyway. Have to be made a probationary, have to spend so much time in that rank, have to go through the rote, proper schooling and now this routine exam.

He wouldn't say he didn't understand it—watching Micah, it made sense —and he wouldn't say that he had any illusions that his Apprenticeship would be any different. But at least he would be learning new things as an Apprentice. Instead of just fumbling his way into some new skill, Sean would be there to show him a new skill, what it looked like, what it did, and how to use it effectively.

Walking out toward the symbol on the floor and facing the Hands, he still wasn't one hundred percent sold on the Timekeeping thing as a whole. He'd never really envisioned himself as a constable or policeman, and his inclination toward soldiering only extended as far as protecting Éire from her enemies, be they German or British. Maybe he just didn't quite feel the loyalty toward the Hands or the Time industry as a whole that would cause him to get upset over someone stealing something that he wasn't sure the Hands had a right to say they owned. Who could claim to own Time, really?

After half a breath of staring at each other, the Zero Hour stood and spoke.

"MacEoghan Dearbhfhine, probationary Timekeeper, you approach the Hands today for your review, your intentions to advance to the rank of Apprentice Timekeeper. Is this correct?"

"Aye, that's why I'm here," MacEoghan answered.

He might have hoped for an immediate procession into the knowledge exam, might have expected a quick rundown of some rules and guidelines and general housekeeping. What he was assailed with, however, was a good ten minutes of absolutely loathsome formalities.

"Do you believe that you have studied diligently under your mentor, have acquired the necessary knowledge, have learned all the necessary skills, and have achieved the necessary mental fortitude needed to not only pass your review but continue your training as an Apprentice Timekeeper and beyond?"

If I didn't, would I be here? Is this where I'm supposed to say Sean is a tyrant or an idiot and he's forcing me here against my will? "I think so."

"Your review will consist of three parts. The first part is a test of knowledge, to be sure that you understand the basics of Time and how it works. The second part is a test of skill, to be sure that you have a solid foundation for the skills you will be learning in the future. The third part is a psychological evaluation, to be sure that you are fit to wield Time and uphold the Laws. Do you understand this?"

Why, no. I thought I was here to receive my license as a veterinarian. "I understand."

And it just—didn't—stop. Everything the Zero Hour said, MacEoghan had to confirm he understood. Was there a malfunction in the translators that he was somehow unaware of? What would happen if he said he didn't understand? How much time could be saved if all that so-called prep time in the empty room was instead spent signing forms to this same effect? Maybe they could have a disclaimer that said that by entering the Inner Sanctum, he was agreeing to all of the rules and anything bad that happened was the result of his own poor planning? If he wasn't ready for this test—this Apprentice review—then clearly he shouldn't be here.

"You are not to discuss your review with anyone, even your mentor," the Zero Hour continued. "Do you understand this?"

"I understand," MacEoghan sighed. Sean had only mentioned it half a dozen times. Were there really Masters out there who didn't disclose all of this information? Were there some probationaries out there in the universe who just walked in here at their Master's behest, utterly oblivious to what was going on?

"The review does not conclude until we have rendered judgment and deemed you worthy of advancement or not. Do you understand this?"

He tried not to roll his eyes. "I understand."

Of course, this meant that the Hands could drag this out for an unholy length of time if they felt like it. At the same time, considering how many reviews they likely presided over in a day, they could also decide to cut it short. They could also decide to forego these atrocious formalities and instead cut right to the review.

"Commence now the first part of the Apprentice Timekeeper review for MacEoghan Dearbhfhine."

Finally! True, MacEoghan was less confident in his straight knowledge than his demonstrable skills, but he would take anything over what he'd just endured. He shifted his stance and glanced around at the assembled Hands. There was no official written language in the Wheel, only some universal symbols, so he knew this was going to be an oral test. For their sake, he hoped they didn't ask any opinion questions, because he had certainly formulated a few just in the last ten minutes.

"The first part of the review is a test of knowledge. It is an oral exam only. Each of the Hands of Time will pose a question. You will have one Base Minute to begin to answer the question. At the end of the Base Minute, if you have not begun to answer the question, you will forfeit the question. At any time in your answer, you may simply state, 'Unknown' and the test will move on, and you will forfeit the question."

God Almighty, more rules and formalities. MacEoghan wanted to claw his eyes out. Would this never end? He didn't even know what the rest of the speech was, only that when the Zero Hour asked if he understood, he couldn't help but reply with an emphatic, if sarcastic, "Aye, I understand."

"Very good. Let's begin."

Are you sure? Really sure this time? You actually mean that we can begin with the questions? Are you absolutely certain there isn't some obscure rule or bylaw you forgot to recite?

But the Zero Hour sat and another Hand stood.

"Name all of the Hands of Time," it commanded.

Micah was better at lists than he was. Micah had absorbed a dozen different ways to memorize dull facts in school, had offered to refresh MacEoghan on some of those ways in order to help with this test. MacEoghan knew those methods just as well; he just hadn't really expected to need them. It wasn't like the question was a surprise. Sean had told them repeatedly that this was likely to be the first question the Hands asked and they had better get it right. Somehow, for all of that, MacEoghan had still expected it to be...different. Somehow.

The answers were in his head, in the same way that there were papers in a filing cabinet. The time to organize them was not in the middle of a big, important meeting, but here he was.

He fumbled through all fifty-one titles, fairly certain that he may have said a couple of them twice and maybe missed a couple, too. Eventually, he indicated that was he done. The Hand sat, and another stood.

"Name the ranks of the Timekeepers, starting with yourself."

Well, it was rote information, but it was more interesting and more pertinent information. He nailed the ranks quickly and easily, and he basically did the same with the ranks of the Harvesters and Merchants.

He supposed it could be argued that the Hands were pertinent information, too. They were, essentially, his bosses, his big bosses all the way at the top of the chain. Except he was unlikely to interact with the Hands as much as Harvesters and Merchants. Actually, he couldn't recall even meeting any Harvesters or Merchants at home. What was the point of all of this, then? If Harvesters were the most likely to turn Runner, shouldn't they go where the trouble was most likely to be? He was no strategist, but that seemed like a logical thing to.

On the other hand, if there was no trouble, then, as it had been pointed out multiple times, there was no real limit to what he could do with Time outside of Timekeeping. There was no rule saying he couldn't be a boxer and use Time in that realm. Not that he would use it excessively, of course, just to protect his face. And who knew what other things might tickle his fancy? Maybe he would become an actor; that sounded like a promising industry to get into, and it was expanding rapidly. Or maybe he would get into mechanics.

His daydreams almost caused him to miss hearing the next question.

"What is a Scout?"

Scouts were those who went out into the wilds of space, searching for information and those worlds and species who had, somehow, never heard of the Time industry. Their job was to bring these new peoples into the fold, even if it was just one single person, just enough to establish a foothold. The bravest of Scouts sought out these new, untouched worlds, while the majority of them actually came behind them to start cataloging information for the Wheel Archives. Everything about a planet or species was cataloged: geography, geology, cultures and people groups, governments, history, biology, flora, fauna, nothing was left out. Depending on how advanced the species was, this information could come from the people themselves, their doctors and scientists and historians, or it could come from observation and using methods available in the Wheel. For example, according to Sean, the Wheel had more advanced knowledge about the human body than even the most up-to-date human doctors did. If anyone ever got sick or hurt and needed answers, check the Wheel Archives before going to the doctor.

But that was neither here nor there. Scouts really didn't have an official ranking system, more of a pecking order. Most Scouts didn't last more than a few years. Given that they needed to be highly trained in all Time Agent disciplines before even being considered for a Scouting position, it was both sad and a tad suspicious. For some, it was simply the price they paid for the job, making contact with potentially hostile aliens. For others, they wouldn't say. Or Sean didn't care enough to really find out. There weren't any human Scouts to ask currently, so who really cared?

The questions then began to morph from reciting textbook information to more subjective material, requiring him to give opinions. They weren't anything so open-ended as, "What is your opinion of the Time industry?" but the wording still allowed for some wiggle room.

"Name all areas of the Food Court, and is it prudent for the Time industry to provide sustenance for all creatures who act as Time Agents?" was one such question. Actually, in MacEoghan's opinion, that was two questions shoehorned together.

The Food Court was actually multiple areas, divided according to the sustenance needs of various creatures. Raw food, cooked food, waste,

251

carrion, things MacEoghan never would have considered food at all, like rocks. As for whether it was prudent, well, the Time industry did not force anyone to dine at its restaurants, but it did eliminate a potential excuse for why a Time Agent wasn't doing his job. For some species, or some cultures or individuals of a species, obtaining sustenance could be a major part of life and take up a great amount of time, regardless of any metabolic changes owing to Time and extended lives. By having food on hand at any given time, a Time Agent could spend less time worrying about his next meal and more time out hunting Runners.

It was also a good way to ensure loyalty, though MacEoghan did not actually say this aloud. He also couldn't come up with any reason why it was bad. Feeding people was arguably the fastest way to make friends, and having the resources to ensure that everyone across the whole universe had access to whatever their body considered food was incredible. He could barely imagine a market on Earth where every possible edible food was available.

Despite his irritation with the exam as a whole, MacEoghan was able to keep track of the questions fairly reasonably, so he knew he was getting close to the end. If MacEoghan had any hope during this test it was that there was a guaranteed maximum of fifty-one questions, so there was a foreseeable end to this exam. Finally, the Zero Hour stood.

"What is Time?"

What kind of stupid question was that? Was he a scientist, a philosopher? Were they looking for a defined answer or something he thought? He couldn't say that he knew any kind of dictionary definition of the word, and he couldn't think of any kind of philosophical explanation either. Time simply was. Well, maybe not quite. There was past, present, and future, cause and effect.

He knew he could just say, "Unknown," and basically shrug off the question. It would be the only question he'd done so, but that alone was enough to annoy him. He had to try, he had to say something.

So he bumbled through a few contrived sentences about the past, present, and future, cause and effect, and some relational dynamic. Maybe this was a question that would be asked at every review just to see how his understanding of Time changed as he progressed through his training and learned to control Time. Were other Time Agents asked the same question? How many different answers did the Hands actually hear? Were there any correct answers, or was this purely philosophical?

When he was finished, there was a moment of pause before the Zero Hour spoke again. It gave no indication of how well it liked his answer, but moved on to the next piece of business.

"Thus concludes the first test of the Apprentice Timekeeper review for MacEoghan Dearbhfhine. Thank you for your time and thoughtful consideration of all your answers. You have performed admirably and are a credit to yourself and your mentor. We will now move immediately into the second test, the test of skill. MacEoghan Dearbhfhine, are you ready?"

MacEoghan felt adrenaline dump into his system even as his brain told his body to settle down. Yes, he was ready to demonstrate his skills and get into a little skirmish, but how long was he going to have to stand here and listen to the Hands recite the entire rulebook?

"The second part of the review is a test of skill, and this test will be done in two parts." *There it is.* "The first test is a standing test. You will be asked to create Bands with specific parameters which will not exceed the reasonable limits expected of a probationary Timekeeper. If we the Hands are satisfied with the results of the standing test, then we will move on to the second test, that is, the reflexive test where you must create Bands reflexively in a variety of scenarios."

The combat portion, MacEoghan thought.

"The test will end when we the Hands are satisfied with your performance," the Zero Hour went on. "Do you have any questions before we begin the test?"

"Can we start now?" MacEoghan blurted. He hadn't really intended to say it out loud, or maybe he had but less annoyed than it sounded. Or maybe he had intended that, too, but— Never mind. It was out there and he wanted to actually start demonstrating his skills instead of listening to them talk and talk and talk.

It was impossible to tell exactly how the Zero Hour reacted to MacEoghan's outburst. The acoustics in the Coliseum also made tone difficult to judge. The Zero Hour sat slowly, saying, "Commence now the first test of the second portion of the review."

Now we're getting somewhere.

The first Hand stood. "Fast Band, hour:second."

Hour:second? That was all? Were they going to punish his outburst by patronizing his skills? Maybe it was his own fault for being so impatient, but he hadn't asked to be bored to death with formalities.

Still, he did as he was asked, trying his hardest not to appear flippant about it. Fast Band, then bring it in and feather it so it settled into the hour:second ratio, where one hour inside was one second outside. According to Sean, it was one of the first standardized ratios that an probationary learned, right after getting used to just the concept of putting up Bands.

Just as soon as he got it in place, it was ripped away. MacEoghan stumbled forward several steps, gasping for air. Now what was that about? Had that been intentional? He had no chance to recover his wits let alone ask the question before the next Hand was ordering him to create a Slow Band of ten seconds:four hours.

So that was how it was going to be, MacEoghan figured. The Hands were just going to be vindictive about it. Had they never heard of constructive criticism? Another thought crossed his mind. Would they fail him for a bad attitude? The Brothers had done that more than a few times, so why not the all-powerful masters of the universe?

The thought was sobering enough that it took the edge off his frustration and desire to metaphorically spit in their faces with each trick they demanded. And as the test wore on with the requests alternating between Fast and Slow and becoming ever more specific in their ratios, he couldn't help but wonder what exactly he'd expected from the test. What had he come here expecting to do, really? Yes, yes, combat and all, he was looking forward to that, but when it came to the basic information and demonstration of skill, had he really expected anything more than a grade school exam for a probationary Timekeeper?

The most interesting thing they asked of him in the skill test was to slide a Band from Fast to Slow, but even that wasn't a show-stopping challenge. One of the most difficult things he had learned so far, yes, but he had done it a time or two, mostly out of curiosity to see if it even could be done. And it could. And he did. It was made a bit more difficult because of how tired he was—this owing mostly to how forcefully the Hands were taking his Bands away from him—but then it was over.

"And so concludes the first part of the second portion of the review," the Zero Hour said formally. "You have performed admirably and may take the second test. Are you ready?"

Might as well. He'd have probably half an hour to recover some of his strength before ever getting to the exam.

"I'm ready," he answered, trying to keep his tone neutral.

"The second part of the test is a test of reflexes. As you do not yet possess the skills to perform Outside Bands, this test will be brief." MacEoghan decided he wasn't going to tell the Hand that he already knew about External Bands; he didn't need to be punished for getting too uppity. "For this test, you must use Fast and Slow Bands in order to defend yourself. Do you have any questions before we begin?"

"Is this open combat?" he wondered. "Am I expected to hurt someone?"

"You are expected to defend yourself, but there is no penalty for attacks or counterattacks."

Well now, this was why he'd shown up today. MacEoghan rolled his neck and shoulders and bounced on his toes. "All right, let's get this show on the road."

Probationary exam, so it probably wasn't intended to be too difficult. How it was balanced among all the different species in the universe with their varying sizes and strengths and weaknesses, he did not know. Honestly, he didn't really care. He was back in the ring and this time, his opponent had the same abilities he did.

He didn't know quite whether it was one of his Reflex Band senses or just his natural fighting sense that initially tipped him off, but he didn't bother to waste time reaching for a full Band and trying to study the situation. He let the Reflexive Band linger just long enough that he was able to step back, turn in, and lash out with a full right hook. He didn't know what he was meeting, if it was an actual attacker or maybe some ranged projectile, but he didn't want to take chances.

Coming face-to-face with the Bat itself was not what he was expecting. At least seven foot tall, a wingspan of at least twenty feet, long, muscular arms with talons more than fingers, just the sight of it took a lot of the wind out of MacEoghan's hook. He could tell he was within an inch of the Bat's flesh, somewhere on its arm, but he swiftly elected to take that Reflexive Band, turn it into a full Fast Band, and tuck and roll out of the way, narrowly missing the claw at the end of the Bat's wing.

The Bat whirled around with theatrical flourish and, not wasting a beat, charged him again. MacEoghan dove forward. Not wanting to lose momentum, he opted for a Slow Band for just a moment. The Bat sailed quickly over him, but as MacEoghan came out of his dive and whipped around, he released the Band just in time to grab the Bat's three-foot tail. His hands slid along the remarkably soft skin until he reached the end and the barnacle-like formation at the end pierced his hands with tiny spines. He yelped at the same time the Bat did.

While he was fighting the urge to let go because of the wound, the Bat had already circled around and was coming in for a full takedown, using its wings like a cloak to keep him in.

"I see you," the Bat hissed.

MacEoghan's confusion saw the end of the match, at least for him. The Bat's tail ripped from his grasp and the creature slammed into him with the gentle caress of a train. The rest of it was a bit of a blur as he hit the ground and rolled, sometimes able to breathe and see light, other times being crushed under an enormous bat-like creature with stunningly soft skin covered in velvety peach fuzz.

Then he was free, lying on the ground, staring at wall or ceiling he could not tell. He'd been knocked out a time or two, and this was feeling a bit like the morning after but right away. Once his other senses let him know he was not in immediate danger, he began the slow process of figuring out where all his limbs were and how to use them to get to a standing position.

"Are you well, MacEoghan Dearbhfhine?" one of the Hands asked.

MacEoghan drunkenly stumbled back to the symbol on the ground. How had he never noticed that there was more than one? He wasn't sure which was which, so he just picked one. He looked up at the Hands and nodded.

"I'm fine. Not the first time that's happened." He tasted blood dripping into his mouth from his nose.

"Thus concludes the second part of the Apprentice Timekeeper review for MacEoghan Dearbhfhine," the Zero Hour decided. All the Hands stood. "The third part of the review, the psychological exam, will commence shortly. You will be returned to your waiting room where food and drink will be provided."

As invigorating as the fight had been, MacEoghan decided he wasn't going to argue with resting for a few minutes, and he dutifully slogged off back toward the tunnel. There, the Bat stood by the opening mechanism, stoic as ever. MacEoghan was inclined to just walk on by, but he paused first and looked at it.

"Can you see?" he wondered. "Is that why you said you could see me?" And why would it have said that, except maybe to try and throw him off?

But the creature did not answer, simply pointed out which waiting room was his. MacEoghan's head was pounding enough that he wasn't overly concerned with it at the moment, and he staggered toward the indicated room.

But when he opened the door, he paused. He'd expected to find Sean and Micah. Instead, he found none other than Kearney and Kane.

"Well, well, look who decided to show up," Kearney sneered, standing from where he'd been sitting on the bench against the wall. "Seems to think he's one of the good guys now."

"Criminal who becomes a cop in order to hide his crimes," Kane agreed.

"How did you get in here?" MacEoghan demanded, squinting as if it might make his headache go away. "Where are Sean and Micah?"

"Took a while to figure out where you'd gone and what happened," Kearney explained. "Got yourselves adopted by a nice family, changed your names, that was a good start. Then you got yourselves some nice formal training by a bleeding heart officer to try and cover up your misdeeds, pretend it was all just some misunderstanding."

"Sean's a real officer and you're not. That much can be verified in the Archives. And there are no rules about how we can use Time outside of the industry. I can use it in boxing if I want to."

"We're not here to talk about boxing. We're here to talk about murder."

"You're no policeman, nor prosecutor, nor judge."

"No, but we know those who are. And just as soon as you're done here, we're going to take a little walk. Or maybe I should just Suppress you here and now and march you out anyway, forfeit this little review. You can try again in...thirty, forty, fifty years? Good things come to those who wait."

MacEoghan's head and heart throbbed in rhythm. "You would have done the same thing, and I didn't even intend for him to die."

"Intent is such a small, small factor," Kane sighed.

"You weren't there. You wouldn't believe—no one believes—what the Brothers do to the boys in their charge. I can't even call it care."

Kearney shrugged. "So you didn't intend to kill him, but you had fantasized about it. Even a little bit? You wouldn't have minded if he were to vanish from the face of the Earth?"

MacEoghan glared at the man. "You're not a prosecutor. And as far as I'm concerned, defending and avenging my twin and countless other boys is hardly a crime."

Kane tsked. " 'If a man even hates his brother, he is guilty of murder.' "

MacEoghan took several menacing steps toward Kane, aware of Kearney approaching behind him. "Don't you dare quote Scripture at me. The Brothers knew how to twist it for their ends, and you're no better than them."

"What are you going to do? Kill me, too? Cut off my cock like you did Brother Andrew?"

MacEoghan got in his face. "You're a small man with a big mouth. There's no use of Time in this place, and there's only the three of us in here. Why don't we see who really has the power here?"

"You have a psychological exam coming up," Kearney mentioned casually.

MacEoghan kept his gaze firmly fixed on Kane. "But it's not right now, is it? I don't think it would take too long to put you on the ground. And once I've beaten you in the ring, maybe I'll drag you two out before the Hands themselves and see how they want to deal with your intimidation and impersonation. I don't think they would appreciate learning that you're claiming to be officers when you're not."

Now Kearney got close on MacEoghan's right side. "No one likes an uppity probationary who thinks he knows everything just because he got a little lucky."

MacEoghan turned his head to look at him. "We'll see who's lucky today."

His first strike, then, was not against Kearney, but Kane. Surprised, Kane stumbled back. At the same time, Kearney, who did not immediately jump to the defensive like MacEoghan might have hoped, lashed out with his own formidable strike, catching MacEoghan in the side of the face.

Immediately MacEoghan knew this was not his brightest idea today. Even talking back to the Hands was looking like a better idea. But there was no getting out of this now, not until he'd won.

Kane recovered quickly and, while MacEoghan was reeling from the blow, his dizziness augmented by preexisting injuries, got in a good one-two punch with a kick for good measure, sending him to the ground. He was no lightweight either. Both men were clearly veteran fighters, even without Time to back them up. And here was MacEoghan, probationary Timekeeper who couldn't even rightly call himself a boxer because he was on no circuit but the street circuit, wherever the wind took him, whichever pub would let him fight a few rounds in exchange for a free meal and a couple free beers. He might have pointed out the strength he'd maintained because of the fishing, but if he wanted to be honest, that was the only reason this fight was even remotely fair.

MacEoghan managed to roll away from a followup strike by Kearney, getting to all fours and using the wall to stand back up. He did remember that he got in two, possibly three good punches, but after that was a fast slide into a deep sleep.

When he came to, his whole body ached and the exhaustion made it so the best he could do was open his eyes and look around. The room was empty save for Sean to his left. MacEoghan did not have the energy to speak or make any real noise, and it was a couple minutes before Sean noticed him awake.

"If you didn't already have a concussion, I'd punch you right in the fucking face," Sean said, not moving from where he sat against the wall.

MacEoghan wanted to ask why, but the best he could do was a small, exhausted sigh.

"I'll just cut to the chase so we don't waste time with twenty questions. That was your psychological exam. That was a hallucination. The drugs they give you allow you to interact with it fully, with all of your senses. The drugs also interact with some fancy technology so that I can also observe it while being hidden from your view. Micah's review was the same way. Don't worry, he didn't see it, only I did." Now Sean shifted his position, though he didn't get much closer. "You're a fucking idiot."

MacEoghan didn't think it was fair to accuse a man who couldn't speak to defend himself. But Sean clearly had a little speech prepared, and MacEoghan was his captive, and intended, audience.

"I know that you've been dealing with Time for a lot of years. You want to learn more, you want to advance. You're not much for sitting still and you don't like authority figures. Fine. Now wake up and realize you're in the real world now. There are methods and hierarchies and authorities that, sometimes, we have to acknowledge and obey whether we like it or not."

MacEoghan did not take a breath so much as forcefully seize it and wheeze out, "Big words coming from someone who fought in the War for Independence and the Civil War."

Now Sean did stand and, taking advantage of MacEoghan's current state, punch him in the face. It was not perfectly on target and MacEoghan could tell it was nowhere near full strength, but he still moaned pitifully.

"I swear to Jesus, Mary, and Joseph, *a MhacEoghan*, if the Hands don't pass you, I will keep you as a probationary for another three full years or until your brother becomes a Journeyman, whichever is longer!" He huffed a sigh and sat back down. "You're lucky they could bring you back."

"What?" MacEoghan rasped.

"The psychological exam. You either realize it's a hallucination, or it will kill you."

"What kind of stupid test is that?"

"It's just how it is."

"How was I supposed to know it was a hallucination if it's intended to engage all of my senses?"

Sean rubbed his face. "If there's no personal use of Time in the Wheel, outside of specific instances like the skills exam, how were they going to Suppress you and drag you out?"

That was it? That didn't seem fair at all. How was he supposed to catch that one little cue? And he was fairly certain he knew how that would have played out.

You can't Suppress me. There's no Time use here.

Well then we'll just kick your ass the old-fashioned way and drag you out unconscious against your will.

And they had very effectively kicked his ass, just not dragged him out. Or would they have been significantly weaker if that was the case? MacEoghan couldn't think too straight about it right now.

"When do we get our results?" It was Micah, thought MacEoghan couldn't see him.

Sean sighed and turned his attention away from MacEoghan. "As soon as your stupid half is feeling up to it."

MacEoghan felt himself burn with embarrassment, though he still felt like it couldn't be entirely his fault. If they wanted to see a real, unfiltered reaction, well, they got it, for better or worse.

It took the better part of an hour, but eventually MacEoghan was able to get to a standing position on his own and walk with some help from Micah. It was slow-going back to the Seat where the Hands were assembled, as impassive as ever in their shrouds.

"Micah Dearbhfhine, MacEoghan Dearbhfhine, you have completed the review in order to advance from probationary Timekeeper to full Apprentice Timekeeper status," the Zero Hour said, standing. "How are you feeling?"

Like they cared, MacEoghan thought. Whether it was Sean's chastisement or his own exhaustion, he himself did not answer, and the most Micah gave was, "We are recovering well."

MacEoghan fully expected there to be another half hour of formalities and empty praise, congratulating them on their intense studying, wealth of knowledge, great skill, and whatever other frills they deemed necessary. Sean had said that the hallucination could kill them, but the boredom was more likely.

"Micah Dearbhfhine," the Zero Hour began, "as to the first part of the review, the oral exam, testing your knowledge of Time, fifty out of fifty-one Hands were satisfied with your performance."

Knowledge test, of course Micah did well. MacEoghan was happy for his twin, really, but it was buried beneath his own burning contempt at the moment. The good news was that they didn't have to go over every single question and have a group discussion on it.

"As to the second part of the review," the Zero Hour went on, "the first test, the standing skill test, forty-two out of fifty-one Hands were satisfied with your performance."

Not so great there, MacEoghan thought, an he was forced to wonder why. Sure, Micah didn't have as many years of practice as he did, but then, almost no one did. And Micah was no slouch; he did know his stuff. Apparently even that wasn't good enough for the Hands.

"As to the second part of the review, the second test, the moving skill test, forty of fifty-one Hands were satisfied with your performance."

Considering the test was combat against the Bat, that hardly seemed fair. Didn't survival count for anything?

"As to the third part of the review, the psychological exam, fifty-one of fifty-one Hands were satisfied with your performance."

Even Sean reacted to that one with an expression that was thoroughly impressed. MacEoghan hoped his expression and body language conveyed something similar. Then he wondered what his brother had seen in his hallucination; it seemed to be participant-specific.

"As to the review overall, forty-eight of fifty-one Hands were satisfied with your review. Congratulations, Micah Dearbhfhine, you passed your review. You are now an Apprentice Timekeeper."

The Zero Hour then turned his attention to MacEoghan, still lightly leaning on Micah.

"MacEoghan Dearbhfhine," the Zero Hour began, "as to the first part of the review, the oral exam, testing your knowledge of Time, thirty-eight out of fifty-one Hands were satisfied with your performance."

Should have seen that one coming. At the very least, he bungled some of the titles, which he was sure angered those Hands.

"As to the second part of the review, the first test, the standing skill test, forty-eight out of fifty-one Hands were satisfied with your performance."

Had he done something wrong? He'd hit all of the Bands with speed and accuracy. Or was it the bad attitude thing?

"As to the second part of the review, the second test, the moving skill test, fifty-one of fifty-one Hands were satisfied with your performance."

Different test, same perfect score, which elicited a similar expression and congratulations from Sean. MacEoghan just wished he felt good enough to accept the praise.

"As to the third part of the review, the psychological exam, twenty-seven of fifty-one Hands were satisfied with your performance."

Ouch. MacEoghan flinched at that and both Micah and Sean made disapproving sounds. Damn it. Sean was right; he was an idiot. A fucking idiot. Damn it. Three more years of being a probationary. Or until Micah made Journeyman. Damn it damn it damn it.

"As to the review overall, thirty-seven of fifty-one Hands were satisfied with your review." The Zero Hour paused, and MacEoghan didn't need an intergalactic interpretor to figure out what it meant. *Here comes the failure.* "You have clearly demonstrated good knowledge and great skill. However, the psychological exam was somewhat concerning."

"I understand," MacEoghan said without being prompted.

"Do you?" The Zero Hour turned its attention to Sean. "His knowledge and skill have granted him the privilege of advancing to Apprentice Timekeeper. However, he and you will remain under probation of the Grandfathers for the foreseeable future, until he can demonstrate clearer, more insightful thinking into what it means to be a Time Agent in service to the Time industry."

"I understand," Sean said stiffly.

The Zero Hour looked back at the twins.

"Congratulations, you have the privilege of advancing to Apprentice Timekeeper status, that is, if you choose it." Micah and MacEoghan exchanged a glance. "Timekeeping is not an easy task, and many probationaries are frightened by the things they see in the psychological exam, as well as what they encounter at home. Time demands much from those who protect it, and it is not a job all can accomplish. Therefore, it is now that we offer you a chance to safely renounce your Apprenticeship, renounce Time, and walk away back to what may be a normal or abnormal life for your species. Your clock will not be broken, and no ill mention of you will come because of it. Your Timekeeping abilities will be Suppressed. The idea is not that it is something you can come back to at a whim, like a hobby, but to provide a safe way out and to protect you in the future. While Suppression itself is not irreversible, the premise is that it is permanent. If you require, you may be given time to consider the options."

MacEoghan knew his answer, but he looked at Micah with some concern. This was exactly the out his brother had been looking for, and he could even get the blessing of the Hands to go with it.

"I'm staying," MacEoghan cut in before anyone else could speak. "I didn't come this far to quit now, and I know I have a long way to go."

"Your decision has been rendered," the Zero Hour confirmed. "And so, MacEoghan Dearbhfhine, do you promise to uphold the Laws of Time, to defend them and execute them in the pursuit of justice both within the Wheel and without, apprehending those who would seek the use it selfishly or for destructive purposes, no matter where they may hide, and bring order and peace to the area you serve?"

"I do." He said it because he knew it was the right answer, not necessarily because he fully believed it.

The Zero Hour then looked expectantly at Micah. After a moment, his twin nodded. "I'll stick with it. There's still a lot I need to learn."

Then attention was given to Sean. "And do you, Sean McKeogh, promise to continue to train Micah Dearbhfhine and MacEoghan Dearbhfhine in the respect of a Timekeeper, to uphold the Laws of Time, to defend them and execute them in the pursuit of justice both within the Wheel and without, teaching him of the wonders and dangers of the universe that he may be wise and bring order and peace to the area you serve?"

"I do," Sean swore.

"And so, Micah Dearbhfhine and MacEoghan Dearbhfhine, you are now a full Apprentice Timekeepers. The use of the Arena is available to you with the oversight of your mentor, as well as several sections of the Archives. Per the standards of human Timekeeper training, it is expected that your Apprentice training take approximately two Base Years. There is much to learn until you become Journeymen. Study well."

"Thank you, we will," Micah said.

Sean shuffled the twins out of the Seat just as fast as he could, before MacEoghan could do anything else stupid that day.

NEXT STEPS
OLDER BROTHER

A ll right, I want to know what the fuck happened at your review, and I want to know now."

After returning to Earth from their review, both MacEoghan and Micah had basically passed out and slept for a day and a half. Sean Banded them with ease so they could sleep and recover, then left them to their regular routine—in this case, the middle of dinner—with hardly a word of either congratulations or farewell. He had returned two days later, allegedly for training, although his mood once they had retreated to their normal training location down the beach was decidedly less than enthusiastic. The strangest part was that he seemed to be upset at both of them.

"I lost my temper," MacEoghan began. "I—"

"I'm not talking about that, although I'm glad you're owning up to it," Sean cut in, his demeanor saying he wasn't above punching MacEoghan in the face a second time. "I'm talking about your psychological exams. Aye, it's a fantasy conjured by your own minds, but there is still an element of truth to it. I want to know that truth, and I think it has to do with Kearney and Kane's original misgivings about you. So, let's hear it."

MacEoghan glanced at Micah who had gone wide-eyed and pale. Neither was keen to relate the tale of their escape from St. Joseph's, but did they have a choice? Sean had seen something was amiss, and the only other story available was what Kearney and Kane conjured up.

"We were sent to St. Joseph's as orphans," MacEoghan began. "I don't know what you believe about the schools, but they're horrendous places. Boys are beaten, locked up like animals, and touched in unspeakable ways. The reasons for it all ranged from slurping your soup too loudly at mealtime to getting a math problem wrong to no reason at all or whatever they made

266

up at the time. I wouldn't let myself be touched inappropriately, so I received a good number of beatings."

"When you say touched—"

"They'd call a boy to the front of the room," Micah continued, face stark white. "Usually a little one, under ten. The Brother might make some pretense of a lecture or a question to answer, but he would put his hand down the boy's trousers, or have the boy do so to him."

"That's absurd." Sean spoke the words, but there was less hostile refusal than most people gave upon hearing such an accusation.

"That wasn't even the worst they did," Micah shot back. Color came back to his skin, although it was red and he was starting to sweat. "When they took the boys and explained how a boy's body works, how a man's body works, any boy who didn't understand was given an object lesson. Forcefully."

"And they did this to you."

"Brother Andrew did, aye. I screamed and I cried and he beat me for it and locked me in a cage."

MacEoghan noticed that his brother was shaking, with rage, with shame, who could say? Micah himself probably didn't even know for sure as tears streamed down his cheeks and he clenched his fists until they were as white as his face had been a moment ago. MacEoghan cleared his throat and went on, "We'd been planning to escape for a while. We knew that with my ability to Band, we'd have a better chance of getting away than any of the other boys who had tried over the years. The night Micah was taken away and didn't come back, I knew that as soon as I found him, we were leaving. No more hesitation.

"I found him, freed him from the cage. We were just going to run, but then he told me what happened. So instead, we went up to Brother Andrew's room. I cut his cock off, Micah defiled him with an iron rod. Then we ran and we kept running. It was hard at first, when we were still young enough to be sent back to the schools. Once we were older, it got easier, and life just went on. Until Kearney and Kane showed up, we had no idea what had happened to Brother Andrew. We just wanted to stop him from hurting any more boys."

"We also switched names," Micah added quietly, having composed himself somewhat. He jerked his head toward MacEoghan. "Micah was always the braver one. He thought that by giving me his name, it would make me braver."

Sean nodded. "I recall you saying something of the sort."

For a long moment, none of them said a word. MacEoghan could feel the relief in his brother, just the fact that someone was giving even a little credence to his story. The fact that someone had listened through the whole story without trying to shout down his accusations with sentiments about how holy and good the Brothers were for running the schools at all. MacEoghan wouldn't say he didn't feel a measure of relief, too, that someone not only knew what he'd done, but might even be giving weight to the reason why he'd done it, and the fact that it wasn't even intentional. He hadn't meant for Brother Andrew to die. His whole goal had been to stop the man from harming any more boys and maybe give a lifelong reminder of what that entailed. And, well, he hadn't technically failed either of those goals.

At the same time, he'd just given a full confession to murder. And both of them had been in on it. Banding might have saved themm from the law for this long, but Sean had the skill to not only track them down and bring them back if they tried to run, but also to Suppress them so they couldn't Band and try to run again.

"You know I've done a lot of fighting," Sean began slowly. "I've fought in the Great War, the Anglo-Irish War, the Civil War. This war across the channel, whatever Emergency they've dubbed it, is the first fight I haven't gotten into. But I've done my share of fighting. And killing. I can no more condemn you for killing Brother Andrew in defense of your twin than I could condemn myself for killing men in defense of my countrymen. And, aye, sometimes I killed my own countrymen."

MacEoghan breathed a sigh of relief.

"As I've told you before, you have to pick your battles, pick your causes. Judging by what you've told me, what Kearney and Kane told me, and what I learned through your exams, I think I have a pretty good idea of what happened. I'm not exactly a great lover of Catholics, though I try to keep that to myself since the end of the Civil War." Sean huffed a sigh and shifted his stance. "But I will tell you this: I am probably the only one who will give you any sympathy for this, and I am probably the only one who would not turn you over immediately for murder. I doubt they'd convict unless you gave them this same confession, but the trouble is more than it's worth.

"And I'll tell you this, too, especially you, *a Mhicah*: It's been a long time. You were an orphan boy then. Well, you're a grown man now and you've got a good family here. I think you know that, since you've expressed your desire to be Suppressed and settle down into normal life with your own family. To that end, you have to move on. Set it aside, focus on your business, focus on the family you want to have. What's done is done. You can't change it, and you especially can't speak of it. Ever. To anyone. Do I make myself clear?"

MacEoghan and Micah glanced at each other again. A little sympathy and no murder charges were apparently the best they were going to get out of this. The twins nodded.

"We understand."

"Good." Sean nodded once. "You're both Apprentices now. I know that means less to you, *a Mhicah*, but you are both Apprentices which means we move forward. Understand?"

"Yes, sir."

"Now then, is there anything else I need to know? Something else important you want to tell me?"

Again the twins glanced at each other. Then, each in his own way, "No, sir."

Sean nodded slowly, studying each of them. Finally, "Good. And I expect that if anything major does happen, I will hear about it. One way is appreciated, another is not."

"Yes, sir."

After still another moment of hard study, Sean finally relaxed and MacEoghan found himself letting out a breath.

"So," Sean began, "you probably noticed from the review that I've been teaching you a little above and beyond probationary work; you have been doing Apprentice training for at least a short time now. External Bands are one of those items. Other skills include Pinpoint Banding and Double Banding." He paused as Micah raised a hand. Then, "Yes?"

"I'm guessing Pinpoint Banding is making the Band small enough that you pinpoint a specific area rather than a whole object," Micah said. "So you could theoretically heal a single cut on your arm without having to experience that full time."

MacEoghan didn't hate his twin, but he wouldn't deny a touch of envy over how Micah could articulate what he himself could probably just do or physically work out. He could probably already Pinpoint Band, had maybe already done it a time or two; he just couldn't explain it.

Sean nodded. "That's right." He looked at MacEoghan. "That's part of how your arm was healed so quickly in Bredavad without you having to experience the full portion of time required."

MacEoghan shrugged. "Makes sense."

Sean looked back at Micah. "Want to take a guess on Double Banding?"

"Holding two Bands at once?" Micah ventured.

"Yes, but not enough. There's more to it."

"Holding two different Bands at once, like a Fast and a Slow?"

MacEoghan piped up, "Holding one Band inside another." He made a motion like stacking his hands. "Double it up."

Sean pointed at him. "That's what I'm looking for." He again glanced at Micah. "You're not wrong, you just weren't completely right. It is possible to place a Slow Band inside of a Fast Band, or vice versa."

"Can you combine a Double Band in a Pinpoint Band?" MacEoghan wondered.

Sean shrugged. "Sure, why not? At higher levels, it's even possible to build a Band that's Fast on one side and Slow on the other."

"Why would you want to do that?" Micah wondered.

"Oh, it's great for setting traps. Because the majority of Runners are Harvesters, they can't see Bands, or not well, but they know enough about them to perceive when they're being used. Using a Slide Band like that, they'll run right into a Band and by the time they perceive it, it's too late."

MacEoghan shifted his stance. "So do we actually get to go out and start hunting down Runners now that we're Apprentices?"

Sean's expression turned into one that said he was still in trouble for his actions during his review. Nevertheless he answered, somewhat stiffly, "I might be persuaded to take you out here and there, assuming I think you're ready and the Runner isn't too dangerous."

"Do Runners get dangerous? If there are no rules about how to use Time outside—"

"Stealing Time is not punished by a slap on the wrist. The Hands of Time are extremely stringent about accounting for every second taken, and the Grandfathers are not shy about doling out punishment." Sean's expression turned grave. "If you knew that your punishment was everything your brother went through and worse, you'd fight against being taken in, wouldn't you?"

Micah cleared his throat. "Do the Grandfathers—?"

"No, no, they don't." Sean shook his head. "It's worse."

"How so?" MacEoghan wondered.

"The Grandfathers are staffed primarily by a species called Borelian. The Borelians have been blessed with an unholy gift to manipulate the body in unimaginable ways, and the most well-trained among them don't even need to touch you to do it. They can rip a man's skeleton out of his skin, cause him to experience hallucinations exactly like what you saw in the Coliseum, and break a man's internal clock so he is entirely unable to even perceive the passage of time."

Micah raised a brow. "How does that work?"

"Imagine if there were no difference between one second and one year in your mind. Even concepts like 'before' and 'after' have only the vaguest of meaning. It's not a memory problem, as if you've simply forgotten something, but the inability to place an event in any semblance of a timeframe. You could feel as though you had just left home after your mum died, but your supper from yesterday was a hundred years ago. You might physically know that one occurred before the other, just because you might physically know that you had to be small before you got big, but your innate sense of time to firmly place one event before the other is gone." Sean continued before either twin could speak. "It's a tough concept to comprehend because of how time-oriented we are, even regular people. But it's a terrible thing to witness in someone."

"You know someone like that?" MacEoghan asked.

"Knew, more accurately. I spoke to him once, left the room, came back a minute later, he thought it had been ten years. I tried to reason with him that he hadn't even left the room, how could it have been ten years? But these temporal terms no longer held any meaning. He could say what happened, but not when." Sean shook his head. "It is a terrible thing, some say even worse than any physical thing a Borelian could do."

"Having your skeleton ripped out of your body doesn't sound all that pleasant," Micah commented.

Sean nodded. "Oh, I agree, absolutely. But at least then you just die. You don't have to go through life, all the years and decades you've acquired, not knowing when is when, not being able to organize your life in any meaningful sense."

"And this is what happens when someone steals Time, the punishment they face?" MacEoghan suggested.

"It's one possibility, yes. Probably not for stealing a few seconds or minutes, but once you get into years or more, what better way to punish someone than to make all of those extra years a negligibly existent hell?"

MacEoghan still couldn't wrap his head around it. Maybe that was the point? Closing your eyes or wearing a blindfold could imitate blindness. Heavy muffs could imitate deafness. Sickness could make it difficult or impossible to smell and taste. Touch was already pretty voluntary. How did one imitate the inability to perceive time? Did he really want to? If that was one of the worst punishments the Grandfathers could dole out, beyond ripping out someone's skeleton or causing hallucinations, why would he want to experiment with it? Blind and deaf men learned to adapt, but was there no adaptation for one who had no sense of time?

"But, enough about that," Sean said, cutting into his thoughts. "You are still just brand new Apprentices and have a lot to learn. Let's start there."

MacEoghan glanced at Micah. His twin was clearly still disturbed by this new line of thought, trying to puzzle it out himself, and not entirely ready to just go back to the start of the conversation. Nevertheless, they both nodded and tried to turn their attention to simpler matters, like Pinpoint Banding.

It sounded simple enough, just creating a really small Band on a really specific area. Putting it into practice was surprisingly difficult. MacEoghan could feel Sean's smirk as he just watched the two of them struggle with their first attempts. Band just one part of themselves, didn't matter which part. A hand, a foot, whatever. It wasn't happening.

"All right, all right, stop a moment," the Master laughed after a few minutes of watching their futility. "I think the first lesson has been learned. It's not that easy."

"Why?" MacEoghan blurted in frustration.

He and Micah straightened their stances. MacEoghan clasped his hands behind him, hoping to appear respectful while also still working on trying to Pinpoint Band his fingers. Already apparently impossible, doing it blindly was no easier.

Sean cleared his throat and began explaining, a shadow of the smirk still on his lips. "Everything is connected in some way. Pulling yourself or anyone else out of Base Time into a Band at all is difficult. That's why there is specific training for it. But, as in this example, our bodies are also connected. This much might seem obvious, but now you understand just how deep it goes. You are trying to pull a specific part of your body, which is connected to every other part of your body, onto a different plane of Time. How can you ask part of your blood to circulate faster or slower? How can you ask one lung to work faster or slower than the other? How can you cut off the nerves sending signals back and forth to your brain?"

MacEoghan glanced at Micah, hoping he'd have some kind of well-thought-out technical explanation. He was still fiddling with his fingers behind him, but he didn't think he was coming up with anything.

"If you're trying to Band a finger," Micah began, "shape the Band around the finger—No. Don't try to start big and make the Band small. Start small and expand it only as much as you need."

Sean nodded, shrugged, and made a gesture. "Go ahead and try."

MacEoghan was already on it. Start small. Maybe even start with a tiny Band outside of himself; that was entirely possible. And from there, he could attach it to his finger, or maybe push his finger into the Band.

Sean raised a brow and looked at him. "You got it yet?"

"What?" MacEoghan wondered innocently.

His Master's tone was amused yet still unimpressed. "Your pecker's in

273

front, so there aren't too many things you could be doing back there with your hands."

MacEoghan felt his skin flush bright red as he unclasped his hands and brought them out front, showing off his attempt at Pinpoint Banding. He had a tiny Fast Band on the side of his hand, like a small red soap bubble.

"It's a start," Sean said. "Keep going."

MacEoghan was still flustered about the man's previous comment, and for a long moment, the best he could do was move the bubble around on his hand with no notable progress. Then, perhaps by accident, the end of his right pinkie poked inside the bubble. It was a bit like getting caught in a mousetrap, and he flinched. Then it felt like when his arm or leg went to sleep, pins and needles. Then he noted a bit of pain in the rest of his arm. When it started to intensify, he released the tiny soap bubble Band and looked at Sean. The man's expression said he knew exactly what had happened, what MacEoghan had felt.

"It can take some getting used to," he acknowledged. "Pinpoint Bands are very much about finesse. They are normally used for treating wounds very quickly, but there are combat uses for them as well. A couple well-placed Pinpoint Bands could very easily paralyze a man."

"If Time is a business, why would we need to know that?" Micah wondered. "Fine, so Harvesters can be violent, but if they can't use Bands like we do, just a regular Fast or Slow Band ought to be enough, shouldn't it?"

"A lot of the time it is. As for your first question, well, speaking only of the Time industry, Intervention and Triage Harvesters don't need to wait for someone to be dying in order to pull the Time out of them. Even some of lesser rank and higher skill can kill at just a touch. Some of the most skilled Triage Harvesters don't even need to touch you, just be within a certain range."

"That's absurd," MacEoghan interrupted.

"Isn't all of this absurd?" Sean countered coolly. "As for Runners who happen to be Timekeepers, or former Timekeepers, well, each side just kept developing bigger and better weapons. Look at the Emergency on the mainland, or any of the recent wars. Why do we have the weapons we have except we need to overcome a particular obstacle? A weapon to us is an obstacle to them, so they seek to overcome that with a bigger weapon or armor, and then we develop something better to overcome that, and up it goes, a kind of wretched, mutually destructive symbiosis."

Micah opened his mouth, but Sean looked at him and started speaking over him. "It wasn't perfect, but your brother got a start. Let's see you try."

Micah closed his mouth, looked ready to open it and say something more, then apparently thought better of it and turned his attention to his hands in front of him. He tried to replicate MacEoghan's method using a small soap bubble on his hand. He maneuvered it around to a cut he'd sustained earlier that morning. MacEoghan watched as that cut started to heal before their eyes and finally disappear. Well, it didn't completely disappear before Micah dropped or lost the Band, yanking his hand away as if from a flame.

"Very good," Sean praised. "I don't think it was quite what you intended, but we'll take it."

"I don't remember the Band itself hurting so much when my bullet wound was healed," MacEoghan commented.

"Practice and finesse," Sean repeated. "As a doctor, Haunstein is very good with anatomy and physiology; he knows how to limit the Band to the affected area only, and how to exclude the nerves that would register it as pain. He's boasted that he can force your body to produce morphine, I think, and counteract the pain, but I think he's also a bit of a braggart." He shrugged. "Whatever the case, he still has more experience than you."

"What about Double Banding?" Micah wondered.

"Aye, he's got more experience in that, too." Sean's eyes glittered with amusement. "Quite honestly, that's kind of what we're doing right now. You are making Bands within Bands. Now, granted, they don't all belong to the same person. If I were to Band one of you a second time, that would be true Double Banding on my part." He shook his head. "One thing at a time. For the moment, Pinpoint Banding will serve you better than Double Banding. And there's no reason you couldn't try both at the same time, a Pinpoint Band inside another Band." He shrugged again. "It's up to you. Right now, your only homework is to work on your Pinpoint Bands, getting them formed and placed where you want on command, just like regular Bands. I might suggest you stick to the basics and maybe healing small wounds; don't go trying to paralyze each other."

"Can that actually be done?" MacEoghan asked, unsure if he wanted to know the answer.

Sean's expression was very frank. "All you're doing is separating the time between when the brain tells the body to do something and when the body receives that message. You can't stop the electrical energy from firing, but you can slow it down."

"And what rank would you have to be to be able to do that? I'm guessing the German who shot me wasn't all that skilled."

"It wouldn't take much more skill than an officer, a Captain at the minimum. Unless, of course, special attention was given to that skill, which would include anatomical knowledge. Haunstein could probably do it very easily. Myself, not so much. As I said, it's only a Pinpoint Band that has been incredibly refined. Like you with your boxing; anyone can make a fist and punch something, but you have the skill to know where, when, and how to make it most effective."

MacEoghan thought about that for a moment. Just a skill that has been refined. But he still needed to be within swinging distance to be effective. Becoming a good shot with a gun at least required the gun, be it pistol or rifle. This was far more deadly and could be done at quite a range just by sheer willpower.

"Don't be working yourself up over it," Sean said, apparently sensing some of his anxiety. "You aren't likely to come across anyone that powerful as an Apprentice. Even I would be hard-pressed to name any Runners who spooked me in that way. You just keep working on your skills where you are, and I'll see you in a few days or maybe a week." His expression and stance grew serious as he pointed sternly at each of them in turn. "And for feck's sake, if any shit happens again, I better hear about it from you first. You understand?"

"Yes, sir," each twin said in turn.

They returned home where Sean wished them a good night and forced them out of the Band. The man vanished instantly and they were left standing there, just after supper on a Saturday night.

Looking around at the younger kids playing games, Sarah cleaning up from supper, and Padraig going for the family Bible to start reading, MacEoghan discerned two things about himself. First, that he was happy. He knew a moment of pure gratitude that he had this family to call his own. He had something to protect and defend, beyond just Micah. The second thing he discerned was that he was frustrated. He was a man grown now, and this training felt like he was sneaking off to go do something naughty that his mum would disapprove of. He should be free to come and go, or even just have a little privacy in his own room without worrying about little brothers running in being a nuisance. Being able to train more openly would certainly feel better. He might even be able to make more meaningful progress if he didn't have to schedule training around home life.

He should be looking for a home of his own. Ideally he might be expected to find a wife at the same time, but he wasn't concerned with that just now.

Padraig grabbed the Bible and started calling everyone into the living room to sit and listen. He sat in his favorite chair and Sarah took her rocking chair. The younger kids sat dutifully at their father's feet while MacEoghan, Micah, and Shay all found their own seats.

MacEoghan kept his posture and expression attentive, but his mind frequently wandered. Did God exist? Was He the same God that was in the Bible, or was He different? Sean had mentioned that there was a Dominion Timekeeper who claimed to have been a Roman soldier and witnessed Jesus after His resurrection. Was that true, or was he just a well-practiced charlatan who thrived on confusing Time Agents? How would anyone really be able to tell?

There were too many questions surrounding Time for MacEoghan to say he had any solid faith. He would never say this out loud, of course, but it was there, deep in his heart. He saw the comfort and joy it brought the rest of them, especially with the war across the channel, but he knew too much to feel the same way.

Padraig finished reading and the kids launched into questions and their own interpretations. Micah answered some questions or countered with his own. MacEoghan noted that his twin seemed very engaged, very...fatherly. He was stepping into a role he hadn't even auditioned for, and the worst part was, he was good at it. He loved these kids not just as younger siblings, but as his own children.

MacEoghan knew a moment of jealousy, but he couldn't say just why. Micah was planning to leave Time and take on the mantel of the family business, which also happened to include starting his own family. MacEoghan was going to stick with Time and explore the world and do as he pleased, occasionally going after some criminal Runners. There was no reason that they both couldn't get what they wanted. Just as soon as the war was over, that was exactly what would happen.

The reading and ensuing lecture ended. Sarah shuffled the youngest of the kids off to bed while the rest of them stayed up a while longer to pursue idle hobbies. Then, one by one, they made their way to bed.

"I'm surprised you were as calm as you were tonight," MacEoghan commented as he shut the door to the room he and Micah shared. "After what Sean had to pry out of you earlier."

"The kids had nothing to do with that," Micah said quietly from the edge of his bed where he was taking his socks off. "And anyway, it was nice to tell someone and have them actually believe me."

"Maybe, but it doesn't change anything."

Micah looked at him. "Just because Sean doesn't tell us what he's doing doesn't mean he isn't doing it. Maybe he'll look into it."

"Look into what? What the Brothers are doing to the boys?" He shook his head. "That's not going to change. The Church is too powerful to let it come to light."

"But we can move faster than light. At least Sean can, and other Timekeepers. He could gather evidence because the Brothers won't be able to clean it up fast enough."

"And then what? It's not like he can take them before the Grandfathers; this has nothing to do with Time. And like I just said, the Church is too powerful. They would never let it go to court, or else they'd just find themselves not guilty." He pointed at Micah. "And excommunicate you forever, if not take you to court for slander or blasphemy."

Micah's expression twisted with grief. "Something has to be done, *a Mhac*. You saw what happened, and you were willing to do anything for me.

You killed a man for me, even if you didn't intend to. But if you were to hear a story like that, you wouldn't feel motivated at all to look into it more and try to bring about some kind of justice?"

MacEoghan sighed. "I don't know. Sean's a nice guy and a good teacher, but I don't know him that well."

His brother's expression hardened. "The only reason most people ignore me is because they feel too much loyalty to the Church to believe that any evil exists within it. Sean holds no such loyalties or illusions."

Well, he couldn't argue with that one. He let out a breath and shrugged. "Maybe you're right; maybe something will get done. Just...don't hold your breath. Even if something happens, it won't be quickly. The war on the mainland is still too prominent and volatile."

Micah nodded. "Aye, you're not wrong there. You still think it's going to come here?"

"Been nothing but bad news for the Allies," MacEoghan said. "Germany is pressing hard into France. France took a beating in the last war; they haven't been able to recover too well from it."

"Germany took a beating in the last war and they're doing whatever they damned well please."

MacEoghan shrugged helplessly. "I don't know. I'm not there. But I do think that it is going to come here, whether we're neutral or not. If the Germans break France, they're going to press on to Britain, and we just happen to be in the vicinity. Britain is going to want our ports and our airspace."

"Who would you rather see invade?" Micah asked peculiarly.

MacEoghan opened his mouth, but nothing came out. It was a dumb question, but not an unfair one, given the circumstances. Finally he decided, "Germany. Britain would never give us up a second time. At least Germany might have some mercy on us like they did with Denmark."

Micah just nodded.

"What about you?" MacEoghan inquired. "Would you rather see German or British soldiers marching down the road or up from the sea?"

Micah tossed this around in his head for a minute. Then, "I think I have to agree with you. Britain has only ever been a conqueror, squatted over us for eight hundred years. They take us back, they wouldn't give us up. Germany knows what it's like to be conquered and ruled, especially by the British. Maybe they would show us some mercy like they have the Danes."

"Of course," MacEoghan said, turning off the light and sitting down on his bed, "the best option is for none of them to come here." He swung his legs up on the mattress and got comfortable. "But if they do, we'll be ready."

His brother did not reply, and for a couple of minutes, the only sound in the room was the squeak, creak, groan, and rustle of mattresses, bed frames, blankets, and pillows.

"*A Mhac,*" Micah said from the darkness, "do you think, with things going bad for the Allies, the war will be over sooner rather than later?"

"I don't know," MacEoghan replied. "Maybe."

Several minutes of silence. Then, just as MacEoghan was drifting off, Micah spoke again. "If an empire is overrun, say if Germany did take France or Britain, what happens to all of their territories?"

Fighting a yawn, MacEoghan answered, "I imagine they would come under the control of Germany."

"Oh."

"You didn't think they would just become independent, did you?"

"Some of them might want to."

MacEoghan shifted position, trying to get comfortable. "Well, that's their problem, between them and Germany."

"Oh." Another pause, then, "What do you think would happen to North Ireland if Germany took over Britain?"

"They would probably come under German control."

"But they're Irish."

MacEoghan grumbled under his breath and said, "They wanted to stay under British rule. If there's no Britain, they get to be under German rule."

"But if they didn't want to be, you think Germany would let them come back to Ireland?"

"I don't know. Maybe."

He could hear Micah shift position. "You think Sean is still part of the IRA?"

"Go to sleep, *a Mhicah,*" MacEoghan sighed.

"But do you think so?"

"Of course I do. He even admitted to it."

"After the war is over, are you going to join him? It wouldn't make much sense to stay here fishing with me, especially after I've been Suppressed."

MacEoghan frowned in the darkness. "The idea crossed my mind. But I also still want to get into boxing."

"The good news is, you can do both. Reunite Ireland and then become a boxer, all without aging a day."

MacEoghan had a hard time discerning his brother's intent. Was he being patronizing or calculatingly neutral? He opted for what he believed to be a safe, "I suppose."

"Well, just make sure you unite Ireland quickly," Micah sighed. "I'd like to come watch your boxing matches. Real boxing matches, not just brawls in a pub for a free beer."

Guilt gnawed at him as he heard his brother shift position some more then finally fall asleep, his breathing slowing and then turning into a soft snore. MacEoghan, who had been trying to sleep the whole time he'd been talking, was now wide awake.

This was was going to end at some point. Seeing how the Allies had been hastily evacuated from Dunkirk, France, just a few weeks ago and now Italy was jumping into the fray against France and Britain, that end seemed to be coming sooner rather than later. MacEoghan mentally paused as he wondered about the likelihood of Italy invading Ireland. He wasn't entirely sure where Italy stood in all of this other than as sort of an ally of Germany, but he didn't think they were overly interested in Ireland.

And what if Germany did offer North Ireland back to Ireland? What would a united Ireland really look like? Would the IRA really be needed anymore? What if North Ireland didn't want to come back? Would the IRA still fight for them, or fight to punish them? What would MacEoghan's role be in all of this?

He turned his head in the general direction of his brother. It wasn't the leaving that bothered him. He would be more than happy to go out on his own. Maybe it was the fact that in twenty, thirty, forty years or more, he would still have his whole life ahead of him while Micah would have his whole life behind him. Maybe they would sit down to have breakfast and catch up on things. MacEoghan would have tales of adventure and liberation and exploration and all the things he still wanted to see. Micah would tell stories about his wife and children and grandchildren.

Why couldn't Micah stay with Time? There were plenty of old men in town with a lifetime of regrets, all the things they wished they could have done differently. The two of them could do that. They could always start over. If Micah wanted to go back and raise another family, he could. If he regretted staying with the family business, then he would have an opportunity to start again. If he regretted getting married and being tied down, he had another chance to join MacEoghan and see the world. There was no need for regrets.

He rolled over and closed his eyes, trying to find sleep. With things going poorly for the Allies, who knew how this war was going to turn out? If Germany did take over Britain and tensions remained high, Micah might still be obligated to keep up with his training in order to keep the family safe. He might be forced by circumstance alone to stay in Time.

He rolled over again, his mind too active with a thousand different scenarios. He couldn't just stay here and pretend that going fishing in the morning was the most important thing in his life. He needed to do something. Anything.

CLOSE TO HOME
YOUNGER BROTHER

FRANCE ASKS PEACE.

FRANCE SURRENDERS.

LA GUERRE EST TERMINÉE. LES SIGNATURES ONT ÉTÉ ECHANGÉES HIER SOIR À 19 H. 35 LE CESSEZ LE FEU FUT SONNÉ CE MATIN À L H. 35

HITLER'S TERMS READ TO FRENCH AS FUEHRER LISTENS IN TRIUMPH.

PARIS FALLS! 'FRANCE DOOMED, BRITAIN NEXT' - NAZIS

Micah couldn't stop staring at the headlines on the newspapers, and when in the truck, the attention of both him and the driver was taken by the radio. Suddenly, the Germans were a lot closer than they used to be.

Only their ingrained habits got them to their next destination safely where they began mechanically offloading the fish, all the while listening to the grumbling of the market owner.

"Keep an eye out for British uniforms," he warned them severely. "Tanks, planes, bicycles, men on foot. Before the Germans come for Britain, the British are going to come for us. You guys ought to keep a special eye out; they're going to want your port and all the surrounding ports."

"Our port isn't deep enough," the driver commented, his voice hollow.

"Because that ever stopped any man from conquering another." The market owner shook his head. "We threw them off once and we could probably hold our own for a time, but trapped rats will do anything. When they become desperate, they'll come in full force."

Micah did not say anything, just focused on whatever his hands were doing at the time. Grab a crate, hand it off, finish this load, get back in the truck. Do not engage with anyone unless absolutely necessary. It was their last stop and now they headed home.

"I think we're about to go out of business," the driver said, turning down the radio.

"Why do you say that?" Micah wondered. "Business is steady."

"Going to be harder to import anything now with the Germans that close, to say nothing of the battering our merchant ships are already taking. The government might end up passing some law about commercial fishing activities, try to make it so we're less likely to be accidentally targeted. People are going to lose their jobs. Prices are already going up." The driver shook his head. "Fish is a luxury food, *a Mhicah*. The time, effort, and equipment required for more than a single fish on a line makes it a luxury. Plants, though, those grow with or without our intervention. When people have to choose between bread and fish, they'll choose the bread."

"The Lord multiplied the loaves and the fish," Micah offered. "He can do the same for us."

The driver barked a laugh. "Aye, He did. And He could. And if He wanted to do it, well, He can start at any time."

The man remained in a cynical mood all the way home. Meanwhile, Micah's attention had diverted from the newspaper headlines and the radio to the books in his father's office. Since agreeing to take over the business, and because he was good with numbers, Micah had effectively taken over most of the bookkeeping. He tried to think over the last couple weeks of business, tried to recall the last few months of business. Sure, costs were up, and maybe they weren't selling quite as much fish, but they weren't in dire straits. They were having to turn down fish, so it wasn't for lack of product that they were cutting back. And people still needed to eat something. Was it as grand or profitable as before the war? No. But they weren't completely cut off either.

Well, it was easy to get wrapped up in the headlines, Micah decided. He had succumbed to it as well, while they were out. Staring at the black on white, especially those publications that Micah knew were technically illegal yet still quietly distributed by the likes of the IRA and other, smaller, similar groups. The government didn't want to alarm the public and cause them to call for war, while some groups did want to sway the public to one side or the other. No doubt the latter was only reinvigorated by this tragic turn of events.

And yet, life in the very south of Ireland just kept moving. Here they were, in the truck, driving home after delivering fish, the same as they did almost every day. The landscape was dappled with sunlight as the sky alternated between gray clouds threatening rain and patches of clear blue splendor. There was no war here, only the countryside, the cliffs, the town, and the ocean.

Still, Micah could not deny there was a knot of dread in his stomach as they parked the truck and he got out, making for the office to begin the day's accounting. Opening up the office door, he saw Padraig reading a newspaper at his desk, expression grim.

Without looking up, Padraig said, "I'm supposing that you've already gotten a fair amount of commentary on the situation from the various grocers and market owners?"

Micah nodded as he sat down and quietly took the accounting book. "Yes, sir. Mr. McKinney especially."

Padraig made a sort of groaning noise as he mildly rolled his eyes and shook his head. "McKinney, that bastard." He huffed a sigh. "So, who do you think it will be first?"

"First for what?"

"To invade. Britain, to expand their military presence and try to keep us out of German hands? Germany, so they have a base to launch their invasion of Britain? Someone else? Italy, maybe?"

Micah opened up to the correct page in the ledger but did not look at the numbers. "I know most people are worried about the British."

"I didn't ask for McKinney's opinion," Padraig cut in, not unkindly. "I asked for yours."

Micah frowned and sighed. "Britain. Germany is going to need time to keep hold of France and get their assets moved so they can hold the territory. In that time, Britain will be thinking about the same thing, but the only place they can go is west into Ireland. Not saying Germany wouldn't try it, but in a race for first, I'd say Britain."

His father nodded thoughtfully. "I had similar thoughts. And what do you think that will mean for our business?"

"Well, on the one hand, we could be forced to close, either directly by order or indirectly through a collapsed market. Everything would be commandeered for military purposes, even our little fishing boats. On the other hand, we could be forced to stay in business in order to keep the invading soldiers fed and act as canaries for a German invasion."

"Canaries," Padraig echoed. "Or bait."

"Aye."

"And what if the Germans get here first?"

Micah let out a breath, hoping it didn't come across as flippant. "I think they'd be more interested in seizing the major ports just to watch their backsides, but they'd be more interested in heading for Britain first."

"Are you sure? Why not take over Ireland like they did Denmark?"

"At least the Danes still govern themselves," Micah pointed out. "And what are you suggesting? What does that have to do with fishing?"

Now Padraig lowered the paper. "Politicians declare the war. Soldiers fight the war. Ordinary men pay for the war. I'd like to not have to pay with my soul."

Micah blinked. "I agree, but...are you suggesting we fight? Fight who? How?"

His father leaned back in his chair, looking a bit distressed. "We may not have a choice, *a Mhicah*. Whether it's the British or the Germans, their intent is to disrupt our lives in order to advance themselves. Regardless of who wins and if they leave the area when this is all over, we will be stuck with the remains. My intent is for there to be something to salvage, a business that I can actually pass on." He made a forceful gesture.

"You try to fight, they'll take the business from us by force," Micah told him. "Irish, British, or German, doesn't matter."

Padraig barked a laugh. "Yes, well, tell that to your brother."

"Why, what's he done?" Micah stood suddenly. "Has he gone off to enlist?"

His father made a lowering motion. "Sit down, he's not gone anywhere. To my knowledge. Yet. But he is certainly of that mind." Padraig's expression turned disapproving. "That fellow you two sometimes meet with, Sean. He's IRA, isn't he?"

Micah swallowed nervously. "He was, at least, during the war. We've speculated that even if he isn't active now, he still has his connections."

"Of course he does, though it's a wonder he's still walking around freely." Padraig sat up and leaned forward, folding his hands in front of him on the desk. "You listen to me, *a Mhicah*, and listen very closely. I don't care if they're British, German, Italian, Japanese, or anyone else, even the IRA. This business is our business, it belongs to our family. I expect you will defend it appropriately. You understand?"

"Yes, sir," Micah said. He hesitated, then, "What if MacEoghan decided to join the IRA or some other group or even the British Army?"

He could see Padraig faltered for half a breath. "Your other half is objectively more inclined to action than you. I'm more surprised he hasn't gone off yet; I think he stays out of loyalty to you. If he goes to the IRA or the British or whoever else, then I can't stop him. But that is his choice and his choice alone for himself alone. If he somehow talks you into going with him, you are not inheriting this business. Do I make myself clear?"

Micah nodded slowly. "Yes, sir."

"I'm not trying to scare or threaten you; I simply want to impress upon you the idea of priorities. If this family and this business is your highest priority, then you'll stay with the family and the business and you'll defend the family and the business. If MacEoghan decides that national pride or winning the war or boxing is his highest priority, then I expect he will make choices to that end. But no business can survive long under wishy-washy leadership. You have already made some decisions, and I want to ensure that you will keep to those decisions. You understand?"

"Yes, sir."

"Good." Padraig folded up his newspaper and stood. He made a vague gesture to the accounting ledger. "You know what to do." He made his way around the desk to the office door. "You know where I'll be."

Afternoon chores, Micah thought, finally picking up the pen and turning his attention to the next blank page. He'd always enjoyed the numbers, but he'd never felt so relieved by them. He gathered up all the receipts Padraig had left on the desk, sorted them, then started in on the math.

When he was finished, Micah looked back over the past few months. As expected, costs had gone up, revenue had gone down, but they weren't in any more trouble than anyone else. Those who had managed to survive the initial scare after the emergency declaration were doing...well, they were doing. Not as good as before, not as bad as they could be. But it was all right, because that emergency was still far away. Just not as far as it used to be.

Even if there was some fallout from the fall of France, it wouldn't last forever. It couldn't, Micah told himself.

And yet, as the war unraveled in the weeks following France's defeat and the fight for Great Britain began, Micah watched the numbers in the ledger grow tighter and tighter, the gap between income and expenses narrowing more than he was comfortable with at a rate faster than he would have believed except he saw it firsthand in his own penmanship.

"We can't keep this up," he told his father one September afternoon. "If we go into winter with the same expenses that we've always had, we're not going to come out of winter with any business at all. We have to cut back. Cut the routes, cut the drivers, cut some of the boats. Bring the business back to where it started."

"Where it started isn't where our best market is," Padraig said. "We can cut back and save money overall, yes, but it will still be the same thin margin. Ten percent of one thousand pounds is one hundred pounds, ten percent of one pound is a dime. You can do a lot more with that hundred pounds than you can with a dime."

Micah stared at his father in disbelief. "So you want to just do nothing? Did you not just hear what I said? We're losing money, and we haven't even changed anything. It's not as though you don't know what you're doing; we're dealing with circumstances very much beyond our control."

"I didn't say do nothing—"

"All right," Micah cut in. He held up one hand and started counting off fingers. "Not doing nothing, that's out. Not cutting back, that's out. What is there left to do? We can't expand. We don't have the money to pay men to run the routes and we certainly aren't going to get any more petrol rations. And what are you going to suggest if those rations get cut?"

"The farmers up the way are having their own struggles," Padraig began, using a tone that Micah had come to know meant he already had some plan in the works. "We pack our fish and send it with them—"

"By horse and cart like it's the fifteenth century going to market?" Micah questioned. "What we don't spend in petrol will be spent on ice."

"The fish will be just fine if we only send out the orders for the local markets on the carts. And we trade the fish for milk and vegetables. It's no real expense to us, and even if we can't pay our workers entirely in coin, we can give them food so they can still feed their families. We save our petrol rations for the longer trips, claim every ration we can so maybe we can get back into some of the markets we had to previously cut."

"The people in town aren't starving for food," Micah said blandly. "Just about everyone's got a garden, a few have goats for milk and meat, and there's always the fish that we don't catch every day. Trading fish for cow's milk and vegetables up the hill won't mean a damn thing in the long-run. The people need petrol to be able to get to places; they have to pay for their electricity and coal or wood for heat; the women need textiles to sew into clothes and quilts, and they need needles to sew with; the men need wood and stone to build houses, copper for wiring and plumbing. These are just the basic necessities, never mind any comforts. Taking fish to market on a horse-drawn cart won't make any of that happen."

Micah looked at his father's face, and for the first time, he saw the fear. It was the very real fear that Padraig Dearbhfhine wouldn't have a business to pass on to any of his sons, not just Micah. It was the fear that he was going to lose everything his father and grandfather had built, that one day he was going to have to tell Sarah that he lost it all, that they had nothing.

"We'll think of something," Micah said quietly.

He turned to leave the office and head to afternoon chores, but Padraig stopped him. Micah looked back.

"If I've got my days right, your friend Sean should be coming by pretty soon, am I right?" When Micah nodded, he went on, "Maybe ask if the IRA is partial to southern fish."

Micah turned just a little and shifted his stance. "Haven't you been talking about defending the business from the Germans, the British, the——"

"If we don't do something, there won't be a business to defend. At least the IRA is made up of Irishmen. Pro-treaty or Anti-treaty, they're still our countrymen and we can be civil toward them. I know the government is doing their best to stay neutral, but if worse comes to worse, we might need the enthusiasm of the IRA to defend us."

Micah nodded wordlessly and headed out.

Sean visited far more often than Padraig knew, but every so often the man made a physical appearance. He dropped by that evening as a matter of fact, just in time for supper. He was kind enough toward the family, and Micah noted how Padraig was just a little friendlier than usual toward the man. Nothing was explicitly said about providing the IRA with fish, potentially in exchange for protection, but as Sean excused himself with the twins, Padraig looked at Micah and said, "Don't forget what we talked about."

Micah just nodded and followed Sean and MacEoghan out of the house.

"Everything all right?" Sean wondered once they were out of earshot.

Micah hesitated then relayed the gist of the conversation, finishing with, "Does the IRA have a taste for fish?"

Sean frowned and did not answer until they were in their usual training spot down the beach. Then, "I'm sorry to hear things aren't going well. Yours isn't the first story of hardship I've heard."

"Are you able to help?" MacEoghan pressed. "You're not affected by petrol rations; you can go anywhere with a portal. Take the fish all over."

Sean gave him a look. "You can't have forgotten the difficulty of portal travel."

"You know what I mean."

Sean looked at Micah. "Why the change of heart? Padraig has always struck me as someone who didn't want to get involved with any politics, especially illegal factions."

"Circumstances are forcing his hand," Micah said flatly. "I'm sure you can appreciate that."

"You come for fish once a week, we do our training at the same time," MacEoghan proposed. "Sounds simple enough." He went on before anyone could speak. "Or, even more simple, I deliver the fish to you, we train, and when I get back, I train Micah."

Sean blinked. "What are you saying?"

"We have the Germans to the south and the British to the east, and everyone seems to think we can just wait it out. I made a promise to defend the family, and I will, but I can't just do nothing. Take me with you, at least for a little while. Once things have been sorted out a bit, then I can fully commit."

Sean shifted his stance. "You want to come with me and join the IRA? That's what you're proposing?"

"Exactly. Once a week, I agree to meet you somewhere outside of town with a load of fish. I can say it needs to be far outside of town, give myself an excuse to be gone most or all of the day. I train with the IRA, I train with you in Time. When I get back, I can give Micah whatever instructions you gave me about Time and he can practice on his own if he wants. If he's not sticking around long, then it's not as important for him to be at every class and master every concept." He looked at Micah. "No offense."

Micah shook his head.

Sean sighed though it grew into something of a frustrated scowl. He turned away and ran his hand through his hair. He walked away a few steps, looked out over the darkening sea, then meandered his way back. After studying the two of them for a minute, he said, "I sort of stepped away after the war, but you never really leave. And this Emergency has seen me getting more involved, especially lately." He huffed another sigh. "I can't just bring you to one of our meetings and sign you up like a school field trip. I'll have to talk to some people."

"You've already been talking to them, I think," MacEoghan said.

"A bit, yes. We're few in number, most of our members imprisoned in order to keep them from influencing the public during this Emergency, so we have to be careful."

"And the fish?" Micah wondered.

Sean gave him a look, but it was one of annoyed resignation. "I imagine they'll appreciate the fish. Things are harder in the cities than places like this, and not everyone has a backyard garden they can pick from when things get scarce. Or when they have to pack up quickly."

"If they don't have money, we can barter."

"We'll see what they think of the idea first. Then we can work on the details. For right now, let's get back to Time training. Have you been working on your Pinpoint and Double Bands?"

Micah was comfortable enough with demonstrating his abilities that he was able to let his mind wander a little. He was less concerned about using the IRA as a means of keeping the business afloat during hard times, and more concerned with how he was going to account for it in the ledger. Barter was simply recorded as zeroing out the monetary values. Two pounds worth of fish, two pounds worth of vegetables, ultimately, it was two pounds all around. But they still had to record their transactions and their benefactors. Records were more likely to be scrutinized amid the rationing, and now they had to contend with the new fears of possible invasion messing up the neutrality ideal. Where were they going, who were they dealing with, and what kind of money was changing hands? Well, they couldn't just list the IRA as a customer or benefactor, and it wouldn't go well for anyone if they listed the IRA members by their names. Granted, fish was less important than, say, petrol or steel, but these things still had to be taken into consideration.

"When you're working on Double Bands," Sean was saying, "regardless if they are the same type or different, it's easier to start with the outer Band and then the inner Band. Then you're only dealing with one plane of Time at a time. It's also easier to construct the second Band as either the same or the reciprocal and then change it. So if you have your first Fast Band which is second:hour, you'll have an easier time starting your second Fast Band as either second:hour, or your second Slow Band as hour:second."

It was a bit hypocritical, Micah thought, for the government to declare the IRA illegal. They had all been IRA at one point, all of them using violence for their own ends in the Anglo-Irish War, and the Civil War. But the Pro-treaty IRA won the Civil War and got into more formal government power. Then they outlawed their Anti-treaty IRA counterparts and suddenly condemned them for all the violence against the British.

"Pinpoint Bands are about finesse," Sean went on. "Obviously there is a certain amount of pressure you need to hold to keep it in tact, but it should be the absolute minimum amount required while forming, reforming, everything. Once you have it where and how you want it, then you can hold tight and strengthen it as necessary. Anything else, light, light, light, like a feather."

Micah didn't blame the Taoiseach for wanting to remain neutral. Ireland just couldn't handle another war, one where they received no real benefit for joining, nor any real consequence for not joining. At the same time, Padraig wasn't wrong when he said that if the British or the Germans decided to make a move, regardless of what Ireland wanted, the IRA could probably mobilize a lot faster and fight with more enthusiasm to kick out any invaders. Except for that bit about most of them being imprisoned.

"Any Band inside another Band is a Double Band, regardless of strength or size. A Pinpoint Band inside another Band is still a Double Band. Everything we're doing here is, really, a Double Band." Sean paused. "You have a question, *a Mhac*?"

Micah looked at his brother who nodded. "Why are we doing this here? Why not use the Arena in the Wheel? That opened up to us after our review, didn't it?"

Sean blinked and shrugged. "We could use it. There isn't much of a benefit to it, though, at this stage of your training. We're still working with the basics. Once we get into combat applications, that's when the Arena becomes more beneficial. And before you ask, that typically comes at the Journeyman stage, when you receive tutelage from other Masters and you might have to learn to fend for yourself for a little while. As an Apprentice, the best you can really do is—"

"Run away."

"Aye." Sean met MacEoghan's gaze. "You're already well-equipped to handle any common street ruffian, even a battlefield full of soldiers. Anyone shows up who's more powerful than you, your better bet really is to run."

MacEoghan made no effort to hide his frustration. Sean gave him a look. "I like your enthusiasm, *a MhacEoghan*. I do. I respect that you want to do something, to feel useful, to help Éire. But even the IRA values thinking and planning before execution. If you are unable to exercise even a small measure of patience and forethought, I'm not going to waste their time—or mine—bringing your case before them. If you just want to jump into the fray, you're a liability, not an asset, whatever Time abilities you may possess. Do you understand me?"

MacEoghan took a breath and nodded. "Yes, sir."

"Good. I'm not saying that as the IRA, as if they're the only ones who think that way. Any respectable man will tell you that doing before thinking only lands you in heaps of trouble."

He moved back to talking about Time before MacEoghan had a chance to say anything. Micah gave him a sympathetic look, but that was all he could do. MacEoghan still looked annoyed, looked annoyed at Micah. What did he want him to say? No, leaping before looking is a good idea? Acting on the spur of the moment never results in catastrophe? Micah wouldn't say he didn't approve of Brother Andrew getting what he deserved, but he highly doubted MacEoghan had had any intention of even seeing the man that night, much less killing him.

They finished up their training and returned to the house. Sean promised that he would bring their concerns to "his friends" and let them know as soon as possible. It might be at the next training, it might not. Just be patient. Then he said good night to Padraig and Sarah and departed into the growing darkness.

"You look a tad frustrated," Padraig observed, looking at MacEoghan. "I take it the conversation didn't go as planned?"

"It went fine," MacEoghan grumbled, pushing his way into the house.

Micah and Padraig made their way inside, closing the door, and watched him head off into another room. Then Padraig looked at Micah who said, "It went about as expected, just not fast enough for him."

Padraig nodded. "He's got a mind to fight, one way or another."

"But why?" Sarah wondered, looking distressed. "How can anyone want to continue fighting after how much we've suffered?"

"He was too young to know that," Padraig reminded her gently.

"Oh, maybe so, but the ones putting these ideas in his head weren't. They know very well what they're doing."

"Means they value their cause more than they fear death," Micah stated.

His mother shook her head. "Means they value their cause more than they value life." She gave her husband a look. "And I don't see you trying to stop him either."

He returned the look. "What do you want me to do? Forbid him? He's a grown man, Sarah."

Now she looked at Micah. "And you? You're clearly the more sensible half. Why don't you talk some of that sense into him?"

Micah hesitated and glanced at Padraig. His father's expression said that he hadn't told Sarah about the new difficulties they were facing in the business. If she didn't know about the looming hardships, she certainly didn't know about their plan involving the IRA to try and keep it afloat.

"I've never been able to tell MacEoghan what to do," he decided. "This issue is not the one that changes that."

Sarah huffed and headed to the kitchen to busy herself. Beside Micah, Padraig let out a sigh of relief. "Thank you, lad." He motioned for Micah to follow him back outside. Once they were out of earshot of Sarah, he went on, "I haven't had the heart to tell her, but I think that time is fast approaching."

"About the business or the IRA?"

"Either. And I have a sneaking suspicion that MacEoghan is going to volunteer to be the go-between."

Micah felt his face flush. "I already told him. And he already volunteered."

Padraig shook his head. "Damn boy."

Micah was unsure if his father was referring to him or MacEoghan.

Padraig sighed. "I guess we're all willing to make sacrifices to get what we want or keep what we have, even if that means doing business with the less savory types."

"Do you ever feel guilty about it?" Micah wondered.

Padraig shrugged. "A bit, I suppose. But there's no pride in starvation, no nobility in having to look your wife in the eye and tell her that you didn't do everything you could to save the business and now you're going to have to scratch and scrape for food and fire. At least in compromise, there's a chance for the family to live on."

Padraig turned to go back inside, but Micah spoke up, saying, "Some would say that just sitting around waiting for something to happen is just as bad. If you let someone kill you, well, then they've killed you."

His father chuckled hhumorlessly as he pushed open the door. "You're a smart man, Micah, but I think you should leave the philosophizing to the philosophers."

Micah frowned and did not say anything more, but neither did he move to follow the man back inside. He knew what he meant, but apparently his father hadn't caught on. Well, they'd all basically made up their minds anyway. Some were just more enthusiastic than others.

He made his way back into the house where Padraig was gathering everyone up for the Bible reading. Micah took his usual spot in a chair beside Shay. At a call from Sarah, MacEoghan meandered his way out to his usual spot. The kids got up close to their father's feet, eyes huge. Padraig mussed Shauna's hair, then leaned back and opened up to the passage he had picked out for that evening.

It was a passage out of 1 Samuel, about King Saul going to war and disobeying the Lord's command. Although Saul was victorious, his disobedience, especially the way he flaunted his disobedience, meant that the Lord was going to revoke his kingship and give it to the little shepherd boy David.

"Who knows the phrase, 'Win the battle but lose the war'?" Padraig asked of the children. Cillian, Ciara, Brendan, and Shauna raised their hands, but Darren and Kayleigh shook their heads. Padraig glanced up at the older children. Micah, MacEoghan, and Shay all bobbed their heads yes. Padraig turned his attention back to the young'uns. "It means that you can get what you want, but in the long-run, it doesn't mean anything. In fact, it can even make things worse."

"But you have to win battles to win a war," Cillian said. "I heard Mr. O'Leary at the warehouse talking about how the Nazis took France. They had to win a battle."

"And we Irish had to win battles against the British to win that war," MacEoghan threw in nonchalantly.

Padraig ignored MacEoghan's remark as he turned his attention to Cillian. "King Saul won this battle, but he lost his kingdom. He got what he wanted in the short-term, but it ultimately cost him everything. If he had listened to the Lord and done as he had commanded, things might have been different."

"Because he didn't kill all the oxen?" Brendan questioned.

"The oxen aren't important. The greater lesson here is obedience to the Lord."

In his peripheral vision, Micah saw MacEoghan shift position. He didn't say anything, at least not until later when they were getting ready for bed.

"He wants to tell me not to go. I know he does. I know you do, too."

Micah gave his twin a look. "Is there a reason I shouldn't want to at least try and stop my twin brother from running off and joining an illegal group of violent political terrorists?"

MacEoghan huffed a sigh. "Because that group is the same one you want to sell fish to in order to keep the family business alive over the winter?"

Micah raised a brow. "You think you need to join in order for them to want to buy fish from us?"

MacEoghan shrugged. "Maybe. There might be other businesses with the same idea. Helping out their own members and their families might be more of a priority. If I'm a member, maybe the business will get priority."

Micah frowned, if only because there was some sense to that. If their father, who had always been so staunchly against the IRA, was now entertaining this idea, who was to say that others weren't doing the same? Prioritizing members and their families would not only keep the IRA functioning at an administrative level, but it would ensure loyalty as well.

"You know what they're going to ask of you, right?" Micah said instead. "You are going to have to go out and harm people."

"Oddly enough, other people would very much like to harm us. Whether we're talking about Britain or Germany—"

"Then join the army!" Micah snapped. "You want to go out and fight, you want to pretend that this is about the Emergency, then join the army. Go to Britain, join their ranks if you want heavy action. Go over to Germany—or France now, I suppose—and join them if you believe in their cause. You want to be part of a standing army, join the Irish army; there is certainly good cause to think we might be invaded and the army will be needed no matter the aggressor. Why the IRA?"

Micah had actually expected to catch MacEoghan on that one. He did not expect his brother to have an answer prepared. "Because I want to fight for the people. The Irish government is the one who sent us to St. Joseph's. They're the ones who are politically in charge of that nightmare. The IRA is for the people."

"The IRA is bloody Catholic," Micah informed him. "Two wings of the same bird, I say."

"Still the people," MacEoghan insisted. "The Taoiseach says to sit and wait. Well, we're sitting and waiting for an invasion. And while we're sitting and waiting, you're in the office looking at a ledger that says we're in trouble."

"And what if the IRA isn't able or willing to buy our fish? What if they don't actually care about the businesses, or they don't have the means to help? Sean admitted that most of them are in prison. Are you going to insist? Are you going to walk away? For Father and I, this is just one avenue of trying to help the business, a small chance and a huge compromise, but one avenue only. What about you?"

"They're still the best chance we have."

"Have for what? Protection? Sean just said it earlier, we're far and away more prepared to defend against the average soldier. But if there are any soldiers who have more power than us, like the one who shot you in Denmark, we've got nothing and our best bet is—"

"Run away, I remember."

Micah sighed. "What is this about, *a Mhac*? Why are you so eager to jump into another fight?"

"I want to help, *a Mhicah*," MacEoghan said, tone exasperated. "I see a problem and I want to fix it. You were hurt, we were both being hurt, and I fixed it. You wanted a family, and you got one. Now, whether anyone wants to admit it or not, Éire is in very real danger. The family business is in danger. I want to help. Sitting around and hoping that things get better isn't an option for me."

Micah did not doubt that MacEoghan was speaking the truth, but he didn't buy that it was the full story. "And how does the IRA fix these problems?"

"Buying the fish, hopefully, like you said. As for the Emergency, they fight for us. I don't know how to explain it any other way. They are Irishmen fighting for Ireland. We just got rid of the British after eight hundred years. Eight centuries of British rule, no doubt many opportunities over the years for them to just give us our freedom as an ally, and it took violence. Now some men want to go fight and die for them? And the Germans? Their war might be against the British, they might treat us well as they did Denmark, but Denmark is still occupied. They are under Nazi control. I don't want to see Éire under anyone's thumb again, not after we just got rid of the British. And we're still not unified."

Micah frowned. "And you blame the Irish government for our time at the school?"

"Aye."

"You want to shut down the schools?"

"I know where you're going with this. Aye, we did learn a lot there. But the power to just freely abuse boys and then sweep it under the holy rug is too much."

Micah nodded slowly. "And how are you going to stop it?"

MacEoghan huffed. "I don't know." He sat down heavily on his bed. "You think I haven't asked myself these same questions over and over again every night? What are they going to ask of me? What purpose does it serve? What cause does it advance? Is that a good cause? Are the actions worth the consequences? What if it's not everything I'm making it out to be? What if they're not as strong as I think? What if their cause or their methods are too much?"

Truthfully, Micah was a little surprised that MacEoghan had thought of such things, but it was also reassuring that his brother wasn't a complete oaf.

"I don't have all the answers," he went on, laying back on his bed. "At this point, it is entirely a leap of faith. I don't know just what I'm getting into, but then, if I have to go dark as a Timekeeper, there's always an opportunity to start over, a new life with no regrets."

"No one is promised tomorrow, *a Mhac*," Micah said quietly, turning off the light and making his way back to his own bed. "That is true in war more than anywhere else."

"War hasn't come here yet," MacEoghan sighed. "And I know I sound like I'm just spoiling for a fight all the time. I'm really not. Boxing is fun and all, but going up to Brother Andrew's room and doing what I did, I was scared. I really didn't mean to kill him. I just wanted to punish him for what he did to you, give him a lesson he wouldn't forget. If I was that eager to fight, I'd be gone by now. I really do what to keep you and the family and Ireland safe."

Micah took an even breath, feeling an unexpected wave of relief, and he nodded in the darkness. "All right. Well, as you yourself have said, no one can really stop you; you're a man grown. Just make sure it's what you want and what you think is the best course of action."

"We won't really know until I get there, I suppose."

But no one is promised tomorrow.

A THIRD ENCOUNTER
OLDER BROTHER

G od Almighty, I can't believe I'm doing this," Sean grumbled.

MacEoghan followed close behind as they wound their way through the streets of Gaillimh. Portal travel was hard, the weather was decidedly poor, and Gaillimh was not on either of their lists for cities they most desired to visit. It was huge and cramped and smelly, at least for MacEoghan. He had become accustomed to looking in any given direction and seeing the ocean, the cliffs, some part of the landscape. Even the town was built according to the flow of the land. The city, well, it was very nearly an island; there was only so far it could go. Buildings in every direction with only the sky above for relief, and even that comfort was snatched from him in a torrent of cold water.

"You offered!" MacEoghan reminded his Master, shouting over the wind.

"Aye, but I didn't think they'd actually accept!"

MacEoghan raised a brow though neither man slowed his step. "Is your opinion of me really still so low?"

Sean sighed, though MacEoghan caught this more from his posture than actually hearing it. "I didn't mean it like that. You'll understand when you meet them."

MacEoghan looked around, stomach in knots. The last time he'd walked these streets, well, he'd been running from the police after trying to steal...something. Probably food, or maybe some money to buy it. He couldn't remember.

Some people felt warmth and belonging when returning to the town they were born or grew up in. MacEoghan had no such inclinations. Truthfully, he didn't want to be here at all. When Sean had first mentioned that this was their destination, MacEoghan had known the first real moment of doubt about his ambitions. Of course, he told himself he was being foolish. The IRA operated all over Ireland, and this was where the leaders, or those high enough to have some kind of pull, happened to be when Sean was able to arrange the meeting. Maybe next time they'd be in Corcaigh or Baile Átha Cliath. If they thought he could be trusted, maybe he'd even end up in Derry or Béal Feirste. He had to be ready for anything, and shying away from a city because he had a few bad memories wasn't a good enough excuse in his book; it certainly wouldn't be good enough in theirs.

He was jerked back to the present moment as a massive gust of wind caused him to stumble and nearly topple over. Sean wasn't having much better luck. Finally the Master Timekeeper led them into a small shop.

"Ha! The things our women make us do, no matter the weather," the shopkeep laughed.

MacEoghan looked around and saw they'd ended up in a dress shop. Several fine gowns adorned the front windows while the rear of the shop displayed more modest attire and even a few suits for the gents who were either waiting back home and going to be surprised by the second purchase, or else unfortunate enough to have to accompany their women on such an excursion. Glancing at Sean, MacEoghan could see this was not their final destination, their secret meeting place.

"Ah, no, we're just ducking for a bit of reprieve," Sean told the shopkeep.

The man nodded. "I can't fault you for that."

"How much farther?" MacEoghan asked of Sean.

"Six blocks," Sean answered, adjusting his coat. He did not look at MacEoghan. "Ready?"

MacEoghan could feel the wind against the outside of the building, the tremor in the windows. He made a noise of resignation. "I guess, unless I want to be stuck in a dress shop all day."

The shopkeep laughed again.

Sean had only to barely push on the door before it was ripped from his hand. MacEoghan's first thought was to Band so they might be able to grab it before it struck the building, perhaps shattering the glass on the brick. The problem was that things like air were unaffected by Bands, impossible to control. Anything caught in their wake, then, was just as difficult to catch as it was not a matter of simply going against the natural Base Plane of Time, but every other physical force as well. In theory, gravity should have also been unaffected, but because there was no real way to separate themselves from gravity, they simply learned how to work with or around it naturally. If they traveled someplace where gravity was different, they might have a harder time of it.

The best Sean was able to do with his Band was make a grab for the door and rely more on his own speed to catch the door and his own strength to ensure it did not escape his grasp a second time. He was able to do it, albeit just barely. The two of them forced the door closed, then went on their way.

MacEoghan looked around, a vague memory suddenly resurfacing. It didn't become clear exactly, but he knew the information well. "Six blocks, going the way we are, that'll take us down to the wharf."

"That is our destination," Sean said, pushing against the wind once more. "Where else is a fisherman likely to go?"

"I'm not here on fishing business."

"As far as anyone else is concerned you are."

"Then why not open a portal a little bit closer?"

Sean shot MacEoghan a look. "You want to try opening the portal next time, you be my guest. I got us as close as I could before I felt it would become unsafe, between my fatigue and having to fight the storm."

"Why does the storm matter? Fine, so Banding doesn't work well with high winds, but a portal?"

"You'll learn in time. Until then, just let me handle the higher logistics."

MacEoghan scowled though Sean couldn't see. Yes, yes, he was only an Apprentice, but why did it feel like every time he learned something, Sean introduced him to ten new things that he didn't know yet and then scolded him for not knowing them? Were these actual things he had to learn, or was the man just making it sound that way to try and keep his pride in check?

The wind and rain only got worse the closer they got to the wharf. No longer obstructed by buildings or twisted by winding streets, the storm punished them with every ounce of force it had, nearly stopping their progress. MacEoghan put his arm up to shield his eyes and try to make out where they were supposed to be going. He saw Sean angle toward a particular building, a warehouse not unlike what he had at home though ten times larger.

After having to fight the wind for so long, when Sean at last opened the man door to one of the warehouses—keeping it firmly in hand—and ushered him inside, he nearly fell over. As it was, he stumbled forward several steps, arms flailing awkwardly until he got his balance. If not for his fishing experience, he probably would have pitched forward onto his face.

"This way," Sean said, striding confidently past him.

There were few workers in the warehouse this late in the afternoon, and none of them paid the pair any mind.

"Are they part of it also?" MacEoghan wondered, grateful to be able to lower his voice.

"No," was all Sean replied.

They headed to an office that, again, was not unlike the one back home where Micah did his accounting. This one was a little bigger with a desk and chair in one corner and a larger table with six chairs in the middle. Sean flipped on the light and bid MacEoghan sit .

"They're not involved, and they can't prove our operations, but they can be persuaded to not question things," Sean told him.

MacEoghan took a seat but did not dare relax. He looked up at Sean. "If you've already got one fishing operation, the IRA isn't going to care about our little fish, are they?"

"That's for them to decide. Wait here and I'll grab them."

MacEoghan felt very uneasy about being left alone in the office, but there was nothing he could do now except think about how he was going to address whoever it was who came to speak with him.

Sean hadn't given him any names to consider, hadn't told him how many would be coming. He really hadn't said anything at all except they'd agreed to meet with him. That suggested at least two, but he really couldn't figure out any other information beyond that. Seeing how they were war veterans, then they knew how to fight, they were probably middle-aged or older, and they expected respect from those lower in rank. And, as Sean had said, they were smart and knew how to plan. His best option, then, would probably be to keep his mouth shut as much as possible. Just listen, answer questions succinctly but honestly, and—

He looked up as the door opened and stood abruptly.

"You're fucking joking."

The words were out before he could think about them, but Kearney and Kane just smiled. A third man walked in behind them, and Sean entered last, closing the door quietly.

"You haven't changed a bit," Kearney said, still grinning.

MacEoghan turned his gaze toward Sean. "Is this your idea of a joke? Did you do this on purpose?"

"Actually, Mr. Dearbhfhine," the third man said calmly, "I did."

MacEoghan suddenly remembered his plan to stay quiet, listen, answer questions, and otherwise keep his mouth shut. He felt his skin flush red as he turned his attention to the third man.

"You may simply call me Cillian; it is not my real name as you may guess." The man sat slowly, making a gesture to invite the rest to do the same. Only Sean remained standing by the door.

Cillian was six foot tall with blond hair and blue-green eyes, clean shaven, and very physically fit. MacEoghan judged him to be about thirty-five years old.

"Sean only mentioned that you had a history with Kearney and Kane," Cillian continued. His voice was not an uninteresting monotone, but it was low and controlled. "It was Kearney and Kane who told me, well, their side of the story. Would you like to tell me yours?"

It sounded like a challenge to MacEoghan, or maybe a trap. Cillian's expression was utterly stony, but Kearney and Kane were not so calm and collected. Kearney wanted to hear MacEoghan stutter and flounder and incriminate himself; he wanted a full confession. Kane was waiting for some cue to attack or arrest or something. MacEoghan was briefly put in mind of his psychological review. Had it really been a hallucination?

"I was a wannabe boxer, fighting in the pubs," MacEoghan began. "Sometimes, people would come to us and ask us to do a little dirty deed, usually rough someone up. Mr. Kearney asked me to find Mr. Kane, scare him, rough him up, retrieve some stolen property. When I caught up to Mr.

Kane, I discovered that it had been a trap. Neither one could take me by themselves, so they lured me into an alley and tried to jump me together."

Kearney's infuriating grin vanished immediately, as did Kane's.

Cillian remained unmoved. "I see. They mentioned that you were accused of killing a priest and instructor at St. Joseph's Industrial School for Boys. Do you fancy yourself a Protestant, Mr. Dearbhfhine?"

"No, sir. I attend Mass every Sunday with my family."

"You deny killing the priest, then."

"That wasn't the question."

MacEoghan and Cillian locked eyes. This man was old enough to have contributed to the Civil War in some fashion, and he carried himself with the cold determination of someone who was determined to not let bygones be bygones.

"Did you kill the priest?" Cillian asked pointedly.

"No, sir, he died of his injuries," MacEoghan replied.

Cillian's gaze could not get any stonier, so it was difficult to gauge just how close to physical violence he really was. "Did you give him those injuries?"

"Do you fancy yourselves agents of the Catholic Church?" MacEoghan rebutted. "I can't imagine that you work for the police, but you seem to be looking for some kind of confession."

"We fight on behalf of Éire, and that includes her clergymen. The Irish people are Catholic."

"I fight for my twin brother and my family, and they happen to be fishermen. Fishermen who are struggling because of this damned Emergency going on."

"Not unlike this lot here in the warehouse, I imagine," Cillian commented, a momentary burst of casual tone catching MacEoghan off-guard. "What are you expecting, then? Selling your labor to us in hopes that we buy your family's fish?" He noted MacEoghan's apparent expression and silence. "We are not a company nor an employer, Mr. Dearbhfhine. There is no pay, no standard working hours, no building to go to every day where you punch in and punch out. The Taoiseach has branded us an illegal organization; many of us are under watch, especially now during this

Emergency because they don't want us trying anything that might disrupt their so-called 'neutrality.' Many have been arrested and imprisoned simply for expressing sympathy."

"We have day jobs," Sean said from where he leaned against the door. "We have homes and families and lives. Everything we do for the IRA is done in secret, on off days and at off hours. We meet, we discuss, we plan, sometimes we execute under the guise of a business trip, a short vacation, any common excuse so it can't be easily traced. Sometimes it's not enough."

"And outside of this room, no one knows anyone or anything," Kane added.

"So if you're just a little farm boy or fisherman from a dull town who wants some excitement in his life, join the bloody English army; they're getting lots of it," Cillian continued. "If you're serious about wanting to fight for Éire and the Irish people, then that means staying in your fecking fishing boat, waiting patiently, and sometimes making excuses as to why you need to go out." He shifted in his seat ever so slightly. "Sean mentioned that you have a bit of difficulty with the patience bit."

"Someone has to do something," was the best MacEoghan could offer. "I'm tired of sitting around being told to just wait and hope and pray that it all blows over."

"I agree, and you're not the only one. We have operations in the works, but even if we agreed to bring you in right now, you would learn none of it. It's a matter of trust and learning how we do things. The IRA is not some kind of festival that you attend and indulge in once and call it good for the year. It is a long-term commitment, even if that means spending a bit of time in jail for it, if you get caught."

"I understand."

Cillian raised a brow. "Do you? You ever spent time in jail? I don't mean overnight so you can sleep off a drunken pub brawl, I mean really spent time. A month, a year, five years. Locked in the same cell, the same building, idling away your time for something you did years ago?"

MacEoghan nodded slowly. "Aye. I have. I was stuck in St. Joseph's Industrial School for Boys, the same bed, the same campus, the same people, the same classes, the same chores. Boys came in, boys left, but the public never did; we were too isolated. No parents, no guardians, no government agents, only a couple visiting priests a year. Anyone who ran away from any of the schools was sent to St. Joseph's where they were beaten and locked up in a small cage for several days before being let out into the congregation. We could be beaten for any reason, no matter how small, or no reason whatsoever. And you don't want to hear what they did to the younger boys."

Cillian's gaze returned to its former icy glow as he sat up and leaned forward, folding his hands in front of him on the table, face a shadowy mask. "I assure you, I do."

"So he had a bad time at school, so what?" Kearney hissed.

"Hush!" Cillian barked. He made a small gesture. "Please, tell me what they did to the younger boys."

MacEoghan hadn't actually expected him to want to hear it, but he couldn't back down now. He had only one option: tell the man everything. Well, almost everything. He still did not expressly admit to harming or killing Brother Andrew; all he said was that he found Micah in the cage, unlocked the cage, and the two of them escaped.

The intensity of Cillian's blue-green gaze only grew the more MacEoghan spoke, to the point where, if his eyes had been glass, MacEoghan was certain they would have shattered. When MacEoghan finished his tale and stopped talking, a heavy silence draped itself over the room. Even Kearney and Kane couldn't find anything to say.

The wind howled outside.

Finally, Cillian spoke. "Even if true, you would shame your brother by telling this story?"

"It is true," MacEoghan informed him, "and you can't punish a crime no one knows happened."

"True enough. And it sounds like you, allegedly, went to some great lengths to punish this crime against your brother."

"Allegedly."

Cillian nodded slowly. "We also, allegedly, go to some great lengths to get justice for Éire and her people." He relaxed just enough that he no longer appeared to be in imminent danger of spontaneously shattering. "You're not old enough to have fought in the wars, but do you remember them at all?"

"No," MacEoghan admitted. "We were orphans on the street; our greatest concern was finding food and a dry place to sleep. Then we were caught and whisked away to school. We learned some things about the wars, but not much."

"That makes you one of the lucky ones, but also regrettably ill-informed. Do you know why we do what we do? Do you know how we were conceived?"

"The IRA has always wanted independence for Éire, led the charge against the British after the Great War. When the War of Independence was won and the separation proposed, the people were split over whether to accept or reject it."

Kearney sighed noticeably, and Kane just looked at the ground and shook his head. Sean remained impassive, and Cillian looked a bit disappointed.

"That is a very...clean, very rote way of telling it, I suppose," Cillian said, shifting position. "Good enough for children in school studying to take a test on a piece of paper."

"I know there is more to war," MacEoghan stated.

"Oh, aye, there is," Kane said at the same time Kearney spat, "Oh, he's figured out that much, has he?"

Cillian silenced them with a look, then turned his attention back to MacEoghan. "Divide and conquer, a simple enough tactic. The British knew they were losing, but the arrogant pricks couldn't let us have everything. So they struck up what they called a compromise, knowing full well that it would divide us.

"Some people may ask, 'But if the people of the North of Ireland are all right with it and want it, why bother?' The answer is that they are Irish. They belong to Éire. They don't get to have the identity of the Irish while being coddled by the British. If they want to be British, they can leave and give the northern lands back to Éire. They want to have it both ways, but the reality is, they can't. Part of their history and culture and identity is suppressed and even lost by remaining under British rule.

"Our goal is simple: reunite the Irish people on Irish land, and anyone who can't handle that can go where they think they will be happier."

"Problem is, sometimes we're still fighting our own," Kearney mused.

Cillian nodded. "Many times it is political, but sometimes it's on the street. People in the northern counties who want to claim their Irish history and the land with it, yet live under British law. You look at them and wonder why they think they can live in two worlds, why they love their oppression. At that point, you have to make your own choice: you can think of them as British invaders, that they are, in fact, not Irish, whatever they claim, however they speak; you can agree with them and let them carry on, in which case we don't want you because you are just as much a traitor; or you can continue to think of them as a misguided brother or sister who needs to be persuaded." He put up a finger. "The last avenue may sound noble, and it might be appropriate in some instances, but if you are unwilling to let any such person slide into that category of being an invader, someone who must be removed, you won't last long."

MacEoghan stared at the man. Kane, who evidently took his silence for confusion, spoke up. "There are allegations that we kill people."

"Considering the Civil War, it is not untrue to say that the IRA has killed people," Cillian went on. "The more successful ones just went into politics afterwards and called us the villains." He shook his head. "We are not assassins. We are not thugs. The Irish and British governments may say that we engage in senseless violence, but everything we do has a purpose. We want to send a message, and we want to effect change in the most efficient manner possible. If Britain were to give up the northern counties tomorrow, we would ensure the smooth transition of Irish returning home and the expulsion of those who wish to remain British subjects, and then our operations would all but cease. It's not our goal people have a problem with. It's our methods."

MacEoghan nodded slowly, studying a spot on the table. He looked up. "So what is your opinion on this Emergency? Half the people think we're going to be invaded by the British, and the other half think we're going to be invaded by the Germans."

"At present, we have no quarrel with the Germans. In fact, we applaud their efforts and apparent ability to cut the British Empire down to size; we Irish are not the only ones to have been liberated recently. Make no mistake, however, we are monitoring the situation very closely. If worse comes to worse, our loyalties always fall squarely with Éire, regardless of what any invader says."

The five men sat or stood in silence for a long minute. MacEoghan still couldn't believe that Kearney and Kane were part of this. And even if they were, did they have to be here, now? Were they really part of the command? Was this intentional by Sean, just to see how he reacted to their presence? Was Cillian a Time Agent as well?

"As much as our loyalty is to Éire," Cillian continued slowly, "we also expect loyalty to the organization. I know what you intend to ask of us, but I want to know if you are still interested even if we said no. We're not here to be used for your personal gain; we are here to achieve a greater goal of a united Éire. Everything else we do is secondary." He made a vague gesture. "And as you can see, we are already well-supplied with fish."

"I understand," MacEoghan said, dipping his head. "I think my brother proposed it in order to make himself feel better about it, my being here."

Now Kearney jumped in. "I don't doubt that you and your twin are very close. I would be lying if I said we would never use him as well, even unwittingly, to carry out an operation with you. But as we've stated before, we are typically under surveillance. We don't advertise our involvement, even to our own families if we can help it."

"Who else knows you're here?" Kane asked. "Your brother might be the heir to the family business, but he's not in charge yet. Does your father know? Your mother? Your siblings?" He looked at Cillian. "A good sympathizer, nothing more. He's too much of a liability, or his family is."

"I'm already known as a restless soul," MacEoghan cut in. "Everyone knows I'm not happy as a mere fisherman. My comings and goings would be nothing out of the ordinary. If I were to make it back into the boxing circuit, that would be even better."

"The boxing circuit is your business," Cillian told him. "We are not influential politicians or celebrities to be able to bribe sporting officials to get you in or out or stage and rig certain matches."

"Maybe not the IRA, but I think I know someone. Or maybe a few someones." MacEoghan shot a glance at Kearney and Kane who glowered at him.

"He'll never make it," Kearney stated flatly. "And he is still a liability. His impatience and hot-headedness has announced his intentions to everyone. They probably already think he's one of us. For all we know, there's a swarm of police waiting outside to arrest all of us."

"Well then, if you're so worried about it, you can train him," Cillian decided.

"What?" Kane demanded. Behind them at the door, Sean was smirking.

"You don't have to show him everything, just enough to get his feet wet, see what he's really made of. You know how it goes; he's not your first."

"Just like that?" Kearney asked in disbelief. "We're not going to have a conversation about it?"

Cillian stood. "We have been having a conversation about it." He rebuttoned his jacket and flipped the collar up, preparing for the storm outside. "I've gotten what I needed, and talk only goes so far. Your job will be to assess his physical value." He made his way to the door, but before he opened it, he turned back and said, "And if he is that much of a liability, you know how to dispose of a body."

Then he left.

MacEoghan couldn't believe that just happened. He had actually been accepted into the IRA. A trainee or probationary, true, but that had actually just happened. Considering Kearney and Kane were both Timekeepers as well, maybe he could learn some real tricks when it came to Banding instead of this rote, formal stuff that Sean was giving him.

"Did he just say that?" Kearney demanded after a moment.

"He did just say that," Sean replied, still smirking.

"Is he out of his fecking mind?"

"I think he's a little tired of listening to you two complain."

Kearney cursed and stood abruptly. "I'm going dark. I don't have to put up with this bullshit."

"And go where?" Sean laughed. "The world's ablaze and you'd rather chance going dark than training him." He made a vague gesture toward MacEoghan.

"United States isn't involved," Kearney informed him. "Canada might be British but they're still an ocean away."

Sean's expression turned even more smug. "So you'd rather live in occupied territory than train someone to fight for your homeland? Oh, I'll bet Cillian would love to hear that."

Kearney just scowled and pushed past him to leave the room. Kane followed wordlessly though his glare spoke volumes.

Sean just shook his head as he closed the door and turned to MacEoghan. "Congratulations. Welcome to the family, I suppose."

"Do they really hate me that much?" MacEoghan wondered, standing. "All because of what I did to Brother Andrew?"

"Kearney's the nephew of a priest. Idolized the man, or so I've gathered. Not real religious himself but, in an odd sort of way, he worships the institution."

"Wouldn't it be good, then, to cleanse that institution of bad actors?"

"Aye, but then that would be to admit that there are bad actors." Sean shrugged. "It's a personal vendetta, not something you or I are likely to change. He'll come around, but his training won't be as friendly as mine."

MacEoghan moved toward the door. "Is Cillian a Time Agent as well? Is he another officer?"

Sean shook his head. "No." He opened the door. "No, he's as average as they come."

They headed out of the little office. The rain still beat against the warehouse though the wind did not sound as strong.

"Even I don't believe that," MacEoghan said.

"Well, if you do well and he likes you, he might tell you about it someday," Sean told him, "but he truly is not a Time Agent."

They crossed the warehouse to the same door they'd entered earlier. "How does this work now? Do I come here? Do they come to me? If Cillian isn't a Time Agent, then he won't understand portal travel as a mode of transportation. We never really talked about the fish, but it was a long-shot anyway."

Sean waved a hand dismissively. "Kearney is going to go complain to Cillian. Cillian is going to tell him to get over it. Kearney's going to complain some more, probably to Kane. Then he'll come complain to me for a bit. Eventually he'll break down and come down to talk to you in person."

Sean opened the door. The wind was still quite strong, but the door was not ripped from his hands and he had no trouble closing it once they were outside.

"Is Kane going to be with him?" MacEoghan wondered.

Sean shrugged. "Maybe, maybe not. Thick as thieves, those two, but really only when they get a chance to bully someone. If Kearney really is going to be your trainer, Kane won't want to subject himself if he doesn't have to. Bad enough he's going to have to hear about it later."

Well, at least there was some hope for the situation. "Can you give me any advice on how to deal with him? You know, so I don't end up acting out what happened in the Wheel?"

Sean gave him a knowing look, then turned serious. "Kearney knows his stuff, at least enough to keep himself and others alive and out of trouble. He's not the best, whatever he believes. He's certainly not Cillian. Listen to him, learn from him, but keep your own wits about you. Just a mite of thought and consideration will see you in a better position than him."

"Is that why Cillian assigned me to him? Am I supposed to be a mirror?"

"There is that thought."

"Is that why they were here at all? Did you orchestrate all of this?"

Sean smirked again. "I'm no conductor. Sometimes the music just plays itself."

MacEoghan sighed though he doubted Sean caught it. "Is this some punishment for me, too? Because of the Wheel?"

They left the wharf. Once in the clutches of the city, the wind died down to almost nothing, though it did little for the pelting rain.

Sean answered, "The Wheel certainly didn't help things, but it's not the only incident. I'm not fooling around when I say you are irresponsible, irrational, and impulsive. I think your love and loyalty to your brother is the only reason things aren't worse for you, but as your lives diverge—especially if you continue with Timekeeping and he doesn't—he won't be able to save you anymore."

"I've done what I thought was best for both of us, tried to keep us alive!" MacEoghan protested. "It was my inaction, not forcing Micah to leave the school, that got him hurt."

314

There wasn't much Sean could say to that, but there was still the matter of Brother Andrew. That had been revenge, plain and simple. He hadn't confronted them, hadn't known about their plans or their escape at all. It had been entirely opportunistic, an opportunity made possible only through Banding.

And yet, wasn't it even a little justified? Getting anyone to believe them had been a non-starter, and the Church wasn't going to do anything about it. God was the final Judge, fine, all MacEoghan did was send him to court.

A long alleyway provided ample cover from both rain and prying eyes so Sean could open a portal for MacEoghan to return home. MacEoghan stepped through to a small copse of trees on the high cliff overlooking the town. The thick trees and thicker underbrush provided more than enough cover on this end, though it also proved very difficult, if not impossible, to navigate quietly.

When MacEoghan finally ripped his way past a dead branch and its many sharp yet brittle twigs, and tumbled out into the open, he found himself being watched by the passengers of a car as it rumbled past him and nosed its way into town. The kids stared at him, and he gave a nod and small wave to the husband. He recognized the occupants as one of the neighbors. According to the government, they were not special enough to receive any extra considerations during this Emergency. Nevertheless, they tried to save one gas ration per week in order to be able to take their kids on a drive to have a picnic at a nice spot about an hour's drive outside of town.

His mother was going to hear about this, he was sure. Might as well hurry home so he could hear the rumors the same time she did and figure out what he was apparently doing.

According to the neighbor's wife, who arrived a few minutes before he did, he was in that copse of trees with a girl. No, she hadn't actually seen the girl, but what else would he be doing in a copse of trees at the top of hill outside of town? And why else would he have been so red and so wet?

The cold wind and rain had indeed made him red and wet, but without being able to explain that bit, well, it was still only a cloudy day at home.

Sarah listened politely, sipping at her midmorning tea, and saw the neighbor's wife out the door with a mild assurance that all was well, and

MacEoghan was a respectable and honorable young man. Then she closed the door and gave him a look.

"What?" he asked dumbly. His mother just held the look until he relented. "I was out for a walk, it sprinkled a bit, and I needed to take a piss."

"Don't use that language in this house," she scolded him. "And you're sure that's all you were doing?"

She would never believe the truth so the best he could give was, "Aye, that's all. When I saw the neighbor, well, I knew what was going to happen, so I came back down."

Now her look turned mischievous. "You knew that she was going to come down here to confront me and look for a way to start some new gossip or rumor in town?"

"And you say I don't pay attention to any of the neighbors," MacEoghan added with his own bit of sarcasm.

She moved past him to continue whatever she had been doing. "Well, in the future, maybe you should pay more attention to their daughters than their wives."

He'd known she would say something like that. He brushed it off with a light laugh and headed back outside. It was still early morning and the boat wasn't back yet. Micah knew exactly what was going on, while Padraig knew only that he was going to potentially negotiate with the IRA about the sale of fish. He likely suspected that MacEoghan would inquire more deeply than that, but for now he was feigning ignorance.

How was he going to tell them that Cillian had said no? They already had a fishing operation that they used for cover, and it was much more believable than some tiny business in the south. Sure, Padraig and Micah had made it clear that it was only one option they were considering, but MacEoghan still didn't like it. He was trying to help. Sure he might become a full IRA member and do good on a national scale, but how much did that matter if things fell apart back home?

Only one option, he told himself, heading into the warehouse. He entered the office. He didn't come here much, or at all, really, unless his father needed to tell or ask him something away from prying ears. Unlike the larger warehouse that smelled like fish, the office smelled like stale fish left to sit in a brine barrel. MacEoghan gagged once, sending up a silent prayer that he wouldn't be here much longer. Whatever Sean and the others said about having a day job, he didn't want this to be his day job. Unfortunately, with things the way they were, he didn't have many other employment options here.

Curiosity getting the better of him, he approached the desk and opened the ledger. There was Micah's handwriting, tight and neat, the labels and figures lining up perfectly through years of rigid and sometimes violent reinforcement.

"Right hand!" the Brothers would snap, making a show of their short rods. "Elbow in! Fingertips tight!"

And here was the product of their yelling and snapping and sharp cracks of the rod: entries in a fish ledger.

MacEoghan looked at each line, the profits, the expenses, the outstanding debts owed to the company and that the company owed. He pursed his lips. Micah was being modest when he said things were looking grim. Peeking back over the last few months to the first page of the book, things were not going well at all. No wonder Padraig was open to the idea of dealing with the IRA. If MacEoghan told him that Cillian had said no, Padraig might become desperate enough to talk to the British. Or the Germans, if they invaded first.

He looked up and swiftly closed the book when he heard the telltale horn of the boats returning. He left the warehouse and went to meet them, helping them tie off and unload. He pulled Micah aside and Banded the two of them.

"How did it go?" Micah asked.

"You didn't tell me things were that bad," MacEoghan hissed. "I looked in the ledger."

"Would it have made a difference?"

MacEoghan let out a breath and grudgingly admitted, "No, I suppose not. And they said they would take it under consideration once they saw how much I proved myself."

Micah frowned. "How long is that going to take? What are they going to have you do?"

"I don't know and I don't know." He hummed a frustrated sigh. "Kearney is my mentor."

"Kearney!" Micah spat. "The one who—"

"Yes. Sean and Kearney and Kane are all part of it, but the main operations leader I met with today is not a Time Agent."

"Was this all just coincidence, then?"

"I don't know. Honestly, I don't think so. I asked Sean and he implied that he did have some pull, and he was kind of using me for his own ends against Kearney."

Micah shook his head. "Don't get wrapped up in this, *a Mhac*. It is not going to end well. Walk away while you still can. Forget about the fish; it was long odds anyway and only one option."

"I already told them I would stick around. They've got me on..." He sighed and only just stopped himself from rolling his eyes. "They've got me on probation. Like I said, Kearney is in charge. He's going to be looking for every reason to throw me out, and he's got enough rank, I think, to do just that."

He could see his brother wasn't convinced.

"I don't like it," Micah stated. "And I don't know how much I would trust Sean either at this point. Unfortunately, we're not in any position to argue right now."

"We'll see what happens," MacEoghan told him, dropping the Band.

We'll see what happens.

FLOATING THE BOAT
YOUNGER BROTHER

A bad day for a fisherman was going out and catching no fish.

A worse day was going out and not being able to catch the fish because they would ultimately have no profitable market value.

Micah had run dozens of figures, trying to figure out how to make things work. If they went ahead and caught a bunch of fish, the price would go down, but maybe more people would buy. But then again, maybe not. Then an already razor thin profit margin would sink into the depths of crushing debt. And, just like it was possible to drown in a shallow bucket, it wouldn't take much debt to shutter the business for good.

He hated to see the frustration and confusion on his younger brothers' faces. Shay understood pretty well, but Cillian struggled to make sense of it, and Brendan just couldn't accept his father telling them to pack up the nets when there were obviously fish swimming around the boat. They'd tried to explain it the best they could over the last few months, but there was no getting through to him it seemed. With his cracking voice, the boy protested the whole way back to shore, as he did every morning when they returned with only a meager haul.

"I hope you can convince them quickly," Micah told his twin. "We're not likely to make it to spring at this rate."

"According to Sean, Kearney is supposed to be coming by tomorrow," MacEoghan said helplessly. "That's all I know."

Micah could rehash his doubts and misgivings about the whole situation, but it would do no good. He could voice his general distaste for the IRA or his suspicions about Sean orchestrating a few too many coincidences, but MacEoghan would only comment that he had agreed to help them and he would honor his word. If Kearney decided to throw him out, fine, but he wasn't going to suddenly walk away after working so hard just to be accepted, even if it was probationary work.

"And what about some of your other leads?" MacEoghan went on. "Anything?"

Micah opened his mouth to give some kind of reassurance, maybe a little hope. After a moment of thought, he just sighed and shook his head. "No."

One fisherman had proposed that each company only catch one or two species of fish, so there was less direct competition. Padraig had pointed out that people were being less finicky about the specific fish, paying more attention to the price. Fishermen who specialized in an expensive species would very quickly go under.

Someone else proposed that all of the companies should merge and share resources; it had worked well enough for some of the smaller crews to get by so far. Unfortunately, there was a bit too much bad blood between some of the fishermen for anyone to agree on who should be in charge.

Micah had looked into that proposal a bit further, perhaps on a slightly smaller scale with one other company.

There had been twelve fishing companies of various sizes when he'd first walked into town years ago, most of them single family businesses, like the Dearbhfhines. Only five remained in business, although some of that was because of the merging of smaller companies.

One of them hated Padraig for no reason that Micah was able to discern, nor that either man was willing to explain.

Two of them were much larger operations, competition only to each other, and circling like sharks as all of the other companies had to make such tough decisions.

The fourth was at the tipping point, but the owner was too proud to merge or otherwise ask for help, and he was willing to go down with his ship. His employees were not so loyal, which only fueled the fire.

The last business was the conglomeration of smaller companies who had merged and made deals and such. From everything Micah understood, they would be more than willing to absorb Padraig's business into theirs, and it was Padraig himself who was still hesitant.

As the boys secured the boat to the dock, Micah moved away from MacEoghan to talk to his father.

"We should talk to them," Micah said, indicating the workers from the company in question, down the way at their own docks and warehouse.

"We're busy," Padraig stated, not looking at him. "They're busy."

"After we've all sent out our trucks."

Padraig scowled but did not immediately reject the idea. But, instead of addressing the issue, he busied himself in the unloading and the sending off of trucks. Padraig alone could do the work of Brendan and Cillian and more besides. The boys watched with worshipful awe as their father worked, and Micah kept quiet. It was all a show, because there was so little to do anymore. Then MacEoghan jumped in a truck and took off.

"And?" Micah goaded, catching up to Padraig before the man could hurry off on some invented errand.

Padraig hesitated, then made a motion to follow him to the office. Once inside, he shut the door quietly and went to the desk. Micah meekly took a seat across from him.

"Have you never thought it a bit odd that I would be more willing to work with the IRA than Michael down there?" Padraig began.

"The thought crossed my mind," Micah replied diplomatically.

"The IRA is or was just a means to an end, an avenue to explore that might let us keep this business going through leaner times. Ultimately, they're a customer. An unsavory customer, true, but only a customer all the same. When this Emergency is over, when things calm down and go back to the way they were, we have no need for them. And they have no need for us. They have no interest in fish, especially not this little operation, obviously. We can go our separate ways and you can take over." Padraig shifted in his seat. "If I go down there and talk to Michael, if we join up with the others, we lose this business. We lose everything we've built, we lose the ability to govern ourselves and our affairs. There won't be any way of getting it back, and I will have nothing to give you."

Micah gave his father a look. "You're not going to have anything to give anyway if we lose the business because we can't pay our employees or our bills. Pride doesn't feed a family."

Padraig met his look. "Oh, if you want to go work for Michael, by all means, go down and talk to him yourself. I'm sure he'd love to have you. Go ahead, walk away from me and all your brothers."

"That's not what I'm saying—"

"Sure sounds like it."

"And what do you suggest?" Micah challenged. "Where are we going to get customers? Where are we going to get money? We don't have time for hope and planning, we have to act now!" He shook his head and calmed his voice. "We don't have time."

Padraig just sighed and put his head in his hands. "Every avenue that I know of, I've exhausted. I've exploited every ration, every credit, every scrap of relief. I've written to every member of every government agency I can find, even called a few, but there's just nothing." He leaned back, slouching in defeat. "Ireland is neutral but we're still being punished by this damned Emergency. This fucking war." He raised a fist as if to slam in on the desk, but ultimately he just calmly laid an open palm on the notched wood.

"And Michael?" Micah asked evenly. He added quickly, "I'm going to stay with this business to the end, even if that means going down with the ship." He let out a breath. "But I'd rather not go down at all if someone is offering a helping hand."

Padraig shook his head absently. "I wanted to give something to my sons like my father gave to me. I didn't want to lose it. This business has already survived several wars, what's one more?"

"Maybe we can negotiate with Michael, see if there is a way we can still somehow retain ownership over the business, stay separate so we can break away after this is over," Micah suggested. "But we have to do it now while we still have our own assets and affairs."

His father sighed, still not looking at him. "You're not wrong there." The man straightened a little, a bit of life coming back to his eyes and posture. "I might be able to come up with a few ideas." He frowned. "And your other half is sure that the IRA isn't willing to help? I consider that our little secret; if we go in with Michael in any fashion, we can't bring that along."

Micah shrugged. "He said it depended on how well he proved himself, but he didn't seem to have high hopes about it."

Padraig nodded slowly. "And am I correct in assuming that, regardless of the state of the business, his interest in the IRA is genuine?"

Micah sighed and reluctantly nodded. "It appears to be."

His father frowned. "You know I don't approve. He knows I don't approve. And this Emergency isn't helping matters. If at all possible, keep trying to talk him out of it. I won't say anything, but I'm not risking the rest of the family or this business if he gets caught. You understand?"

"I understand."

"Good." He made a shooing motion and took the ledger book to himself. "Go on, then. I'll see if I can't fashion something better than unconditional surrender." He looked up as Micah stood. "Don't say anything to him yet. Don't ask about it, don't even hint. Understand?"

"Yes, sir."

Padraig said nothing, just turned his attention to the ledger. Micah frowned, waited a moment longer, then left the office.

Chores were taken care of easily enough, and Micah spent his bit of free time wandering around town. It was quieter than he was comfortable with. A number of shops had closed in the last couple years, many of them unable to get in stock. Because of this crisis, no new shops could open. The shops that were able to remain open still had signs stating that stock could be low and ordering anything was dubious. Assuming it could be gotten, it would take a longer amount of time and cost extra.

The town was close-knit, but there were a few homes no longer occupied, a few more in the process of becoming unoccupied as people hoped for a sale or decided they couldn't wait any longer.

Micah stopped in front of one such home, a sale sign in the window and stuck into the ground near the road. He knew the family from Mass but he couldn't say he knew them personally. Father, mother, five children under twelve. He was a woodworker, if Micah recalled correctly, and, while not rich, he'd never seemed to have any problems.

The front door opened and the oldest child, a boy of twelve whose name escaped Micah, walked out. Micah could see the boy's mother watching from a window while she tended to a smaller child.

"Mama wants to know if you need something," the boy said.

"No, not really," Micah answered, feeling his skin flush. "Do you know how much they want for the house?"

The boy shrugged. "Ten thousand? Twelve, maybe?"

Micah nodded. "Where are you going?"

"Papa says we're going to America, place called Ohio." The boy giggled and repeated the name several times, finishing with, "I don't know where that is, though."

Micah shrugged wearily. "I don't know either. Why America?"

A woman's voice answered, and the wife stepped out of the house, toddler in her arms. "Because there's nothing for us here anymore. Germans to the south, Britain to the east. It's only a matter of time."

"But your husband is a woodworker," Micah said. "He seems to stay busy, doesn't he? Wouldn't a move to a city be better? You could come back later."

She shook her head. "I've got family in America, and they say it's the best place on God's green earth, especially Ohio. Lots of open land good for farming, steady work for Brendan without having to worry about your neighbors invading just because they're sore."

"But this is your home."

"Aye, it is. Or it was." She bounced the toddler in her arms. "But we have to do what's best for the children." She indicated the twelve year old. "What hope is there here for Junior? All my life it's been nothing but war and poverty. The Great War, the Anglo-Irish War, the Civil War, the Depression, now this Emergency that could very well turn into a war. What kind of life is that? Not one I want for my children."

Micah frowned but could not disagree. Instead he asked, "What are you asking for the house?"

Still bouncing the toddler, she glanced back at the structure in question. "We'd like twelve, but if we were to get ten, we could pack up and be out by next week." She looked back at him. "You interested?"

He shook his head. "I haven't got that kind of money, ma'am, but my brother might."

She nodded. "Aye, you do have another half, don't you? To hear your mother tell it, he's just chewing on the bit trying to get out of here. Having his own home might help to alleviate some of that, make it easier to find a nice girl and settle down."

"It would," Micah agreed. "I'll let him know."

As he departed, he knew he had no real intention of telling MacEoghan about the house, at least not with any real hope that he would buy it. Would it be good for him? Yes, absolutely. MacEoghan was a man grown who needed and wanted to get out and live his own life. Was it likely to happen? No, not with his fiery ambition to be a Timekeeper and member of the IRA.

Maybe MacEoghan would buy the house for him, Micah. At least that way, whenever MacEoghan came strolling back into town he would have a place to stay that was quiet and peaceful. Well, for the time being. Once Micah started a family of his own, that peace and quiet would disappear.

By the time Micah returned home, he had come to the conclusion that it wasn't worth telling MacEoghan about the house. It wasn't as though it was the only house for sale, and MacEoghan wasn't blind to goings-on in town. If his biggest complaint was having to stay at home with Padraig and Sarah, that could have been solved long ago. Having a place of his own was not going to tame his wild heart. At least, Micah figured, keeping him home let everyone keep a closer eye on him, especially with this IRA business.

Padraig made no mention of the business or the ledger whatsoever at dinner, and Micah did not ask. He wanted to, certainly, but for the moment, he would see what his father could come up with.

With the business as small as it was now, there was less to do after dinner which meant more free time. MacEoghan left without telling anyone where he was going. Micah decided to take a walk down the rocky shore. Maybe he'd get lucky and find some clams or other goodies.

He headed down away from town first, then back up toward the docks and the warehouses. There were a few people milling about on the docks, out for walks or casting a hopeful line or skipping rocks. Micah paid them no mind, but one of them apparently paid him mind.

"You're one of the Dearbhfhine twins, aren't you?"

Micah, still down on the shore at low tide, strained to look up at the dock where a figure, presumably a man, was hunched over and talking to him.

"I am," he replied uncertainly.

"Would you mind coming up here so I don't have to shout at you?"

Micah nodded and made his way back up to the dock. The man waited patiently, not saying a word. He looked familiar except Micah knew he wasn't from town, and he dressed too well to be one of the market workers they interacted with on deliveries.

"Micah Dearbhfhine, sir," he introduced himself. "Can I help you?"

The man looked around, his expression almost bored. Then, without warning, he enveloped the two of them in a Band so strong it caused Micah to stumble in place.

"Honestly, I might have hoped your brother would have warned you about me," the man said.

"Kearney," Micah stated.

"Very good, you know who I am. Do you know why I'm here?"

Micah gave the man a look. "MacEoghan said you're supposed to be training him. So why are you talking to me?"

As suddenly and forcefully as the Band went up, it dissipated. Again, Micah stumbled in place.

"I'm here to inquire about some fish," Kearney informed him. "I understand you go out early in the morning, but perhaps you have some left over? Something you couldn't sell?"

Micah studied the man, his expression and posture. "MacEoghan said you all told him that he would have to prove himself first."

Kearney raised a brow. "Did he? Actually, he was told a solid no, we aren't going to help."

"So you're here to patronize me? Or make an offer that you will help but only if I join, too?"

"Hardly. This offer isn't coming from the IRA, it's coming from me."

Micah raised a brow. "You already can't stand MacEoghan; why would you want to do this?"

"Because it serves my interests. Sean may have told you that Timekeepers get salaries from the Hands of Time. Probationaries barely make enough to pay for their own burial, but my salary is a little more substantial. The currency in the Wheel is called the turn. Turns can be converted into any other currency in the universe—but not the other way around, in order to keep the value high. Right now, the United States Dollar is the strongest currency in the world—"

"Money laundering," Micah cut in. He glared at Kearney. "And you want to call me and MacEoghan criminals."

"By definition, you're harboring one fugitive and talking to another. Do you want to save your business or not?"

"How do I know you won't flip on us and sell us out first chance you get?"

"Because it would be much more fun and much more consequential to turn your brother over to the authorities for his involvement in the IRA. Yes, I can do it without implicating myself; I've done it before and I'll do it again."

Micah had not stopped glaring at Kearney. "And what if I say no?"

Kearney shrugged and took a step back. "Then I can leave right now and we will never speak of this again."

"And you won't punish MacEoghan for it."

"No, never." He took another step. "If that's really what you want...?"

Micah hesitated. He could see why people didn't like the man, could only imagine what it was going to be like for his hot-headed twin to have to train under this man. At the same time, wasn't this exactly what he had been proposing? Whether it was the IRA or Kearney personally, they were dealing with shady customers and potentially falsifying ledgers. Just because Kearney was an ass, it didn't change the crime itself.

"Give me a couple days to think about it and figure out how we might do it from our end," he said at last.

Kearney grinned and did a sort of half-bow gesture. "Of course. I would tell you to take all the time you need, except I can't wait that long, and don't suspect you have that much time anyway."

The most that Micah was able to relax himself was an annoyed glower. "Do you know something I don't? Have you been talking to MacEoghan?"

"I know a lot of things you don't," the man replied smugly. "And I expect to be speaking to your other half in the next day or two. If you were able to quickly think things over and perhaps pass along your final answer through your brother, that would be most expedient."

Micah nodded. "I'll let you know."

Kearney dipped his head, not losing an ounce of self-satisfaction. "I await your reply."

Before he could leave, Micah asked, "What kind of business do you have that requires such an elaborate cover-up of your money? Cashing in your Timekeeper salary, turning currency over probably multiple times, pretending to give a rat's ass about some small fishing business in the south of Ireland...what do you have going on?"

The man raised a brow. "Why do you think I'm inclined to tell you of my business? It's my business; let it be. It's not any worse or any more incriminating than that of the IRA. Good day."

And he left, making his way along the docks until he reached the warehouse and vanished around a corner. Micah watched him go.

Sean was using MacEoghan to get to Kearney. Kearney wanted to use the fishing business to launder money. Who was this man? What was so horrible about it that the two of them had to be kept in the dark like this? What did they have to do to earn enough trust from either of them to find out what was going on? Would telling them put them in danger? Would it make them not want to help? Well, not knowing was making Micah not want to help.

He might have passed on telling MacEoghan about the house, but he wasn't going to leave his twin out of this loop. He was going to have to tell his father, too, and see what he thought. Was it better to help the IRA and their malevolent deeds, or help an international money launderer? Were there any Time aspects to this, or was this entirely within Earth-side jurisdiction? How did that all work?

Micah found his father a few docks down, sitting in one of the boats, looking lost in thought, open book on his lap; it appeared to be some kind of manual. He looked older than Micah remembered, or maybe it was the way the sun hit his face and accentuated all the wrinkles in his skin. Micah tapped lightly on the hull. His father startled, looked up, closed the book, sat up straight, and made a motion for Micah to join him. Micah took a seat on an empty crate.

"I haven't talked to Michael yet, but I have some ideas," Padraig said, stretching.

"Well, I just had an interesting conversation of my own," Micah told him, and relayed the talk he'd just had with Kearney.

Padraig did not say anything, but Micah could see that, though he wasn't sure what to make of it, he also wasn't thrilled by the idea in general.

"So this man is part of the IRA, but he's not acting on their behalf," Padraig clarified.

Micah nodded. "That's right. The IRA isn't interested in helping, whatever their reasons. But he has his own agenda that such an arrangement might fulfill; he didn't say exactly what his business or agenda was, just that it wasn't worse than the IRA."

Padraig scoffed. "Well, that's a low bar and small comfort."

Micah shrugged. "I'm just repeating what he told me."

"What did you say this man's name was?"

"Lorcan Kearney. He keeps company with a man named Nolan Kane."

His father thought a moment, then shook his head. "Neither one sounds familiar, but that's not too surprising, I suppose. I don't tend to keep company with dishonest types." He huffed a sigh. "Bad company corrupts good morals. But we're not going to have a company if we don't do something."

"You think we should take his offer?" Micah wondered.

"Mark my words, I don't want to. And I'm not going to give an answer right now. If we've got a day or two, let's use that day or two. Then I guess we're either dealing with Michael or this Kearney fellow."

Despite the numerous conversations and the seemingly inevitability of this decision, now that Padraig said it aloud, Micah suddenly felt a rock knot up his gut. This was it. This was their final gambit to save the business, and it came down to either working with Kearney and his money laundering or potentially surrendering all control of the business to Michael. What a choice.

"You know, Brendan the woodworker, they're leaving, heading to America," Micah mentioned.

Padraig gave him a look. "So now you're just writing us off and running away to another country?"

Micah blinked like he'd been slapped. "What? No, I—"

"Brendan and his wife both come from families who flee when things get tough. Fled to America when things got tough during the Famine. Fled from the north during the war. Now they're going to take up that cowardly mantle and flee themselves." Padraig shook his head, expression grave. "Well, we're not. Maybe we'll have to deal with the IRA or this shady agent, maybe we'll have to put in with Michael. But we don't flee. I'm tolerant of a lot of things, but that isn't one of them. You understand me?"

Micah nodded seriously. "Yes, sir."

"Good." Padraig shifted, stretched, yawned, shifted again, but did not stand. "Today would be a nice day if not for this damned Emergency hanging over our heads."

Micah looked out over the water and tried to relax. "Ocean's still blue, sky's still blue. Even the sun is out today for a bit." He glanced back at his father. "I'd say it's a nice day."

Padraig managed something resembling a smile. "Aye, I suppose you're right. Good Lord's trying to cheer us up when we're down. Guess we shouldn't cling to such bitterness out of spite." He hummed anxiously. "Although, if He could spare a moment, maybe He could show us an honest way to save the business, something that doesn't require working with the IRA or their shady agents or any of our enemies."

Micah shrugged. "We're enemies of God, but He still works with us."

Padraig made a scowling, dismissive sort of sound and stood slowly. "Bah! He don't need us." He stretched, making loud noises all the while, and then relaxed. "But I do need to take a leak." He stopped Micah before he could leave. "Like before, don't say anything. Don't speak, don't hint. You and I will talk some more about this over the next couple days."

"Should I tell MacEoghan?"

His father hesitated, then nodded. "You might as well, since he seems to be our go-between. And maybe, with how shady this all sounds, you can use it to try and talk him out of the whole business."

Micah nodded. "I can try."

"All you can do, and we both know how stubborn he can be." Padraig shook his head. "If you didn't look alike, I'd never know you were brothers." He waved a hand. "All right, go on."

Micah left the boat and headed out on the docks, slowly making his way toward home. He spotted MacEoghan approaching from a different direction and managed to flag him down so they could continue walking elsewhere and speak privately.

"Everything all right?" MacEoghan wondered, his tone suggesting this was a question of formality; he knew everything was not all right and was likely instead expecting a report on how not all right everything actually was.

So Micah relayed all the conversations he'd had throughout the day, even starting with the woodworker's house as a way to prepare himself to deliver the onslaught of more serious news. Kearney was up to something, was offering the company a deal, but it was all for his own ends. Micah tried to play it up as best he could about money laundering and a whole host of other suspicions and speculations, including wondering aloud whether Sean had any knowledge of this and how this all tied together with the IRA or Timekeeping.

MacEoghan did appear disturbed by this turn of events, and Micah knew a moment of hope that his brother would walk away from one or the other or both. Maybe they were only dealing with a few bad apples, but was it really worth the risk?

"I don't know what Kearney's up to," Micah concluded, "but he's been too shifty and too elusive even before all this, with you. I don't think he can be trusted on any level with anything. He's going to find a way to bring this down on us, hard. He's been too involved in our lives for it not to be intentional. If he can't get us for murder, why not embezzlement or money laundering?"

"But we could out him as part of the IRA," MacEoghan said weakly.

"Accusation only. At best, you're just a new recruit who can't possibly know everyone and by then you've just outed yourself."

His brother frowned and made a sound of frustration. He shook his head. "I don't know. Being part of the IRA, I mean, they're not a formal army, they have lives and jobs. This could just be that." Who he was trying to convince, Micah did not know. "I suppose I could ask Sean. Worst that happens is he doesn't tell me anything."

"No, the worst that happens is he lies to you and you believe him."

Now MacEoghan sobered up a little. "And what do you suggest? I automatically assume him to be a liar?"

"He hasn't exactly been the most forthcoming. Maybe he won't lie, but he won't give you the full truth."

"Why don't you ask him then? At the next training, ask him all the things you seem to think I'm too afraid or too dumb to ask."

"Maybe I will. And maybe you can press Kearney for some answers, too, when you go out with him."

"Oh, you're going to let me? You're not afraid he's a bad influence?"

Micah waved a hand. "I think Kearney is a pompous fool, thinks he's sneaky but is probably just as run-of-the-mill as anyone else. It's Sean I'm less trusting of."

MacEoghan looked like he wanted to be upset but couldn't quite muster the appropriate amount of anger. In the end, he settled for, "If the world weren't so messed up right now, I might try to contact Timekeepers in other Districts or Regions, see if they have any insight."

"The world is messed up, yes, but not all of it," Micah offered. "You think the Timekeepers in North America might know something?"

MacEoghan raised a brow. "Why would they? There might not be many Timekeepers in the world, but it's not as though we go out for a family picnic on a regular basis. I was just referring to Timekeepers on the mainland."

"Only the mainland? You think Britain doesn't have Timekeepers?"

"I'm not going to out Sean, Kearney, and Kane as IRA to them. And, all things considering, how could I trust what an Englishman tells me about them? If I were to ask, 'What do you know about Sean?' and the answer is that he's a liar and a conman and a thief, is that because he is, or because the Englishman thinks so?"

"Aren't you doing the same thing to this imaginary Brit now?" Micah teased. "How do you know you wouldn't find an honest Englishman? What if he said that Sean is a good and honest man? Are you still going to disbelieve him? What if he is honest but he says Sean is dishonest?"

"Would you stop?" MacEoghan cut in. "You've made your point. And I'm not going to ask an Englishman his opinion of an Irishman."

Micah shrugged casually. "So, what are you going to do?"

The answer Micah had been looking for was something along the lines of, "Maybe I should ask some questions and rethink my decision to join the IRA and pursue this Timekeeping business."

Instead he got, "What are you going to do? He made the offer to you, it's your business."

Micah sighed and tried not to slump. "It's not really my business, and it never will be if we don't do something. We might have to say yes. If nothing else, it might buy us a few days to see what his actual plans are, what shady business he's got going."

"That's one way to look at it."

"And the next time I do see Sean, I might have a few questions for him."

MacEoghan said nothing to that.

It was two days before Sean did show up for regular training, this time earlier in the morning once the boat had returned. Neither twin was happy to see Kearney with him. He paid respect to Padraig briefly before telling him that he would be stealing his twin boys. Padraig scowled but nodded. Sean thanked him, and the four of them headed down to their usual training spot on the beach.

"Why is he here?" Micah asked, indicating Kearney.

"To get your answer," Kearney replied, looking at him. He glanced at MacEoghan. "And then I'll be taking him with me afterwards."

Sean opened his mouth to speak, but Micah wasn't done. "What kind of business are you running—?"

"What kind are you?" Kearney shot back. "The fact that you are even considering deals with the IRA, with me, you're going to have to do some creative accounting of your own, so don't get high and mighty on your morals with me."

Micah glared at him. "We do it to survive, not as a matter of course."

"And who is approaching whom in order to survive?" Kearney raised a brow. "I won't force you to take the deal. I'm not going to reward your brother if you do or penalize him if you don't. This is strictly business."

Micah glanced at Sean who gave a nearly imperceptible nod. He took an even breath, tried to keep it from turning into a sigh, and gave Kearney a stiff nod. "All right. We'll do it."

Kearney responded with his own stiff nod. "Good. I expect we will see each other on a bi-weekly basis."

"Is that twice a week or every other week?"

The man raised a brow. "Which do you think?"

Illicit business, Micah thought resignedly. Every other week to keep suspicions low.

"Don't worry about the details," Kearney went on. "You aren't the only business I'm helping through these tough times."

"If you two are quite done," Sean said, stepping in before either twin could speak, "then maybe we can accomplish some other business, like our regular Timekeeper training."

"When do we get to go out and actually go after Runners?" MacEoghan wondered as a Fast Band went up around them. "There have to be a few of them around with the war and all."

Sean nodded. "There are, certainly. And, just as in Denmark, there are other Timekeepers as well, not all of them friendly."

"Are there no Runners trying to flee to Britain or Ireland?" Micah questioned.

"Remember when I told you that most Runners don't have especially advanced abilities? You know portal travel is difficult, the vast majority of Runners don't have any experience creating them, and those who do have little or no experience with blind portals. The only other real option is by boat and even that has been greatly reduced and restricted. There are no Runners 'fleeing' to Britain or Ireland, no, and everything here is usually pretty quiet. You two were the most exciting thing to happen in a while." There were a few seconds of incoherent babble as the three of them tried to talk over one another, but Sean won out, saying, "If I hear of anything and it doesn't sound overtly dangerous, I will, if possible, come and get you."

His word was the best they were going to get, really. Micah glanced at MacEoghan. MacEoghan glanced at Micah.

They didn't learn anything new that day; it was all review and strengthening the skills they already possessed. Fast, Slow, Internal, External, Double, Pinpoint, and so on. Kearney did not offer up any tips or criticisms, for which Micah was grateful. At the same time, he couldn't help but feel a tiny twinge of jealousy that Kearney was probably going to teach MacEoghan some more advanced things while they were out, ahem, working.

But why should he be jealous? He wasn't going to be a Timekeeper forever, just until things settled down on the mainland. After that, he was going to be Suppressed so he could live his normal life with a normal family.

He glanced at Kearney again. He shouldn't be dealing with this man and his shady business. This shouldn't be happening at all. Had he done something terribly wrong in his accounting that this was all his fault? Was this just an inevitable slide from poor decisions and practices years ago? Were they truly just victims of circumstance? What was he going to do if even Kearney's deals couldn't help them? What if Kearney did turn on them and they got into huge trouble? He looked at MacEoghan. His brother would have a chance to start over. Another life, another chance to get it right, no regrets.

"All right, good work," Sean said, gently removing all Bands and depositing them back in Base Time. "Keep working at it. I'll do my best to introduce some new concepts over the next few months, and you'll be well on your way to your Journeyman test. It's nowhere near as bad as your Apprentice review, I promise."

Micah just nodded.

Breaking his hour or so of silence, Kearney spoke up. "This is all well and good, yes, but MacEoghan and I have work to do." He made a motion at MacEoghan even as he looked at Micah. "I'll be by in a few days to get things set up, and then we'll be in business."

I can't wait.

DUAL APPRENTICE
OLDER BROTHER

The first thing you'll need are papers," Kearney declared once they recovered from the portal. "Make this person part of your life. He is your life. This is not a mask to wear, but a person to be."

They emerged from the alley into a respectably busy but not overcrowded street. Regular business hours had ended and the nightlife was in full swing. Men got off work and headed for the pub, and even a few ladies were out and about enjoying themselves in the twilight, the scene becoming ever more glitzy as the sun went down and the street lights came on.

"A person is more than just himself," MacEoghan said, looking around at all the people. "They have friends, family. Are we all pretending to be one big family, then?"

"No one is pretending anything. We are exactly who we are." Before MacEoghan could speak, Kearney continued, "I forgot to ask. Can you do an English accent? More to the point, can you do one well for extended periods of time?"

MacEoghan thought a moment, then altered his voice. "I don't interact with the English much, so I don't know that I could imitate them very well."

Kearney made a dissatisfied sort of noise. "Assuming this all pans out, you're going to have to work on it."

"I don't know that I could pass as an Englishman anyway." MacEoghan scratched at his beard, about two inches long at the moment. "No matter which way you shave me, I still look Irish."

"There's some English with red-tinted hair. Shows up in the Scottish, too. Besides, English is only twenty percent looks, eighty percent attitude." Kearney glanced at him. "And anyway, you might have to shave it off."

"Why?"

Now the man sneered at him. "For gad's sake, it's not just red, it's brown and blond, too." He shook his head. "It's far too memorable. Your hair's not too bad, brown, maybe a bit ruddy in the right light, but nothing unusual about it."

MacEoghan frowned. He rather liked his beard. "Wouldn't it be better to keep the beard, and then if things do get tight, I can shave it off?"

Again Kearney shook his head. "It would only work once for you. Only works once for most men, but especially for you. Better to stay clean, let them think your beard is a good, normal brown or red, if they should think that you might try to grow it out instead. Then you have every advantage when it isn't what they are looking for." He gestured around to the crowds. "And you'll notice that in the city, very few beards. Easier to blend in."

The man had never missed a step, and they now turned the corner into another alley. They ducked around the back of the building where Kearney produced a key for a locked door.

The door led to a small room, maybe ten by ten, full of papers and filing cabinets. In the center was a small, round, wooden table with two creaky, wooden chairs. On the table were more papers and a couple mechanical machines whose use MacEoghan did not know. A man sat in each chair, both with glasses, hovering over papers in front of them, fine pens at the ready.

"Evening, gentlemen," Kearney greeted. "I have our new recruit. What's his name?"

"Connor Walsh, twenty-two year old from Béal Feirste," one man replied, not looking up from his paper. He was an older man in his sixties or so, thin to the point of being gaunt, balding, bony fingers gripping his pen with arthritic determination. Several scars on the left side of his face and a missing lower leg testified to his time in the trenches.

The second man wordlessly handed Kearney a bundle of papers which he in turn handed to MacEoghan.

MacEoghan opened up the bundle. Military record, a stack of letters, some more reading he could not readily identify. He looked at Kearney. "He's a real person."

"He *was* a real person," the second man replied. He remained hunched over his papers. He was a man in his forties, thick-rimmed glasses, big nose, dark hair, clean-shaven, nothing especially remarkable about him. "Poor lad didn't survive the Great War. Lucky for us, his mum sided with us in the Civil War."

MacEoghan looked at Kearney who gestured to the papers. "She gave us those papers to help with our operations. Letters between them while he was in the trenches. His service record. Learn who he is. Become him. Should you make it through your probationary period, she'll be your point of contact in Béal Feirste, and your alibi."

"Won't her friends and family and neighbors know that I'm not him?" MacEoghan wondered.

"We'll address that if you make it that far," Kearney informed him, a touch of smugness in his voice. "Right now, I want you to read through all those letters, all the papers and records."

"What? I thought we were doing training tonight."

"We are. Adapting to a new persona is part of that training. Or did you think we were going to go out and bomb some British military camp somewhere?"

Kearney gave him a look, then squeezed around the younger man at the table and disappeared into the next room. MacEoghan stared at the door he'd walked through.

"Have a seat, son," the older man told him. He vaguely indicated a chair in the corner that had a stack of files on top. "Just set those on the floor, pull up a seat, start reading."

MacEoghan had the ability to read, he just didn't like to. He didn't enjoy just sitting and reading for its own sake, or for most any reason, actually. There was so much more that he could be doing with himself, even if it was just going out and fishing. Even the nightly Bible reading left a bit of a sour taste in his mouth and unease in his mind, but that may have had to do with the Brothers more than the material or the activity.

Reluctantly, he cleaned off the chair, maneuvered it toward the table and the dim light the men were working under, and started flipping through the pages.

"Read them in order," the younger man said. "Story only makes sense from beginning to end."

With his mood now in free fall, MacEoghan stopped mindlessly shuffling and just started reading. For at least a few minutes, he did nothing more than stare at ink on paper, hoping his brain was reading what his eyes were seeing. Then a word jumped out at him. Then a phrase. Then curiosity bade him read a sentence, then a paragraph, then a whole letter.

The next thing he knew, he was reading one letter after another, a story of naivete, bravery, and fear unfolding before his eyes. Connor was not twenty-two years old when he died; he was nineteen. He'd only been sixteen when the Great War broke out. With his pa long gone, it was up to Connor to be the patriarch, and that meant, in his eyes, lying about his age and going to war. His mother did not want him to go—better for him to stay home and keep the little ones safe and fed.

It wouldn't be long, Connor promised. Before the leaves turn, they were told. Before the snow falls. Everyone expected this to be a short war, even the Germans. Not even a war, just a bit of a conflict. A skirmish, even. He would go, do his duty, get some excitement, then come back to entertain the kids with heroic stories of grandeur from the front lines.

But that skirmish quickly turned into a conflict and from there into a war that stretched around the world. Everywhere one looked, war, with no reprieve. Connor's letters morphed from almost joking around, light-hearted, and hopeful, to something very dark, very distressing. Although Connor never told his mother the terrible details about what was going on, MacEoghan could get a sense of what he was hiding. Endless gunfire, sleepless nights, friends dying left and right and he's still standing. At least, until he became that dead friend on someone's right or left.

The whole time, Connor's mother pleaded with him to come home. She included a prayer or Bible verse at the end of each letter and said that she and the little ones were waiting for him to come home.

"He was a good lad," the older gentlemen commented. "Survived a lot of shit. Just not enough."

"You knew him?" MacEoghan questioned.

"A bit, in passing. By that time in the war, everyone, on both sides, was splitting into two camps: jaded, glassy-eyed, nearly catatonic but for the shellshock; and savage, mindless, monsters intent on killing everyone around them, foe and friend, because they had been fighting for so long that they had forgotten everything else, everything human."

"And which had Connor become?" Truthfully, he wasn't sure he wanted to know the answer.

"He was dawdling between both when I knew him. Some days he was a walking dead man. Other days he was picking fights with anyone and everyone and once had to be dragged back into the trench because he thought he was going to storm the enemy trench and kill them all single-handedly."

"How did he die?"

"Taken out by a bullet as he made that heroic charge across no man's land. Oh, we took the enemy trench, but he never made it." The old man made a vague gesture to the papers in MacEoghan's hand. "That last letter, it was in his jacket. Never got a chance to send it to his mum."

"How did she get it, then?"

"She didn't. I took it when we dragged the dead back to the trench to rummage through pockets and distribute his worldly goods. I told myself I'd find his mum and deliver the letter. Then I read it." He shook his head. "She didn't need to see that."

MacEoghan nodded slowly. It was darker than the other letters, showing some of the madness that had begun to overtake the poor lad.

"How am I supposed to impersonate him?" he wondered. "As a naive farm boy, or a veteran on the brink of insanity?"

"You know his history," the old man told him. "You know his mind. He survived that charge, took the trench, won twenty fecking yards of ground for our side, and somehow made it back home. You're not the same boy who kissed your mum goodbye before signing your life away. You've seen things, done things. And yet, life goes on. Here you are in Baile Átha Cliath now, with its rich life and culture, everyone trying to stay optimistic in the face of this Emergency."

"But I know what it's like when a city could be under attack at any moment," MacEoghan added.

"Aye, I suppose you do."

He shifted position. "What about you? You did all of this, too, yet you're sitting here quietly. Who's to say that's not what Connor would be doing?"

340

"I'm an old man of sixty years and half a leg. You expect me to charge into battle?"

MacEoghan frowned. "You came home from the war, tried to warn me about what it was like, but I didn't listen. I'm too young, too rash, too eager for adventure and excitement. And in the wake of the Civil War, I came to view those in North Ireland as hostages held by a foreign power so strong they could even convince some people to hate themselves and their brothers. My mum is hostage there also, but she will not flee to save herself. She wants to free as many hostages as possible. But there are those who would expose the operation, so we have to be careful."

Now the old man chuckled. "You're starting to get it, I think. Learn all you can about Connor Walsh. Read those letters until you start speaking them in your sleep. Study them until you no longer respond to your own name. You must become this man."

MacEoghan again shifted position, noting the interior door was opening. "How am I supposed to become him if operations are only carried out every so often? If everything is clandestine—"

"You must be able to switch personas at a moment's notice," Kearney cut in, closing the door behind him. "Fully and completely. You must reach a point where even you are unsure which person is real and which is the mask. There are some among us who rotate between five different lives, and even they may not be able to say for sure who they truly are."

"Five?" MacEoghan questioned.

"One for the north, one for the south, one for England, and now one for both Germany and France. If the United States were to join the war, a sixth life may be required."

"And one for the Soviets?"

There was a collective shaking of heads from those gathered. It was the younger man at the table who finally looked up and answered. "No. There are no identities with the Soviets, only prisoners. Only death. We have no dealings with them. It is safer that way."

The stern rigidity was clear, but MacEoghan also detected a certain current of fear in the statement as well. These men were willing to deal with Hitler's Nazi regime, currently marching its way all over Europe, against the wishes of their home government and the surrounding allies, in order to advance their own cause. But they would not touch the Soviets, refused to deal with them in any fashion. Even Kearney had a wariness about him when discussing the Red Army.

"For the moment," Kearney said, his tone pivoting the conversation back to its normal course, "if you are back home in your little fishing village, you are free to be who you are. When you leave your safe village, when you're around any of us, you are Connor Walsh."

"I understand," MacEoghan told him.

"What is your name?"

"Mac—Connor Walsh."

Kearney grabbed his shoulder. "I'm sorry, I must have dirt in my ears. What did you say your name was?"

"Connor Walsh."

"Who?"

"Connor Walsh."

"Who?"

"Connor Walsh."

"What's your name?"

"Connor Walsh."

"One more time."

"My name is Connor Walsh," MacEoghan insisted. "I'm twenty-two years old from Béal Feirste."

Kearney fixed him in a hard stare for several long seconds. MacEoghan could feel his heart racing in his chest. He wanted to Band and buy himself a moment to breathe, but he had a suspicion that Kearney wouldn't allow him such a luxury. At last, the man backed down, took a step back, and held out his hand. "Nice to meet you, Mr. Walsh."

MacEoghan eyed the man's hand suspiciously, then reached out to take it. Nothing nefarious happened, just a simple handshake. Then it was over, no harm done. Kearney went to the exterior door. "Shall we go out and have a pint, Mr. Walsh?"

That sounded like a mighty fine idea, MacEoghan thought. He nodded once and stepped outside, Kearney following.

"From here to the street is the length of time you have to figure out your mannerisms," Kearney told him, pausing to loosen his jacket. "How do you walk, how do you talk, how observant are you of your surroundings, or how observant do you appear to be? Mannerisms make a man as much as his formal identity and his words. If you're a careless man, you should become cautious. A stupid man should appear intelligent." He gave MacEoghan a pointed look. "And a man quick to anger should learn patience. In this way you will never be identified, nor could you be mistaken for your persona. Never forget the value of a convincing appearance."

MacEoghan's first thought, as they made their way toward the street, was to basically impersonate Micah. They were always accused of being complete opposites, so why not? Patient, subservient, dutiful, everything their parents expected. Then he considered what a dilemma that could cause. If anyone did track down "Connor Walsh" and tried to associate him with MacEoghan, then, by mannerisms alone, even if their physicality was a bit different, they would go after Micah by mistake. MacEoghan may have wished his twin was a little more enthusiastic about what he was trying to accomplish, but he couldn't put him in danger like that. This association alone was already likely to cause him some trouble, being a twin.

If he was supposed to be his own opposite, but he couldn't be Micah, what was he supposed to do? The walk to the street wasn't that far, and he hadn't absorbed enough of Connor's personality from the letters to really guess at such nuances. Could he maybe just figure it out as he went along?

Then they reached the sidewalk and turned down the road. A light drizzle had begun and the light from the street lamps reflected brilliantly on the wet pavement. MacEoghan followed Kearney across the street amid several vehicles and a large group of cyclists, and they turned down the road again.

"Have you been to Baile Átha Cliath before, Mr. Walsh?" Kearney inquired in a tone that was unusually friendly.

No, he told himself. Kearney and Walsh were friends. Friendly, anyway. Maybe business partners? Either way, Kearney and Connor were friends in a way that Kearney and MacEoghan were not.

"No, never," MacEoghan replied. Even as he said it, he doubted himself. Had Connor ever been to Baile Átha Cliath, more often called Dublin? He didn't think so as it was never mentioned in his letters. He looked around. "It is a big city. Quite bright."

"Aye," Kearney said. "We don't have the same blackout rules that the north does; we can actually enjoy ourselves for a time after work."

He turned and opened the door to a pub. MacEoghan was genuinely surprised by how busy the place was. Actually, he was surprised by quite a lot going on around him. His memories of Gaillimh were few, with most of his life spent in relative isolation either at the school or in the fishing village, with only brief visits here and there when he was boxing. Even then, Baile Átha Cliath was for professional fighters and remained only a dream for him. Maybe he would have the chance to continue his career?

He mentally shook his head as they sat down at a table. No, he was here on a mission. Here, he was Connor Walsh. MacEoghan the boxer was back home.

"So, Mr. Walsh, tell me about yourself," Kearney said, unfolding a napkin to place on his lap. "What brings you this way?"

Well, "joining the IRA" was not a good answer in such a public place, MacEoghan knew, but what was he supposed to say? He didn't know his business, didn't know anything about this man he was supposed to be impersonating. He was having to build up a dead man.

He shrugged. "Trying to help my family, I suppose. More opportunities for work in the city, maybe better housing."

A waitress approached but words were unnecessary as Kearney just held up two fingers.

"Are you a regular here?" MacEoghan inquired, trying to wrestle some control within the conversation. "You know her name?"

"I suppose you could say I'm a regular," Kearney answered. "As for Mindy, well, she's a bit young for me, I think." He shifted position. "You don't have a girl back home, then?"

Did he? No, he couldn't. He was impersonating someone, but he wasn't actually living that life. He shook his head. "No, not anymore. She was less than supportive of my views on the war."

Kearney chuckled. "Which one?"

"Pick one."

The man's expression turned unreadable, and MacEoghan had a sense that it was not the best answer he could have come up with.

"So if you don't have a girl, who's your family? Where's your father?"

"He died, a long time ago. Mum's still alive, though." That much he knew for certain. "Got the little ones still. Well, I say they're little, but they all grow up eventually."

The waitress, Mindy, returned with their drinks. Kearney lifted his in a mild toast. "Aye, they do grow up, for better or worse."

"What'll it be?" Mindy inquired, flashing MacEoghan a smile.

"What'll you let me have?" MacEoghan wondered.

"Rations do make things a bit difficult, true. But we have potato soup, beef barley soup, lamb roast, salad—"

"I'll take the lamb roast," Kearney cut in.

"Potato soup," MacEoghan decided.

Mindy barely gave Kearney a second look as she walked away.

"Going to be hard to convince you to set up shop here, I can tell," Kearney commented, his tone smirking.

MacEoghan watched Mindy disappear into the kitchen, then turned back around. "I don't know what you mean."

He took a drink and couldn't help but blanch. "Rationing barley should be more than a crime; it should be a sin."

Now Kearney laughed and raised his glass. "I'll drink to that."

MacEoghan clinked his glass and drank as expected, but he wasn't being witty or facetious or acting as Connor; the beer really wasn't all that good. He set his glass down, leaned back, and stared at it. He didn't want to commit the sin of leaving a pint unfinished, but he also didn't want to commit the sin of subjecting his body to its contents. Across the table, Kearney had composed himself and was speaking again.

"So, if you're here to help your family, what's your trade? Iron, glass, lumber, shipyard, business?"

MacEoghan recalled a statement in one of Connor's letters, that his grandfather had left the glassworks in Wales, seeking to be rid of heavy industry and crowded places. They'd settled on the outskirts of Béal Feirste with the intent of finding a larger plot of land to farm, but it never happened.

345

Connor's mother had pleaded with him to come back home, find that plot of land, and live peacefully.

"I think my mum would skin me if I went into the glassworks," he answered after a moment. "But I'm no stranger to farming or fishing or business or doing whatever needs to be done."

Again Kearney flashed him a disapproving look, disguised by a drink. MacEoghan knew a moment of irritation. He had been given only a short time to study, been told that he had to decide a lot of information in a very short period of time, and was now expected to act out a full persona to perfection. What did Kearney expect from him? Was this part of everyone's training, or was this just part of the man's personal plot to find any excuse to get him kicked out of the IRA?

"Your determination is admirable," the man commented. "And there's nothing wrong with being open to learning new things. However, my company values specialization, the ability to hone in on one or two key abilities and exploit them to their fullest potential. It is not merely something you 'try' for a few years because it interests you at the time; it requires dedication, commitment, even for a lifetime, almost like having a mistress."

"And what abilities do you see in me?"

MacEoghan couldn't be sure, but he liked to believe that Kearney was caught off-guard by the question. The man wanted him to be and act a certain way, well, maybe he could define just what that certain way was.

"You say you're a farm lad. You certainly look good and strong."

"Thank you, sir."

"Unfortunately, that is not what we're looking for. Not only, anyway. A monkey can be trained to do a task. Any man can use a shovel or swing a pick."

MacEoghan nodded. "True enough, but not every man can break or drive a horse properly. Not every man can catch a greased pig. It takes skill."

Kearney just bobbed his head once, but before he could speak, the waitress returned with the potato soup and lamb roast.

"Looks delightful, dear," Kearney said.

MacEoghan wistfully agreed, then, "So, what's a pretty lady like you doing here? Doesn't it get a bit...rough?"

"It can," Mindy sighed, still smiling, "but it puts food on the table without having to risk danger in a dirty factory or work the streets."

Her expression was both smug and teasing as she walked away. Again, MacEoghan watched her go, ignoring whatever Kearney was saying across from him. Finally the man cleared his throat and MacEoghan twisted back around.

"As I was saying," Kearney went on, cutting open the fork-tender roast, "those are important tasks. What I'm interested in is the skill. Breaking a horse requires an observation of method and a great deal of planning and forethought. Catching a greased pig requires the ability to think on one's feet, compensate on the fly, and, admittedly, a bit of luck as well." The potato soup was better quality than the beer, for which MacEoghan was thankful. "We'll not have you breaking horses or catching pigs, but there will be other tasks which require the skills I just outlined."

"I can learn a method," MacEoghan told him. "Thinking on the fly, well, that depends on the goal."

"The method is simple enough. Parcel delivery is not a difficult task. Local deliveries can be made by boys."

Parcel delivery? That was Kearney's business? Or was it just a pretense? Did it have anything to do with the shady offer he'd made to Micah? It would make sense, especially if there was international money laundering involved. Yet the man made it sound like the business was completely separate from the IRA. Was that a lie? What was he missing? Would he ever find out? Would he find out too late?

He fished out a few potatoes from his soup and ate them. "You think of me as a boy, then?"

"I don't know what to think of you; we barely know each other and you've not yet worked for me. I cannot simply hand over my most difficult jobs on blind faith. My clients may be of the understanding that war causes delays, but they would still like to receive their parcels."

So maybe his business was not as separate from the IRA as he would have others believe.

"Are you adverse to such things?" Kearney inquired. "As I said, moving parcels around Ireland is simple enough. You could be here to Corcaigh and back and never realize there was a war going on just a stone's throw away. Cross the border into North Ireland, England, or even Scotland, and that could be a very different story. You could be stopped, searched, even detained."

"Why would the English detain an Irish parcel carrier?" MacEoghan asked, genuinely curious.

"Confiscate goods to boost the war effort, for one. It's bloody near impossible to send food across the border. English soldiers will seize a sack of flour, send two measures to the troops and half a measure to the civilians. It's a damn crime. Not just food, either, but anything that could be used on the front lines or in the field hospitals. Textiles, needles and thread, flint, shoes, alcohol, all of it. Even things you wouldn't think of. Heard of a farmer in the north, got too close to the border, Englishmen seized the straw on his wagon. Got to send it to the boys, they said, for bedding and fire to keep warm."

Even if that were the only reason, MacEoghan would have been sufficiently annoyed, taking another bite of his soup to keep from talking, even as Kearney continued.

"And if it's not for the war, that want to make sure you're not IRA. They don't want anyone coming up on their backside, especially their neighbors, taking advantage of them while in a weakened state."

MacEoghan swallowed. "And badgering Irish farmers and couriers over straw and small goods is supposed to make the people sympathetic to their war?"

Kearney scoffed, taking another piece of tender roast on his fork. "They don't care about our sympathy. They can't conscript our men so they take what they can get."

"If things are so bad, why bother shipping anything to England or the north?"

"People still need goods. People still need jobs, don't you?" Kearney gave him a look. "I know maybe I made it sound frightening, as if an Englishman might jump out of the bushes at any time if you're within ten miles of the border, but it's not all bad. Plenty of people, even couriers, go back and forth without any trouble."

MacEoghan nodded and tipped his bowl up to finish off the broth. When he lowered the bowl, he found Kearney giving him a very disapproving look.

"You're not in the barn anymore, son, you are in a respectable establishment," the man informed him with an undisguised glare. "I suggest you act like it."

MacEoghan cleared his throat and slowly moved his hands away from the bowl. After a moment of thought, he picked up his napkin to wipe his mouth. Kearney still looked annoyed but said nothing more about it, just finished his lamb roast. As he ate, MacEoghan watched Mindy slip around the dining room with drinks and food.

"When would you have me start working for you?" he found himself asking, his eyes still on the pretty waitress, even staring at the door to the kitchen where she disappeared.

"Well, I would give you a few test runs first, to make sure you can do the job and do it well. I don't want to entrust a delivery to someone who is going to balk at the first sign of trouble on the road. It's not just the soldiers you have to worry about. The British are under constant threat from the Germans, and their government restricts their movement and goods in many ways."

"Highwaymen," MacEoghan stated, finally turning his gaze back to Kearney.

"Exactly. They don't care what's in the parcel—it could be food, it could be ash—only that it is more than what they had ten minutes prior to your ambling by."

MacEoghan might have had more to say, but Mindy returned and scooped up their empty dishes. She flashed a tantalizing smile at him. "So, how was the food?"

"Beautiful," he answered dumbly.

Her expression turned coy. "Beautiful? That's not a word I would normally use to describe soup."

He coughed to hide his embarrassment, feeling the heat of his skin and Kearney's smirking gaze. "Well, I mean, presentation is half the meal, isn't it?"

Mindy's expression never wavered as she shifted her stance. "That's pretty high praise for a restaurant with no stars."

"Well, I think I'm looking at one."

She laughed. "Oh, you're a smooth talker, aren't you? What's your name?"

Only at the last second did MacEoghan recall himself and answer, "Connor. Yourself?"

"Mindy. It's very nice to meet you, Connor. Maybe I'll see you again sometime."

She walked away before he could reply. MacEoghan again watched her leave, then glanced back at Kearney who was still smirking.

"What?" MacEoghan asked.

"You have to ask?" Kearney retorted. He put his napkin and some bills on the table, then stood, grabbing his overcoat. MacEoghan followed suit. "It may be more productive to discuss business elsewhere. Somewhere less...distracting."

MacEoghan didn't disagree, nor did he think that Kearney was incorrect in any silent assumptions; he just wasn't going to apologize for any of it. Mindy was pretty: pale with bright blue eyes, long legs, fiery red curls bouncing over a rather appealing bodice. Whether or not he worked for Kearney, he was going to have to come back and maybe find out where she lived.

But for the moment, he just followed Kearney down the sidewalk, back across the street, down a different alley than before, then finally ending up back at the same building with the same locked door and the same two men at the same table.

"How was dinner?" the younger man asked.

"Oh, fork-tender," Kearney reported, showing soft emotion for the first time MacEoghan had ever seen. "They must have George back in the kitchen tonight, absolutely superb." He jerked a thumb at MacEoghan. "Apparently this one has an eye for aesthetics. He found his soup 'beautiful' this evening."

MacEoghan felt his face flush red again.

"Oh, the soup was beautiful, was it?" the older man snickered.

"How much of a liability is he?" the younger man asked, his tone mocking but expression serious.

Kearney sat in the same chair MacEoghan had earlier. "Well, he remembered himself when she asked his name, but fuck me if he didn't want to follow her home."

"All the lads do, Kearney," the older man said. "That's why we use her."

"What?" MacEoghan blurted.

"Damn it, man, are you thick?" Kearney questioned. "Mindy's one of ours. One of the best damn spies we've ever had, and you know why." It was a statement that defied challenge. He shifted position. "First test is just remembering who you're supposed to be, especially when your guard is down and your cock is up."

MacEoghan didn't know he could feel any more humiliated. "I did give her the correct name, though."

Kearney sighed. "Yes, you did. And it's the only reason we're having this conversation. Given the wrong name, we would have parted ways and that would have been the end of an otherwise lucrative career with the IRA." His tone and expression were heavily sarcastic. "As it is, we can proceed to the second test, running parcels as I described, which I hope you heard."

"I heard just fine."

"Good. Then tell me the name of the farmer who had his straw stolen."

MacEoghan gave him a look. "You never said his name."

Kearney nodded. "Oh, yes, I did. Were you paying attention to me, or watching Mindy?"

MacEoghan would admit a bit of confusion. He was sure the man hadn't named the farmer. They were talking about problems that could arise for couriers, and Kearney had mentioned that the straw was stolen to send to the troops on the front lines. He shook his head. "You didn't mention his name."

Kearney waved a hand flippantly. "Well then you weren't paying very close attention, were you? You were gawking at the pretty waitress."

"She wasn't even at the table. She had just taken our orders and gone back to the kitchen. Me and you were talking about problems on the road. You never mentioned the farmer's name."

Now the man's expression turned knowing. "Very good. Know this. People are bloody liars, not all of it intentionally, mind you. Some people just work with what they know, even if it's incorrect. But there are those who will try to confuse you, make you believe things you know aren't or couldn't be true, make you go along despite knowing that something isn't true or right."

"And using a fake identity of a real dead man isn't the same thing?" MacEoghan wondered. "Lying to Mindy—even though she was apparently expecting it—about my name isn't the same?"

"We desire unification, *a Chonnor*. We are told, repeatedly, that the partition is what everyone wants. It's what's best. It's almost logical, even natural. And people go along with it, because they're tired of fighting, tired of war, especially among our own, and I don't blame them. They look back on the last thirty years and sigh; they just want it to be over, regardless of the outcome. We aim to fix that. Sometimes it means using the enemy's tactics against him." Kearney shifted position. "Now, if you have a problem with any of this, I suggest you leave now. You're going to lie to people. They're going to lie to you. You may have to rough up some people, and at the same time, others are going to try and rough you up. Even unto death."

"Torture," MacEoghan stated.

Kearney's expression twisted and he made a so-so gesture. "I wouldn't call it torture. I wouldn't go that far, no. We're not invaders like the British or the Germans. We're not seeking indefinite expansion of an empire, creating wars and causing havoc, and demand to know information about the movements of the enemy. We need information, yes, but there is really very little call for torture or anything of that nature when all you're trying to do is persuade a few politicians to move the property lines and the fencing back to where they should be."

MacEoghan met his expression. "So then what kind of parcels am I delivering? Sweet rolls for mum?"

"In the beginning, sure. I can't give you anything of consequence yet."

MacEoghan understood, but he didn't have to be happy about it. Somehow, this whole IRA thing was not turning out how he expected. Of course, he didn't know just what he had expected. The Civil War was over. Unless they wanted to reopen it, raise up their army and try to face both the formal Irish Army and the British at the same time—even he knew that was akin to suicide—then things would have to be done a little more quietly, more strategically.

As if sensing his thoughts, Kearney said, "If you want action, excitement, something to keep you constantly moving, an activity where you can hit someone but not too hard, go back to the boxing ring. You're good at it; you'll probably go somewhere. Or, as others have said, hop the border and join the British troops on the battlefield. Or the Germans for all I care. Or, if things go sideways as many suspect, just wait a bit and either side could come to us.

"I am not at liberty to tell you our greater plans. We may not be formal soldiers, but it is expected that we will fight if called upon. I cannot tell you if and when that will be. For right now, you are an untested recruit. You get jobs that are inconsequential and insignificant. Prove that you can do that, those parcels may change and become more significant. But if you just want to jump in with guns blazing, this isn't the operation for you."

"I want to defend Éire," MacEoghan said lamely. "I want to put things back to rights, keep the British and the Germans off our land, and let our people breathe again with no interference."

"An admirable goal, but regrettably naive when it comes to larger politics," the younger man at the table commented. "Éire may get its border properly arranged, but isolation hasn't been a viable option for any country for decades."

MacEoghan glanced at the younger man, then the older man, and finally back at Kearney. The man stood and made a motion to follow. MacEoghan did so, but they only stepped outside to the alley.

"You need to decide your goals and your priorities," Kearney told him, not unkindly. "If you want physicality, you know where to find it. If you want to help your family and save their fishing business, this isn't it. If you want to help Éire, you may have to come to terms with the fact that it won't be exciting all the time, or even most of the time. You'll be working with limited information for seemingly no benefit to the cause." He shifted his stance. "I'll give you a few days to think about it. But know that once you commit, you're committed. We're not going to have this talk every time I send you out on a job. It does no one any good if you can't be dependable, if one day you're engaged and the next day you're not. Do you understand?"

MacEoghan sighed but nodded. "I understand."

"Once you make that choice, I'll give you some pointers on the use of Time as well. Comes in handy on these missions sometimes."

MacEoghan continued to bob a nod wordlessly as Kearney opened a portal back home. Neither one said any word of farewell as he stepped through.

He went to his face on the ground, sand and rock cutting his face and irritating his eyes. He may have blacked out; he wasn't entirely sure. He got to all fours, shifted his weight so he could brush off his face and try to clear his eyes. For a moment, he thought he was going to heave all that potato soup, but as he shifted around to a more comfortable position, his stomach settled and he could breathe. After another minute or two, he stood on wobbly legs and brushed himself off. Once he was oriented, locating the house down the way, he started off in that direction.

What did he want? What was he looking for? What was he trying to accomplish? He thought he was going to fight for Éire, not merely run errands for her.

He paused a stone's throw from the house, noticing Padraig inside. Every morning, his father went out on the boat, fighting wave and fish to make a living for his family. But that wasn't all he did. He also kept books, mended equipment, and dealt with people. It was part of being in business. And at home, he was good and kind to his wife and children, even to him, MacEoghan, who had certainly grieved the man plenty in the last year or so. There was no shame in doing chores and running errands. Sewing fishing nets wasn't glamorous, but it was necessary.

But there might not be a business if something didn't change quickly. Micah was working perfectly well in the office. Maybe MacEoghan could work the other avenues.

TEST RUN
OLDER BROTHER

According to Kearney, methods rarely mattered in low-level operations, although some things could be specified just to see if he was paying attention and willing to take orders or perhaps to identify him to a contact. But for this first test run, most of the means were up to him. However he thought he could best do the job, do that, and they would discuss the particulars later.

It was a simple enough task: deliver a parcel from Dún Dealgan to Béal Feirste. He didn't know what was in the parcel, only that he, as Connor, had to take it to "his mum" in Béal Feirste. If anyone asked, it was a sweet roll, a gift from son to mother to cheer her up in dark times. As long as the parcel arrived in tact, he received the return parcel, returned to Dún Dealgan in one piece, and his fake identity wasn't found out, the mission would be counted a success. But, as Kearney had reiterated more than once, if he was found out, he was too low on the totem pole for the IRA to want to risk its neck for him; he would be considered a wannabe recruit not affiliated with the organization.

He'd given his Connor persona some thought over the past few days, read over the letters and other papers some more, thought about the conversation with the old man and with Kearney in the pub. He figured he had a good idea of how he wanted to portray himself that would not lend suspicion to either himself or Micah. Of course, he hadn't really had a chance to practice this persona, and border agents were not what he would consider easing into the waters.

Gas rations were a strict inconvenience, but not yet intolerable. In Britain, everything was about conservation, conserving fuel for the soldiers and their many vehicles of war. In Ireland, it had more to do with making sure they would have enough fuel to get through the war and its many blockades. Personal vehicles were frowned upon unless they happened to be horse-drawn or carrying at full capacity.

Because of this, it was surprisingly easy to hitch rides to just about anywhere. There was usually someone who was raring to go somewhere and just needed a good excuse. Giving a ride to a chap, or a few chaps, was both neighborly and patriotic. When one of those fellows hitching a ride was going to take his mum a present in occupied and terrified Béal Feirste, well, who could say no to that request?

The car was packed full with six people when they finally got on the road north to Béal Feirste.

"You know, Adrian," the driver said, addressing one of the passengers, "you don't have to go back. There's more than enough people around here who'd be happy to have you and your wife stay a while, at least until the war is over."

"Amber would like that very much," Adrian replied, "but her mother is too ill to look after herself, or to travel."

"And there's no one else who can help her? Your wife should be here with you, at least."

"Amber's an only daughter, and all six of her brothers went to fight in the war."

"Are none of those brothers married?"

"Two are, aye, but Lucille doesn't like either of them, never has. Tolerates them for Christmas and Easter supper, as the Good Lord commands, but doesn't want much to do with them otherwise."

MacEoghan did not comment, though the other men in the car grunted and bobbed their heads as if in some understanding.

"And what about you, Danny?" the driver inquired of another passenger. "Why not bring your wife with you on this little venture?"

"Into territory that is both occupied and at war?" the man in question demanded. "Absolutely not! The fact that I'm going on business at some of the factories should be more than enough to deter that thought." He huffed a sigh. "I know my wife worries, and she would enjoy getting out every now and again, but her place is at home with the children."

"Your youngest is fourteen," a third passenger commented. "She's not changing his nappies and spoon feeding him anymore. He ought to be at work himself here soon."

"Well then he ought to be helping her while I'm gone," Danny retorted. He shook his head with a sharp snapping motion. "No. Absolutely not. Maybe once this Emergency is concluded, then she and I and all the boys will go on a nice drive together, like we used to do."

There were more grunts of agreement, some grumbling about how things used to be but they all got messed up on account of the Emergency, or the war, depending on which side of the border one resided.

"And what about you, stranger? Connor, wasn't it?" the driver asked. "Going to take a present to your mum?"

MacEoghan cleared his throat and shifted in his seat. "I am, yes."

"What are you bringing her?" Adrian wondered. "What's in the bag?"

Unsure if he should, but seeing no reason he shouldn't, MacEoghan opened his satchel and peeled back to flap to show off the box inside. Danny whistled.

"Maggie's Bakery." The man nodded. "You are a good son, aren't you? Or you're trying to make up for something."

MacEoghan closed the bag and shrugged, trying to get comfortable. "Just trying to cheer her up a little."

"Is she ill, too?"

"No. I've tried to get her to come south and stay with me, but she won't have it. She still believes in a united Ireland, and she still believes in Béal Feirste, and she's going to stay right where she is."

"Sounds like a stubborn old crow," the driver observed. "I can respect that, I suppose. Judging by your age, she's probably seen all sorts of horrors."

MacEoghan nodded. "Born in occupied Ireland, watched the Great War, the War of Independence, and the Civil War. She just happened to land on the wrong side of the line in the end."

"There shouldn't be a line," Adrian growled. "Half our country shouldn't be at war while the other half is...well, relatively safe."

"It's hardly half," another passenger, who had been silent thus far, sighed. "Six counties. Six bloody counties, who agreed—"

"It doesn't matter if they agreed," Danny cut in. "I can agree to a lot of things, but that doesn't mean they're good for me. And besides, most of those counties are nationalist counties. But how do you suppose they were taken anyway, if that's the case? Shady deals and the voice of the few whining and crying until they got their way."

The silent passenger rolled his eyes. "Oh, for heaven's sake, your exaggeration is astounding."

"If you agree with it, why are you here?" Danny challenged.

"I have some family here. I hitched a ride to come down and visit. Now I'm going home." He gave Danny a look. "Seems I should have waited for the next bus."

"Maybe you should have."

"Gentlemen, please," the driver interrupted, his tone nervous. "We're all going to the same place, but for our own reasons. If we can tolerate each other for just a little while, we can go our separate ways in peace."

"Oh, can we?" the antagonistic passenger inquired. He looked at Danny. "Can I? Will you let me? Or is that something that might not be good for us, to go our separate ways?"

Before Danny could reply, the driver spoke again. "I swear by God Almighty, I will pull over and leave you two stranded on the side of the road. Now sit down and shut up."

The arguing men glared at each other for another long moment before settling into their seats. The tension between them, however, was still such that no one dared to speak a word the rest of the way to the border where they were stopped by two customs officers.

"Morning, gentlemen," the first officer greeted.

"Morning, Liam," the driver replied.

"Still ferrying souls across the Styx?"

"You know, the Greeks failed to mention that it was a two-way service."

The first officer nodded while the second walked around the car, giving everything and everyone a glance over. The first officer leaned over casually on the sill of the window. "All right, who's in the gang today, and what have you got?"

MacEoghan was suddenly aware that he was the only one with a bag.

358

"What's in the bag?" the first officer, Liam, asked.

He opened the flap and showed the officer the box from Maggie's Bakery. "Just a present for my mum."

The officer raised a brow, but his expression was almost jealous. "A good son you are."

For a moment, MacEoghan seriously wondered whether the officer was going to confiscate the sweet roll for some absurd reason. Indeed, the man held out a hand and made a gesture. "Let me see it."

Was there any good way to refuse? Could he talk his way out of it? What would happen if the parcel was confiscated? How would it be for him to fail his first mission? The curtain of his confidence lifted to reveal only his stupid cockiness. He had no idea what he was doing. He didn't know what to do, or what he could do. Truthfully, he'd never crossed the border, even when he was a boxer, however much he might have bragged so. He had never left the country in his life. Somehow, he had just assumed that everything outside of Ireland, although different, was also the same.

Hoping his dread didn't show on his face, he handed over the box, unsure if the object inside was even a sweet roll since it had been given to him as is. The officer opened the lid and pushed aside some wax paper. The smell that wafted out was indeed that of a sweet roll, or some other delicious baked good. In his mind, MacEoghan could just see him lifting the delightful baked good and taking a huge bite out of it. As it was, he couldn't be sure the officer didn't intentionally brush the icing with his finger just so he could have a little taste anyway.

On the other side of the vehicle, the second officer was talking to Danny. It was apparently not the man's first time crossing the border, although the officer was quite keen on ascertaining the reason for his interest in the factories in Béal Feirste.

"We've been warned to keep an eye out for IRA agents trying to cause mischief during the war," the officer was saying. "Factories are prime targets for hostilities and recruitment."

"You think I'm not aware of that?" Danny wondered smoothly. "I go there to make sure my workers are working and not causing trouble. The war, the IRA, the bloody unions, it's a wonder any work can get done anymore. You used to be able to trust people enough to leave them alone to do their bloody job. It's not difficult, but somehow..." He sighed and shook his head dramatically.

MacEoghan flinched at a tap on the shoulder, but it was only the officer handing his box back to him. He peeked inside; the roll was still there, albeit with a minor finger swipe over the icing.

"Just remember," Liam said, "working men enjoy a bit of luxury every now and again, too. I'm sure you can relate."

MacEoghan resisted the urge to sneer, reminding himself that Connor was a more agreeable man. "What flavor do you like?"

Liam nodded toward the box. "One of those—for each of us—will do just nicely. And if you don't remember, well, there is a duty fee." The officer shrugged. "I'll let you off free right now since it's your first time; just remember in the future."

"I'll try to remember."

On the other side of the vehicle, the second officer had moved on to the passenger who had argued with Danny. "Welcome back, Peter. Another successful trip to visit your sister?"

"Depends on how you define success, I suppose," Peter answered. "I'm happy to see her, she's happy to me. I just can't convince her to move back home closer to family."

"I'm sorry to hear that." The officer shrugged. "But, to each his own."

Peter waved a hand. "No more of that progressive talk. Our father forbade her to leave, but she went anyway. Ran off with a man who filled her head with nationalist ideals."

"I remember."

Liam turned his attention to the driver, gesturing toward Danny and Peter. "Must have been a fun ride with these two sitting together, aye?"

The driver gave him a look. "You have no idea."

The second officer straightened and returned to his counterpart. "Nothing out of the ordinary."

Liam nodded. "Same." He took a step back and swept his arm forward. "All right, off you go. We'll see you when you come back through."

The driver tipped his hat and stepped on the gas. Within minutes the checkpoint had vanished from view.

"So you see, *a Chonnor*," the driver said, "getting across the border isn't all that scary."

"I was expecting him to steal my sweet roll," MacEoghan told him.

"Liam and Marcus aren't too bad," Danny stated, "but there are a few who might have."

"Frank," Adrian grumbled.

"Forget Frank, how about Erik or John?" Peter added in surprise agreement. "Greedy little shits."

So maybe MacEoghan really had gotten lucky. Maybe Kearney had been banking on him running into less amenable customs officers who would have confiscated the roll, forcing him to argue for it or steal it back via Time. Who knew what would happen on the ride back? He didn't know what kind of "gift" his "mum" was going to give him; what if it was just as desirable for customs officers who were just as bored or greedy or hungry?

But it was behind him now. He had to focus on the present moment. He was now officially in North Ireland and he still had his package to be delivered. That had to count for something, right? He could be proud of himself for a few minutes.

North Ireland didn't look all that different from Éire Ireland, and it only served to further cement MacEoghan's resolve that there shouldn't be such a distinction. Éire was Ireland was Éire, and her people were all one. North Ireland would be delivered from both the war and the Crown. There was no other option.

"All right, just like every time," the driver said, cutting into MacEoghan's thoughts. "I'm going to drop you all off downtown, and you'll make your own way to where you have to be. If anyone plans on riding with me back to Dún Dealgan, I'll be leaving about five o'clock from the same place."

Everyone else apparently knew the drill, and MacEoghan bobbed along with the nods. Of course, everyone else had also been to Béal Feirste or lived there; they knew their business, where they were going, and so on. The most he had was an address and a satchel which held a box containing a sweet roll. Obviously he couldn't ask anyone in the car how to get to the address; after all, he should know where his own mother lived, right?

Well, he would figure that out when they arrived and he had a few minutes to stretch his legs, look around, and get a feel for the place.

Béal Feirste, or, as the English called it, Belfast, was situated on a river, and everything about the city's geography reflected this. Streets were winding in accordance with the river's course, and many parks had been designed to overlook one part of the river or another. Boats ran up and down the river with various cargo, steam and coal smoke billowing from their stacks. Although obviously a different place than Baile Átha Cliath or Gaillimh, Béal Feirste was still very much an Irish city. Whatever anxiety MacEoghan had felt at the border crossing, it mostly faded away as he realized that things weren't so different here. After all, he was still in Éire, whatever the British maps dictated.

They pulled up to a street corner and climbed out of the car. The driver reminded them about the pickup time, then drove off. The other passengers hastily turned and went on their way, with only brief farewell pleasantries from Adrian and Danny. MacEoghan did not miss the nasty look Danny shot at Peter, nor the smugness and smirking that Peter gave in reply.

MacEoghan also turned and started in a direction, if only so he didn't look completely lost. After all, what good son wouldn't want to deliver this delicious sweet roll to his mum posthaste?

Once the sight of Béal Feirste and the feeling of being in a new place wore off, MacEoghan started to notice the less pleasant differences between North Ireland and Éire. Éire had rations on gas and a few other essential items, but it was still more of an inconvenience. North Ireland had a stranglehold on just about everything. There were buses running, a few trams, a taxi or two, but almost no personal motorized vehicles. People rode bikes everywhere, or just walked. A number of stores were closed, some simply so, others boarded up. Many stores had signs up either indicating what they didn't have, or what they did. The market seemed to be the liveliest place, though it, too, was less vibrant than he might have expected for a city this big.

Everything was being diverted to the war effort, MacEoghan thought. A war these people had no business being in. A war that their countrymen were relatively safe from, except, perhaps, for any stupid decisions made by

British or German leadership.

It shouldn't be like this. How can anyone just sit by and accept what's been done? Maybe people are tired of conflict, but some things are worth fighting for. Britain isn't worth it, but Éire—a united Éire—is.

He managed to flag down a taxi, clambering inside and rattling off the address.

"Fit young man like you taking a cab only that far?" the driver said with a sneer. He shook his head as he pulled away from the curb, grumbling, "If I didn't need the money so bad, I'd tell you to get out and take a bicycle. All the way to bloody London to join the war, lazy louse. Might do you some good."

Connor kept his mouth shut, but MacEoghan was going through a hundred comebacks in his mind.

Although, in all reality, had he known where the address was, he really might have just taken a bicycle, or even walked. Might have even been a little faster, considering all the pedestrian traffic.

Just a couple miles, if that, from where he had flagged down the taxi, sat a long row of common housing, endless units on either side of a narrow alley, an eight-foot brick wall and wooden gate keeping out the riffraff. Every window was exactly the same, every door spaced at precise intervals, every chimney puffing the same smoke.

MacEoghan paid the cabbie, stepped out of the vehicle, and headed through the gate. He tried to project some sense of optimism, a son bringing a present to his mother. His one saving grace was that this was not where Connor had been born and raised, so he didn't have to deal with nosy neighbors who could pick out a phony a mile away. The woman he was meeting, Melinda, had relocated after that house was destroyed in a fire during the Civil War. She moved several times after that before settling in this residence just a couple years ago.

The only thing that really separated one brick unit from another was the creativity in the tiny gardens which were also separated by brick walls about six feet tall. Grasses, mostly, but it appeared that some women had managed to cultivate shade-loving flowers as well. These provided the only color in an otherwise drab landscape. The clothes that the children wore were dull, earthen colors; even the little girls had to make do with yellow faded to gray or red faded to brown. Only a little hair bauble here and there gave any of them any color.

Some of the units had numbers on the door. MacEoghan suspected they were all supposed to be this way, but some numbers had fallen off or been stolen or disappeared by some other means. Some doors had the numbers simply painted on.

MacEoghan found the door he was looking for, entered the tiny garden that, like the rest, was no more than twelve feet across from wall to wall, and six feet deep from alley to door. Putting on his best face, he knocked on the door. He heard some movement inside, and a moment later, the door opened.

It was all he could do to hide his shock. Reading Connor's letters, he had expected a woman of maybe forty years with a gaggle of children running around. And, with a sudden epiphany, that had probably been true twenty years prior when Connor had gone off to war. But that was twenty years ago or more. If this woman had been forty years old at the time, she was at least sixty now, and she certainly looked like it. Her hair was gray, back hunched, arms feeble, shoulders frail. MacEoghan knew immediately why she was an operative for the IRA, because no one would ever suspect her.

Nonetheless, Melinda lit up at the sight of him. Or, more accurately, she lit up at the sight of his coat and satchel. They had indeed belonged to Connor and to every impostor after him.

"Well, this is a surprise!" Melinda gushed. Thin, white skin turned pink as she took MacEoghan's hand and held it to her cheek. "Oh, I love it when my little birds return to the nest!"

With his other hand, MacEoghan opened the satchel and retrieved the box containing the sweet roll. "Brought something for you."

The old woman giggled in delight like a young girl at the sight of the treat. She turned and motioned for him to come inside.

Once inside, MacEoghan thought they were going to drop all pretense and discuss business. Melinda had other ideas as she fetched a couple of small plates, then brought down some teacups for tea. Any time he tried to speak, she shushed him and carried on about her own business. Once the water was on for tea, she took the roll, cut it in half, and placed each half on a small plate. When the water was ready, she measured out some tea and prepared the beverage. With everything ready, they retired into a living room half the size of the garden to drink tea and eat half a sweet roll.

"I see you already got into the roll," the old woman teased, turning her half so he could see where the officer had swiped a taste.

Rather than mention the officer, MacEoghan just shrugged and said, "It was a long drive; I couldn't help myself."

She waved a hand. "Oh, you. Always causing trouble for your mama."

"Some things never change."

He ate the roll—which was, in fact, quite delicious—and drank the tea, glad that he was getting something for his efforts at least. The two of them made small talk about the weather, the drive from Dún Dealgan to Béal Feirste, and some gossip about the neighbors two units down. MacEoghan tried to be attentive to the gossip, wondering if there were any codes or clues he needed to be aware of, but, to him, it just sounded like Melinda was the nosy old neighbor he'd been worried about earlier.

"She works at the rope factory, you know," Melinda was saying. "Fine work for fine fingers, or that's what they say. Well, sounds like the supervisor there is rather fond of her...dexterity, if you know what I mean. Not just her, of course, but any lady with slender hands. And he's not such a slender man himself, mind you. Course, fishing isn't going so well up here, not with all the iron and munitions shipments on the river, and then the potential for blockade or attack in open waters. So, business is bad, and the man gets bored, I suppose."

MacEoghan nodded, unsure how he was supposed to respond.

"Now, the women over at the smiths, they don't have such problems. They might be slender gals, true, but they're working with metal and hot iron. Any man who touches them is liable to get burned. Course, lot of women there don't last so long. It's hot, thankless work. They do it just because the men are off to war and someone needs to keep the fire lit."

MacEoghan listened to her for the better part of two hours and several cups of tea, feeling his hopes of meaningful IRA work slip away with each passing moment and change of topic from one line of gossip to another. He tried to remember names, places, dates and times, but it felt useless. Back in

January, the authorities had seized a bunch of ammunition that the IRA had been stockpiling. Why couldn't he be assigned to some work on that case? Fine, so he couldn't be trusted with anything highly secretive yet, but couldn't this woman give him something more than some idle gossip that she'd gotten from a neighbor ten units to the south?

"Oh, and before you go," Melinda said at last, standing, "I have something for you."

This would be his return parcel, to prove that he had indeed met with her. It turned out to be a small, silver, heart-shaped locket. When he opened it, wondering if he was going to find some kind of real information inside that would help the IRA, he discovered only a photo of a young woman. Judging by features, this was Melinda thirty or more years ago.

Nevertheless, with his return parcel now secured, he dropped it in a pocket and made to leave. Melinda followed him to the door.

"Thank you so much for visiting," she told him, her expression joyful enough to make him feel guilty for departing so hastily and, to be honest, ungratefully. "You have no idea the comfort it brings to spend such a lovely afternoon with someone."

She opened the door and he stepped outside. Still feeling a bit guilty, he turned back around, bent, and kissed her on the cheek. Again she made a sound of delight like a little girl, and waved him goodbye.

At least a locket would be easier to get past the customs officers than a delectable pastry, he thought, exiting the alley and turning up the road toward Béal Feirste proper. He didn't need to call a taxi; he still had time, and it was a nice day. Cloudy, but still nice.

He whiled away his afternoon, trying to familiarize himself with the city a little, just in case he got sent back on a future mission. He hadn't thought to ask if he would be expected to assume Connor's persona for an extended period. Kearney had said that he should become so intimate with the persona that he wouldn't be able to remember whether he was Connor or MacEoghan. Except he wasn't the only one who had ever been Connor over the years. What had happened to the others? Or had Connor's whole life and identity and sacrifice simply been boiled down into nothing more than a training tool for IRA hopefuls?

He met up with the driver at the appointed time and place, climbing in the car with only a brief how-do-you-do.

"Your mum not like the sweet roll?" the driver wondered. "That was from Maggie's Bakery. She'll be hard-pressed to find anything better anywhere in the country."

"No, no, she was very happy for it," MacEoghan told him. "Just not looking forward to going back, I suppose."

"Aye, it can be hard. Separated families are a crying shame. At the same time, unless a fit young man like you wants to be conscripted, I suggest you do go back."

Two new passengers joined them for the ride south. This was a far more amiable ride as conversation was centered on more pleasant topics such as family, cooking, gardening, and sports. No mention was made of war or politics of any leaning. It helped to ease some of MacEoghan's anxiety as they approached the border. It was the same two guards as before.

"So, how'd your mama like the sweet roll?" Liam inquired.

"She loved it," MacEoghan informed him. "And she still loves me enough to give me half."

The officer laughed. "All right, good on you. Just don't forget what we talked about earlier, hm?"

MacEoghan assured him he remembered, even as he quietly told himself that next time, he would ride a bike across the border and use a Fast Band to bypass customs without having to pay tithes to bored and greedy border patrol. They didn't search his pockets and he said nothing about the locket, but that didn't mean that less friendly officers wouldn't try something.

Then they were on their way, no one any worse for wear. Conversation resumed, and it was an enjoyable ride overall. They reached Dún Dealgan in good time where the driver again dropped them off at a street corner. Everyone said their goodbyes and went their separate ways.

MacEoghan walked down the street as casually as he could manage, searching out a small cobbler's nook, tucked away between two larger clothing stores. One of these stores was closed, gone out of business due to the blockades and difficulty in securing materials; the other store wasn't far behind. But the cobbler still plied his trade, and his door was unlocked.

The room wasn't bigger than any of the tiny gardens in the housing units in Béal Feirste where Melinda lived. A middle-aged man was hunched over a pair of shoes while Kearney watched with something of a disapproving scowl. He looked up as the bell over the door jingled, though when he recognized MacEoghan, his expression hardly changed.

"Let me guess: somebody stole your sweet roll?" Kearney asked with a bit of a sneer.

MacEoghan raised a brow. "No. Not at all. Actually, Melinda split it with me."

The cobbler snickered, his eyes still on his work. Kearney did not seem overly pleased by the news, though the best his expression did was soften to something like annoyance. "And the return parcel?"

MacEoghan dug in a coat pocket and produced the silver locket, letting it slide through his fingers into Kearney's outstretched palm. The man opened it up, then used a small razor blade to slip the picture out of its place. Then he turned the picture over, enthralled by something on the back.

"What did she tell you?" Kearney asked, replacing the picture.

"About what?"

The man looked up at him, his expression more thoroughly irritated. "About anything."

MacEoghan shrugged. "I mean, nothing seemed all that important. Just gossip for lonely old women."

The cobber sighed dramatically and made a tsking sort of noise, still not looking up from his work.

"What?" MacEoghan looked at Kearney.

"God Almighty, are you thick in the head?" Kearney had a posture that said he was about three seconds from just walking out the door without elaborating. "You think she's just going to blurt out names, dates, places, and sensitive information?"

"Well...Maybe?"

Kearney shook his head. "No. I can't...I'm not...No. Just no."

The man made to leave, but now the cobbler spoke. "Come on, Kearney. No one is born with these skills."

"Aye, but a little intuitive thinking and rationale goes a long way."

The cobbler sighed again and finally looked up at MacEoghan. "Do you remember what the old woman told you? Whatever you think about it doesn't matter; do you remember what she said?"

MacEoghan gave him an uncertain glance, then looked at Kearney and repeated back most of what Melinda had told him. Maybe it wasn't verbatim, and he might have missed or mixed up a few details, but he did remember. It still sounded like gossip for old women, but if Kearney found it interesting, well, MacEoghan would tell him what he wanted to know.

After a few minutes of prattle, Kearney held up a hand, his expression intrigued.

"Say that again," he ordered.

MacEoghan blinked, momentarily forgetting everything he'd just been talking about. Then, "A woman named Adele is working at the rope factory and having to deal with a supervisor who isn't being proper towards her. Or any of the pretty women."

"Which supervisor?"

"I don't think she said a name, just that he isn't especially fit or handsome."

Kearney nodded slowly. "All right." He gave MacEoghan a look. "Maybe you're not quite so useless after all. What else did Melinda say, about anything?"

So MacEoghan continued to recount the old woman's gossip, though his mind was now more interested in whatever secret code had been embedded in the gossip regarding Adele and the rope factory. It seemed to center around the fat, ugly supervisor. Was she calling out a secret operative? A traitor? A spy? Was it possible he was a friend instead, but spoken poorly of in order to disguise such affiliation? Would Kearney ever tell?

He finished recounting his tale and waited for a reaction. Other than the one time he had MacEoghan repeat something, Kearney hadn't said a word or given much indication of what he thought of all the news. How did he know what was code and what was, really, just idle gossip from a lonely old woman living in very close quarters with her neighbors? Were there specific names that they used? Had there been some coded message written on the back of the picture in the locket?

Well, given this almost-blunder, he didn't think he was likely to find out any time soon. On the other hand, it would have been nice to know that he was supposed to pay attention to every bit of gossip Melinda espoused. His mission, as explained to him, was to deliver the package and bring something back that would prove he had done as ordered. No mention was made of acquiring additional information.

But then, wouldn't a good spy look for every opportunity to gather information?

On the other hand, he was brand new at this. As the cobbler said, no one was born with these skills. He didn't understand what was expected of him.

Was Kearney trying to fail him intentionally? It wasn't impossible, he figured, but still annoying. Was this really all still about Brother Andrew? Was the man trying to take out some kind of vengeance against Cillian for assigning MacEoghan to him in the first place?

Kearney sighed. "All right. If nothing else, you appear to have an excellent memory. That alone is worth its weight."

"If it all checks out, he may have a better memory than you did starting out," the cobbler added with a cheeky grin. He glanced at MacEoghan. "Exercise that brain, boy. The more you can keep in your head, the less you have to write down, and the less of a paper trail there is for anyone else to find."

"It has its advantages and disadvantages," Kearney cut in. "True, there's no paper trail for our enemies to find, but it could also be that information dies with you, too, with no way for it to be found or passed on to our people."

Maybe it was his tone, or his body language, or just some idea that was finally settling into place. Die? MacEoghan was in this to fight for a united Éire, fully independent of Britain and her wars and woes. But was he really willing to die for that idea? Perhaps if there were a real conflict, another War of Independence or second Civil War, that would make a difference. But just this political maneuvering and spy work? All of this espionage that no one saw or knew about or cared about, may or may not support? It was one thing to defend the family from German or English invaders as soldiers came form the sea or the land. This was something very different. One, his father would support and even help. The other, he grudgingly tolerated only due to greater circumstances.

It all came down to, then, how much was he, MacEoghan, willing to tolerate? Stolen land and subjugated people were not less of a problem just because one side had settled back, cozy and comfortable in their castles and the other side was too tired to fight anymore. The work wasn't done; it had simply changed. And who knew? Real fighting could break out. If that happened, he wanted to have a little more knowledge and understanding of the situation in order to be more effective in the fight.

Now if only he could understand what Sean wanted out of all of this...

"Your work here is done," Kearney declared at last. "Your mission was a success and you have proven some worth. So, I suppose we can bring you back a second time, teach you some more essential skills."

"I appreciate the vote of confidence," MacEoghan told him, trying to keep his tone neutral.

"Don't let it go to your head. This was the easiest mission by far. Wait until we start sending you places with real, damning information. Stuff that could actually get you arrested. Wait until the government learns your face. God help you—and your family, especially your brother—if they learn your real name." Kearney shook his head. "You have a long way to go." He folded his arms. "But for the moment, it's time to send you home."

With that, Kearney thanked the cobbler and headed to the door, MacEoghan following. They left the cobbler's nook, walked down the street, and entered another building. Once inside the door, they walked down a hall to a certain room that turned out to be little more than a broom closet.

"Tell your brother I'll be by in a few days," Kearney said.

MacEoghan just nodded. There in the broom closet, Kearney opened a portal into the same copse of trees MacEoghan had used before, and made a gesture. MacEoghan took a breath and stepped through.

Red-faced, shaking, he picked himself up off the ground and decided to wait and compose himself before stepping out of the copse and potentially being spotted by another nosy neighbor.

It was almost completely dark out by now, and navigating the steep, cliffside road was only slightly dangerous. The silver lining was that it hadn't rained recently, so the road and rocks were dry. Once he got to town, most of the houses still had lights on in windows or stoops, and his walk became far less treacherous. Upon reaching his home near the beach, he could see the typical evening routine as his mother gathered everyone up for the nightly reading.

Taking a breath, he opened the door.

"Mac!" one of the girls, Kayleigh, cried. She was seated already and did not move, but she pointed and looked at their mother, smiling hugely. "See, Mama? MacEoghan is right here!"

There was no such thing as a sneaky entrance in this house.

His mother approached him, taking his arm and turning as if to guide him to his usual spot.

"Where have you been?" she hissed under her breath, starting a slow walk to the family room.

"Out, like I told you this morning," he murmured back.

"Don't worry me like that again. Winter's coming, the war on the mainland is getting worse, who knows what could happen? We need you here more than the IRA needs you out there."

Then they were among the children where they both put on good faces and took their customary seats. MacEoghan glanced at Micah, but his twin had his gaze firmly fixed on the Bible in their father's hands. He wore a look of concern and fatigue.

What did Éire—united or partitioned—mean at all if his family at home was suffering?

LEDGER
YOUNGER BROTHER

In good times, the average person would usually buy one or two fish every few days, maybe more on Fridays. For fishmongers or market owners serving a small town, a few crates a day were generally sufficient to keep up with demand without running out too early or having too much unsold product at the end of the day. With the war on the mainland, the blockades, and the rationing, most people were down to one or two fish for Friday dinner, and the vendors had to adjust their buying practices accordingly.

This problem was not unique to the Dearbhfhine fishermen, nor anyone in the south. Business practices could only account for so much. Personal connections and history and favors could only drum up so much support. At the end of the day, the money simply wasn't there, and debt collectors didn't want to be paid in fish.

So it came as some surprise—and not without some suspicion—when Padraig Dearbhfhine suddenly secured a client who bought forty crates of fish every other week. Well, officially, it was his client, because he owned the business. It was Micah who actually dealt with the man.

Most of the time, it was simply a representative of the company, one of two who would show up regularly. But every so often, Kearney himself would make an appearance. He came early on Friday mornings and waited for them at the docks. The first forty crates went directly to him, and whatever was left got sent out on the trucks for normal delivery.

Micah didn't like seeing Kearney on the docks, didn't like dealing with him. He preferred the representatives. They were friendlier men who liked to joke around and offer encouragement, whom he could pretend were legitimate clients. Seeing Kearney on the docks only ruined that illusion. There was a money laundering scheme going on through an illegitimate company, and there was almost a guarantee that the funds were being funneled through the IRA at some point. The crates of fish were only a distraction.

"How well will the orphans eat today?" Kearney inquired as they stepped off the boat. It was the same question he always asked, in the same smarmy tone.

The crates of fish might have been a distraction, but they had to go somewhere. If Kearney had any redeeming qualities, it was that he wouldn't let perfectly good food go to waste. Wherever the money came from, however it got into his hands, the fish would go to a good cause. Most of the time, it went to orphans and the poor so that they could be good Catholics and observe a proper Friday meal.

"As well as they always do," Micah informed him, putting himself between Kearney and the rest of the family as they brought in the haul for processing.

"Good. Then our arrangement stands."

Micah gave him a look. "Nothing has changed in the last three months on our end. If something isn't making it where it needs to go, it has nothing to do with us. Not that I think you care about the fish after this point."

"More than you think," Kearney told him. "If I put in my books that I bought and donated forty crates of fish, well, I ought to have some idea of where those forty crates ended up."

"As I said, nothing has changed here. I might suggest you talk to your other representatives."

"Perhaps."

Then Kearney made a gesture, and the two of them retired to the office where the man handed over a familiar envelope. "The same, then, as always. With a little extra for each of you. As always."

"Including MacEoghan?" Micah asked, walking around the desk to grab a paper to write out a receipt and other forged papers.

Kearney sighed. "Your brother has the strength. He has the determination. He even has an excellent memory. Unfortunately, I think his boxing opponents may have knocked his noggin a few more times than is good for him. He lacks a certain...discernment, the shrewdness that you possess."

"If that's a compliment, I'll take it." He looked up briefly. "But I'm not joining."

"No, of course not. You're too shrewd for that." The man's tone was mocking. "You're more focused on business and the predictable things in life."

Micah signed the receipt, then swept the paper around so Kearney could sign as well. "Quite honestly, you are the most predictable thing about business these days. That, and the knowledge that it's only going to get worse."

Now Kearney's expression turned knowing. "Oh, you like having that knowledge, do you? You don't want to be as naively optimistic as the other fishermen, as the other businesses in town, all drinking that curated, censored, media drivel that says everything is going well and the war on the mainland should be over soon? You like knowing that you need to plan for the long haul? All you have to do is outlast the other fishermen and then you've cornered the market."

The man set the pen down with such care that it didn't make a sound, and Micah found it uniquely unnerving as he met his gaze. "What do you know, and what do you want?"

"I'm willing to up my order to forty crates of fish delivered every week. The payment will be doubled accordingly, maybe even a little extra, but I want something more, too."

"I already told you, I'm not joining the IRA. My father would let this business sink before he saw another son—"

"I'm not talking about the IRA," Kearney interrupted. "I may prefer to have you over your brother, but God knows having both of you would be a nightmare. For me."

Micah blinked and shook his head. "So what do you want?"

"I know your Timekeeper Journeyman test is coming up in the spring—"

"I'm leaving Time, too."

"Not before the end of the war, you're not. MacEoghan has informed me of that much. I can respect that; you want to have some kind of advantage if the Germans or the British do come marching up from the sea or down from the cliffs. But as we've already established, this war isn't ending any time soon. That means you're going to have some time as a Journeyman, and as a Journeyman, you will be expected to travel to other Districts and train under other Masters."

Micah smirked. "I thought you just said you didn't want to have to train both me and MacEoghan?"

Kearney met his smirk. "I'm not talking about me." He shifted his stance. "My company isn't just some shell company sprung up overnight in order to accommodate some opportunistic scalping and money laundering during a conflict. It has reach. It has influence. It is, primarily, a sort of haven for Time Agents when they need to disappear, go dark, and lay low between lives. The representatives who come by, they are Time Agents, just trying to stay busy but stay out of the war as much as possible."

"They work for you, and you reward them with new lives," Micah stated.

"The Wheel of Time can forge any paperwork you need to become anyone you want. At least on paper. I merely provide their lives with substance. Where they grew up, who their friends were, where they went to school, where they worked. Everything I'm doing for your brother in the IRA, I can do for anyone for any reason, any life."

"And somewhere, something has gone wrong."

"Aye, you might say that. And unfortunately for me, I am too...present in my own dealings to take care of this matter myself. I'm here. I'm there. I'm all over the place. Even if my name changes, my face does not. And that's a problem."

Micah nodded. "Well, you might have noticed, but my face, if not my self, is currently associated with you in the IRA."

"Then I suppose it's a good thing this little errand would take you out of Ireland where your brother isn't known."

The two of them stared at each other for a long minute.

"What is this errand? Then I'll decide."

"I need you to find someone. A thief, more accurately—"

"A money launderer is complaining about a thief?" Micah folded his arms. "Now there's irony for you."

Kearney's expression said he was not amused. "I'm not talking about money. I'm talking about information."

Micah nodded slowly. "He has information about all those fake lives you're churning out."

The man gave a barely perceptible nod. "Shrewd, and smart." He shifted his stance. "As you can imagine, the liability here is...stunning, to say the least."

"You expect this thief to give or sell the information to the Germans or the British?"

Kearney shrugged. "Or any interested party. What would the Soviets make of the information? Spies, everywhere. Same with any of the smaller governments and resistances within Soviet territory. The Finns, the Poles. The French might take an interest in it. Or the Americans."

"Why? They're not in the war."

Kearney ran his fingers over the edge of the desk, seemingly nonchalantly. "My sources tracked this thief to a flight to Newfoundland, Canada, three weeks ago."

Micah raised a brow. "A flight? Military?"

"Passenger. Not difficult to track because of how new they are, but exceptionally difficult to obtain tickets. My guess is, he was planning this for a while, maybe indulged in some of those identities in order to secure connections to get one of those tickets."

Micah nodded, then shrugged. "Three weeks is a long time. He could be anywhere. And my Journeyman test isn't until the spring at the earliest."

"With the war, I expect he will stay put in Canada or the United States. If he wanted to be in the action, get lost in the chaos, he very easily could have. Unfortunately, the war is also what is limiting my ability to send anyone after him. I am known, as are my people—he knows who they are and who they could be. The best I can do is monitor any incoming flights and civilian ships and hope to catch him at an airport or a dock. Again, time and resources, neither of which is infinite."

Micah sat down in the chair opposite Kearney and tried to get comfortable. "So you want me to do a favor for you next year based on information that is already three weeks old. And you're offering to double your current money laundering now. Do I have that right?" He shook his head. "If your company—whatever it really is—is as strong and influential as you say, there's more to this than meets the eye. Surely there must be Canadian or American Time Agents who could help you."

Kearney shrugged and nodded. "It is true that if he were to turn up and be apprehended in that time that I would have no need for such a favor. In that case, you may consider the extra fish as payments for your brother's services."

Micah didn't like the sound of this. Kearney was right about one thing; he was shrewd and discerning. Even if what the man said about this alleged thief was true, there were too many unknowns. At the same time, doubling the fish would help tremendously right now...

"This man must be either an experienced thief," he reasoned slowly, "or your business is really hurting on account of the war."

"With the Wheel of Time able to change its own currency into any local currency, money has rarely been an issue," Kearney said. "But right now, almost all manpower and resources are being diverted to the various fronts."

"And the Canadian or American Time Agents?"

Kearney hesitated for half a second. Then, "I don't know them well enough to trust them with this. Besides that, Canada is involved in the war. The United States is not, but if they were to join, well, it's too unpredictable."

"You need someone from a neutral country with the freedom and directive to move around."

"Exactly."

He still didn't trust it, didn't like how much trust Kearney appeared to be extending to him. Recognizing discernment in a man was one thing, but to pay for a favor months in advance, knowing that the favor might not even be necessary by then...

But he couldn't just turn down the money.

Or maybe that was the point. If the thief was found before spring, then that favor was wrapped up, but how about some other favor Kearney might conjure up? Was this thief favor merely a smokescreen for something else?

But he couldn't just turn down the money. Kearney may have been right about outlasting the other fishermen and cornering the market, but the first step to that was outlasting the other fishermen. And if their business did go under, well, Micah would suddenly have plenty of time to go look for that thief.

"You are free to refuse my offer, of course," Kearney pressed lightly. "Or take some time to think it over. Talk to your father about it."

"Talk to him about what?" Micah cut in. "Our shady business partner is willing to double his order in exchange for me doing a favor for him in Canada next year?"

Kearney shrugged. "Perhaps. There is no IRA in Canada, so it isn't as though he has to worry about that. And clearly you're not running off to war."

Micah rolled his eyes and shook his head. Then, "Why not send MacEoghan to do this? If nothing else, it would get him out of your hair for a while."

"I'm not convinced he would be the right man for the job. I need the man apprehended and the information recovered, all as neatly as possible. Information regarding Time Agents is a little more sensitive than even IRA documents. Governments are racing to weaponize nuclear power while we bend the fabric of the universe, maybe even reality itself. The fewer people who are aware of such abilities and activities, the better."

Now Micah nodded emphatically. "Well, on that we can agree." He shifted in his seat. "I'll think about it. Come back next week for another order of fish, and you'll have your answer."

"I'll be sure to set aside extra money for large tips."

The man departed without even an attempted handshake to refuse. Micah felt a twinge of guilt over it, as it was terribly impolite, but he just did not like dealing with this man or his business.

He hadn't really said anything about it to Sean beyond general distaste, but he had a notion to bring up the topic the next time he saw him. With luck, that would be before next week. After all, Sean was Irish. He was neutral. He wasn't involved in the war. He was a Master Timekeeper. Sure, Kearney and Sean might not see eye-to-eye, but if this information was all that important, involving the identities of various Time Agents, surely petty differences could be set aside?

But the extra money...

Why did it have to come back to the money? Why did it always have to come back to the money? Was there no other avenue they could pursue? None at all? Well, it wasn't as though his father hadn't been looking into less shady dealings, to clean both the books and his conscience.

Even as he thought it, the door to the office opened again and Padraig walked in, his expression mildly displeased.

"Is he discontinuing the deal?" Padraig inquired, his tone hopeful even as his expression conveyed an element of severe fear.

Always the money.

"No," Micah told him, finding some relief himself as he watched his father relax. Then he sighed and said, "But he did make a secondary offer." He tapped his fingers on the top of the desk. "He is willing to double his order, provided I do him a favor." He put up a hand. "Nothing to do with the IRA."

Padraig took a seat across from him. "What is the snake asking for, then?"

"He was vague on the details, but it had something to do with retrieving some property stolen from him."

It dawned on Micah that it was the exact same ploy he'd used when he first met MacEoghan, when he and Kane had tried to jump him in the alley and arrest him. It was the same ploy that had driven MacEoghan out of boxing. Was he trying the same thing on Micah? Was Kearney trying to drive them out of the fishing business? No, he could simply rescind his offer and let nature take its course. Was he trying to drive them out of town? Out of Time? Was this a roundabout way of getting MacEoghan kicked out of the IRA?

"I have a notion that it's hardly so straightforward," Padraig was saying. "When did he expect you to do this favor?"

"Next year. And he would keep up the double order until then."

His father shook his head. "No. I may have become accustomed to the smell, but even I smell fish here."

Micah nodded. "Aye, I was thinking the same thing. At the same time, the money—"

"—isn't worth your soul. Or your freedom if you end up behind bars." Padraig sighed. "Was he rescinding the standing offer if you refused?"

Now Micah shook his head. "No. This was intended to be a bonus." He let a certain amount of sarcasm and disbelief bleed through his words.

"Well, you're having doubts. I certainly have doubts. I suggest we ignore this obviously poisoned carrot and continue on as we are."

Micah stood and stretched. "I was thinking the same."

Padraig also got to his feet, more slowly. "The extra money would certainly be helpful, but money isn't everything. It mustn't be."

"No, of course not. But I figured I should let you know what was going on."

His father chuckled. "Aye. But look at who's sitting where."

Micah blinked, then realized he was on the business side of the desk while his father was in the guest position. As if sensing his sudden insecurity, Padraig put up a hand, saying, "No, don't. I think you've earned it." He nodded slowly. "Take a walk to get that man out of your head, then come back and do the books like normal."

The two of them left the room. Padraig wandered off to get work done, and Micah headed out to stand on the dock and look out at the sea, or the bay anyway. He hoped this emergency would end soon. Time was proving to be a trickier business than anticipated, and he certainly wanted to distance himself from his brother's dealings with the IRA.

"Everything all right?"

Micah turned at his brother's voice. MacEoghan's body language and expression suggested he had seen Kearney but had not actually talked to the man. Reluctantly, Micah shared both the conversation and his misgivings.

"Do you know anything about his business?" Micah wondered. "What his real dealings are, his goals? If he's going to try the same trick on me that he pulled on you...it doesn't seem smart, does it?"

MacEoghan shook his head and shrugged. "I don't know what he wants or what he does. I'm sorry, I don't. I'd like to know that myself."

Micah shifted his stance. "So why not find out? You say he's got you training in spy work, why not turn it back on him?"

"You can't think he hasn't already considered that. Besides, I'm not a very good spy. He says I'm too clumsy, too brash."

Micah sighed and looked away. He wasn't wrong. Being clumsy, brash, and hot-headed was, even if indirectly, what got MacEoghan into the IRA in the first place.

"You can find out, though," MacEoghan said.

Micah looked at him. "What?"

"You could find out what he's up to."

Micah stared at his brother for a long moment. Then, "What? No."

"He's holding the door wide open."

"Aye, and he'll cut my head off as soon as I look in the room."

"Keep your friends close, keep your enemies closer," MacEoghan stated simply.

Micah was surprised his brother knew that axiom, and was even more surprised he had a grasp of how it might be applied. He also knew a moment of irritation, not only that it was being used against him but that MacEoghan seemed to be so selective in his ability to discern motivations and strategic thinking.

"*A Mhac*, this wild idea to go to Canada might just be bait," Micah reminded him. "I agree to it, he lets it simmer for a couple months, then shuts it down. Maybe this alleged theft never even happened, just like he did with you. But because I made the agreement, now I have to do some other favor for him, something worse."

"If he asks you to do something questionable, I'll do it," MacEoghan told him. "I'll take the heat and the consequences; you don't have to get your hands dirty." His expression was sincere. "On the other hand, maybe you can use your more refined book learning and make it so you agree only to this trip to Canada and nothing more. If he wants to buy a bunch of fish from us, that's his business, but your only concern is going to Canada. Whether this thief exists or not, if he's caught or not, you agree to one specific favor, nothing more."

Where was this MacEoghan when it came to making decisions for himself? How could he see so clearly for others, but when it came to things like getting involved with Kearney or the IRA in the first place, he was worse than a blind man?

"I suppose," Micah conceded slowly. "At the very least, he might have to be more creative in his attempt to get around the stipulation."

"And if these documents that were stolen are so important to his business, well, you'll have some insight into his business and whatever it is he's up to."

"There is that. And if this thief is crippling him so badly, if I do find the documents, I'll obtain that same leverage."

"So there you go."

Micah sighed and shifted his stance again. "I still don't like it. It feels just as dirty as anything you're doing."

MacEoghan gave him a look but didn't say anything.

"Is it worth it, though?" Micah wondered. "If I'm leaving Time, why should I get wrapped up in his dealings?"

"Money for the business," MacEoghan said, his tone as much of a shrug as his actual gesture. "And, if he does have the ability to reinvent our lives, maybe he can help in other ways."

"Except I don't want his help, and I'm not convinced that this is all for charity."

MacEoghan shrugged again. "I don't know what to tell you. Nothing I say is going to make you trust him. Nothing he says is going to make you trust him. So either you trust him enough to go along with this and possibly find out what he's up to, or you play it safe and refuse his offer."

Play it safe. Micah hesitated. He didn't like the phrase. It felt cowardly. And yet, not playing it safe was how people got into serious trouble. Were risks worth rewards? Was it better to have jagged highs and lows, or a calm constant?

They needed the money. He didn't want to deal with Kearney. But he already was dealing with the man. He didn't know the man's business. Here he had an opportunity to figure it out, even a little. It felt a little too good to be true. Kearney knew Micah was a hard sell, so he'd waited until the situation was truly dire before approaching with this little carrot on a stick. He'd like to talk to Sean about this, but he wasn't sure when they'd see him again, nor was he entirely sure how much he trusted him, either, after his own IRA affiliation had been revealed and his manipulation of MacEoghan.

Unfortunately for him, he did not see either Sean or Kearney during that week. Nor did MacEoghan disappear for half a day or a day to work for

Kearney. Perhaps it was deliberate, perhaps not. All Micah knew when the next week rolled around and the shady business man showed up on the dock was that Kearney was expecting an answer.

"I would ask if you've given my proposal any thought," Kearney said, closing the office door behind him, "except I suspect that you have thought about little else this entire week."

"You're right, although I don't think it requires too much intelligence to ascertain such," Micah countered, sitting down behind the desk. "My little sister could tell that I've been uniquely distracted."

He didn't like the expression that crossed the man's face. "Accept or reject, I'm curious to hear your answer."

"You're offering to double your order," Micah stated. "Forty crates of fish every week, paid appropriately."

"Correct."

"In return, you want me to go to Canada to find this man who stole important documents from you. In theory, this would not happen until the spring or summer after my Journeyman test."

"It would make it easier to disguise your departure."

Micah grinned. "That's not what I asked."

Kearney's face was neutral. "There was no question."

"Is that the favor? Going to Canada to find this man and your documents?"

"Unless he is apprehended between now and then—"

"Yes or no, Mr. Kearney?" He did not give the man a chance to answer as he sat up. "See, I have a theory. You pulled this stunt on my brother, giving him one task and surprising him with something entirely different. I think you're trying to do the same to me. Have me agree to one favor, and suddenly that need dissolves. But you're not a charitable man, and this fish won't pay for itself. So you put me up to a new task, one perhaps less savory but no less obligatory. If I don't do it, you'll throw MacEoghan out of the IRA, and not in a pleasant way." He continued, "It also occurred to me that you may, in fact, have dealings in Canada. I mean nothing, but if you can get my face over there—that is, MacEoghan's face—then you can carry out some business without either of us being the wiser. And possibly getting

MacEoghan thrown out of the IRA, and not pleasantly." He leaned back in the chair once more, tenting his fingers together. "So, how close am I?"

Kearney slowly took a seat, never breaking eye contact. "You're a thinker. I like that. Truly, I wish I could have you over your brother. As it is, I'm glad to do business with you."

"How close am I?" Micah repeated.

Kearney leaned back and got comfortable. "I told you that I had the docks and airports monitored for the man's return. What does that tell you about him?"

"He's not highly trained. An Apprentice, maybe Journeyman, can't open portals by himself yet, isn't working with anyone who can. Fleeing to Canada, most likely a British citizen, taking advantage of the free movement."

"Now, if you were a British citizen, or a citizen of anywhere in Europe right now, would you want to return to war so soon? The media may tell us that it's going well and should be wrapped up soon, but anyone who has eyes and ears, who watches soldiers and artillery ravage the countryside, can say otherwise with absolute confidence. Yes, spring and summer may seem far away, but you think he would really go anywhere right now?"

"Let him sit for a while, false sense of security," Micah said. "But then, how important are these documents really if you can afford to let them sit?"

"This man has no political power nor influence; he himself is no great academic mind. If he had any military prowess, he would be immediately conscripted into the fighting." Kearney smirked lightly. "He is a nobody. He will not be able to get an audience with anyone who matters, at least, not right away. But he could, given time, use the information in those documents and the services in the Wheel of Time to make himself a somebody who is capable of garnering such an audience."

Micah nodded slowly. "Understandable."

"It would also take a short time to get your papers in order. You are not British with the luxury of free movement. You are Irish of Éire."

"As MacEoghan likes to frequently remind us. But your point is taken."

Kearney shifted in his seat. "So, we find ourselves coming back to the original question. Are you going to help me, or should I look elsewhere?"

Micah sat up once again. "I will agree to go to Canada, to look for this man and your documents. That is what I am agreeing to, nothing more. And I want to hear you say it."

The man's expression turned bemused. "Very well. To ease your conscience, I will state aloud that I am asking you to go to Canada in the spring or summer, after your Journeyman test, to look for this man and my documents."

Micah dipped his head slightly. "Exactly. And naturally I will need more information about the man I am looking for."

Kearney stood. "That information will come as your test and departure date draws nearer. I don't need more documents simply floating out there in the wind."

"Fair enough." Micah stood and held out his hand. "Forty crates of fish, then, for next week?"

"And every week, until spring or summer at least," Kearney said, accepting his grasp. "After that, who knows?"

Despite the strict terms and hearing the man repeat them out loud, watching Kearney leave, Micah still got a sick feeling in his stomach that he had bitten off more than he could chew and was going to pay for it dearly.

But there was nothing to be done about it now. The deal had been made, sealed with a handshake. Next week, they would be supplying forty crates of fish to his business—whatever it really was—and, come spring or summer, he would be making a trip to Canada. Travel papers aside, it might take him that long just to figure out how he was going to disguise the trip to his parents. Padraig had made his position very clear. How could Micah explain this without sounding like a coward fleeing to North America? He didn't know how long this was going to take, but he had a hunch it was going to be longer than a simple day trip. He'd told Padraig about the shady deal, and they'd informally agreed to ignore it and stick with the forty crates every other week. What would the man say when Micah informed him that they would indeed have to pack forty crates every week now instead?

"Why not fifty crates, and you can leave next month?" was apparently the answer. "Or seventy, and you can go next week? Or a hundred, leave tomorrow and be a coward!"

Padraig Dearbhfhine paced angrily around the office while Micah stood behind the desk. "We're not in such dire straits that you have to sell your soul to that man! Slavery hasn't been a viable answer for—"

"We're a slave to everyone," Micah told him. "We're a slave to England, being their neighbors, constantly at risk of invasion if it pleased them or they thought it necessary and proper for themselves. We're a slave to Europe, our entire country crippled because of war and blockades. We may be independent and we may be neutral, but we are not unaffected. You know that as well as I do."

"So we fish for ourselves."

Micah couldn't stop a look of disbelief. "To what end? We are slaves to our government, too; we call them taxes. But taxes can't be paid in fish; you've said that yourself often enough."

Padraig made a sort of snorting, grunting sound. "Bad enough your brother works for this man, but I thought you were smarter than that."

"I'm trying to save this business." Padraig started to protest, but Micah spoke over him. "Fine. Disinherit me, disown me entirely, but I am trying to make it so there *is* something to inherit. Whether it's me or Shay or Cillian or Brendan or anyone else, if you want to leave them a business, you need a business to leave them." He sighed. "I'm trying to make that happen."

"With blood money," Padraig hissed. "Blood of our own countrymen, blood of our neighbors. I may not like the English, but that doesn't make it right." He slapped his palm on the table. "This is a business of integrity!" A second slap. "Of character!"

"But it is a business," Micah insisted. "And all we're doing is selling fish. We go out, catch the fish, sell the fish or ship it to market. We don't interview every customer to make sure they haven't lied that day, or cheated, or stolen, or taken the Lord's name in vain. We just sell them fish."

His father growled something under his breath and stormed out of the room.

Micah let out a breath and collapsed back into his chair. Well, his worst case scenario where his father disinherited and disowned him hadn't come to pass, so that was a positive thing. Not that he couldn't do so later, but in the moment, well, he'd call it a draw.

Padraig did not return to the office while Micah was doing the books. There was no mention of the deal during the day, nor around the supper table, although everyone could feel the tension between the two. It wasn't until bedtime that MacEoghan dared to bring it up, the twins lying in their beds in the dark.

"We still have a roof over our heads, so that's a good thing," he ventured. "Do you still have a business to inherit?"

Micah sighed. "If he's disinherited me, he hasn't said so to my face. But then, he's not one to make rash decisions. He'll tell me in a few days."

"He might not. You explained your reasoning to me and I think it's sound."

"*A Mhac*, I don't know if you've noticed, but he doesn't exactly consult your opinion of what is sound."

"Maybe not. Doesn't mean I'm wrong." Micah could hear his brother shifting position. "The fishing business is his life. It's all he's ever known, all he ever expected to know."

"Built by his dad and granddad, survived multiple wars, I know," Micah sighed.

"Exactly. He doesn't want to be the one to lose it. He wants to be the one to save it. He doesn't want to put that burden on you. He wants to be able to hand down a good business with no worries, not have to look at you and feel as though he's handed you a sinking ship."

Micah looked in his brother's general direction. "Where is all this sagely advice coming from, and why do you never listen to any yourself?"

His brother laughed but quickly strangled himself so as not to wake anyone else. "Isn't that the nature of advice, to freely espouse but always ignore?"

"Well that explains a lot about you, then."

"And what's that supposed to mean?" MacEoghan's tone was good-natured.

"What if I had told you to join the IRA?"

"Then that would be encouragement, not advice."

Micah sighed dramatically and rolled his eyes though his brother couldn't see. "*A Mhac*, what am I going to do with you?"

He could imagine his brother's shrug. "Who knows? Kearney asks that question quite a bit, but I don't think he's as friendly as you are about it."

"That's not a comforting thing to consider. Does he still have you doing 'minor spy missions' as you call them?"

MacEoghan shifted position in his bed. "He suggested something about going to London around Christmas, but he doesn't give me any details until the day of a mission."

"Sounds a little more serious," Micah relented, trying to keep his tone neutral. "Going to London, I mean."

"Aye, I expect so."

"Are you nervous?"

"A little," MacEoghan admitted. "A little excited, too."

Micah hesitated. "*A Mhac*, you talk about spying and having to learn this new identity and wear it well. Have you ever considered that Kearney isn't who he says he is? That Sean isn't who he says he is?"

He didn't miss the half-second pause before his brother answered, "Of course. That's the nature of things. That's how they protect themselves."

"It's a world of lies. And they're teaching you how to be a liar, too. Come back to reality, where your family is, and where everyone is who they say they are."

"The reality is, Éire is divided when it shouldn't be." MacEoghan's tone hardened. "We're trying to fix that. There are those who stood with Éire against the English, but now they want to stop and let things lie because it's easier." He went on before Micah could speak. "Six counties, *a Mhicah*. Just six. Four of them are known nationalist majority, but they're ruled by separatists."

"I know," Micah said quietly. "You've said it all before."

"Then why make me explain it again?"

"Kearney complains about you, and even you admit you might not be the brightest, that your talents lie elsewhere. Spying is one thing. Boxing is one thing. Are you prepared to kill for these people? Are you prepared to die for them?"

For as prickly as his brother was about the subject, Micah still did not miss the hesitation or uncertainty as MacEoghan shifted again, getting comfortable in bed in an effort to buy himself time. In the end, the best his twin could come up with was, "I'll do what Éire requires of me."

There were any number of things Micah could have said to that, but the conversation was well over. Time for bed. Soon enough, it would time to get up and get back out on the boat to go fishing.

Forty crates next week. And if things didn't turn around for Kearney, it would be Canada next year.

WAR WOUNDS
OLDER BROTHER

Everyone in their group was IRA, though no one used his real name. At first, such a prospect was very exciting, very mysterious and alluring. Now, MacEoghan couldn't deny that the thought made him a little uneasy. He didn't know who these men were, didn't know their identities, their motives, their ambitions. It should have been all the same, of course, to liberate the north and bring it back into the united, independent nation. And yet, who was to say that some weren't furthering their own agendas under the convenience of anonymity and rotating identities? Kearney was a prime example of that, but why should it be limited to him?

He told himself he was just being paranoid, or maybe his brother's paranoia was rubbing off on him. But something about it stuck in a way that he was very uncomfortable with. In the army, be it Irish or British, safely at home or fighting in mainland Europe, every soldier knew who his brother was. He knew the name and business of his commander. When someone achieved something great, everyone knew about it. There was honor, glory, and, most importantly, results.

This sneaking around business was nothing like that. He wanted to fight for his people, and he was doing everything but. He didn't know his brothers or commanders. And, assuming anyone ever achieved anything, no one knew about it. There appeared to be absolutely nothing to show for their efforts.

"So why are we going to London?" he asked, trying not to sound like a whiny child.

"The city has been bombed heavily, and communication with our operatives have stopped," one of the men answered. "We're going to find out where the line has been cut, whether it's at the source, or somewhere in between."

Operatives in London. Ostensibly to somehow influence Parliament or whatever pertinent government officials into giving up the northern counties, or something to that effect. And yet, like the operatives purported to be charged with the same task on the Irish side, no mention was ever made of them. Nothing ever showed up in a newspaper, no rumors made the rounds. MacEoghan never heard any news of talks or negotiations or ideas or influences or anything. The door had been shut on the "northern issue" and it appeared to remain heavily fortified.

The crossing into England was far more heavily guarded than the remote highway between Éire and the partition. If MacEoghan had to hazard a guess, they were preparing for a potential German invasion, too, should the Nazis decide to land in Éire first and push east. Everyone crossing the channel was searched. Gates and fences were reinforced, more soldiers were on watch with tired, leery eyes. Had they just come home from Europe, or was this their first assignment before shipping out? Perhaps both, judging by the ages of the soldiers, some old, some young.

The boat docked and there ensued the chaos of offloading passengers and cargo. Kearney and the rest of them collected their bags. MacEoghan tried to keep a straight face as a group of four soldiers, two with dogs, approached them, slowly circling.

"Where do you think you're going?" the lead man inquired. His tone was not friendly. It was barely in the realm of neutral. Anyone who wasn't on guard with him was a potential threat, and that included the free Irish.

"London, sir," Kearney told him.

"With supplies?" The soldier gestured to where large containers were being loaded into a vehicle, a paper announcing "Kearney" was to pick up the vehicle once it was ready.

"Bringing supplies, sir. Just trying to help the civilians."

Two of the other soldiers halted the loading process, opened up a couple of crates, and began rummaging around. True to Kearney's word, they did have some supplies: blankets, coats, hats, non-perishable food, sewing kits, simple pots and pans.

"No need to trouble a soldier who already has a much more important task," Kearney went on. "We can deliver the goods ourselves."

The solider before them glanced toward the vehicle. MacEoghan wanted to turn and look, see if he could glimpse the reaction from the soldiers still rummaging, but he forced himself to remain where he was and keep his eyes forward.

"It's a kind gesture, sir," the interrogating soldier said at last, his tone causing the tension to dissipate almost instantly. "Good to know that we can still be neighborly."

"If the government did it, we'd risk losing our neutrality," Kearney said calmly. "That doesn't mean we don't want to help."

The crates were cleared and the two officers joined their leader. "Every little bit helps. A lot of children have been sent to the country, but if you come across any, might be you can get a few out of the danger zone, eh?"

"We'll see what we can do."

And just like that, they were waved through to England.

"So..." MacEoghan hesitated, wondering if he should ask. "How much of that did you mean? Are we going to actually do any of that stuff?"

"The children, hardly. We're not a babysitting service. And enough of our children were orphaned during the wars that maybe they ought to consider what that feels like."

Even if MacEoghan wanted to raise the point that they were just children who didn't understand what was going on, he knew how that would go. They were four men in a car. They might be able to pick up three, four, possibly five children, whisk them away somewhere safe. But there were likely still thousands of them wandering the city. They couldn't rescue all of them.

And, furthermore, children eventually grew up. And they would become the enemy.

But at what age did that really happen? At what point did innocence become culpability? Was it possible for the children to not become the enemy if they were not taught to look down on and even hate others? Surely simple existence did not automatically condemn one to death. Action or inaction may prove damning, but simply being—something which one's parents ultimately decided—shouldn't be the only reason.

"The blankets and supplies," Kearney went on, "those will be distributed as planned."

MacEoghan still only received information on a need-to-know basis. He knew they were going to London, distributing supplies, and ascertaining the status of certain agents. But was that really all? The English were extremely vulnerable right now. With the Germans crouching at the channel, bombing London and other places day and night for months now, invasion was almost certain. Maybe the British could be persuaded to give up the northern counties in exchange for Irish support. Maybe the Germans, should they actually invade and occupy Britain, could be persuaded to give the counties back in exchange for an alliance. And if any extra persuasion was needed, well, the IRA was clearly alive and well.

MacEoghan's stomach twisted into knots. He would see how this mission went, but he could almost hear his brother giving him a big, fat "I told you so" lecture. Suddenly annoyed, he looked around at the others in the vehicle. They were committed. They were tough. They had set a goal and now they were going to see it through. If diplomatic avenues to peace were possible, they wouldn't even be in this predicament; the whole fight would have ended years ago. Diplomacy had failed. It wasn't unlike the war on the mainland. There had been talks and diplomacy and conferences for years leading up to the outbreak of the war. When words lost their power, the parties only had two options: quietly acquiesce and maintain the status quo, or force a change. They, like the Germans, were forcing change.

It eased the tension in his stomach but did not erase it completely. And as they neared London, his anxiety only grew. The city skyline just didn't look right. It was cracked and crumbled, like a mouth full of chipped or missing teeth. A layer of dust coated everything for at least a couple miles outside the city. MacEoghan looked around and saw perfectly good fields, fallow for the season, with enormous holes in the center of them, or large boulders or trees or miscellaneous oddities that could not have gotten in their present position except by terrible force. Family homes, obliterated like a kid kicking over an anthill.

"People cry over the few bombs that fell out of German planes over Baile Átha Cliath, and other areas," the man sitting next to MacEoghan said, perhaps seeing something in his face, "but few can appreciate what a war of this magnitude really is." He looked out the window thoughtfully. "If the

Germans wanted to start a scrap, if they wanted to kill people and destroy our cities, they could do it."

MacEoghan knew a moment of horrific dread, a realization that his whole identity as Connor was as flimsy as the forged papers he possessed. Connor was a war veteran, had spent countless months, even years, in conditions far, far worse than this. Some days he was sane, some days he barely existed, and some days he was little better than a beast lurking in the muddy trenches. Then he was just supposed to come home and be the hero and pretend that it was all knights and formations and heroics, like in the stories? He was supposed to just...move on?

As they reached the city proper—some streets looking untouched, others almost nonexistent—he had another inclination about the ensuing wars, the War of Independence, the Civil War. Streets, where people were supposed to walk about freely as they went about chores and errands; buildings, where goods might be bought and sold, services rendered, or apartments rented; everything that was supposed to be comforting and familiar, horribly divided and even dangerous. Friendly competitors turned deadly rivals, kindly neighbors pitted against one another whether they wanted it or not. Every man a policeman, ensuring the loyalty of everyone who dared tread his territory.

He was jolted back to the present as the car came to a stop and the engine went quiet. They were parked on the curb of a particular street. No building had escaped damage, but most appeared to be in usable condition. Shattered windows were covered up any way they could be, doors held open or closed with string while crude signs denoted the interior accommodations. Most appeared to have been turned into emergency shelters for displaced people, but there appeared to still be some functioning businesses: a general store, a clothing shop, a hardware store, even a small furniture store. And people still appeared to be going about some business as usual. Men kept their caps clean, ladies sported fine skirts, and children still ran about in dirty pants to the dismay of their parents.

"The cracks in the impenetrable armor of an empire continue to widen," Kearney murmured quietly. "They will keep hold of anything they can, even if that means their own destruction."

The blankets and supplies wouldn't be going to anyone here, then, MacEoghan concluded. He watched an elderly woman enter a store, carrying a few empty burlap bags. The store sign was damaged, but writing on the window indicated it was a general store. A widow, perhaps, just trying to make it another day, another week. Maybe she had coal for her stove, or kerosene, or maybe not. Maybe the store wouldn't have any, or she wouldn't have enough money. Maybe she would have to choose between food and fuel, and end up with an insufficient amount of each.

A crash behind MacEoghan startled him, and he whirled around to see one of the other men had broken down a door into another building. It, too, was in terrible condition, although not unusable for the desperate.

"Not abandoned," the violent man said, his tone a question as he stared at the door, hanging limply on busted hinges.

Kearney walked into the building. MacEoghan went to the door and watched him cross the room. It appeared to be a small store of some kind, although looters had already made quick work of it, rendering its original purpose almost entirely unidentifiable. If he had to take a guess, he might have said another general store.

"No, but the back door is most lucrative," Kearney reported from inside. A moment later, he reappeared, his expression rather unamused. He made a sharp, annoyed gesture. "Come inside. Put that door back up right, and get it closed. Barricade it if you must. And hope that no one takes enough notice to call the authorities on a band of brigand looters."

If anyone did decide to call the authorities, it wasn't in the five or so minutes it took them to right the door and barricade it.

When they were finished, MacEoghan chanced a look around. It did not appear to be a general store as first believed, but a sewing and crafting store. Any and all bolts of fabric were gone, save for a few dirty scraps peeking out from under an overturned box. A few small spools of thread had rolled into corners, and only the glint from intermittent sunshine indicated the presence of fine needles on the floor. A busted bottle of glue had solidified into a mass on the floor. Elsewhere, unidentifiable objects littered the floor and a few shelves, torn, dirty, and abandoned.

"Why do you say it's not abandoned?" MacEoghan wondered.

"Footprints," Kearney stated, pointing to a set of tracks leading from the back door to a set of stairs behind the front counter. He glanced up the stairs. "If it is them, it's recent."

"I don't see any prints leaving, so they're probably still here," the fourth man observed, leading the way up the steps.

The four of them made their way up, the steps creaking ominously under their weight. MacEoghan was fairly certain he felt the entire assembly bow, then slowly breathe a sigh of relief as each man made it to the top. The upper floor felt only marginally more stable.

There were two doors at the top of the stairs, facing each other with a small window between them overlooking more of the ruined city. The number one was painted on one door, and the number two etched into the other. The footprints appeared to lead to door one, so they turned their attention in that direction. The man at the lead knocked. When there was no answer, he tried the knob. Locked.

"We know you're in there," the man said. "Doors don't lock themselves."

A moment later, there was a muffled male voice from the other side. "A bird in flight is a hunter's delight."

"A bird in a tree is a sight to see."

The knob rattled, unlocked, and the door opened. The man standing there was in his late thirties or early forties, thinning brown hair, narrow face, lean frame. His clothes were a bit disheveled but by no means filthy. He looked over the four of them, then nodded and stood aside to let them in.

The flat was tidy, if sparse. A couple beds, a stove, a table with some mismatched chairs, a few basic necessities. Two more men sat at the table, bigger in frame and size than the man at the door, but in no more fortuitous straits.

"You'll pardon our lack of reports," the man at the door said, closing it behind them. "We've been a bit preoccupied."

"We've brought some supplies," Kearney began, his tone dismissive. "Blankets, clothes, a bit of coal and oil, some food."

"We thank you kindly, Kearney," one of the men at the table said, "but that won't stop the Germans from raining holy hell on our heads."

The third man nodded. "Spent not a few nights, wondering if our chances would be better trying to survive the drop if the building were to collapse, or hope it fell in such a way that we might not be buried alive on the ground."

Kearney was clearly not enthused by their talk, and he stiffly turned his head to nod at the rest of them to go out and retrieve the supplies from the car. MacEoghan wondered if the man might have withheld the goods because of real or perceived insolence, but they couldn't return to the border with them and he would still rather the goods went to Irishmen.

MacEoghan got the task of carrying the coal and oil, which he did without complaint. If nothing else, this was a good thing. They were bringing much-needed supplies to people who were in dire need of goods. That he could do without wondering or worrying. Even Miach wouldn't be able to chastise him for doing this small act of kindness.

By the time they had brought all the goods upstairs, the conversation had turned from the woes of the day to whatever report Kearney had come to extract.

"There's a fucking war going on out there, what do you expect?" the largest of the men growled, his tone suggesting this was a protest to something Kearney had said. The man shifted in his seat and managed an even sigh. "There were rumors—rumors only—of Britain offering up the partition in exchange for Ireland's alliance and participation in the war. We don't know if there is any substance to these rumors or any finer details."

The lanky doorman spoke up. "I heard a rumor that the partition was considering their own bid for independence, take advantage of Britain's weakened state. Not British, but not part of Éire either."

Now there was a thought, MacEoghan mused silently.

"Ah, that's bollocks," the third man murmured. "They've got too many men fighting on the frontlines, too much invested in the war effort."

"And rumors are the best you can do? What of action? Unrest? Laws? Anything?" Kearney pressed.

The big man cursed. "We've got bombs dropping on our heads day and night. Everyone in this whole damned city is just trying to survive."

"Which ought to make it easier to take back what is rightfully ours, no?"

"Aye, sure, if the partition was just a bauble and not a land full of people."

"Most of whom want to end the partition. So what's the problem?"

"What do you think?" the third man inquired. "Bloody politics. It's always bloody politics. If things can't be done the nice way, they have to be done the hard way. Problem is, no one wants to do anything. Britain doesn't have the resources to defend the partition in a drawn-out conflict. Ireland doesn't want another civil war; they don't want to enter this war; and they don't want to risk a second war with Britain, no matter how weak the British may be. No one wants to talk. No one wants to fight. So everything stays exactly the same."

The man who had broken down the front door of the building shifted his stance. "And that's where we come in."

"Our chances might be better if we simply wait it out," the lanky man suggested. "As you seem not to have noticed, but we are under constant threat of bombing and invasion. Germans have tried before, they'll try again. They might actually have a shot at winning this war. When the spoils are divided, we might be able to regain the partition without needing to do much of anything on our part."

The big man nodded. "Cost of resources is too high. We don't have anything we can afford to waste in risky gambles here or there. We wait, the rubbish might dispose of itself."

"And since Éire hasn't been bombed to shit and we haven't lost our best men, we'll be in the best position to recover and enhance our status economically and politically," the third man added hopefully.

MacEoghan was persuaded. Kearney was not.

"Are you giving up?" the head man challenged icily. "Quitting? Are you contenting yourselves to—"

"We're not contenting ourselves to anything," the big man cut in, standing. The other man at the table also stood. "We're looking at the way things are. You get to sit at home and be inconvenienced by an occasional flyover, maybe a small bomb dropped haphazardly in a field because some young German twat can't read a fucking map. You get to complain about fuel rations on your way here and there. But we're out here where it matters, where shit's actually happening. Far as I'm concerned, you don't get to tell us how it is. We decide for ourselves because right now, it's a matter of survival."

His expression never changing, Kearney reached into his coat, withdrew a small pistol, and shot the big man in the knee. The man crumpled to the ground, shrieking in pain. The other two men cursed, glanced at Kearney, then rushed to their comrade's aid. MacEoghan, ears ringing and head cottony, could only stare at the scene unfolding before him. The other two men from his group did not appear surprised by this turn of events.

"You want a war wound? There's your war wound," Kearney stated coldly, replacing his gun. "Now you can return home to collect your fine pension."

The big man had ceased shrieking, but he was still wheezing with guttural groans. One of his friends was quick to tip some alcohol in his mouth while the other began hastily examining and bandaging the wound.

"Gentlemen, I suggest you think long and hard about what you're doing here. You were sent here with a purpose, a mission to pursue. You were sent here before the war broke out, true, but not so long ago that such a thing was somehow unfeasible. You, like all of us, swore to uphold the ultimate mission: a united Éire. You, like all of us, knew that a peaceful resolution was unlikely, and that we should be prepared for any eventuality. Now, if you are unable to fulfill this oath because things are a little difficult, because some events have transpired which are a bit inconvenient, then I suggest you say so now."

Somehow, MacEoghan got the sense that if any man were to make such an utterance, it would likely be his last.

"I can respect that mail may be long in coming," Kearney went on, ignoring the two men still tending to their friend. "Perhaps you ran out of supplies to write letters, maybe telegram lines have been severed, who can say for sure? Whatever the case, guidance from the home base was lacking, which is why we were sent to investigate. Who knows, maybe you had indeed perished in the bombings? But now that we have established that you are alive and you are still willing to carry out the ultimate mission, some things may have to change. Humanitarian missions are an easy way into the country, so you will not want for basic needs. And those who are running these missions—" His tone made it clear who that would be. "—will take your reports and bring new orders as needed." Only now did he seem to truly regard the man whose knee was no longer functional. "For now, your only orders are to rest and recover and prepare for whatever may come. We'll see how the next couple weeks treat you."

With that, he made a motion, and the four of them who had entered the country just earlier that day now turned and left the flat. This time they went down the stairs one at a time, and by the time MacEoghan made it to the car, Kearney was anxious to leave.

"I think I would have preferred to find them dead," one of the other two men stated distastefully.

"My first instinct is to agree, but the fucker wasn't wrong," Kearney growled. "Men are a valuable resource, and we can't afford to waste any. They've been entrenched in life here for too long, ingrained themselves in too many important events, to be able to replace them easily. A busted knee sends an effective message, I think, and it won't be out of place for the current goings-on."

The man sitting next to MacEoghan in the back elbowed him in the ribs. "What do you think, Connor? Your face said this is your first taste of blood."

"No," MacEoghan protested, immediately feeling like a child. He composed his voice. "But can we really afford to disable our own?"

"Discipline, Connor, discipline," Kearney stated. "Every good army enforces strict discipline on its soldiers, or else the battle and the war is already lost. He clearly did not want to fight; I simply enforced his wish. But that doesn't mean he is useless."

"And how, exactly, does it further our ultimate mission?"

"It delivers a swift kick in the hind end, that maybe they'll get something done. The city has certainly been ravaged, but you will recall that no bombs fell while we were there. There is ample time to make progress."

MacEoghan still had questions, but he dared not voice them aloud. What progress did Kearney expect the men to make? What specifically did he want them to do? Break down the doors of Parliament and demand they end the partition? Maybe assassinate some politicians or burn down the building? Britain wasn't surrendering to the Germans while their cities were literally being bombed out of existence. Did Kearney truly expect them to surrender the partition because of manipulative wordplay or comparatively minor disturbances or disruptions? Wouldn't their better bet be to head to North Ireland and see if they couldn't get the counties themselves to separate? It wasn't as if the British could spare many men to deal with such problems. That seemed like a much more feasible course of action. Or maybe that was happening simultaneously. MacEoghan didn't know, and he didn't like not knowing.

They reached the border and crossed without incident, Kearney exchanging uncomfortably pleasant greetings with the on-duty soldiers. Then they picked up another car on the Irish side and carried on their way. The other two men lived in small villages within ten minutes of the channel, and Kearney dropped them off without much more than a bland farewell. MacEoghan expected an equally uneventful return to his own village, whether by car or by portal, but as they continued rumbling down the road and turned off on the wrong road, he began to wonder. Five minutes in, when they had bypassed all other roads that might reasonably take them back to the correct route, he began to worry.

"Where—?"

"This way."

MacEoghan blinked.

"Why—?"

"You'll see."

Kearney was physically smaller than MacEoghan, in terms of height, weight, and general bulk. MacEoghan had little trouble believing that in a straight fight, such as a boxing ring, that he would be able to easily defend himself. Given that Kearney was a Master Timekeeper, MacEoghan was less certain of such a fact. And he wouldn't be surprised if Kane was going to be involved in whatever was happening next.

Kearney rolled the car to a stop in a place that could be effectively described as the middle of nowhere. A dirt road in a gently sloping valley, the trees on either side thick enough to constitute a forest but not so dense as to completely obscure one's view or greatly conceal large hidden dangers, though the rapidly disappearing sun was not their ally in that regard.

"Where are we?" MacEoghan wondered.

"Here." Kearney opened his door. "Get out."

He didn't want to get out. At this point, with invisible fleas crawling on his skin, he wanted to go home, get a lecture from his mother, eat some supper, and go to bed. Cautiously, he opened the door and climbed out of the car. More fleas erupted onto his skin as a cool breeze hit him and rustled the tree branches overhead.

"We're going to have a bit of a candid chat," Kearney said behind him.

MacEoghan turned and was surprised that the man wasn't pointing his pistol at him to make a point.

"What did you expect when you asked—*begged*—to join the IRA? You dislike spy work and covert intelligence gathering, you disapprove of discipline, you claim to desire action yet balk at the prospect of violence. Did you expect our differences to be settled in the boxing ring?" Kearney did not wait for an answer. "A child plays in his mum's garden where it is safe, the rules are many but predictable, and punishment is only as tough as it needs to be. You stepped out of that garden, expecting the bigger things in life to be similar. They are not. This greater purpose is not safe, the rules are few and unpredictable, and punishment is often cruel. But the rewards are much greater. You need to decide what you want."

"And if I decide poorly, you're going to bury me in these woods, is that it?" MacEoghan wondered. "Doesn't seem like much of a choice."

"The choice is always yours."

MacEoghan raised a brow. "Is it? Then I choose family. You've got Micah working for you on some cockamamie scheme to go to Canada, I'm going with him. Whether he leaves Time before or after, he's going to need someone to watch his back."

Kearney had plenty more experience than MacEoghan when it came to personas, identities, disguises, and control over facial expressions and body language. And yet, MacEoghan liked to believe that the man faltered for just a fraction of a second, a shadow of surprise crossing his face. He hadn't expected this. He wanted yes or no; he wasn't prepared for the third option.

"A change of position, then?" the man inquired.

"A change of position, employment, however you want to phrase it," MacEoghan stated. He shifted his stance. "This war has everyone uptight. No one gives a shit about the partition just now, not when the whole United

Kingdom is under threat. Any political maneuvering is far above our ability to influence, and violence will only attract unwanted attention. Do I want to see a united Ireland? Aye. But we're stuck just now, and my brother is in greater danger, danger that I might be able to do something about."

Kearney stared at him for a long moment, murky gray eyes doing little to conceal the turning of gears in his mind.

"You've been looking for any excuse to get rid of me," MacEoghan pressed, "but you haven't been able to fully justify it to Cillian, and you can't simply let me go. Maybe this is a compromise."

Another long moment of silence passed between them, the shadows getting longer around them. MacEoghan knew, of course, that this was because the sun was setting, but it still made him uneasy just now.

In Time, most Bands were technically considered External; they were held outside the body and were visible, sometimes encompassing just the user, but sometimes involving others as well, such as when Sean Banded the three of them for training. But there were also Internal Bands, those that were held just under the skin so they could not be seen, even to other Time Agents. These were much more difficult to create and hold, given the contours of the body, but MacEoghan suspected that Kearney was doing such a thing now, Internal Banding in order that MacEoghan wouldn't notice he was Banding and to give himself more time to consider his options.

"It's a tempting offer," the man acknowledged. "Unfortunately, I'll have to send it by Cillian first. We have no operations in Canada currently, so I can't just send you there on a whim, even if you are working for me."

"That doesn't sound like my problem," MacEoghan said.

Kearney's look made him instantly regret his words, but nothing came of it. Instead, the man simply climbed back in the car without a word. MacEoghan hastily followed suit before he could drive off without him.

"I should have turned you in when I had the chance," the man grumbled, starting the car. "The problems you don't solve only get bigger and harder to get rid of."

"Tell me about it," MacEoghan murmured intentionally.

The car lurched forward and they puttered along in grudging, tense silence. Just a few miles up the road, MacEoghan recognized where they were. Whatever route that Kearney had taken in order to worry and confuse him was apparently not all that far from where they needed to be. And, just a few minutes later, they were creeping down the steep road into town. Kearney stopped near the docks and stared disapprovingly at MacEoghan as he got out.

"It doesn't necessarily mean you won't still be called upon for work, given that your brother won't be going anywhere until after your Journeyman's test anyway," Kearney told him.

"Just let me know what Cillian decides," MacEoghan retorted and shut the car door.

He waited until the car was well out of sight before breathing a sigh of relief and turning to go home.

He had never been so happy to see the house by the water, with its creaky floors, faded walls, and roof constantly in need of repair. Compared to the buildings in London, this was Solomon's Temple. Nor had he ever been so happy to see his mother and father, his siblings, even his annoying twin brother with his disapproving yet genuinely concerned expression. These people loved him, respected him, truly wanted the best for him, even when he was wayward and impulsive.

His father gave him a short lecture, his mother a long one. Then everyone sat down to supper, and afterwards the Bible reading and a bit of leisure time before bed. MacEoghan headed outside, vaguely gesturing for Micah to come with him.

The two of them did not speak until they reached the water's edge, turned, and walked until they were well out of earshot.

"You look like you've seen a ghost," Micah observed. "What happened?"

"We went to London today," MacEoghan said.

"How is it? They've been getting bombed and raided for months now."

MacEoghan nodded. "None today, thankfully, although I think I might have preferred that."

He explained what happened, the drive, lying to the guards at the border, the awful sight of London half-obliterated by the Luftwaffe.

"And you couldn't help any of them," Micah stated, tone sympathetic.

MacEoghan shook his head. "No. Honestly, it didn't bother me too much.

Not because I didn't care, but because it would be such a laughable task with the supplies we had, bailing out a boat with a teaspoon. And besides, they weren't just for show; those supplies were going to men who needed them."

He went on to explain the scene in the building, the downstairs that had been looted, the upstairs that was in sorry shape but very likely one of the nicer accommodations still standing. He related the conversation, the men's complaints, and Kearney's response, including the shot that maimed the one man. Then he described the drive back, how cool Kearney had been with the border guards, dropping off the other members of their party, and finally the drive into the woods and the tense confrontation that followed.

When he was done, Micah stared at him for a long moment. Then, "Have you considered maybe going to the police? Or the military? Or somebody?"

"And tell them what?" MacEoghan countered. "It's not as if the government doesn't know about the IRA. It's not as if they don't know that the IRA is trying to take advantage of the war and everything else to further their own agenda. As for people, no one uses their real name, and I have no doubt that they're keeping an eye on me, you, and anyone we could tell, like the police." He shook his head. "Besides, Kearney's a Timekeeper. No Earth-side authority is a threat to him. And he's dangerous enough that he would come after me, you, and the rest of the family. How are we supposed to defend them against him?"

Micah frowned and let out a stunted sigh as he looked out over the sea and the shadowy, jagged rocks jutting up through the spectral foam.

"I messed up," MacEoghan admitted. "I got involved with something...I don't even know that I don't still believe in the cause, but the people...I got involved with some very bad men. And you are well within your rights to say 'I told you so.' "

"One of those men is still our Timekeeper Master," Micah pointed out. "And, well, I told you so."

Despite having just told his brother that he was within his rights to say that very phrase, MacEoghan still felt rather defensive about it. "I'm sorry. All right? You were right. Maybe we can just get this task in Canada done and over with and have nothing more to do with any of this. Maybe the task in Canada will resolve itself and we don't have to worry about it anyway."

He couldn't bring himself to believe his own words, and he could see Micah wasn't buying it either.

"Has Sean said anything to you at all?" MacEoghan wondered.

Micah shook his head. "No. He accepts that I'm just going through the motions and have no intention of getting deeply involved in anything."

The good son, MacEoghan reflected. Easy-going, polite, level-headed, always putting others first and thinking things through. And, now, having to rescue his hot-headed twin brother from another mess he'd gotten himself into. Except this time, his potential enemies were a little more consequential than a couple of humiliated boxers.

"All right, so, it sounds like you might be going to Canada with me," Micah stated, his tone shifting. "What do we do until then?"

MacEoghan took an even breath. "How's the business doing? Are we going to survive until spring?"

"Assuming Kearney doesn't rescind his standing order, we should." Micah's tone was not accusatory, but MacEoghan felt the sting all the same. "Pa is still unhappy about the arrangement; I think he is seriously considering giving the business over to Shay while I'm away."

"If we both go, it's all but guaranteed," MacEoghan murmured.

Micah just nodded. "But the business will survive to go to someone. I told him that's what mattered, so I have to live with my words, too."

He didn't deserve that, but before MacEoghan could say so, he added, "But, it was your involvement with the IRA that introduced us to Kearney and got us that security."

MacEoghan could only shake his head. Was it really worth it? He didn't know. "When is Sean supposed to come around next?"

"Next week, I think. And I imagine that Kearney will tell him all about what's happened."

MacEoghan shrugged, suddenly fatigued. "I mean, if we're both Journeymen, we both have to go to other Districts to train. It's not as if he can just tell one or both of us no, we can't go to Canada."

"True," Micah acknowledged. "Between you and me, I'm more worried that he'll support the idea, and not because he wants us to stick together as brothers."

Because MacEoghan really wanted to consider that, too. He sighed and turned back toward the house. "Well, I don't think anything is going to be happening right away. We should probably get back, try to get some sleep tonight."

They did return home and carry on with the evening as normal, but sleep remained terribly elusive for both of them. And soon enough, their father was stomping through the house, rousing everyone for a new day.

SIDES
YOUNGER BROTHER

The weeks passed. Kearney continued with his double order of fish, most often sending his representatives, but occasionally coming himself. No mention was ever made about the alleged excursion to Canada, whether it was still on and Micah should prepare, or if it had resolved and was no longer necessary. As the man handed over his customary envelope in the latter part of March, Micah was not inclined to inquire about it.

As usual, Padraig waited until after Kearney had left before walking into the office.

"Are we doing well enough otherwise that we don't need his contributions yet?" he growled, sitting across from Micah.

"I wouldn't turn down a helping hand just yet," Micah told him, not for the first time. "The war isn't over yet, the *Blue Maiden* still needs repairs, and steel is at a premium."

"I know it is!" Padraig snapped. He grumbled a sigh. "We are one of only two remaining fishing companies, the only one that hasn't joined up with the two feuding conglomerations. Surely we're doing better than we were last fall?"

Micah shrugged. "We make a pound, prices go up two pounds. By straight numbers, we're doing better than last fall, but based on the economy, we're about the same as we have been."

Padraig cursed, then muttered a prayer and crossed himself. He shook his head. "The newspapers and the radio say that the war isn't that bad, that things are looking up, should be back to normal soon. The bombing of London has stopped, the Nazis are on the run. Well then why the hell are our ports full of Allied ships in need of fuel and repair? Why can German planes still wander over our skies and drop bombs on us?" He scoffed. "I may dislike the IRA, but at least your brother brings real news of the world. Years, to hear him tell it. Years left in the war! How are we supposed to survive for years?!"

"The same way your father and uncle and grandfather did, and brought the business with them through multiple wars," Micah offered helplessly.

His father sighed once again, more sadly this time. "I wish you could have met them." Now he looked at Micah. "They'd like you; I know they would. You've got a good, shrewd business mind."

Micah accepted the compliment, though only at face value. Padraig had not officially stated that he was turning the business over to Shay, but it was coming. Just as soon as Micah—and MacEoghan—left for Canada, it would all go to his younger brother. Months ago, when Micah first made his deal with the devil Kearney, he might have hoped that the task would have resolved itself. Now, he wasn't so sure.

But he was saving the business, just as he had promised to do. He was ensuring that Padraig Dearbhfhine had something to pass down. He might have been many things, but he would not be accused of being a liar or disingenuous with his word.

"...they could squeeze us," Padraig was saying.

Micah shifted in his seat and cleared his throat. "Sorry, what?"

"The conglomerates. They're big enough, they can try to squeeze us. Drop prices until we're forced to surrender, join them or go out of business. Then they have only each other to compete with."

There was a notion. What did Kearney have to hold against him if there was no business to manipulate, no money to change hands?

"They're allied out of necessity," Micah said. "They're still honorable men."

Padraig put up a finger. "Some of them are. Not all of them. The ones who aren't tend to be the ones running the show."

"Unfortunately, even if they did try something like that, there's nothing we can do about it. Best we can do right now is everything we've been doing."

His father grunted and left the office without another word, Micah staring after him. There was nothing more they could do. A simple, unfortunate fact of life. And, truth be told, he was getting a little tired of his father trying to pretend otherwise. Things were different than they had been in his father's and grandfather's time. Ireland was a free nation now, trying to stay out of a new global conflict and keep itself together after a civil war. The world was bigger now, too. Machines were bigger, goods and materials and services competing on a global scale. It wasn't just them. They weren't the only ones who were hurting, but there was also no one to turn to for help.

He turned his attention back to the books. Simple numbers, simple math. Math didn't care about politics, he told himself. Math didn't even care about war. There were plenty of stories of small forces outlasting and even triumphantly defeating more numerous foes. Why shouldn't that happen in business also? They didn't have to be the biggest, best, richest, and most powerful. They just needed to survive.

At the moment, that was all they were doing.

Numbers and math, he told himself. Addition, subtraction, multiplication, division, zero through nine. Money and goods. Whatever part they played in Kearney's money laundering, well, he was just another customer. Was it weird that he bought so much fish? Yes. But his money was as good as anyone else's. In fact, it might even be better because it was actual cash and not some promise written on a check. Everything perfectly absolute and finalized.

He finished up the office work, put the money in the safe to deposit later, closed up the books, then leaned back in his seat, looking out the single small window to his right. It was springtime now, or close enough. April was less than a week away. Wet, winter misery was slowly giving way to the first inklings of green grass, daffodils, and tulips. That alone was enough to take the edge off the worry, Micah thought. No matter what, the sun still rose, the tide still came and went. The clouds cared not for the concerns of ants.

He was halfway to standing when the door opened again and he was surprised to see Sean there. The man had always come in the late afternoon or early evening, always at home and never at work. To see him here, now, Micah almost didn't know how to greet him.

"This is a surprise," was the best he could come up with as Sean entered the room, closed the door, and came to take his outstretched hand. "Although

411

I'm guessing the reason for this more formal visit is...not the most pleasant."

"Neither good news nor bad," the man said, sitting casually. "Simply some information."

"About what? MacEoghan is your IRA prodigy." MacEoghan's excursions with Kearney and the IRA had become increasingly infrequent over the last few months.

"Prodigy, hardly," Sean said, his tone suggesting he picked up on Micah's dry comment. "No, this has more to do with the little errand Kearney is sending you on."

Micah felt his shoulder's slump, metaphorically if not physically also. So, it hadn't been quietly resolved. Worse, Sean appeared to be in on it. He tried to cover up his disappointment with a question. "Our delivery routes aren't long these days; should we wait until MacEoghan gets back before you tell me anything?"

Sean waved a hand. "I have no doubt you can relay the information just fine. Besides, I agree with Kearney and, really, most everyone, that you are the more level-headed twin and better to consult in matters of business."

Micah raised a brow and shifted in his seat. "How do you mean exactly? I know I'm level-headed, but what is this about? And why are you giving me this information and not Kearney?"

"He will at some point, or he should. I'm just here to explain the rest of the story as it were."

Micah said nothing.

"Believe it or not, Kearney and I agree on a lot of things," Sean began. "The reunification of Éire, for example. We fought together in the War for Independence and the Civil War. His business of spying, disguises, and forged identities serves its purpose in matters of state, war, and Time."

"But...?" Micah prompted.

"When you work in the business of identity, when names and lives can be swapped like hats, it can easily come back to bite you."

"Kearney implied that this was an Apprentice Time Agent, maybe an early Journeyman, since he has to travel by normal means and not portal. He also suggested that he's unfit for military service in some way, by age or physical impairment."

Sean shook his head. "Not in the slightest. If my own information is correct, the man you're dealing with is a professional mercenary and a Lieutenant-trained Master. Slavic in origin, he was taken captive by Arab slavers, pressed into military service for the likes of the Abbasids and other powerful families in the ninth century. What information I could find suggests that whenever he has popped up in history, it has always been as a mercenary. The Renaissance and Reformation, the Industrial Revolution, any scattering of small wars and petty conflicts. Where there's war, there's money to be made."

"Having information on dozens or hundreds of Time Agents and other military soldiers and spies would command a hefty price," Micah commented absently. "But why go to Canada? And why was Kearney so wrong in his assessment about the culprit?"

"Actor outfoxes actor, perhaps?" Sean suggested, his tone saying he didn't necessarily believe that. "My greater suspicion, and the other reason I'm here, is that I'm not convinced Kearney is wholly a victim."

"You think he staged the theft?" It made sense, now that he thought about it. Why else would a thief steal such important documents, then flee to a, really, uninvolved country, and sit on them for months? "For what purpose?"

"If I knew that, this conversation would be going much differently, if we were having it at all." Sean's tone and posture were frustrated. "If not for the records in the Wheel of Time, no one would know Kearney's real name. Honestly, I'm not even convinced that it is his real name. I don't think he even remembers his real name. He's been in this business of identity since at least the American War for Independence, forging names and lives for spies on both sides."

"Hm. Funny. He said he didn't know any North American Time Agents."

Sean shrugged. "That could be true. Most Time Agents don't last more than one hundred fifty, maybe two hundred years. The stress of constant change gets to them." He made a trigger pulling motion under his chin. "Kearney's one of the rare ones. He thrives on the constant change."

"And the thousand-year-old mercenary?"

"If you consider that in ancient times, mercenaries tended not to reach middle age..." The man's look finished the sentence. "As far as I'm

413

concerned, it's just more reason to think they're somehow working together, executing a greater plan."

"All right, fine, but then why stage it as a theft? Why ask me to go after him? I'm leaving Time anyway."

"I wish I knew, but it must be a very specific reason. A standard theft, regular Runner, that would fall entirely within the jurisdiction of the Region Four Manager and his underlings."

"Have they been informed of the situation?"

"They know there is a Runner somewhere in Canada who is in possession of the documents. They have been advised not to actively pursue until we can determine what the man intends to with them. We don't want to spook him."

Micah nodded. "Fair enough. Does this Runner have a name, or something I can call him?"

"His last known alias is Michael Bielski. Obviously, with a suitcase full of stolen identities, he could be literally anyone." Sean reached into a pocket inside his jacket and retrieved a couple of folded papers. He slid them across the desk, and Micah unfolded a sketch and a photograph, though the photo had been taken from a distance, watching the man walk down the street.

Five-foot-six or thereabouts, remarkably athletic build, short dark hair, clean-shaven. His facial features were narrow for a Slav, and the sketch suggested his nose had been broken a few times. But what was a few times over a few centuries? The sketch portrayed a coldness about him that one would expect from a hardened mercenary, but the photograph depicted a man simply out and about on regular business.

"Where and when was this photo taken?"

"A month or so ago, in Ottawa."

"That's Canada's capital, isn't it?" Sean nodded. "Are there any Time Agents in Canada's government?"

"Not in their Parliament, though there are a few in more local and provincial governments."

Micah frowned and leaned back, still staring at the photograph and the sketch. "Has any contact at all been made with this guy, even second- or third-hand rumors? Has he said anything about what he's doing or what he wants?"

"Any contact has been simple small talk on the street. He is very reserved and seems to move around enough that anyone who follows him, well, they're following him. He's not dumb."

"Are you sure he even still has the documents?"

"We don't know that either."

"So what the hell do you expect me to do?"

"Unless something changes in the next few weeks, go to Ottawa, Ontario, meet up with the District Captain. He'll be able to give you the most recent information. Track down Bielski, and first figure out if he has the documents. If he does, work to retrieve them. If you can, find out who he's working for and what Kearney's role is in all of this."

Micah continued to stare at the angry eyes of the sketch. "Why ask me? Why not turn this over to the Allied High Command? If we can forge identities and hide Time, surely it must be no great feat to simply forge this as the potential exposure of a common spy network, no Time involved?"

"Because the information, the identities aren't just British, French, and so on. Kearney's business knows no allegiances. Simply put, we have information that Allied High Command doesn't. And Allied High Command would very likely see that as a big problem, to say nothing of the information itself. We have to handle this internally, quietly."

Micah nodded slowly and looked at Sean. "So, when do we leave?"

Sean shifted position. "I finally got permission to schedule your Journeyman tests. They'll take place before the end of the month, roughly three weeks. After that, I will do my best to arrange passage over to Canada, by ship or by plane, I can't say. Between the blockades and everything else, it's not going to be easy to do, so when I say jump, you jump."

Micah really didn't like the sound of that, but he understood completely and knew his only option would be to agree.

"Kearney is working on your papers as we speak," Sean went on. "And he's working with an agent in Canadian customs to get you in."

"That might be a problem?" Micah wondered.

"Some countries are reluctant to admit refugees; they don't want to overwhelm their own systems. Ireland may be neutral, but we're close enough."

Micah nodded. "Understood."

"Don't worry about that right now, though," Sean told him, his tone changing to something more optimistic. "For the moment, when your brother gets back, we'll head out for some training, some last-minute polishing of your abilities before your Journeyman test."

Deliveries were few these days, and it wasn't long before the trucks returned. Micah and Sean stepped out of the office and waved MacEoghan over to join them. As they were leaving the wharf, they passed by their father who was on his way to see if anything could be done for their languishing boat. Padraig said nothing, just gave them the barest of nods and continued on his way.

Three weeks, Micah realized with a silent jolt. Even if it took another week for Sean to secure passage for them to Canada, that still wasn't a lot of time. Three, maybe four, weeks until they left home. The only stable, loving home Micah could remember. Forfeiting his inheritance in the name of securing that inheritance. It was necessary, and he had been planning for this for months, so why did it still hurt so much?

"All right," Sean said, cutting into his thoughts. They had reached their usual spot, but the man did not put up a Fast Band like he normally did. Had they been training in the evening like normal, this wouldn't be a problem, but it was the early afternoon and there were far more people out and about, children running up and down the rocky shoreline. "I want one of you to hold the Fast Band this time."

It wasn't unexpected or unreasonable, Micah thought. If he wanted to be honest, he was surprised Sean didn't make them do it more often.

He did not voice his opinions aloud, nor interfere when MacEoghan took the task upon himself, enveloping the three of them in a red-tinged Fast Band, bringing life around them to a halt.

Sean's Fast Bands were very form-fitting, for lack of better term. They encompassed the three of them, but little else. MacEoghan's Fast Band was less precise, appearing as more of a misshapen dome when it included others. It was still very close to the three of them, but there was a lot of open space still. A small insect on a rock at their feet was also part of the Fast Band; in one of Sean's Bands, it would have been safely excluded.

At Sean's prompting, MacEoghan managed to wrestle the dome into something more conforming. The small insect was pushed out of the Band, and much of the empty space was removed.

"Very good," their Master praised. "Now, Band yourself—a Slow Band—and effectively take yourself out of this Band."

A bubble within a bubble, Micah thought, watching the blue tint of a Slow Band slowly envelope his brother. His twin's subtle movements slowed until he appeared to stop, frozen in time, or maybe outside of it.

"I'm going to do the same," Sean announced. "When I'm done, I want you to do it also."

Without waiting for a reply, Sean pulled MacEoghan's Slow Band over him like a blanket. Micah watched him slow down and finally stop. The Fast Band still encompassed the three of them, but the barrier between Fast and Slow was rapidly thinning, and he was about to make it even thinner. Like Sean, he grabbed onto the Slow Band and pulled it around himself. He was not so swift and dexterous as his Master, but he got it done.

And there they stood, the three of them, in a Slow Band inside a Fast Band, removed from Base Time yet still interacting with it. MacEoghan was starting to sweat, and a chill breeze ruffled their hair.

Sean did not say anything, gave no further instructions, just stood there and watched MacEoghan sweat, holding the contradicting Bands. It was not unexpected, Micah thought, but it was slightly unnerving. And how strange it must have looked to anyone who happened to glance over. Three men, standing there on the rocky shore, staring at each other, saying nothing, one of them sweating and looking as though he were actively doing hard labor despite doing nothing.

After a good five minutes of Sean saying nothing, with MacEoghan now drenched in sweat and his knees beginning to shake, Micah jumped in. He separated the Bands, taking over the Fast Band and leaving the Slow Band for MacEoghan. His brother gasped with relief and shifted his stance, as though shifting a load that had suddenly grown significantly lighter.

"Good," Sean said, gently taking the Slow Bands from MacEoghan and Micah and then dissolving them, thrusting the three of them back into the Fast Band.

"Wait, that was what you wanted to happen?" Micah asked. "Why not say so? We're not going to be testing together, are we?"

"No, but a little initiative goes a long way."

What was that supposed to mean? Did Sean want them to work together or not? Had he been planning this, and to what end? Now that they knew, he couldn't reasonably have them do the same thing in reverse. Or was this some kind of oblique observation about Micah's less-impulsive nature and trying to encourage him to step up and intervene a little more? MacEoghan would have jumped in much sooner; he just knew it. Considering he, Micah, was already agreeing to this absurd mission to Canada, far out of his comfort zone, he would have appreciated a little more time to enjoy said comfort zone instead of being subtly manipulated out of it again.

Micah mentally shook his head and tried to focus on the present moment. He still had control of the Fast Band that was shielding their training activities from prying eyes, and Sean had not indicated he wanted that to change.

"Internal Bands, External Bands, Double Bands, Pinpoint Bands, the four basic types of Bands, five if you include Reflexive Bands," Sean stated. "And the most basic use for these are the self, the whole body, in a stationary manner." He made a flamboyant gesture. "Why don't we take a walk?"

The stationary manner was one of the first things probationary Timekeepers learned, keeping their Bands around them in about a three-foot area, and keeping the strength of the Band constant. Those with two brain cells to rub together figured out, before their formal Apprenticeship, how to more securely tether their Bands to themselves to be able to move around freely. Even holding an External Band around the three of them and walking down the beach was no great feat for Micah; keeping balance on some of the slippery rocks was more challenging at times.

Then Sean started getting involved. It started out innocuously enough. He scooped up a handful of small stones and started lightly throwing them at Micah. Micah either had to dodge or, as he more likely suspected was the point, Band the stones until he was safely past them. Either action caused his concentration to waver, but he could manage it. At least until Sean started throwing bigger rocks, and more than one at a time and Banding them, making them harder to dodge or get a grip on, speaking Time-wise. Micah twisted and dodged, swatted a few away, tried to break the Bands or take them over himself.

Eventually MacEoghan jumped in, taking over at least part of the defense. By now, because of Micah's dancing, they were moving faster, almost at a slow jog, with Sean still throwing rocks, now at both of them, and looking like he was enjoying every second of it.

Micah paused in his jog and managed to buy himself a few seconds as Sean and MacEoghan slipped past, the former still tossing rocks at the latter.

"A Mhac!" Micah gasped, wiping sweat from his brow. *"A Mhac!"*

"Cad?" MacEoghan wondered, swatting away one rock while snapping the Band on another.

"Déan dearmad ar na carraigeacha! Clúdach Seán!" (Forget the rocks! Band Sean!)

It took a few seconds for MacEoghan to grasp the idea and actually implement it. But, soon enough, he had Sean in a Slow Band, safely contained within the Fast Band and away from them. He was in the middle of a laugh, one rock in one hand ready to throw, four rocks in the other. The rocks had continued to increase in size, from annoying pebbles to something about the size of a baseball.

The twins took a moment to relax and breathe and use Pinpoint Bands to heal any bruises they may have acquired from the sick game.

"I hate him some days," Micah huffed.

"Maybe, but it wasn't a bad lesson," MacEoghan said. "You think I should let him back in?"

Micah gave his twin a look, then went and confiscated all of the rocks in Sean's hands. Before he could do anything with them, MacEoghan snatched them out of his hands and threw them at Sean, striking him in the shoulders, chest, and hip. Micah raised a brow at his twin.

"He wanted us to stop the rocks," MacEoghan said defensively. "And here he can't stop the rocks himself." He shrugged. "Seems only fair if you ask me."

Micah said nothing to that and MacEoghan let the man back into the Fast Band.

Sean immediately reacted to the pain from the rocks being chucked at him, but he still maintained a good nature about it, laughing in between grunts. Nonetheless, Micah and MacEoghan did not relax their postures until Sean relaxed his.

"Holding concentration while multitasking," the Master Timekeeper said, a smile still in his voice. "Granted, it can be a pain in the arse, but it is an essential skill. You two have each other for support, but it may not always be like that. So, why don't we try that again, but with less third-party interference?"

That did not sound like fun, but they didn't have much choice. Micah was dismissed from the Fast Band first, to give him a break and let him breathe for all of three seconds before Sean and MacEoghan also dropped out of the Fast Band. MacEoghan was sweating again, but not bruised or bloody as he might have expected.

There was no running up and down the shore this time, nor did Sean throw rocks two or three or five at a time. He still Banded them, but Micah was permitted to be mostly stationary as he warded off the projectiles. He didn't know if there was a set time limit for the exercise, or maybe he had to defend against an arbitrary number of rocks, but although it went on much longer than he wanted, it did end eventually.

Again he briefly considered how strange it must have seemed to anyone who happened to be watching them, or could even see them now, given that they had run a fair distance down the shore. First, that they had covered that distance in an impossibly short amount of time, and second that they were suddenly so worn out, rather disproportionately compared to the distance they traveled. But no one appeared to be looking their way, nor pointing out the odd shenanigans.

"All right," Sean said, his tone a relief. He made a gesture to some larger rocks nearby. "Go ahead and sit down."

Upon sitting on the rock, Micah decided he would have preferred just walking back rather than having crusty barnacles sticking into his thighs and buttocks. He was tired, but he wasn't dead.

"MacEoghan, are you still planning on going to Canada with your brother?" Sean inquired, turning serious again.

420

"Of course I am." MacEoghan sounded both certain of the answer and a bit offended by the question. "Someone has to watch out for him."

Sean did not react to MacEoghan's terse response, but instead calmly brought him up to speed on the nature of the mission. Micah, who had pocketed the photograph and the sketch, showed them to him.

"So, you want Micah to find the documents and any incriminating evidence against Kearney," MacEoghan stated.

"Against Kearney. Against any Time Agents who could be involved. Hell, if you can find incriminating evidence against anyone, I'd take it, given the state of the war."

MacEoghan nodded. "When we were meeting with Cillian that first time in the warehouse, and I was assigned to Kearney, he and Kane made comment about leaving for Canada just to avoid being my mentor."

Sean managed a small smile and nodded. "I remember."

"Does Kearney go to Canada often?" Micah inquired. "Does he have any favorite cities, locations, people?"

"I know little about his business there, unfortunately. Given that Bielski was last spotted in Ottawa, I would start there."

"Does anyone know if he goes to the United States, too? Ottawa is close to the border, isn't it?"

"In more recent times, he's been there a time or two, but I only know that minor fact, and that only because of his complaints about Americans."

MacEoghan shifted uncomfortably on his spot on the rock. "What do you want done about Bielski? Capture? Return? What? He's a mercenary—"

"A very old and experienced mercenary," Sean clarified. "I highly suggest that you determine who is involved and find or correctly speculate a motive or endgame before engaging the man directly so you don't end up over your head." He shifted his stance and continued before either twin could speak. "And on that, our support will be limited—Kearney, Kane, myself. Again, we don't want to spook him and have him run, release the files, or do something else foolish. If Kearney is in on this, I don't want anything getting back to him either. Your support will come primarily from the Region Four District Three Time Agents, inasmuch as there is a Runner who needs to be apprehended."

Micah shifted position and cleared his throat. "Sean, I don't know if you know this, but Canadians speak with an accent. I can do a British accent just fine, but I don't know that I could do a Canadian one for any long period of time. Or an American one for that matter. And if I drop it for even a syllable —pretending I'm speaking to him or he's within hearing distance—he's going to know we're onto him."

To his relief, Sean nodded, appearing unconcerned. "That's one of the advantages you'll have being in North America. So many waves of immigrants over the years, it's hard to tell who's who. What is a Canadian? What is an American?"

"Someone of British descent in North America who speaks with a funny accent?" MacEoghan grumbled distastefully.

"You've been spending too much time with Kearney," Sean said flatly. "Aye, they're British, but also Scottish and Welsh and Dutch and German and French and Swedish and Norwegian. And, most importantly, Irish. With this war and everything that led up to it, believe me, no one will even bat an eye."

Micah had his doubts, but his only options were to either trust Sean or basically swap his natural speech for a Canadian accent in the span of three to four weeks.

"Do we still have to take a plane or a boat over, or are you going to deliver us via a portal?" he inquired instead.

"We need to keep this as quiet as possible, which means going through all the proper avenues," Sean answered, a hint of regret in his voice. "There's also a bit of work that needs to be taken care of in Customs. This is my own arrangement, apart from Kearney. I'm hoping it will trip him up if he decides to try anything nefarious against you. It's nothing huge, but it'll act as a buffer if something goes wrong."

MacEoghan stood, brushing dirt and broken barnacles from his seat. Micah followed suit. "And what's that? The buffer, I mean?"

"You'll see when we get to that point. I won't say it aloud."

Micah's doubts only compounded, but he did not voice those aloud either. A thought niggled at the back of his mind. What would happen if it turned out that Sean was the nefarious actor in this? What if Kearney had sent the documents away intentionally and Sean was trying to recover them? Was he being too paranoid? After all, this whole mission had been Kearney's idea in the first place. Micah didn't know what to make of the whole situation, but the only direction he could go was forward.

"You never really answered my question about what to do about Bielski," MacEoghan butted in. "Like you said, he's an old, experienced mercenary. But how dangerous is he?"

"I would consider him very dangerous," Sean answered, his tone one of mild disbelief that MacEoghan felt the need to clarify the statement. "I would advise against underestimating him, with or without Time abilities. Your priority should be the documents; let the District Three Time Agents worry about Bielski."

Micah could see his brother was both disheartened and annoyed at the order, but he didn't argue.

"So," Sean said, "I will let you two continue to practice on your own—I have every confidence in you—and I will be back to tell you the exact time of your Journeyman review, and to pick you up."

The three of them made their way back up the rocky shore toward home. They only walked, and no one threw rocks of any size. It was still early afternoon. To anyone else's eyes, the trio had done little more than go for a walk down the beach and then return, although the sweat and overall fatigue of the twins could certainly prompt some questions. If anyone asked, they were horsing around and got a little close to the water. But no one did ask, most—of those who even noticed—preferring to stew in their own ideas of what the brothers were up to with their male companion and formulate rumors.

"Do you know if Kearney has anything more planned for me between now and then?" MacEoghan wondered.

"I don't believe so, but I don't want to promise anything," Sean answered. "Things have been...chaotic lately."

"How so?" Micah inquired, trying to keep the acid out of his voice as much as possible.

Sean paused in his walk, and the twins followed suit. The man was frowning, his posture uncertain. After a moment, he nodded and said, "It seems that even if Éire won't declare a side, the IRA has. Certain high-ranking members, such as Cillian, have gone to attempt to negotiate with the Nazis. Bring down the British in exchange for the partition."

Micah blinked at the news. "Are the Germans really gaining so much ground? Are they about to win the war?"

"You'd never know it, the way the state newspapers are printing these days," Sean retorted sourly. "But they have made significant gains. Blitzkrieg, they call it, a fast and violent escalation with overwhelming firepower, take out the enemy before they have a chance to react. And it's working. The British stand alone right now."

"Is there no resistance?" MacEoghan asked.

Sean shrugged. "Oh, of course there is. The French Resistance is alive and well. The Belgians, the Poles, the Danes, and so on. But they're on the defense, with no real offensive capabilities right now."

"What about the Soviets? I thought the IRA didn't want to tangle with them?"

"We don't. From what I understand, Cillian and the others aren't volunteering as boots on the ground or reinforcements for the Germans throughout Europe; their interest lies solely in delivering the killing blow to the British and taking back the partition."

"And then acting as the Nazis' enforcers in the region afterwards." MacEoghan's tone was unmistakably bitter, and heavy with regret.

Sean's expression was apologetic. "Very likely, yes." He sighed. "I had no say in the matter. No one at our level did. Even Cillian is the lowest-ranking member to attend these negotiations."

"Are very many IRA onboard with this?" Micah asked.

Now the man's expression turned severe. "Many in the IRA don't know about this. Our mission is singular: take back the partition, reunite Éire as one land and one people. Operations in England are nothing new." He gestured to MacEoghan. "You know that. Especially now."

"So Cillian returns, sends men out on strategic missions with German funds and weapons, maybe even has them link up with special Nazi infiltrators, Germany defeats Britain, we get the partition and increase Éire's standing in the United Kingdom and throughout Europe. Win-win for everyone." MacEoghan's tone was still dubious.

"Yes."

"Does anyone in Parliament know about this?" Micah asked, feeling moderately alarmed.

"And why tell us?" MacEoghan added.

Sean frowned deeper and shifted his stance. "I'm no traitor. I love Éire. I believe in her still, in the ability to be one, united people again." He shook his head. "But I think they're making a huge mistake with this move." He folded his arms. "And, honestly, I can't be sure that this incident with Kearney's documents isn't related somehow."

"Moving important documents out of the country in case things go south," Micah stated, "protected by a mercenary with a lot of experience in hiding and fighting."

Sean nodded gravely. "Exactly. And possibly trying to get you two out of the way so he can work more freely. Call it a hunch, but if you hadn't suggested it yourselves, I think he would have suggested you both go anyway."

It made a frightening amount of sense, and Micah's stomach twisted and tightened. "You think we should still go? It sounds like his documents aren't in any real danger."

The man nodded. "I do. I think you should go before this gets ugly. If Cillian and the others are successful, we're looking at nothing less than war. If he's unsuccessful, for whatever reason, there's still a good chance that things will get even worse for us. The Irish government won't just execute a few ringleaders, they'll go after everyone." He huffed a disgruntled sigh. "And most of our people are still imprisoned right now to prevent us from doing anything stupid during the war."

Micah stole a glance at his brother. There was a good chance that only his or Kearney's Timekeeping abilities were keeping him out of prison, but that didn't mean he wasn't watched or under suspicion. Would the authorities follow them to Canada? Would the Canadians care?

"Is Bielski part of the IRA?" Micah asked. "I know you said he's Slavic, but maybe an identity...?"

Sean shook his head. "No. He's part of the mainland European network, deals primarily with eastern Europe, the Slavic regions as you might expect.

Specifically he deals with the Związek Walki Zbrojnej, the Polish Resistance."

MacEoghan shook his head, expression puzzled as he folded his arms and shifted his stance. "How in bloody hell did he get pulled away from that to run an errand for Kearney?" He shook his head again and looked at Micah. "We have to find this guy."

"We have to find the documents," Micah corrected. "A thousand-year-old Slavic mercenary working in occupied Poland is not someone I'm keen to mess with."

"But—"

"And the faster we get those documents, the faster I can get back home and maybe Pa won't be too angry with me."

MacEoghan sighed but said nothing and looked back at Sean.

"The documents are more important," Sean said evenly. "How you go about it is up to you. For right now, though, keep working on your Bands and preparing for your Journeyman review."

With that, they continued, again, up the shore toward home. Sean dropped them off with a muted farewell, then ambled away. Micah and MacEoghan headed to the docks to help with afternoon chores.

Double the fish, double the pay, just trying to keep the business afloat, Micah mused. Was it all really worth it? A simple errand was one thing, but this was very quickly spiraling out of control. And how much would any of it matter if the IRA did enter into an alliance with the Germans and bring hell to bear on the land? What if Micah did retrieve the documents, only for the other end of the bargain to collapse anyway?

He grabbed one of the nets and started looking over it for holes or weak spots. If they did end up in a war, would he ever be able to walk away from Time? Would he be able to settle down and have a family? Would it be a world he wanted for a family?

LICENSE TO TRAVEL
YOUNGER BROTHER

Given that the Wheel of Time had to somehow coordinate the comings and goings of thousands of species from across the universe, scheduling a Timekeeper review was less simple than standard business days with business hours. It could come on any day at any time, such as right in the middle of Mass.

Neither twin was devastated by having to play hooky from Mass, but there was still a small rock of guilt in Micah's stomach over the deception, watching his mother herd the rest of the children out of the house and up the slope, all while pretending to have a tragic bowel irritation which would only disrupt the congregation.

It might not have been necessary at all, except Sean had informed them that, unlike most times when they could just leave the portal open, thereby stopping time at home so it was as if they'd never left, this one would be intentionally closed. That meant time would pass normally at home. They two, assuming they passed their review, would reopen the portal themselves from the other side to come home.

The twins waited for Sean to arrive, sitting at the kitchen table.

"You ready for this?" MacEoghan asked.

"Well, there isn't a psychological exam this time, so it can't be too bad," Micah reasoned.

"You think they'd make us fight each other in the demonstration?"

"I don't think so, no. We're kind of an exception, I think. How would they arrange such a thing for all the Masters who only have one Apprentice?"

"Just schedule two students at the same time." MacEoghan shrugged. "Take one after another for the knowledge portion, bring both out for the demonstration. Doesn't seem that difficult to me."

Micah shifted in his seat. "Do you know something I don't, or do you actually want to fight me?"

His twin shrugged again. "I don't know for sure about the review, but it would be interesting to pit my skills against yours. We both know I could beat you in a fair fight. What if Time were involved?"

It was an intriguing idea, Micah would admit, but before either of them could act on the suggestion, there was a knock at the door and Sean let himself in.

"Good, my suspicions were correct," he commented, closing the door behind him.

"Suspicions?" Micah wondered.

"That you would stay home from Mass rather than try to sneak away in the middle of service." He looked them both over. "Are you ready?"

"We haven't been staring at each other for fun," MacEoghan replied, standing eagerly.

Standing silently, Micah was ready for the review, but he wasn't sure that he was ready for what came after. What had he agreed to? What was he about to get himself into?

"Great," Sean was saying. "I'll open the portal there and force it closed. When you two are done and passed and officially Journeymen, your first lesson will be opening a portal back home."

"Is that standard, or just something you do with your Apprentices?" Micah asked.

Sean shrugged. "Fairly standard. Not a requirement, just something that most or all the Masters of Earth agreed to at some point in the past and it stuck."

Before anyone could say more, he took a step back and, with the usual tremendous amount of effort, opened a portal to the Wheel of Time. Micah and MacEoghan did not question or wait to be told, just stepped through as soon as they deemed it safe. As soon as one person was through, the technology of the Wheel started taking over, relieving Sean of his burden enough that he could step through with no issue.

Nothing had changed about the Wheel since the last time Micah had been there, and although he knew what to expect, it still surprised him. An impossibly large room filled with rows upon rows of doors. Up and down the aisles, aliens mingled with all the amicability of aloof strangers on the street. And why not? How much did Micah really expect to have in common with an alien just three feet tall with three eyes and four-fingered hands? Did those aliens have any concept of fishing? Did they live with their families? Did they have regular religious services?

Micah looked around as they made their way to the front of the room to grab translators. Speaking of God, did He still exist here? If man was created in God's image, what did that mean for the rest of them? Was it possible for an alien to become a saint?

He remembered having such questions before, but they had faded like a bad dream once he had returned to Earth and his comfortable, normal life. Did other aliens feel the same way? Did anyone stare in wonder at the bipedal creature with a patch of hair on his head, patchier hair on his face, five fingers on his hands, then go home and try to sleep off what they perceived to be a nightmare? Was he intimidating? Were he and MacEoghan, as twins, intimidating to anyone? Did other species have a concept of twins?

If MacEoghan was having similar thoughts or questions, his body language testified to none of it. He had a look and a posture similar to when he was about to go out into the boxing ring. He was ready. He was excited.

They traversed the floors, walls, and ceiling of the Cube with ease, making their way to the portal that would take them to the Seat of the Hands, the grand coliseum that was somehow not the Coliseum. As before, they had to wait in line, effectively take a number, then wait even longer until a secretary came to retrieve them. Then they were led through the building to another room where they would wait even longer.

The waiting room also hadn't changed in the time they'd been gone. Plain, white, devoid of any real furniture, no windows.

"What do you think will happen if the family gets home and we're not there?" MacEoghan wondered, his tone suggesting this was only just now crossing his mind. He walked around the room, one hand sliding along the wall.

"I can't imagine they'll be too worried until tonight," Micah answered. He sat on the floor. It was not wood, stone, metal, or any material he was familiar with; he knew only that it was hard and uncomfortable. "Although Mum and Pa will be rightly sore at us for skipping service, and we'll probably have to endure some manner of punishment for it."

His brother gave him a look. "*A Mhicah*, we're not children anymore. We're grown men. What is Mum going to do, send us to bed without supper?"

"What if that's exactly what she does?" Micah countered, raising a teasing brow. "Are you going to be the one to tell her no and take food anyway? Aye, we're men grown, but we still live under her roof."

"He's not wrong," Sean threw in, sitting on the shelf that was maybe supposed to pass for a bench. "Your mother will always be able to tell you what to do, no matter how old you are."

MacEoghan considered that for a long moment, or Micah thought he did. His twin did not stop his walk about the room, and his back was presently to him. When he came back around, his expression said he had already moved on to some other line of thought, though he apparently did not feel the need to share that line at this time.

"Have you made arrangements for our passage to Canada?" Micah inquired instead.

Sean nodded. "You'll be flying over."

"A plane?" MacEoghan asked. "Not a boat? Or a portal?"

Their Master shook his head. "Boat's too likely to be sunk these days, by Axis or Allied alike."

"And a plane won't be shot down? Why not just use a portal?"

"Bielski took a plane to Canada when he is more than capable of portal travel himself. I want you to retrace his steps exactly, see if you can ferret out a reason. Maybe there is no reason other than he was trying to be unpredictable—why *not* use a portal?—but I don't want to potentially miss clues or important information on account of being impatient."

It seemed like a valid reason, but Micah wasn't sure how he felt about flying. Flying itself was probably fine, but there was still that potential to be shot down over the Atlantic.

"How are we going to afford the tickets? Passenger flights are impossibly expensive."

"Kearney is making that donation." Sean's expression was knowing, his mouth a smirk. Micah still didn't like it.

He decided to change the subject. "Have you heard anything more about Bielski? If he's been spotted anywhere else? What he's up to?"

"Still in Ottawa as of last week," Sean answered. "And he's been spotted in the company of some lower-level government officials, likely trying to get an audience with members of Parliament."

"And the documents?"

"Unaccounted for. The local Time Agents searched his flat top to bottom. Nothing. Either he keeps them on his person at all times, or he's hiding them somewhere else." Sean continued before Micah could speak. "They'll fill you in on the details when you get there."

The door opened and a monstrous alien standing a good fourteen feet tall ducked into the room. It had the general shape of a giraffe, but there was a certain quality to it that spoke of a peacock, hair that fit together more like feathers, with an iridescence and pattern reminisce of the unmistakable bird. This was tragically disrupted by the presence of what appeared to be vines entangling the whole body, but may have, in some wild sense, been a real part of the alien's physiology, like impossibly long fingers.

"MacEoghan," Sean said, overriding whatever the creature had to say and making an accompanying motion. "You're up."

MacEoghan abandoned his route and followed the giraffe-peacock thing out of the room.

Micah looked at Sean. "Using each of us to cover up the other's mistakes?"

"Yes, though I don't think it's quite necessary this time. You've both learned well."

"What was that thing?"

Sean shifted position. "Like the Bat, no one really knows anything about it, its species, its home world. It's the only one of its kind that I've ever seen, and they're only ever here. This one is called the Day. And that's all anyone really knows."

Micah nodded absently. As much as he wanted to distract himself from this impending review, he also knew that he needed to focus on it in order to do well. And why should he be anxious about it? It was just a knowledge test and a skill test. The first didn't bother him in the slightest, and the second, well, if he could survive Sean throwing rocks at him, he could probably survive anything. Although, memories of having to face the Bat in combat last time were providing a pretty good clue as to why he was nervous this time around.

He was also fairly certain that it was about time for Mass to be over. His parents would stand around talking for a while. Shay, now basically a man, would be trying to get the attention of one of the girls. The younger siblings who were growing up would also be exploring that weird thing called love as boys and girls each suddenly realized the other existed, and the very youngest would still be playing, glad for the warmer weather and the many puddles to jump in, much to their mother's dismay.

Once everyone was caught up on the latest news and gossip and got hungry, they'd leave the church and head home. There, they would discover the twins were missing. Moreover, there would be no sign that they had done anything during the day, nor would there by any sign of the gastric distress they had both pleaded in order to get out of Mass. Sarah would be worried that something happened to them, maybe head over to see if they'd gone to wait for the doctor to get out of Mass. Once it was confirmed that the twins had not gone to the doctor and had instead jaunted off somewhere, both Padraig and Sarah would spend the rest of the day preparing whatever speech and punishment they deemed most suitable.

"How soon are we leaving for Canada?" Micah asked. He didn't like the thought of being at odds with his parents when he departed. At least a few days would give him time to endure his punishment and get back into their good graces.

"Eight days," Sean informed him. "It was the best I could do without shoving you on a boat just as soon as we returned."

That was fine with him. A day over a week, he could handle that. He could recover from whatever this review was going to be like, accept his punishment for playing hooky from Mass, and spend a few days saying goodbye to everyone before leaving for Canada.

The door opened again and the giraffe-peacock, the Day, ducked inside.

"Where's MacEoghan?" Micah wondered, trying to peer around the large creature.

"Recovering," the Day responded shortly. "It is now your turn to go before the Hands for your Journeyman review."

Micah looked at Sean, but the man did not appear concerned. Recovering? There was no psychological exam this time, no drugs to mess with their minds. Was he recovering from the skill test? Were they facing the Bat again? Or maybe the Day this time? Micah took an even breath, considered backing out, saying he was planning to leave Time anyway. Except for that damned mission to Canada and this thousand-year-old Slavic mercenary and the documents he stole.

Reluctantly, he nodded and followed the Day out of the room. If he had any hope, it was that MacEoghan's exam hadn't seemed to take very long. Had he lost track of time, or was it just a matter of this exam, this time as a Journeyman, being only a stepping stone between Apprenticeship and Mastery? He wouldn't have a problem with that. He might have even felt good about it, except he still didn't like not knowing where his twin was.

Back to the ominous iron gate that separated the inner track from the coliseum arena itself, a unique and raw vintage physicality terribly at odds with the otherwise highly technological decor of the rest of the Seat. The Day cranked the wheel over and over, heavy chains opening this gate and the one at the far end of the tunnel. Any confidence or hope Micah might have had concerning this review evaporated, and he stepped anxiously under the first gate and made his way down the tunnel to the Inner Sanctum of the Hands.

White marble also stood at odds with the rest of the Coliseum decor, but at least it was pleasant to look upon. There was no indication of anything that had happened during MacEoghan's review. No hair, no dust or dirt, no blood, absolutely nothing. It was as though the whole room had been deep-cleaned just before Micah's arrival.

He walked to the indicated spot on the floor, then turned to face the Hands.

Introductions were a tired formality, though someone's ego apparently still demanded they be observed to their fullest extent. Once those were finished, a short speech was given, detailing how the review would proceed.

As before, one Hand would ask a question, and he would have to answer, for a maximum of fifty-one questions.

Micah briefly wondered if there were times when it was unnecessary for all of the Hands to ask a question. Or maybe not all of the Hands were present. Studying the assembly, it looked like there were fifty-one present, but maybe there were only forty-eight.

"Describe the properties of a Band."

Micah was so intent on studying the Hands and possibly counting them, worrying about unnecessary details, that the question caught him off-guard, and he was unable to answer for at least a few seconds. The problem was, he only had a limited time to answer.

"The properties of a Band," he began awkwardly, trying to collect his thoughts and bring them back to the present moment. "The outer layer separates the Band from Base Time or, in the case of, for example, Double Bands, any other Bands. It is theoretically connected to the in-between dimension which regulates the use of Time and Energy. The inner layer is the new Plane of Time, moving faster or slower than Base Time around it. Should the Band move, or when it is dispersed, it creates a wake, which is where the outer layer reconciles the Plane of Time that was created inside the inner layer with either the inner layer of another Band, as in the case of a Double Band, or Base Time itself."

No notes were taken, no feedback given. Straight into the next question.

"Describe the interaction with and manipulation of a wake."

Micah cleared his throat and nodded. "For normal people, running into a wake may produce sudden clumsiness as they are momentarily exposed to Time differentials over different parts of the body; sensations of vertigo or brief confusion for the same reason; and feelings of déjà vu. This is where their interaction often ends. For someone who has been exposed to Time, especially Timekeepers, he is able to effectively grab the wake material. From there he can reform the Band around himself, or follow the wake to its source and possibly slip into that Band, such as a river current into a body of water."

The third Hand stood. "Why are the majority of nascent Time abilities skewed toward Timekeeping rather than Harvesting?"

"Time Agents are most often first exposed through Bands or by traversing a portal. Timekeeping deals with Time on a macro level, the interaction of all things within Time, Base Time, Bands, the Planes of Time, and so on. Harvesting deals with Time on a comparatively micro level, a singular organism's relationship to Time in a more...esoteric way. It is very difficult to cultivate this mindset, relationship, and skill from bare bones. Often it is easier to expose a candidate to macro Time, then refine the understanding down to a micro level."

In that brief moment between one Hand sitting and another standing, Micah wondered how MacEoghan had fared in this portion of his review. He did not doubt that MacEoghan knew the material, but being able to express that knowledge coherently was not always in his arsenal of abilities.

"Is there any advantage to a Timekeeper being afflicted with accelerated aging rather than slowed aging?"

The vast majority of Timekeepers experienced slowed aging due to their abilities, but every so often, it worked in the opposite direction.

"A Timekeeper is forced to acquire and hone his skills much more quickly, before the accelerated aging takes real effect. Thus these Timekeepers possess greater discipline than their average, slow-afflicted counterparts."

Sean had basically given them that answer to simply recite. It was a plausible and even polite answer, but the part the Hands really looked for was the fact that such Timekeepers had to buy more Time Capsules if they wanted to stave off the accelerated aging.

Micah had once asked what the knowledge exams of the higher ranks were like. Sean explained that the Master exam was still pretty limited to the mechanics of Timekeeping, and maybe some basic knowledge of other disciplines. Once one got into the officer reviews, the knowledge exam turned more towards culture, politics, leadership, management, ethics, and any topic that was not always so fortunate to have more clear-cut right or wrong answers. The Captain exam reportedly required near-flawless recitation of the entire Laws of Time.

"What are the advantages of training under multiple Masters during your Journeyman period?" the next Hand asked.

"It gives an opportunity to learn new tricks and techniques that one's common Master may not be aware of. Because of the requirement to travel to other Districts, if not Regions, it also begins to foster cross-cultural appreciation and understanding which can be built on in later ranks and training."

Another recited answer. Given the war that was going on back home, Micah really wondered how true such a concept could possibly be. Europeans traveled frequently, and it was usually to conquer or kill each other. Had Adolf Hitler felt cross-cultural appreciation and understanding when he walked the streets of Paris? If so, such appreciation evidently wasn't strong enough to make him want to give the country back to the people of said culture.

"What is a variable Band?" came the next question.

"A variable Band is a Band which does not have a set strength, and even parameters may be only loosely defined, which makes them a greater technical challenge for a Timekeeper since they are prone to collapse. This type of Band relies on the theory of the in-between dimension to filter Time and Energy at a constantly shifting rate, thereby continuously changing the strength of the Band. A good Timekeeper who is aware of or more...in tune with his variable Band can often self-compensate to function normally, but anyone else is at a distinct disadvantage until they can attune themselves to the properties of the Band, a process that can take time."

And if that theoretical other person were an adversary, those were moments he could not afford to waste, he added silently.

There were no trick questions, no gotchas, nothing that felt designed to denigrate Micah or block him from advancing. Perhaps it had only felt that way in the Apprentice exam because it was his first time doing something like this, and now that he was more prepared and knew what to expect, he could more rationally tackle the exam.

Fifty-one Hands, fifty-one questions, or else he had miscounted. It didn't matter to him, really, because he actually felt very confident this time around. He was almost ashamed that he was leaving Time. Well, if nothing else, he would be able to do some good work before then. Assuming the thousand-year-old mercenary didn't kill him first. Maybe he should do some research on the guy before they left here. That would probably be a smart thing to do. On the other hand, hadn't Sean already done that?

"So concludes the first part of the exam," someone said, jerking him from his thoughts. "We will proceed directly into the second part of the review, the skill test."

Right. That. The thing that MacEoghan thought would be fun to pit them against each other. Where had his brother gotten such an insane idea? Was he really that desperate for a fight that he was looking at his own brother?

On the other hand, facing the Day as an opponent was not an appealing alternative. There was no standing skill test this time to demonstrate his rote abilities. No, the Hands opened up the exam straight into combat.

Micah immediately reached for a Fast Band, trying to buy himself time, and maybe a little distance. He didn't know whether the Day would use its head to actually attack, but he could easily envision it snaking around behind him to keep him corralled within pummeling distance. As it drew closer— sensing his Fast Band and erecting one of its own—he also got an answer to his earlier curiosity. The vines were not merely for decoration, but they did appear to be prehensile appendages. The Day did not have any "arms" or "hands" or "fingers" to speak of, but he bet that it could use these viney appendages to far more devastating effect.

The Day continued to advance, unwrapping the vines from its body until it must have had a dozen or more appendages flayed out, ranging in length from three to twenty feet. It was a horrifying vision, and Micah was rooted to the ground the same as if a bear or wolf or some other predator were charging him.

He wasn't going to beat it physically. All he had was Time. But it had Time, too. It did this for a living, testing Timekeepers. Did Harvesters have to do this?

His indecision resulted in him being effortlessly wrapped in a long vine about the waist and lifted into the air. Being moved from his position helped to jar the paralyzing thoughts, but now he was in a new, far more terrifying predicament. A second vine wrapped around his ankles.

Up close and personal, while the vines did indeed look like vines, they had the dexterity and feel of crushing tentacles, a great leviathan come to crush a small fishing boat. Beating on them with his fists wasn't going to do anything; it was too strong.

A thought struck him. Everything weakened with age. Could he try to age the vines? If he could wrap them in a Fast Band so they aged, then put that Band inside of a Slow Band so that maybe the Day wouldn't notice...

The vines slowed, hardened, creaked. The tentacle feel was replaced by brittle wood. Micah was able to shift his position and crack them open. Before he could drop out of the restraints, a third vine had sneaked up below him and yanked him free.

He repeated his trick of aging the vines, each time getting closer and closer to the ground. When he was close enough that he wasn't worried about breaking his neck if he ended up in a free fall, he aged the vines, broke free, and continued to twist and Band wildly, hoping to keep any more sneaky vines at bay.

Then he was back on the ground. It was not a soft landing, but he took advantage of his better position, stood, and sprinted away a dozen yards.

The Day was down to two vines approximately three feet long. Breathing hard, Micah had a minor revelation that his Band trick to age the vines might not have been all that clever. His Bands had been strong, yes, but not so strong that he himself was barely aware of them. At most, he'd aged the vines only a few years. If the vines were so susceptible to aging...

He let out a breath as he watched the Day utilize Bands of its own to regrow the vines. There it was.

With age came wisdom, and, it seemed, reflexes and a desire for revenge. Or maybe it was just part of the act. Micah found it hard to believe that it would have just let him use his little trick, even the first time. The Day did this every day; it had to have dealt with all manner of tricks and gimmicks from Timekeepers trying to pass a test.

Another idea came to Micah as a vine slithered around one wrist. Being as flexible as they were, the vines likely had some feeling in them. Looking at the Day's legs, he wondered if its...feet? hooves?...had the same. Or were they like fingernails, with no feeling at all?

The next step the Day took, Micah Banded just before the foot came down. He again concentrated on a single area, growing out the nail or hoof a significant length on that one foot. Then he released the Band.

If he was any judge of alien expression and body language—and he was not—the sudden change in foot dynamics seemed to genuinely surprise the Day. It was unable to step as it had originally intended, yet physics dictated that it continue to move. The large mass that was a fourteen-foot giraffe-peacock with prehensile vines for fingers pitched forward. Micah Banded the vines holding him, broke free, tumbled to the ground, and scrambled a safe distance away.

The Day was able to Band and save itself from crashing awkwardly to the floor, but then it stopped. It corrected its foot, breaking off the excess growth of keratin. Then, if Micah was any judge of alien body language—and he was not—it backed down from the fight, wrapping up its vines against its body in a nonthreatening state, and moving back some yards.

Had...had he just won? Sure, if the Day were actually trying to kill him, it probably still had a lot of fight left, but when it came to this exam...had he passed? He didn't know why he found that so surprising, but here he was. Maybe he'd just mentally written it off in his mind anyway, telling himself that he was leaving Time so it didn't matter. Now he'd just bested his opponent, maybe even genuinely gotten the drop on it with his little fingernail trick.

Somehow, in the face of a massive war back home, all this business with the fishing and the IRA and a mission to Canada, he didn't know what to make of a success. He didn't know how to handle it, didn't believe it was real. There had to be something more. Honestly, for as terrifying as it had been to be held fast in those vines, this fight had almost felt...easy.

It was the clarity of it all, he decided. The fishing business was facing an intangible enemy he had no way to fight. The IRA and Europe as a whole were facing tangible enemies that felt unbeatable. Here, now, him versus the Day, everything had become remarkably simple. He knew his opponent, and he knew he had the means to hurt it, to defeat it. Honestly, it felt good.

"Thus concludes the second part of the Journeyman Timekeeper review for Micah Dearbhfhine," the Zero Hour stated. "As there is no third part, you will be taken for recovery. We will reconvene when a decision has been made."

And that was that. The Hands stood in unison. The Day, not two minutes ago throwing him around with prehensile vines, now acted as his escort. Micah followed it out of the room and down the tunnel. They paused so the Day could close the gates, and then they were on their way to a small room where MacEoghan was already waiting. From the looks of things, he was growing quite impatient. His expression was hopeful when the door opened, but it was only to deliver Micah. The Day said nothing to either of them, just turned around and closed the door behind it.

"How did it go?" MacEoghan demanded.

"Surprisingly easy," Micah answered. "You?"

"Same. How did you beat the Day? Or did you?"

So Micah explained his strategy of aging the vines and growing out the hoof. MacEoghan listened, his expression amused. Micah finished with, "How did you do it?"

"I did something similar, but I also used Bands to distract it."

Micah folded his arms. "How is that?"

MacEoghan shrugged as if the answer were obvious. "Well, strong Bands give off light don't they? Flash a bunch of small Bands in rapid succession around its head, it didn't know which way was up. Bought me time and let me get in a few good hits."

Micah nodded. Actually, that probably would have been a good idea, about the lights. "You actually tried to punch it?"

Again his twin shrugged. "A joint is a joint, and most are only supposed to bend one way. I tried to make them bend the other way." He made a so-so gesture. "Success was...admittedly limited. The Day has some pretty big joints."

Micah raised a brow and shifted his stance, folding his arms dramatically. "So what were you planning on doing to me if they had pitted us against each other like you wanted? Were you going to try that on me, flashing lights to distract while you put every joint out of place?"

His brother flushed deep red. "Ah, well..." He awkwardly cleared his throat. "Maybe that wasn't my best idea. Fighting you, I mean. I don't know what they would have expected of us. A timed match? Points? Just keep going until one of us taps out?" Now he matched Micah's expression. "Why?

You want to try to when we get home? You beat the Day so now you're feeling a bit cocky yourself, think you can take on your older brother?"

Micah took a step forward, getting into a stance. "Only by a couple minutes."

MacEoghan also got into a stance. Before they could make contact, however, the door opened and the Day appeared.

"Is there a problem?" the creature inquired.

The twins straightened and faced the Day. It was MacEoghan who answered, "No. No problem at all."

"Then you are both to come with me for your results."

They returned to the Inner Sanctum where the Hands and Sean were waiting. Did they ever actually leave this room, or did they simply debate where they were?

"Micah Dearbhfhine, MacEoghan Dearbhfhine, you have completed the review in order to advance from Apprentice Timekeeper to Journeyman Timekeeper status," the Zero Hour said, standing. He wasted no time in giving the results. "Micah Dearbhfhine, as to the first part of the review, the oral exam, testing your knowledge of Time, fifty out of fifty-one Hands were satisfied with your performance."

Another almost-perfect score. Micah was feeling really good about himself and he glanced at MacEoghan, feeling a bit smug.

"MacEoghan Dearbhfhine, as to the first part of the review, the oral exam, testing your knowledge of Time, forty-two out of fifty-one Hands were satisfied with your performance."

Not terrible, not great. MacEoghan shrugged.

"Micah Dearbhfhine, as to the second part of the review, the skill test, forty-five out of fifty-one Hands were satisfied with your performance."

He thought he'd done pretty well, up until MacEoghan mentioned the flashing lights distraction. Only then did Micah consider that maybe he wasn't as spectacular as he'd thought. Still, it was a respectable score.

"MacEoghan Dearbhfhine, as to the second part of the review, the skill test, forty-nine out of fifty-one Hands were satisfied with your performance."

Micah didn't know what the threshold was for a passing grade, but he knew that they had both far exceeded that threshold.

"And so, Micah Dearbhfhine and MacEoghan Dearbhfhine, you are now full Journeyman Timekeepers. It is required that you study under a minimum of three Masters from different Districts. Per the standards of human Timekeeper training, it is expected that your Journeyman training take approximately three Base Years. There is much to learn until you become Masters. Study well." The Zero Hour turned to Sean. "You and MacEoghan Dearbhfhine have also been released from probation with the Grandfathers."

"Thank you," Sean said sincerely with half a bow.

With that, they were dismissed. Micah could see MacEoghan was enthusiastic, though he contained his excitement until they were out of the Coliseum.

"Canada, here we come!" he blurted.

The smug satisfaction of passing his review slowly receded from Micah's mind. Right. Canada. There was more that they were expected to do now. More that he was expected to do now, seeing how he wouldn't be leaving Time until after the war, and the war was not giving any signs of resolving quickly. Up next, then, was Canada.

"Well, it will be a few days before you leave," Sean told him, though the man was grinning. "Use them to spend quality time with your family, make sure they know you love them."

Micah could appreciate the sentiment, even if his twin appeared to brush it off nonchalantly.

They returned to the portal room and returned their translators. Then the twins followed Sean down a row of portals. Micah glanced left and right through each one, amazed at the scenes from other worlds. Grand forests, open deserts, ridiculously large cities, and scenes he could not readily relate to anything he was familiar with. The walk to the end of the row of open portals felt like at least a few miles, but eventually they did reach a spot where there were no more open portals, merely open floor extending into a vast and almost endless metal cube.

"This is where we'll start," Sean stated. "Opening portals for beginners."

MacEoghan nodded emphatically. "Let's do it."

"Portals can be opened by universal coordinates or by feel, though many typically use some combination of the two."

"The difference between following a map and just knowing where to go," Micah offered.

"Exactly. Portals are no different, except you're condensing the entire middle of the trip into a single, infinitesimally narrow doorway. All that really exists is the starting point and the ending point." Sean made a vague gesture around them. "The first portal for a Journeyman starts here in order to take advantage of the Wheel's power to take and hold a portal once it is established."

"How is it able to do that? How is it able to facilitate all this travel from around the universe?"

Sean shrugged. "Honestly, I don't know. The technical details are beyond my understanding. I just know it works."

It was the best answer they were going to get for the moment. Right now, they had to get home. They had to face their parents' wrath for skipping out on Mass.

"Where do you think we should go?" MacEoghan wondered. "The shore?"

"It's Sunday, *a Mhac*," Micah said. "There'll be people up and down the shoreline." He shook his head. "No, let's go to the office. It's small, private, and I'm very well familiar with it."

MacEoghan did not object.

"A good choice," Sean commented. "Now then, consider the office. Consider how it looks, how it sounds, feels, smells, all of it. Just like anyone or anything else that you want to Band, consider the office, its place in Time, its place in Space. It is wholly unique in the universe. No other thing exists in that same space."

It was an odd consideration, yet it made perfect sense. Micah also suspected that he had to consider the office in relation to the Wheel. Take both places, and connect them. Easier said than done, he thought, but he would give it a shot.

A portal sputtered to life, flickering like a bad light bulb in the empty slot before them. Micah glimpsed the office on the other side for just a moment, but he latched onto it. He became aware of sweat dripping down his forehead and under his arms.

"Something's not right," he said, even as the portal opened fully. He released his hold, handing over control of the portal to the Wheel's technology.

Sean studied the portal. "Looks right to me."

Micah shook his head. "No, not the portal itself. The...the feel..of the office. I could feel it, and I could feel around it, the building and the town." He shook his head. "Something's not right. It doesn't feel right."

Before anyone could ask him what he meant, he grabbed MacEoghan's arm and stepped through.

LIFE AND LIMB
OLDER BROTHER

The office was quiet when they stumbled through, but MacEoghan knew immediately that his brother was right. Something was off. It took him a second to pinpoint anything in the room, for the change here was subtle.

Micah was not a stringent housekeeper, nor the most organized of office managers, but he was clean and generally tidy. He didn't leave stuff just lying around, never left a mess uncleaned, especially over Sunday. The office now was not dirty or ransacked. If MacEoghan had to pick a word in his sluggish mind that was still recovering from walking through a portal, he might have said mildly disheveled. One book had fallen to the floor, the others were knocked out of place and hanging over the edge of the shelf. Some papers had also floated to the floor. Dust and dirt coated everything as if no housekeeping had been done for some days. Turning around to survey the whole room, blinking and forcing himself to right his senses, the window was cracked and the doorframe was cockeyed so that the door looked like it was wedged in place, maybe even stuck.

MacEoghan gingerly touched the doorknob, unlocked it, then twisted. It gave appropriately, but the door itself was indeed stuck. He threw himself against the door, but it wouldn't budge. A second time, same result.

"*A Mhac!*" Micah barked behind him. "Pull!"

The door was still stuck, but putting his weight into a mighty pull at least produced the results he was looking for.

Outside in the warehouse, it was more of the same. No widespread destruction, but noticeable damage. Vehicles had been jarred out of place, bumpers touching each other. One of the garage doors had seen its hinges damaged and was balancing precariously in place. There was more dust and dirt, but there was also sunlight where there should not have been sunlight.

Looking up, MacEoghan saw holes punched in the ceiling, rocks on the ground indicating the culprit.

MacEoghan dashed for the man door, intending to heave it open and being surprised when it was not stuck, but loose. He recovered his balance and darted outside. He was immediately presented with a view of the docks, or what was left of them. Several boats were missing, and others jutted up from where they rested awkwardly on the harbor floor. Floating planks and beams from the docks had congealed into a massive berg floating on the tide, occasionally bumping into one of the navigation buoys marking the safe entrance and exit to the harbor.

Few boats were spared at all, but he could not immediately see any of his father's fishing vessels. He knew, of course, that none of the fishermen would have been out on a Sunday, but it was small comfort.

"What happened here?"

MacEoghan turned. Micah had spoken, cautiously emerging from the warehouse, Sean behind him. His twin looked utterly flabbergasted by the scene, but Sean regarded everything with the cool determination of someone who, regrettably, knew the answer.

"Luftwaffe."

"Are we at war?" MacEoghan demanded.

Sean walked around the side of the building, toward the road that snaked into town. The twins followed.

"This wasn't war," Sean stated. "There would be no town left if it was."

MacEoghan recalled the scene in London, the broken teeth of the city skyline; buildings empty and deformed like battered skulls; debris piled everywhere as people tried to simply make a way from here to there. This, truly, was not that, but he felt an ache in his heart deeper than anything he'd felt in London. Most buildings appeared to be in tact, though everything was quite dirty. He saw some broken windows, a few holes in roofs. There was a crater in the top of a nearby cliff and large rocks and boulders in the street below.

People were out and about already, picking up debris, moving rocks, sweeping dusty porches and stoops. Children climbed on a particularly large boulder that was lodged in the side of the general store, while the wife of the owner of said store got after them to get down so they didn't hurt themselves and start helping clean up.

"Not war," Sean repeated, "only lost German pilots." He shifted his stance and folded his arms. "Three bombs, maybe four. Overly excited pilots, seeing land but not paying attention to where they were. Same story as before when they hit Baile Átha Cliath."

MacEoghan turned to see Micah carefully making his way along the dock closest to the warehouse. Some planks were missing and part of the walkway sagged into the water, but Micah hardly seemed to notice. MacEoghan left Sean to his contemplative analysis and followed his brother out.

"Maybe the boats were just knocked loose," Micah said, his face pale as death, expression lifeless, voice strained. "The ropes or the posts they were tied to, maybe they just separated." Tears rolled down his cheeks.

MacEoghan put a hand on his brother's shoulder. As soon as he did, Micah broke down, stumbling to one of the posts and only just catching himself as he wept. MacEoghan just put a hand on his back and waited.

Micah had sold his soul to protect this business. He had been willing to forfeit his inheritance just to ensure there was an inheritance to give, committed himself, maybe even his life, to the schemes of a shady businessman. And for what? For it to be destroyed because some eighteen year old German pilot couldn't read a map and distinguish between east and west, or north and south?

Micah calmed down and composed himself. He looked at MacEoghan, but his expression bore no trace of relief.

"Father's not here," he said.

"Isn't that a good thing?" MacEoghan wondered. As soon as he said it, he knew the answer. Family came first, business second. And if the business wasn't being tended to...

The two of them jogged back to the street. Sean had already made his way down the road and was speaking to people. When he spied the brothers approaching, he moved to intercept.

"Happened right after Mass, as everyone was mingling and going home," he reported. "Three bombs, as I suspected. One at the docks, one struck the top of the cliff there, and the third...hit the church."

"What?" Micah demanded.

"It's not uncommon," Sean said, his tone carefully neutral. "One of the biggest buildings in any city, nice high steeple reaching into the sky, bells announcing everything from Mass to weddings to incoming bombers."

"Pilots can't read a map but they know how to bomb a church?"

MacEoghan was more surprised that his brother cared so much. Micah hated Mass, hated the Church, and he wasn't too fond of God either. He almost never said any of this out loud in public, but when they lay awake in the dark, talking when they should be sleeping, MacEoghan heard his twin's real feelings about things. Sure, maybe they were out in public now, but Micah was not in a right enough mind to be able to pretend anything. Where was this concern coming from?

"I can't answer that," Sean told him. "I think our best bet right now is to split up. You two need to find your family. I'm going to ask a few more questions around here, and I'll come find you before I leave."

It was the best plan any of them had at the moment. Sean stuck around the area while the twins broke off and headed for home.

The houses by the shore looked relatively untouched, and MacEoghan knew a moment of hope. He could tell that some rocks had fallen from the surrounding cliffs, knocked loose from the shuddering vibrations of the area being bombed, but there did not appear to be any damage other than dust. The roofs were in tact, the windows and doors set correctly—well, familiarly —in their frames. Porches were warped, but, again, undamaged by the recent attack. And yet, for all of these good signs, there was still something off about the whole scene.

It wasn't until MacEoghan was standing on the porch reaching for the door that he pinpointed what that off thing was. There was no activity. He heard nothing inside. No conversation, no laughter, no crying. When he did open the door, the house looked exactly as they had left it. None of the younger kids came running to meet them. No food was on the stove. In fact, there was no heat whatsoever.

"Hello?" MacEoghan called. "Anybody home?"

Now he heard some movement from the back of the house. A voice. More movement. Then, "*A Mhac?* Is that you?"

It was Brendan. The thirteen-year-old peeked his head around the corner. He, too, was pale in the skin, but the relief in his expression was more than evident. He looked behind him. "It's Mac!"

Nine-year-old Kayleigh was the first to burst forth, weaving her way through rooms and around furniture to throw herself at MacEoghan's waist, then Micah's waist, crying inconsolably. Behind her, more reserved, was twelve-year-old Shauna being led by fifteen-year-old Ciara. Shauna hung back, shy, while Ciara approached to give both twins a more respectable hug, her tears staining their shoulders.

"What happened?" MacEoghan asked. "Where is everyone else?"

Ciara pulled away, sniffed, wiped her eyes, tried to compose herself but failed miserably for several long minutes.

"Mass was just finished, and everyone was starting to leave," she finally managed. "We heard the planes from inside the church. We thought they were far away, but when we got outside, they were right on top of us." She wiped her eyes again. "Mum gathered us up, wanted us to hurry home. Papa gathered the older boys, started trying to help people any way they could. Brendan wanted to go back and help Papa, but I had hold of him. But Darren got away from us. Mum ran back to get him."

Her words faded, but her expression and her tears finished the story.

"No," Micah whispered softly, shaking his head. "No." Pause. "Shay?"

"Shay, Cillian, Darren, Mum, and Papa," Ciara said. "Papa and Shay were trying to help old Mr. Bodger out of the church, but he doesn't move very fast, you know. The bomb itself killed them, I think. Cillian had just intercepted Darren to hand him back to Mum, but the debris from the church..."

The best MacEoghan could do was hold his sister. She did not cry, but he could hear and feel her shocked wheezes in his shoulder, along with an occasional silent sob. Micah, meanwhile, had made his way to the couch where the rest of the kids climbed on top of him, seeking comfort and safety. MacEoghan could see his brother was in just as much shock, but he was still something familiar for the kids.

Ciara pulled away and punched MacEoghan in the shoulder in sudden wrath. "And where were you two?! Playing hooky from Mass today!"

Of course they had known that they were going to have to face some kind of punishment for their actions, but now that knowledge was only weighed down by tremendous guilt. They should have been here. The bombing happened just after Mass, and it was nearing evening now. They could have helped with cleanup, with...identifying the bodies, burying them.

Except, without the Journeyman review, they would have had no reason to skip Mass. And they would have been right there with their father and Shay and Cillian, trying to help people as much as they could. And they, too, would likely be dead.

Ciara turned and, apparently having broken through some of her shock, went about building a fire in the stove. MacEoghan watched her for a moment, startling at a knock on the door. The interloper did not wait for an answer, but cautiously opened the door and peeked in. It was Sean. He made silent eye contact with MacEoghan and Micah and motioned for them outside.

The kids ran from Micah when he roused and attached themselves to Ciara who immediately launched in a line of distraction questions, asking what they wanted for supper. The last thing MacEoghan heard as he pulled the front door closed behind him was Kayleigh blubbering that she didn't want supper, she wanted Mama.

"I'm so sorry," Sean began, his tone and expression sincere.

"What have you learned?" MacEoghan was perhaps the only one who hadn't shed tears, but he was exhausted.

"Eleven dead, dozens more injured to varying degrees with a few likely to contribute to the death toll in the next day or two."

Micah did not bother with formality, just sat right where he was, scooting back just enough to lean against the house. He closed his eyes. "We were supposed to be here."

"And you would be dead if you were," Sean informed him, echoing MacEoghan's earlier suspicions.

"Great. So what are we supposed to do?" His tone and expression suggested he had relapsed into shock.

MacEoghan looked at Sean and lowered his voice. "We can't go to Canada now—"

"Why not?!" Micah jumped to his feet. "We have nothing else."

"We have four kids in there who need looking after," MacEoghan told him.

Micah stalked up to him. "Oh, now family means something to you?"

"It has always meant something to me."

"Has it? How did that go with the IRA exactly? And Father?"

"I did that for—"

"And now your German friends just—"

Sean forced himself between them. "Enough!" He huffed a sigh. "*A Mhicah*, you're talking nonsense. *A Mhac*, shut up."

He paused and let the silence settle between them. MacEoghan wouldn't say he didn't understand that Micah was hurting. But he was hurting, too. He no more believed this to be Micah's fault than anyone else's.

"There is nothing we could have done to stop the Germans," Sean said, very matter-of-fact. "We couldn't redirect them, couldn't tell them anything. Now, maybe we could have been of some help here, Banding to get people out of harm's way, but there is no guarantee that it would have worked. Fire doesn't Band well, and explosions don't Band hardly at all. It's too violent of a chemical reaction to be contained by a Band. You'd have to be a Warden or Dominion Timekeeper to even hope to pull off something like that. And the situational awareness to be able to predict the movement of shrapnel and debris and people..." He took an even breath. "It's shit luck is what it is. I wish I had a better explanation, something to make it make sense, but it is just shit luck."

It was an unacceptable answer for both twins; at least they could agree on that, exchanging frustrated glances. Micah shifted his gaze to Sean, and MacEoghan hoped his twin wasn't about to unleash an accusatory tirade on him now. Instead, he just slumped back down to a sitting position.

"Usually," Sean began slowly, perhaps picking up on Micah's roaming displeasure, "where there's one Luftwaffe squad, there are more. I'm going to go and see if there are any other locations that have seen some action, and I will leave you two to take care of your own affairs. I'll be back in a few days to check up on you."

"What about Canada?" Micah asked.

"Don't worry about Canada right now," Sean told him. "You take care of your siblings and bury the dead. After a few days, when the worst of the shock has worn off, then we can talk about Canada."

MacEoghan shrugged. "What is Kearney going to do, anyway, if we don't go? The boats are gone. He's not buying any more fish; he'll have to launder money somewhere else. And as for me..." He sighed and shifted his stance. "I want to support Éire, but the IRA is about to make a deal with the same people who just murdered half our family. If it was intentional, fuck them. If it was unintentional, then they're obviously too fucking stupid to ally with, if they can't figure out the difference between Éire and England after how many 'accidental' bombings?"

Sean nodded. "I can't say I don't understand, or that I disagree. As for Kearney, let me deal with him for the time being. You just stay here, get cleaned up, figure out what you're going to do. All right?"

Did they have much of a choice? Time could do many things, but it only ever moved forward. Reluctantly, the twins nodded. Sean again expressed his condolences, wished them a good night, then headed out into the growing dark towards town. MacEoghan and Micah remained on the porch, not speaking for several minutes.

"Shit luck," Micah said bitterly. He looked up at MacEoghan from where he still sat against the house. "Is that all we can chock our lives up to? Just shit luck?" He shrugged and continued talking. "Whore for a mother, abuse at the school, transient life on the road, and now this?"

MacEoghan folded his arms and leaned against one of the posts on the porch. "I don't know."

"And now what?"

"Now, I suppose we go in and see what Ciara is making for supper."

Neither one of them moved for several minutes still. It was MacEoghan who broke the trance, forcing himself to break from his position and reach for the door. As he was opening it, Micah reluctantly got to his feet.

Simple stew for dinner, mostly broth with a few vegetables brought up from the cellar and some strips of dried meat. Judging by the look on Ciara's face, it was all she was able to manage at the moment. Her lips were pressed tightly together and every so often she would blink away tears. MacEoghan

452

didn't know a lot about the dinner routine in the kitchen, but he could recognize that she was making familiar motions and still somehow expecting their mother to also exercise her routine, like two puzzle pieces fitting together perfectly. But when that second piece failed to materialize, Ciara had to figure out how to balance her work with this extra work she was suddenly expected to do.

It was like that for everyone that evening. They all sat at their familiar spots at the table. But there were empty chairs, and Padraig was not there to pray over the meal. No one volunteered, and they ate in silence. To be more accurate, they all took bites of their food, then slowly abandoned the activity. Instead, they stumbled blindly into the living room, again, right into their routine, their usual spots. But Padraig was not there to read the nightly Scriptures. This time, Kayleigh grabbed the worn Bible and brought it to MacEoghan, her green eyes pleading.

MacEoghan sighed and took the Bible. He opened it up to his father's bookmark and was immediately struck by the book's interior. There were some smudges and dirty fingerprints; verses were underlined or starred, and there were notes in the margins. The handwriting was mostly Padraig, but then there were also some notes written by Sarah in her fine penmanship.

He read the passage, trying to immerse himself in the story, focus on the words. But he wasn't as good as his father, nor could he come up with any sensible questions to ask afterwards. Maybe because the only question anyone cared about right now was simply: Why?

Micah got up and left just as soon as he perceived MacEoghan was done reading. No one tried to stop him. No one got after him. When MacEoghan finally made for bed, he found his twin fast asleep.

The following morning was like a panicked mystery contained in a Band that wavered between Fast and Slow. Padraig was not up before dawn, telling everyone to wake up and be ready to catch fish. MacEoghan still woke with a start, his mind terrified that he had overslept. Looking over at Micah, he discovered his brother was gone and immediately worried that he was already on the boat. Still half-asleep, MacEoghan stumbled out of bed, barely recalling the events of the previous day until he was halfway to the kitchen and realized there was very little activity. Sarah was not in the kitchen, brewing coffee and cooking oatmeal. There was only Ciara and Brendan, quietly staring at a pot on the stove.

"Where's Micah?" MacEoghan asked.

"He went to the docks," Brendan answered. "But he said we weren't fishing today. He said there weren't any boats left."

"Is that true?" Ciara wondered. "Are they all gone?"

MacEoghan frowned but nodded. "It looked that way, yes."

Tears formed in her eyes. "What are we going to do? Fishing was—is everything here."

"I know!" MacEoghan snapped his mouth shut and took an even breath. Then, more calmly, "I know. But maybe we'll get lucky. Maybe one of the boats just disconnected from the docks, floated away, and then came back."

He didn't believe that for a second, but he decided a tiny bit of hope—however false—might be better than an endless string of bad news.

"Where are Shauna and Kayleigh? Still sleeping?"

Ciara managed a barely perceptible nod. "It's best for them, I think."

MacEoghan just nodded and headed out the door, not waiting for breakfast. He made his way to the docks where all of the fishermen had gathered.

As it turned out, a couple of boats had indeed merely become disconnected from the docks and floated out, and one had indeed managed to float its way back where it was promptly rescued. It was only a small boat, but half a dozen men jumped in and, upon confirming it was reasonably seaworthy, pushed off to go out and have a look around, see if they could rescue any more boats, or at least some supplies.

MacEoghan did not see Micah outside anywhere, and he knew he hadn't been on the rescue boat. Curious, he turned and headed to the warehouse. The mandoor was ajar, loose on its hinges. The office door had also been opened, though it was wedged shut just enough that it would not flop open with every gust of wind. MacEoghan didn't want to barge in, but there was no gentle way to force the door open.

The office was clean, the dust and dirt swept up, papers filed, books neatly put away. Micah sat at the desk, leaning back in the chair, staring toward the cracked window but looking at nothing.

"They've got a small rescue boat going out," MacEoghan began. "Guess a few boats did float away."

Micah shook his head slowly. "All of ours are accounted for. I looked." He sighed. "No. We're done."

"Maybe the business, but we could still—"

"*A MhacEoghan.*" Micah's expression was very frank. "There were dozens of boats out there. Dozens of boats with a dozen men going out every morning. And they're going to recover, what, four? Five if they're lucky? Maybe one or two could be salvaged in time? There are hundreds of men out there who just lost their job. Fishermen, mechanics, processors, delivery drivers." He held up a finger. "And we were the one company that tried to hold out, tried—tried to...snub our noses at the growing monopoly." He let his hand flop back down. "Well, they got it. They are not going to let us in, not when they have their own employees to think about."

He wasn't wrong, and that was the worst part. MacEoghan may not have been involved in the office dealings or business politics, but their father still complained about them when they were out casting nets. He had a good idea of what was going on. And Micah was right. There was nothing left. They had absolutely no cards to play. The business was gone, sunk in about thirty feet of salt water.

"All right," he said. He wasn't going to fight it. He couldn't. "So, what do we do?"

"Everything here is still in good shape," Micah answered. He still stared blankly out the window. "The building needs a few repairs, obviously, but the trucks, the tools, that's all still in good condition. We can try to sell it off, make some money." He held up a hand as MacEoghan opened his mouth to protest. "I know. They're going to offer us a mere fraction of their worth, but it does us no good to keep them." He shook his head. "We can't stay here. Hundreds of men are out of work, which means hundreds of men are going to be looking for jobs."

"If we act now, we can probably get a couple of jobs while all those men are still looking at the docks," MacEoghan offered.

Again Micah shook his head, but this time he turned to look at him. "No. We're going to Canada."

MacEoghan gave his brother a look. "Surely you're not suggesting we leave the kids here to fend for themselves?"

"No. We can take them to Aunt Bethany up north."

Aunt Bethany was Sarah's older sister and universally regarded as a bit of an odd duck, one of those relatives visited only around Christmas and Easter because it was proper and expected among family members. But, while maybe a little bizarre, she and her husband Harold were good people and they loved the kids.

"*A Mhicah*, I don't think anyone would stand in your way if you wanted to punch Kearney in the face if he tried to demand his due," MacEoghan told him. "If anything, I'd like to take a few swings myself."

His twin's expression was flat. "I'm not going for Kearney."

MacEoghan raised his brows. "And you're not going because you suddenly changed your mind about possibly confronting a thousand-year-old mercenary in your quest to steal back sensitive documents."

"You're right. I'm going because I want to. Because I need to." He shifted in his seat. "I want to go somewhere where there is no war. No constant fear, no pain and suffering."

"I hate to tell you this, but pain and suffering are pretty universal," MadEoghan said. "Canada has troops in the war."

"Yes, but Canada is not in the war. There are no battlefields there, no constant barrage of German bombers. Whether it's one bomb or a thousand, I'm tired of it." Micah sighed. Then, quieter. "I'm tired of it." Louder, "The War for Independence, the Civil War, the school, now this."

"*A Mhicah*, we weren't around for the War of Independence, and we weren't old enough to appreciate the Civil War."

"No, but it was still there, always looming, even after it was over. Everything the adults did revolved around that war, how they acted, how they thought. Now is no different. The IRA is proof of that."

"So you plan to go to Canada and never come back?"

His brother faltered. "I won't say never. But at the very least, not until the end of the war."

MacEoghan frowned but nodded. "I'd be lying if I said I didn't understand. But how are we going to explain it to the kids?"

Micah managed a small smile. "They're hardly kids anymore. Ciara's fifteen. Even little Kayleigh is eight, nine, ten years old."

"We were ten when we first arrived at St. Joseph's. We were kids."

The smile vanished. "We couldn't raise them anyway. You know that. And at least they have family to go to."

That much, at least, was true. The brothers headed home and broke the news to Ciara—and, by default, Brendan, who was eavesdropping, badly, from around the corner.

"There's nothing for us here," MacEoghan explained, or tried to. "The fishing business is gone, and there aren't enough other jobs in town to accommodate everyone. Aunt Bethany can take care of you until you're ready and able to make your own way."

"And what about you? Are you going to work in the factories in the city?" Ciara wondered.

He shook his head. "No. We'll be making our way to Canada—"

"So you're just going to abandon us."

MacEoghan had a brief memory of their older brother. One day he was there, the next he wasn't. And they never knew what happened to him. Maybe he'd gone to work at the factories, intending to come back, but something happened and he just vanished into thin air. MacEoghan took an even breath. "No. There's no war in Canada, or there isn't yet. Maybe—"

"So you're going to be cowards and run away, and have us run, too."

MacEoghan didn't know if Ciara was just echoing what their father had always grumbled, or if she had absorbed the same beliefs. Nevertheless, he couldn't stop an indignant, "Playing hooky saved our lives yesterday so we could come back and save yours."

Ciara burst into tears and ran away, down to the room she shared with Shauna and Kayleigh. Guilt immediately began gnawing at MacEoghan and he could feel Micah's accusing gaze. Why should he be accusatory? Just last night he'd been chewing on MacEoghan about the IRA and the Germans. MacEoghan might feel guilty about making Ciara cry, but Micah was just as much a culprit.

Nevertheless, two days later, MacEoghan borrowed a vehicle from a neighbor and the six of them headed north to Aunt Bethany's house. It was about an hour and a half away, over hill and dale, to a place where it seemed war had never touched in all the eons of life. It was a small farm, where chickens scattered as the car rolled up the drive, a cow ambled up to the fence to greet them, and three goats were climbing all over the car just as soon as the engine went quiet.

Aunt Bethany, with clothing of strange and asymmetrical style and wild patterns, came running from her garden, shrieking joyfully and gathering up Shauna and Kayleigh in her arms. Her joy seemed to lift the girls' spirits, and it trickled up the line to Brendan, Ciara, and finally to Micah and MacEoghan.

"Oh, how lovely it is to see you all!" the woman gushed. She turned and, with a voice louder than an air raid siren, called, "Harold! Come and see who's come to visit! Oh, and bring the kids!" She looked around. "Goodness, this is only half the herd. Where's the other half?"

The mood instantly dropped. Aunt Bethany, although a bit queer, was not stupid. She picked up on the shift immediately. *"A Mhac, a Mhicah?* Where...are the others?"

Within twenty minutes, all of the women and girls were bawling in Aunt Bethany's kitchen, their wails matched only by the whistling of the tea kettle. Once they had settled down some, MacEoghan explained the plan. Aunt Bethany listened with wide, red eyes, not saying a word.

"Of course, of course we'll take them," she said when he finished, nodding emphatically and wiping her nose with a sodden handkerchief. "They're...always such a joy. Yes, of course." Another sniff, another useless wipe. "And will you send for them, once you're settled in Canada?"

"Aunt Bethany, if we were capable of raising three girls and a boy, we wouldn't be asking this of you," Micah told her. "Really, we're hoping to wait out the war."

She waved a hand. "Oh, it won't be long now, and this Emergency will all be over. But I understand."

"Besides that," MacEoghan said, "most around these parts consider us cowards for leaving." He looked at Ciara who made a face at him. It might have been more threatening except for her red-rimmed eyes and puffy cheeks.

"Oh, pish posh. You do what you think is right. If that means going to Canada, then by all means, go to Canada. And if that means coming back later, then you're always welcome here."

MacEoghan and Micah thanked her, gave her hugs, and said goodbye to both their siblings and their cousins.

Outside, the car was now the plaything of five goats, and half a dozen sheep were licking the front and rear bumpers. A couple of the younger cousins ran out to playfully chase the animals away and keep the path clear for them to back out and get on the road.

"Do you think we're doing the right thing?" Micah asked once they were underway, returning home.

"This was your idea," MacEoghan reminded him.

"That doesn't mean it's a good one."

MacEoghan sighed. "I think it's the right thing, yes. We'll go to Canada, do whatever asinine mission Kearney has set out for us, then wait a bit until the war is over. After that, we can come back. I don't know where we'll live, but that might be something we figure out as we go."

"Sounds like our life story so far."

MacEoghan said nothing to that, and the rest of the drive was silent. They returned the car to their neighbor, then walked toward home. It would be big and empty and quiet now, but that was all right. Or that was what MacEoghan told himself.

They spied the person near the porch from a hundred yards away. At twenty yards, they identified Sean. He identified them also, for his posture relaxed, and he returned to stand on the porch and leisurely wait for them. Getting closer, MacEoghan saw his expression was puzzled and curious, but he did not ask any questions directly.

"We took the kids to stay with a family member," Micah volunteered. "Whenever you're ready for us to go to Canada, we'll go."

Sean blinked, apparently surprised. Or maybe he was just surprised to hear it come from Micah. "Are you sure? I don't want—"

"We're sure," MacEoghan confirmed.

Sean studied them for a long moment, perhaps looking for the punchline to a joke or some sort of terms for their journey. Finally he nodded. "All right, then. Well, I may be able to get you out a little earlier, as soon as tomorrow. Because of this bombing—certainly not Germany's first mistake, although it may be their least popular—the Luftwaffe appear to be in some chaos and steering clear of the United Kingdom, at least for a few days. I'm going to try and get you out before they resume their activities."

"That would be appreciated."

"Pack up whatever you think you're going to need and stick around the house. I'll come and get you, but when I say go, we go. Understood?"

The brothers nodded, and Sean departed, purpose driving his steps. They watched him go and stared at the spot where he disappeared. Then they turned their attention to the ocean. War or peace, the sun still rose and set, the tide rose and fell, and the clouds drifted lazily by.

"So," Micah said. "We're really going to do this."

MacEoghan nodded. "Looks like it."

They headed back inside the house. Head knowledge hit MacEoghan right in the heart as he closed the door behind him and was struck by the silence and the cold. No conversation, no laughter, no tea, no fire, not even the comfort of snoring and shifting in bed. Only perfect stillness.

MacEoghan forced himself forward, following Micah on wooden legs. After the last few days, trying to make plans and fix everyone else's problems, now he suddenly found time to examine himself.

He never outright cried, but he would be lying to himself if no one else if he said he did not shed tears as he packed up a small bag. Whatever their plans, whatever their future, whatever they said about returning to Éire after the war, it would never be the same. All of this was coming to an end, never to be revisited. Their parents were gone. They might have gotten lucky, finding Padraig and Sarah after their nightmare of a childhood, but it wasn't going to happen a third time, not as grown men. They were on their own. Once again, they were all they had.

It hurt in a way he could not truly describe, and he fell asleep, feeling very much like an empty cup. He had nothing. There was no going back. Ever. There was only the way forward. And he couldn't help but feel as though he had squandered the last few years chasing something that didn't exist, ignoring what was right in front of him.

As they had every day that week, MacEoghan and Micah were awake very early, still waiting for their father to go stomping by, yelling at everyone to wake up and get moving, there were fish to be caught. But it never came. There was no fishing. There was no tantalizing smell of coffee and breakfast. There was only the quiet, the perfect stillness.

And a knock at the door.

The brothers Banded to get through their morning routine in only a few seconds, then grabbed their bags and headed to the front door where Sean was waiting for them. Instead of motioning for them to come out, he pushed his way in.

"We're not bothering with a vehicle," he told them. "We're going by direct portal."

"Direct portal to...Canada?" Micah inquired.

"Well...no. Again, I want to trace Bielski's steps as closely as possible, which means taking a plane. We're going to the airport. There's been an arrangement between the Powers That Be to allow a short window for some civilians to escape the carnage before the Germans resume their air and sea campaigns." Sean took a breath and situated himself in the middle of the living room. "I know you've only had the one experience in the Wheel opening portals, but I could use some help, make this as painless as possible. Many hands and light work and all that."

MacEoghan understood the principle, but he wasn't convinced it translated well to shouldering the burden of Time-related activities. Maybe it had more to do with his inexperience in opening portals. Sean directed the thing where it needed to open, and all MacEoghan did was lend some of his strength to opening it big enough for the three of them to pass through unscathed. Micah helped also, but MacEoghan still didn't know just how much of the burden any one of them actually shouldered.

Then they were through, landing in a men's restroom. Sean immediately Banded their group so they could regain their strength and composure without being questioned whether they had been engaging in any unseemly activities. Once they were settled down, he dropped the Band. Then he rummaged around in a pocket and pulled out some papers and a couple booklets.

461

"Plane tickets, passports, and any official documents you may need," he told them.

MacEoghan opened up the passport, then blinked in confusion. "Micaiah Durvin?"

"Close enough to your real name that no one should bat an eye, but should hopefully obscure any affiliation with the IRA, Time, anything and anyone questionable. Canada is still tied to Britain after all."

"Micah Durvin," Micah commented on Sean's other side, reading his passport.

It was a plausible enough explanation, MacEoghan figured, but it only served to put another nail in the coffin of this part of his life. He'd gone from Miach to Micah to MacEoghan and now Micaiah. What was next? Michael? Michael Davis, maybe?

"All right, go on now," Sean said, making a shooing motion. "Small window of opportunity, like I said. Go get on that plane. When you land in Canada, the Captain of District Three should be there to meet you. He'll keep me apprised of the situation. Good luck."

It was the only farewell the brothers would get as they hustled out of the bathroom and got in line. They didn't know which line, but any line was as good as any other. Hundreds of people were already crowding around, some waving money in the air or holding up children, shouting and pleading with all manner of reasons why they should be allowed to go. With tickets and passports in hand, the brothers were waved through easily and shown to the tarmac. From there, they were hustled onto a small plane.

MacEoghan didn't know what to think. Didn't know what to do, if there was anything he could do. All of the passengers here—all fifteen of them— were women of means and their children. Likely their husbands had bought passage for them, sending them away for safety until the end of the war. What must they think of two healthy fighting age Irishmen onboard? Did anyone even notice them? No one looked excited, or anything even remotely close to happy. These people were fleeing in terror, concerned only for their own welfare.

Truthfully, MacEoghan had never felt like more of a coward, more deserving of Ciara's scorn. Nor had he ever felt like more of a hypocrite with his work in the IRA. He thought of what he'd seen in London. That was months ago. What must it look like now?

"You ready?" he asked Micah.

Micah looked at him. There was fear in his eyes, sure, but also a severe determination as he nodded.

"Together forever?"

"Together forever."

AUTHOR'S NOTE
YOUNGER SISTER

I knew I was going to write the twins' story since way back in...I think it was *Stopwatch* (*The Chivalrous Welshman #4*) that I first mentioned that they had Books. Being young, dumb, and ambitious, I even determined that they had five whole Books. Of course, back then, it was a problem for Tomorrow Me. Yesterday Me thought Tomorrow Me was going to have the same ambition, drive, ideas, and personality, albeit with a little more fame.

Well, it's tomorrow, Tomorrow Me became Today Me, and the almost one decade of differences between Yesterday Me and Today Me are massive. My writing has evolved so much over the years, both in terms of ideas, style, and execution, that I don't think Yesterday Me and Today Me would recognize each other. But I can say that I approached this series far differently than I would have ten or even five years ago.

For one, my writing overall has drastically improved. After several million words and more than a dozen books, it has gotten better. Plus, writing the rest of *The Timekeeper Chronicles* before circling back to tackle this series has given me a lot more to work with. Yesterday Me was considerate enough to drop some details of the twins' story along the way, through *The Chivalrous Welshman* and *The Hands of Time*, that I could pick up and use as road markers while I drafted this story. From that, the rules of the world have already been established by this point; I'm no longer trying to just figure it out as I go, in terms of how the Time industry works, what it means to be a Timekeeper, and so on. The characters are also well-established, who they are, who they were, who they're going to be. Even if this is your very first *Timekeeper Chronicles* book, the information is there for you to simply discover; I do not have to learn it with you. Now, this doesn't mean that my older writing was terrible, just...less-developed.

With all of that, then, it kind of feels like *The Timekeeper Chronicles* is really just beginning. Again. Putting off the twins' story until now has proven to be a great benefit for me, for the story, and, ultimately, for you. This book was hard enough to write for a number of reasons, most of them relating to the content, and it's not going to get any easier going forward as we trudge, reluctantly, straight into World War II.

If you have been reading the other books, you may have your suspicions about the Slavic mercenary. You may wonder about a certain lady friend, or a couple lady friends. You may be wondering about any number of things, those little details Yesterday Me was kind enough to drop in odd places.

That's the beauty of having so much backing going into this. It's a reward for the faithful and a grand reveal for the uninitiated. As *The Timekeeper Chronicles* as a whole comes to a close, I hope you find as much joy and discovery as I have. And maybe a little forgiveness for the mistakes and missteps of Yesterday Me.

- Brooke Shaffer